Rachel Pollack is a novelist and poet as we~~ll~~ symbolism of Tarot cards. Her recent no~~v~~ been described as 'brilliant' and 'magical' f where myth and dreams have broken throu~~gh~~ ~~..~~ ~~orld.~~ Her two-volume study of the Tarot, *78 Degre~~es~~ ~~of~~ wisdom*, is recognized in many countries as a standard text. Her other books on Tarot include the official text for *Salvador Dali's Tarot*, and *The New Tarot*. She is also the author of the novels *Golden Vanity* and *Alqua Dreams*. Rachel Pollack's work has been translated into French, German, Danish, Dutch, Spanish and Japanese. A former university lecturer, bar cleaner, IBM production planner, bottler of patchouli oil, and bookseller, she now writes full time. She has lived in Amsterdam in the Netherlands for the past fifteen years.

Caitlín Matthews is a writer active within the Western Esoteric Tradition, about which she co-wrote a two-volume history, *The Western Way*, with John Matthews, her partner in the mythic and Arthurian fields. With him she has designed *The Arthurian Tarot*. Her other books include *Mabon and the Mysteries of Britain* and *Arthur and the Sovereignty of Britain* – a two-volume study of the Mabinogion – and *The Elements of Celtic Tradition*. She is co-editor, with Prudence Jones, of *Voices from the Circle*. She spends a lot of time in the Celtic fifth and sixth centuries, an era which she is currently reconstructing for a series of forthcoming novels. She has lectured in Britain, Europe and America, but, as a poet, singer and harpist, her lectures nearly always turn into storytelling and workshop.

Also by Rachel Pollack
Unquenchable Fire

TAROT TALES

EDITED BY

Rachel Pollack and Caitlín Matthews

A LEGEND BOOK

LONDON SYDNEY AUCKLAND JOHANNESBURG

Tarot Tales
Copyright © Rachel Pollack and Caitlín Matthews 1989

First published in 1989 by Legend

An imprint of
Century Hutchinson Ltd
Brookmount House, 62–65 Chandos Place
London WC2BN 4NW

Century Hutchinson South Africa (Pty) Ltd
PO Box 337, Bergvlei 2012
South Africa

Century Hutchinson Australia (Pty) Ltd
89–91 Albion Street, Surry Hills
NSW 2010 Australia

Century Hutchinson New Zealand Limited
PO Box 40–086, Glenfield, Auckland 10
New Zealand

British Library Cataloguing in Publication Data
Tarot tales
I. Pollack, Rachel   II. Matthews,
Caitlín, *1952–*
823'.01'08 [FS]

ISBN 0–7126–2471–6

Printed and bound in Great Britain by
Mackays of Chatham PLC, Chatham, Kent

Phototypeset by Input Typesetting Ltd, London

*To Mary K Greer
and to all storytellers*

Acknowledgements

Tarot cards from *Mythic Tarot*, page 16, © Tricia Newell, reproduced by permission of Tricia Newell.

Tarot cards from Rider Waite pack, pages 71 to 72, 137 to 138, 218 to 219, 251 and cover artwork, reproduced by permission of Rider and Co.

Tarot cards from Marseilles pack, pages 89, 160 to 161, 178, 241, 273, © Baptiste Paul Grimaud, reproduced by permission of France Cartes, Paris.

Tarot cards from Crowley pack, pages 52 to 53, reproduced by permission of Aquarian Press.

Tarot cards from *Magickal Tarot*, pages 121 to 122, reproduced by permission of Aquarian Press.

Tarot cards from Mantegna pack, pages 203 to 205, reproduced by permission of Edizione del Solleone, Milan.

Tarot cards from Hermetic pack, page 178, reproduced by permission of US Games.

Tarot cards from Cary Yale Visconti pack, pages 106 to 108, reproduced by permission of US Games.

Tarot cards from *Shining Woman Tarot*, page 287, reproduced by permission of Rachel Pollack.

Tarot cards from Voyager pack, page 33, © James Wanless and Ken Knutson, reproduced by permission of Merrill-West Publishing.

CONTENTS

FOREWORD

We all want to hear about ourselves. When someone pro-
duces a Tarot pack at work or at a party, we flock round
to have our fortunes told. We are both eager and fearful,
curious yet cautious. When the Tarot-reader spreads the
cards and starts relating what she has found there, we hush
and listen in exactly the same way as we do for a storyteller.

Humankind has a thirst for stories which is unquenchable. Periods of our lives are marked by our reading of
certain novels; these colour and nourish our inner lives.
Not having a book to read is psychologically traumatic –
the psychic equivalent of not having anything to eat. We
choose our reading as carefully as any gourmet planning a
dinner party. Only certain books will suit certain needs,
and it's not at all unusual to have several books for different
times and occasions. We stock our bags with reading
material against the desert hours spent in hospital waiting
rooms, dentists' reception rooms, or long train journeys.
To have nothing to read is intolerable.

This quest for the right book for our condition is not a
modern phenomenon, although it may seem so. If we take
the oral tradition of the Celtic peoples as an example, we
find that storytellers were well versed in telling the right
story for the right occasion. They told appropriate stories
of wooings and abductions at weddings, stories of tragic
deaths and impossible tasks at wakes, applying the medicine
of story to their listeners and involving them in a larger,
mythic world. In the interminable months of winter, stories
taking eight or nine nights were commonly told. Today we
have television soap opera, serial novels or ongoing trilogies
to look forward to. Protected by modern technology against

boredom, cold and vigorous physical effort, we while away our leisure hours with story.

In our quest for the perfect book, we are supplementing our inner lives with story. By careful selection of the right story, we unconsciously inform ourselves about our psychological needs and set about meeting them. We vicariously enact, through story, the deeds of others, empathizing with them, suffering with them. We are taken out of ourselves and, by means of certain powerful stories, given the cleansing of catharsis.

The saving stories of the world religions act in much the same way, for these put each personal life into the greater context of a god or goddess, a hero or messiah, a king or queen who has discovered the bridge between earthly and spiritual life. The novels of today do not, of course, necessarily reproduce this experience of alignment with other worlds but they do broaden our personal, perhaps sometimes circumscribed, lives.

The story is almost universally listened to but seldom read. The telling of a story is an immediate and primal experience which cannot really be repeated. Rather there is a renewal, for the story is itself recreated in the hearer's heart, though a roomful of listeners each hear the story in their own subjective way. Even so does the storyteller vary his or her pitch, depending on the audience, thus giving each telling a new emphasis.

In exactly the same way, the Tarot – a seemingly limited pack of only seventy-eight cards with different images – can always be spread to give a new and totally original part of a querent's story. This originality is part of the intrinsic survival plan of the oral tradition which has its own rippling effect through life.

The oral tradition is not dead. Anecdotes and jokes still well up and out from their source in an unrestrainable urge of natural wit. And though stories have become more formalized in our society, becoming the raw material of writers, scriptwriters and media people, they still have their part to play. Despite our proud boasts of literacy, we have undoubtedly become symbolically illiterate. The Tarot's

images act as a corrective to our conscious, rational awareness, giving access to the worlds which our ancestors would
have recognized with ease.

Tarot Tales has grown out of such a tradition of storytelling and, as such, defies classification into a genre. Indeed,
the Tarot establishes a kind of literary anarchy when used
for storytelling. This has given a great deal of freedom to the
writers in this collection, allowing their stories to develop
without the limitations imposed by accepted literary forms.
It was interesting to see the reactions of some writers whom
we approached but who felt unable to submit a story. Some
were obviously disturbed by the fact that the Tarot was, to
their minds, only an esoteric device. It could not be associated with writing a story.

Perhaps it is this very point – that divination and storytelling are inextricably intertwined – that has given the writers
in this collection such a satisfying challenge?

The Tarot has been called 'the Devil's Picturebook' but
its uses are both more profound and more holistic than that
title implies. But just as the devil does not have all the best
tunes, neither does he have all the best stories. The Tarot
as a storytelling device can bring us to the roots of our own
personal story or involve us in a greater narrative. It is the
images of the Tarot that have triggered the stories in this
collection. They are the hooks on which the stories hang.

The creative process of finding the story's direction is
precisely that used by the Tarot-reader for orienting a client's spread. In the lay of the cards is an unknown destination which the Tarot-reader or storyteller is there to interpret. Out of many possibilities, the twin alchemies of
creation and interpretation produce an original elixir.

We hope that you will enjoy this diverse collection of
stories and find the one which you most need at this moment. Perhaps you may also take out your pack and spread
the cards to see what story will be revealed, for there is no
end to the variety of Tarot Tales?

Caitlín Matthews

A MACHINE FOR CONSTRUCTING STORIES

'This book is made first of pictures – the Tarot playing cards – and secondly of written words. Through the sequence of pictures stories are told, which the written word tries to reconstruct and interpret.' So begins Italo Calvino's 'Note' to his *Castle of Crossed Destinies*. In that book, the Italian master created an enchanted castle, in which a group of stranded travellers, unable to speak, must lay out Tarot cards to tell their tales. The tales, however, are filtered through the mind of the narrator, who always assumes the correctness of his interpretations. And so, the cards for Calvino become not simply an entry into fantasy, but a demonstration of the deconstructionist thesis that each reader creates the story out of an autonomous text.

The same thing happens when we lay the cards for a reading. They do not *say* anything. They give us only a group of pictures in predetermined positions. From these we create a tale, a fiction, of a person's life. If we are lucky that fiction will give the person a deeper understanding of herself and her situation.

Like most Tarot enthusiasts I came to the cards with the hope and excitement of telling the future and absorbing mystical teachings. Quite early it occurred to me that the cards do something else with their bright images. We could discover Oedipus in the Chariot with its two sphinxes, or Odysseus in the bearded man sitting outside the archway in the Rider pack Ten of Pentacles. What if we mixed the cards at random, not to tell fortunes, but to tell stories?

For a long time the idea never went beyond occasional experiments, or the use of individual pictures to help fill in

12

gaps in some novel or tale. I came across various books, most notably Charles Williams's *The Greater Trumps*, in which the cards serve as theme or framework. There was also Philip K Dick's *The Man In The High Castle*, in which Dick created a series of characters and a general situation, and then let the I Ching determine the characters' actions and the course of events. Except for Calvino, however, no one had let the cards themselves create the story.

Several years ago I began collecting decks for a book on new Tarots. An interesting development became clear. A number of artists had gone away from the strict symbolism of earlier decks to create pictures showing actions and characters, as in a tale or series of tales. Some of these followed pre-selected texts. The *Dante Tarot* joins the traditional card images to specific lines from the *Divine Comedy* and other works. The *Mythic Tarot* (see Gwyneth Jones's story, 'The Lovers'), illustrates various Greek myths (not Oedipus). Other decks, however, did not limit themselves to any external works, but opened up the various possibilities of story. The *Solleone Tarot*, by Elisabetta Cassari, showed witches and sorcerers, corrupt judges and power-mad bishops, peasant revolutionaries and brutal knights. Cassari's *Future Solleone* transferred the same idea to science fiction.

In 1987 I attended the second Merlin Conference, in London. For my contribution I decided to tell a story, using the *Solleone Tarot*. I mixed the cards two or three times until one picture, a woman running with a stick, seemed to click something into place and I had the beginning of a tale of a woman who curses herself and her family. If the beginning came quickly, the end remained stubborn, causing me some nervous moments until an hour before my scheduled appearance, when the cards finally yielded up a suitable ending.

Caitlín Matthews was at the Merlin Conference. Shortly afterwards I received a story from her in the mail. Intrigued by a gap in Celtic myth, she asked her Tarot deck to tell her of the hidden life of Tailtiu, 'The Goddess of the Land'. Delighted by the results, Caitlín had a suggestion. Wouldn't it be exciting if we could put together a whole book of such stories?

We contacted a group of writers, some of them students of the Tarot, others fiction writers with an interest in the cards or in divination, still others storytellers who enjoyed an experimental challenge. There were no restrictions on the kind of story – and so we find here adventures, contemporary satires, historical comedies and far future science fiction, realism and fantasies. We set only one guideline: Tarot cards had to be involved in the creation of the tale.

Some of the writers did stories on Tarot themes, others used the pictures as aids in developing an idea or a plot. Quite a few fulfilled Calvino's ideal: a tale told in pictures and interpreted in words.

Rachel Pollack

CHAPTER ONE

THE LOVERS

Gwyneth Jones

Psyche's quest for Cupid is a timeless task which is pursued in many traditions, from the myths of Rome to the border ballads of Scotland. This truly wonderful version by Gwyneth Jones brings the story into our own time. The rigours of love lend Psyche her maturity of spirit – analogous to Jupiter's gift of immortality which he gives her in *The Golden Ass*, the classical source of the Cupid and Psyche story. Her selfless search for her beloved is perhaps epitomized by a verse from *The Black Bull of Norroway*, a Scots border story, whose heroine, like Psyche, has to fulfil many impossible tasks:

> Seven lang years I served for you,
> The glassy hill I climbed for you,
> The bluid-stained shirt I wrang for you,
> Will you not wake and turn to me?

The radiance of the candle flame lay only for a moment across his face, only for a moment its light shone on the lips and eyelids that she had so often kissed; and her long held breath was released in a soft sigh of relief. This was a human face, a lovely face, the rumour that she was married to a monster had all been lies.

Then the light went out. The little wind that had snuffed the candle flame grew fierce and strong. It roared in her ears. Suddenly frightened she reached for her lover's warm body. He wasn't there. Her hands clutched on nothing, there was nothingness all around her . . . Gradually she became aware that she was in a new place, still all alone. She was standing barefoot on some rough rocky surface, shivering in her thin nightgown. The air was cold and dank. Somehow she was aware that this place was buried deep underground.

FIVE OF CUPS

SEVEN OF CUPS

EIGHT OF CUPS

Then the voice came. She couldn't tell from where, it might be only in her mind. It was a woman's voice, rich and strong and calm; it spoke with stern regret of the consequences of her folly. She had betrayed her lover, she had failed him. She had lost the right forever to be his bride.

Psyche was terrified of the dark. 'Oh please,' she sobbed, 'please, I'll do anything. Only let me have my chance to win him back.'

The voice was kind.

'Trust me, Psyche. If you perform the tasks I set you honestly and well, in the end I promise you will be free to return to your lover, completely free.'

Something dropped from the darkness.

'Your first task. My son's nightshirt is badly marked with smoky tallow drips, because a silly girl held a candle to his face last night; as if she could not recognize without such crude assistance the wonder and beauty that she held in her arms. Wash my son's shirt, Psyche. You will find water close by.'

She groped on the floor, picked up the shirt and began to stumble around in the utter darkness, listening for the sound of water. It was a long time, it might have been hours or weeks or years, before she found her way to the underground stream. The water was numbing cold, when she thrust the shirt into it the linen folds immediately became heavy as lead, and a strong biting current dragged against the frail strength of her arms.

'But how will I know?' she cried.

'Know what, Psyche?'

'It is so dark. I can't see my own hands. How will I know when the shirt is clean?'

The voice was noble and gentle as ever; Psyche felt guilty at her suspicion that somebody was laughing unkindly.

'My son's shirts are very fine linen and need long and careful washing. You must scrub on faithfully, like a good washerwoman, until the whiteness of that shirt illumines the whole cavern. So it will be easy for you to tell when your work is done. You see, I am doing all I can to help you, Psyche. Don't you think you should thank me?'

She wanted to scream that the task was impossible, that this wasn't justice, it was vengeance – but she wanted her lover more. Psyche learned her first lesson. 'Thank you, Lady,' she said quietly; and began to scrub.

How many years? There were no days, no nights, no seasons, there was nothing but the work. Her hands were raw and she hauled the heavy, slimy linen out of the water, slept beside it like the dead; woke and scrubbed again and again until her fingers were covered in weeping sores. She grew old learning how much cold and darkness and pain and back-breaking toil she was able to bear; and at last the shirt was white and, blind as a worm, she was released from darkness by its light. Then there was – what was there? The terrible gleaning of the battle fields. The water of youth to be carried out of the desert (and the sun devoured the water out of her cupped hands when she'd taken three steps away from the fountain. How many times did that happen? – before she learned to protect it with her own shadow, walking backwards over the knife-sharp burning rocks). And then the rose of knowledge had to be plucked from its savage briars. And then, in an oven fired by the flames of that rose, with the water of youth and the flour ground from death's cold stone, Psyche must bake the Lady's bread, which must be lighter than a feather and sweeter than breath. Over and over the harvest was gathered but the rose's petals fell before they could be kindled; the fire was kindled but the bread was soured with tears and would not rise . . .

But there came an hour, a day, a season when the tasks were all done, and nothing remained but for Psyche to take the roads behind the sun and before the moon, out of the Other World and back into the light of common day.

And finally she was once more alone in the dark, cold rough stone underfoot. She heard voices. She walked towards them (quite indifferent to darkness now), and in a very short time found herself in a broad well-lit passageway full of shuffling bodies. She slipped through them, not sure whether these brightly clothed figures were real or more of the Lady's phantasms. No one seemed to notice her. She

came to the cavern's mouth and stepped out into harsh
sunlight.

She held her head, she rubbed her arms, she looked down
at her own body in amazement. There were air-conditioned
coaches in the car park; and an artistic modern pavilion
serving light refreshments: coffee, *chai*, local cakes stuffed
with nuts and honey. Signboards explained in several different languages that these caves had once been believed to
lead down to Hades. There were guided tours through them
three times a day, as far as the banks of the Dark River.

No further. Psyche had been much further; but it seemed,
miraculously, that she had been allowed to return.

Psyche had always known that the country ruled by her
lover's mother was old and mysterious and magical, filled
with ancient ruins and the shadows of forgotten mysteries.
It was very strange to return to it (after how long?) and
find that she had become the ancient one. Standing in that
brash modern car park she felt like a whisper from a world
of ghosts, a word in a lost language; she felt as if she had
been dead for thousands of years. She walked through the
blaring of motor horns and the wail of music from the
tourists' distant countries, picked her way out to the road;
stood with the local people and climbed on the next bus
into town. She was going to have to tell the driver she had
no money. She hoped he would have pity on her – poor,
ragged, calloused, twisted old crone. She sat on the bus
preparing herself to beg (she could do anything now). But
when the driver came she looked down and found a purse
on her lap, a small shoulder bag at her feet. She opened the
purse and gave him money.

Her hands were not the crone's hands. They didn't look
so very different from Psyche's hands of long ago.

She looked at herself in shop windows. She was dressed
in summer clothes, a little too light for the chill that set in
towards sunset. She had scarcely aged at all, except for her
hair which was more silver now than fair. Sandals on her
feet, money and papers in her purse. It was as if she had
gone out to take that tourist excursion on a whim, closed

her eyes for a moment and dreamed everything: her love, her loss, her trial and her punishment.

She found herself in a small hotel in the tourist town, and since it was late in the season she had no trouble booking a modest room. She sat on her small white covered bed, the pillows and coverlet embroidered crustily with the Lady's emblems (as was still the custom in remote places); and tried to grasp the fact of her triumph. She had won the prize and passed the test and paid the penalty. She was free. She was even still young.

All she had to do now was to rejoin her lover. Unless things had changed very much – and it seemed as if nothing at all had changed – she knew where to find him. He would be living as before not in the capital where the mundane government of his people was carried on, but in his mother's palace in the Old City, which was buried deep in these ruin-haunted mountains. It was not even far to travel: a few hours' journey at the most over those hair-raising roads, to the other side of the spectacular, glacier-riven peak they called the Glass Mountain. She could be with him before dawn.

At that thought Psyche jumped up and hurried out into the street, wondering why she had delayed at all. She would hire a car. She passed the phone, the only phone the place possessed, in the hotel lobby; glanced at it, remembered 'phone calls' for the first time but couldn't wait.

She ran around the streets, deserted now in the cold of the evening, into the lobby of a big hotel and ran to the reception desk.

'I need to hire a car –

'Can I hire a car here? Is the office still open?'

Two young women and a boy, attractively dressed in a homogenized version of the mountain costume, went on with what they were doing, placidly.

'Excuse me!!' shouted Psyche, in English. She had been speaking the language of the country; perhaps these servants only answered to foreigners. She banged on the desk. The women and the boy didn't even glance up. A sheaf of loose papers under her hand did not stir.

Psyche left the hotel grounds, slowly, frowning. She went to the bus station next, and there failed to buy a ticket. She tried to climb on the night bus without one – and, as in a dream, a nightmare, her hand grasped nothing, her foot stepped on nothing. She went back to her hotel and tried to place a call to the Old Palace, using the lobby phone. Her hand went through the handset as if one of the two wasn't there.

In the morning she discovered that there was an airport now, with light planes carrying on a regular service in the season to a small strip outside the Old City. She knew that it would be no good but she had learned to be thorough so she tried anyway. She was a ghost in the airline office, too. She could not buy a plane ticket.

She packed her small bag, she paid her bill. With a smiling face and a feeling almost that the world had returned to normal after a brief spell of madness, she set out in her thin clothes and summer sandals to climb the mountain road. The modern town ended. She walked through a stand of pines and beside a row of pretty peasant cottages, their steep roofs weighed down with boulders in the old style. A car engine started up behind her. The engine roared closer. Psyche turned . . . and the road had become the street where she had found her little hotel, just getting noisy with its morning traffic.

She tried again.

She tried again.

No majestic voice spoke from the sky, or in her mind. But Psyche understood. The trials were not over yet, after all. She was still exiled from the human race though they seemed to be all around her. No human hand had been joined with hers, rubbing and scrubbing in the dark stream long ago. She had been living in another world, and she was trapped there still. No one could follow where she must go – not even now, so near the end. She must scale the Glass Mountain as she had wrung that shirt: all alone, and still, it seemed, wrapped in a kind of darkness.

Meanwhile, in the Old City, preparations were being made for the marriage of Madame's son. He was to marry the beauty, the singer who was called La Sensuala, who was famous far outside her own country and a scandal within it. But La Sensuala was a licensed scandal, and not half such a rebel or so dangerous as the name they gave her suggested. People wondered if this time, Madame la Présidente might really let the young man take a wife. She had been for so long the only woman who ruled in this man's world, in this ancient country; nobody believed she would tolerate a rival. But apparently La Sensuala had somehow won her approval.

On the icy cliffs of silence Psyche wandered – she who had not even considered this possibility. She thought of her lover waiting, of his years of loneliness. She wanted to smooth his soft rough hair, to hold him in the hollow of her shoulder; kiss and tell him this was the end of their suffering and the beginning of all delight. Her body was sore, her vision shaken by the cold waste's glassy shining. But though her eyes were blinded and her feet were broken she never faltered, and never for a moment dreamed of turning back.

She was sitting on a heap of stones by a hill track, tying up her battered feet again after bathing them in a little stream, when a dirty old truck stopped beside her, and she knew that she had returned again from the world outside time. The driver told her that the Présidente's son was getting married.

'Again?' murmured Psyche, showing no sign of horror.

He laughed heartily. 'Not really. There was no proper wedding the other time, you see. It was just a little bit of a secret affair. La Sensuala has forgiven him, I'm sure.'

'I'm sure you're right,' said Psyche. 'A woman in love will forgive anything.'

She still knew that all she had to do was to reach her lover. This other bride was one of the Lady's cruelties, nothing more. She had kept her side of the bargain. The prize must be hers as long as she never faltered. La Sensuala's house was an inward-turned, old-fashioned building, with late roses still blooming in the courtyards inside its blind walls. Psyche asked her way there and persuaded the cook to take her on as a kitchenmaid; they needed extra staff because the bride-to-be was doing a lot of entertaining. She really was dressed in rags now, but nobody minded that. La Sensuala travelled round the world in jet planes but in the back rooms of her house time had been standing still for a thousand years. The new kitchenmaid slept on the scullery floor, and they called her 'little mutton fat' because she couldn't get the smell of the washing up out of her hair. She was safe. Her lover's mother would never expect to find her here, never know her if she did.

Once, when she was carrying a pile of dirty table linen across a courtyard, she saw the Présidente's son. He was older, but not much older. He didn't look at her. She didn't want him to; not until the moment came when the abyss of years healed over and everything was made right. Several times as she went about her business she saw La Sensuala – a tall woman always wrapped in bright-coloured shawls, with a sheaf of tawny hair. Psyche wasn't in the least jealous. She didn't give the other woman a second thought, not even to feel sorry for her.

On a chain around her neck she wore, as she had always worn since the night her lover first came to her, a golden key. It was the key, he had told her, to every secret door in the Old Palace. In fact it was a tiny thing, just a love token, incised all over with little doves, one of the Lady's favourite emblems. But not all Madame's powers, or her vindictive jealousy, had managed to part Psyche from this charm. It had become a symbol to her of the truth of her love and his.

One night when she was helping (behind the scenes) to serve one of the cook's elaborate and wonderful meals, she managed to drop the golden key into what she thought was her lover's dish.

She washed her face, she changed her rags, she tried to comb her hair. None of it mattered. The major-domo, a magnificent creature in a portly white waistcoat and scarlet cummerbund, appeared at the back scullery door.

'Did any person here,' he asked, 'drop a foreign body into one of Cook's dishes?'

'It was me,' confessed Psyche.

'La Sensuala wishes to see you,' he told her, as if he could hardly believe it.

Psyche went running to meet her lover. She pushed through clouds of silk curtains, stumbled over gorgeous rugs, tripped over cushions; and was ushered, rather brusquely, into a small glowing room. The woman with the tawny hair turned from a curvaceous window that looked inward into one of the rose-garden courts, and held up Psyche's key in one hand; in the other, one exactly similar.

'You,' she said.

She was a very wise woman. She wasn't confused by the rags or the grease at all. She burst into a storm of passionate tears.

La Sensuala insisted that Psyche must be bathed, dressed, combed, fed. She stayed by her rival all the while; holding her hand, stroking her silver-fair hair, biting her lip and exclaiming over the state of Psyche's worn body and her hard-working hands. It was as if at last someone had seen through the veil of glamour thrown by the Lady between her victim and the rest of humanity; and poor worn and weary Psyche was pitied and cradled in loving arms. La Sensuala said, 'I know all about you. He never speaks of you, but I know he has never forgotten you. Sometimes I wake in the night and he is not beside me. He is only across the room maybe, or else he comes back in an hour and says he was restless and went for a stroll . . . But I think of you then, Psyche. And I am afraid he is still searching for you, though he himself believes that he gave up hope long ago.'

Of course he is still searching, thought Psyche. And you are merely another of his mother's tricks. But she said nothing, she didn't want to be unkind.

Then, in La Sensuala's little glowing parlour, they bargained like two market women.

'Give me one night,' said Psyche.

'Take three – '

'One night, when I will take your place and be smuggled into his private rooms in the Old Palace for a love tryst.'

'Does everybody in the kitchen know about our meetings?'

'Of course we do. And so does the Lady, without a doubt. And approves of the arrangement, or at least allows it.'

'I can arrange for him to come here. I mean, privately, at night, apart from the public times. Meet him in my house, Psyche. It will be safer for you.'

'La Sensuala, you are too generous.'

Poor golden singer, she thought. I am so much stronger than she is. I have so much more to offer.

La Sensuala wiped her eyes and smiled. 'Don't you see? I love him, too. I would rather know, even the worst. I want to be sure.'

'So it's agreed. One night.'

'Three. And here.'

'If you insist, three. But in the palace.'

'Agreed.'

They clasped hands: the silver hair and the sheaves of gold mingled. Outside in the rose court a flight of doves rose clattering and wheeled across the narrow sky. It was only three nights now to the wedding. But for three nights more, Madame ruled alone.

It was dark inside the Old Palace. It had always been dark in here. How cold it was, too – and what a dank strange smell the air had, like somewhere underground. Still she groped her way onward, following the light carried by the servant who would lead her to her lover's chamber. How very cold this passage was. Here was the door, however: massive and ancient like all the palace furniture. And her guide had discreetly vanished.

She saw a large dim shape, she hopped, skipped over the icy floor, and dropping La Sensuala's shawls sat down, as she thought, on the bed.

It was not a bed. She sat on a cold smooth stone in pitch darkness; and knew she had been tricked.

'Where am I?'

'In my son's bedchamber, child, as you wished to be; where he will surely come to sleep at last.'

'I am in a tomb.'

'The family vault, no less.'

'La Sensuala –!'

'No, she is innocent. What does she know of our world, Psyche? Unless I choose to teach her, that is; but that's no concern of yours. The passages above you have been sealed for many years. They are still sealed now, and will remain so until the next royal funeral. Sleep well, Psyche.'

'But I have paid! I did everything you asked!'

'Then you are safe, Psyche. In *this* world no one breaks the law or goes back on a bargain. If you have kept faith with your quest, you will find a way out.'

Then there was silence. When she was sure she was alone, Psyche began to laugh. She unfastened the fine chain from her neck and held in her hand the trinket that La Sensuala had returned to her. The key, the key to all his mother's secrets. She passed her hand, holding it, over the surface and sides of the coffin table, and at last there came a tiny chink of metal on metal.

In another moment the stone door was open, Psyche was running sure-footed in the cold darkness down and down a spiral staircase. At the foot of the stair she found a level passage where the air smelled fresh. The passage twisted and turned, it split into two. Psyche stumbled over long smooth staves, and round things that rolled and rattled. But she was not afraid of the dead or the dark or even of being buried alive. Elated by her own calm and coolness she followed the breath of freshness still; and at last came scrambling out from underground. Strange shapes loomed around her: she was in the old cemetery outside the city walls. The sky was grey and dim. Psyche ran like the wind: through the ancient royal gateway, up the wide avenue between rows of time-blurred guardian statues, up to the palace walls; and just as she touched them a pitiless finger of warm light struck her on the shoulder.

And that was one night gone.

La Sensuala had not explained to her bridegroom why she was letting him spend these last bachelor nights alone. But strangely enough, he, too, was thinking of Psyche. The first night he spent alone, brooding and dreaming. On the

second night he left the palace and walked the city streets.
He was trying to remember what it had been like to be
young, to love so absolutely; to be so helpless. He had
learned how to live with his mother now. La Sensuala was
safe because she threatened no one. He knew that in time
the Lady would give him all the power any man could
desire; and this marriage was the first instalment. She was
not unwilling, she wanted him to have his share of the
world she ruled. It was only Psyche who had caused the
trouble between them.

'Psyche – '

He spoke her name in the chill silvery dawn, and a
woman's figure wrapped in glowing shawls crossed the
street ahead of him. She was coming away from the palace,
bowed as if under a heavy burden. He cried again 'Psyche!'
– though it was Sensuala he thought he saw. The woman
turned her face.

The Lady's son felt a shock almost like terror. For a
moment his first love stood in front of him, absolutely
young and pure and beautiful. The light changed, the
shadows vanished: an old crone pulled her shawl around
her sunken cheeks and scurried away.

And that was two nights gone.

La Sensuala was frightened. 'Supposing she tricks you
again?' she wailed. 'Oh Psyche, promise me one thing. Let
me bring you together in daylight, in some ordinary way,
if you don't meet tonight. Or else how will I ever know,
how will I ever be sure?'

'It would do you no good,' Psyche told her. 'You can't
ever be sure of his love, not the way you long to be. Only
of your own.'

'But will you promise?'

'No, I will not. Would you want me to come back from
the dead, and try and see if I could make your husband
follow me to my grave? Don't be scared – I only meant
you to understand how dangerous a promise can be if you
make it when the Lady is listening. And she is always
listening, naturally. I know the rules, you see. I know how
the wheels go round. I have felt them, going over me.'

'Anyway – ' Psyche smiled: it was like a flash of edged steel in the soft, richly coloured room. 'There'll be no more tricks. He and I must meet tonight. The sun won't rise before I am in his arms, the stars won't move until that moment comes.'

It was dark again. When she heard his step she meant to light a candle, but just for a while she would sit without light and taste for the last time how it felt to be alone in the dark. Here was their bed. Here she sat, and soon her lover would come through the door . . .

What would she say to him? Would she tell him about washing a shirt in darkness, and how the cold of the water burned? Would she tell him how long and strange and cruel it all was? Would she tell him, lying in his warm arms, how it felt to walk alone on the cliffs of ice . . .

La Sensuala, thought Psyche, would have wept and created on the bank of the Dark River, and complained she had a hangnail and she was catching cold. And maybe, who knows, the Lady would have been forced to give in. Strength isn't what you need, not always, to win human happiness. Strength is the reward of suffering, not a defence against it.

Slowly, as if spellbound once more, she got to her feet. She had been sitting here for a long time.

She crept through the gloomy old-fashioned halls of Madame's palace, wondering where her lover had been delayed. She crept by the kitchens, and heard two young servants talking to each other.

'He came down here looking for a girl, can you imagine?'

'That didn't take long! So where's he off to now?'

'To La Sensuala's. He reckons if it wasn't here it was there he saw the kitchenmaid he fancies!'

The two boys roared with laughter.

Psyche ran.

She ran, and she knew that within the silent houses as she passed life paused between a breath and a breath, the fingers of all the clocks had ceased to move; and above the hunched ancient roofs and towers the dance of the sky was still.

And there they were in La Sensuala's parlour, clinging close in candlelight, the lovers. They were both of them in tears.

Psyche stood in the doorway, transfixed. Her beloved, her dear one turned and stood, and took one step away from La Sensuala.

'I saw your face,' he whispered. 'Yesterday, in the grey dawn, I saw you. I would never have believed I would know you again unless I had you in my arms. It was only for a moment, wasn't it, and only by candlelight. You vanished – again – but then I knew you were somewhere near, I just had to remember where. Oh Psyche –'

La Sensuala stood up too, but didn't try to get between them.

'Husband,' she said, in a sad little voice. 'You lost the key to your treasure chest and made yourself a new one. But now the first key is found. Which are you going to keep?'

Psyche's beloved took one more step. He held out his arms. She heard him calling, 'Psyche? Psyche?' But what was happening? She could see him there, and yet there was a mist between them. It was the same as in that town at the foot of the Glass Mountain. She could not touch or be touched, she was wrapped in invisible darkness.

'Lady, you can't do this!' she cried. 'The price is paid and he is mine, he is mine. If you break your promise you will stop the stars in their courses. I *know you cannot* break your promises . . .'

Psyche felt herself becoming crystal and diamond. In the caverns, in the desert and the wilderness of her longing, she had been washed and burned and scoured into perfection. She tried to run forward, offering her dear one all these riches . . . but even as she moved, she understood; she saw what the lovers saw.

La Sensuala was sobbing bitterly. Her beloved was being carried off by a monster: a burning, impossible thing of ice and fire . . . not human at all. Once again the Lady had found a way to destroy the happiness of her son and the woman he loved.

Psyche understood then how devious and invincible the Lady's law could be. And yet she felt sure that the choice was real. Nothing that she had gained on her quest could be carried back into her first world; but to reach her lover she had only to become his bride again. If she could only fall weeping into his arms, there would be no more shining mist and invisible darkness, and La Sensuala would be forgotten. Psyche was free, quite free; just as the Lady had promised.

She sighed.

'Psyche?' she repeated, as if puzzled. La Sensuala was crying, the young man torn between past and present looking bewildered and miserable. 'Psyche? No, I don't think so. In fact, I'm sure you must be thinking of someone else – someone who died a long time ago.'

Outside in the chilly sky of sunrise the doves rose and rattled across the sky like gunfire.

'Quickly!' cried Psyche. 'You'd better go, the two of you. Hurry, she must not catch you here together. She'll come around; but give her time, don't provoke her. . . .'

The lovers fled.

Psyche was left alone.

She blew out the candles and waited. The room grew cold.

She lifted her head, smiling.

'Ah, there you are, my Lady. Welcome back. And what is the next task to be? Something quite impossible, I hope. I want work.'

Gwyneth Jones Born in Manchester, UK, educated at Notre Dame Convent High School and the University of Sussex, Brighton, Gwyneth Jones's subsequent career has taken in a variety of daytime jobs: waiting tables, accounts clerk, cook, chambermaid, writing silly articles for magazines, VDU operator, school dinner lady, civil servant; and lately, child care. She has had published several books for children, most of them under the pseudonym, Ann Halam; three adult novels; and various articles, reviews, and short stories. All her fiction fits, more or less, loosely under the heading of science fiction and/or fantasy, and her special interest is in the continuity of human imagination: the striking identities between stories written today, and those known for thousands of years.

CHAPTER TWO

REMBRANDTS OF THINGS PAST

Sheila Finch

At one time the Catholic Church denounced the Tarot as 'the Devil's Picturebook' (a notion celebrated in this volume by R J Stewart). Since that time, mystical enthusiasts have proclaimed the cards the 'royal road' to God. And today we find people using Tarot for 'past-life regressions'. Sheila Finch has moulded all these elements into a seamless and very funny tale of a certain well-known personality who would like to change the past.

The laser-etched sign on the large glass door of the secluded California mountain clinic said: *Doctor C 'Gus' Young, Past Life Adjustment Therapy*. The computer code for appointments was UPAINTIHEAL.

The aerial tram came up the steep escarpment from Palm Springs several times a day, exchanging parched desert, clogged freeways and over-priced condos for solitude, snow and big-horn sheep. There was always at least one client per day among the tourists disembarking. The clients would present themselves to the jitney driver, then bump up another thousand feet through the pine forest to Gus Young's ashram on a southern slope of the San Jacinto Mountains. Today there were two.

'Do you have an appointment this morning, too?' one of the clients asked, as the jitney skittered over the icy mountain road.

She was an overweight, tanned blonde, older than she looked at first glance, wearing diamond earrings so large they would have had to be cubic zirconias on anyone except

Magician

Moon

Devil's Play

one of Dr Young's clients. She pulled a mink jacket up under her chin and exhaled cloudily in the cold air.

'I'm supposed to be here at ten-thirty for my final Adjustment. At least, I *think* it's today. I have a screen test tomorrow. I'm an actress, you know?'

'I don't have an appointment.' The second visitor inclined his head politely. A tall man, with sandy hair and a freckled complexion, he wore a black track suit with a conspicuous designer label and high-top shoes already wet from the snow. 'I'll just wait.'

'But Gus doesn't – ' The blonde stared at him. 'Don't I know you from somewhere?'

'Everybody knows me,' the man said complacently.

'Huh?'

'I have that kind of face.'

'Oh,' she said doubtfully. 'How did you get clearance? Gus's so afraid of nuts coming up here.'

The man lifted one eyebrow. When he smiled, the freckles crowded together on his cheeks.

'You're a TV reporter, aren't you?' she guessed. 'Yes, of course. CBS, NBC?'

'Let's just say an observer of human nature,' he demurred, examining his fingernails for sand.

'I just *adore* reporters!' the blonde said.

They arrived at the imposing glass door to Dr Young's ashram. The jitney came to a halt and they climbed down. The ashram was a modern, bright pink adobe building with an oddly jarring steeply pitched roof. The balcony projected far out over the almost ten-thousand-foot drop to the desert floor where tentacles of smog twined through bald streets of new housing and shopping centres with cute names. To the south, a jumble of planes, hangars and troop facilities marked sprawling March Air Force Base.

'Hard to get your breath up here!' The woman stopped for a moment in front of the door.

'Nearer to heaven, and all that,' the man murmured.

She hesitantly raised one hand towards the gleaming alphanumeric pad set in the adobe wall. Her fingers moved slowly. Nothing happened. She tried again. An amber warning light blinked malevolently. The man in the black track suit raised one eyebrow.

'Gee! I forgot the code for today.' She reddened. 'I'm a little nervous. The start of my new life, you know?'

'Allow me,' he said. He ran his fingers over the pad. A moment later, the door swung open.

'How'd you do that?'

'An affinity for machines,' he explained.

She rewarded him with a smile as brilliant as her diamonds. In the hallway, a thin, middle-aged woman in a bright cotton dress gestured for them to come inside.

'Hi, Luz,' the blonde said breathily.

They went in to dark wood, white carpets, vivid paintings, and warmth.

'Marilyn, my dear!'

An older man, grey hair tied back in a ponytail, came to greet them. He was smoking a pipe and his feet were bare under an embroidered orange dashiki.

'It's so *fab* to be here again, Gus!' Marilyn said.

Dr C 'Gus' Young beamed. 'Come in!'

Gus had a very faint European accent that might or might not have been put on with the dashiki. He set the pipe down on a glass ashtray, and the waiting Luz immediately bore it and Marilyn's mink jacket away.

Marilyn ran one hand over her baby-fine hair. 'Is my painting ready?'

'Waiting for you to put your final touch to the image that will set you free from the destructive past,' Gus said. 'Today we start your feet down the path of the future towards success and happiness.'

'I guess I'm getting to be happy already,' she said doubtfully.

Gus clasped Marilyn's hands in his. Therapist and client gazed into each other's eyes. The second visitor cleared his throat discreetly.

'Who's this?' Gus dropped Marilyn's hands abruptly. 'You know I don't allow guests.'

'Not a guest,' the other man said. He was at least a head taller than Dr Young and had to bend to meet the therapist's eyes. 'I've waited a *very* long time to find someone with your skill.'

'I don't see anyone without an appointment.'

'I heard about your work so recently, there wasn't time to make an appointment,' the tall visitor explained.

'He's a reporter,' Marilyn said. 'Network news. But he's okay, you know?'

'A reporter?' Gus's voice went up the scale. 'I *definitely* don't see reporters!'

'Oh, Gus! Pretty please? I don't mind him sitting in on my session,' Marilyn begged. 'He'd write real fab stuff about you. Wouldn't you?' She turned her bright gaze on the stranger.

'I'll be most discreet.' The tall man nodded politely to Marilyn.

She gave him a shy smile. 'I don't even know your name.'

'Frank,' he said. 'Frank – '

'First names only here!' the therapist snapped. Then he relented. 'Well, I could use a friendly voice from the fourth estate. Goodness knows I seem to be deliberately misunderstood most of the time.'

Marilyn clapped her hands.

'Come along then.' Gus herded the two ahead of him into another room.

The second room had high ceilings, more of the white carpet and a view from one glass wall up a tumble of boulders to nearby San Jacinto peak itself. Clear, northern light filled the room, an artist's light. A computer with an elongated keyboard stood on a desk by the glass wall, all gleaming surfaces and silvery key-pads.

'This is Rembrandt,' Gus said.

Over the computer, a row of coloured lights winked from a long panel; silvery needles made slow revolutions of dials or took exotic measurements. Twisted cables spilled out from under the computer and ran to what appeared to be an artist's easel in the middle of the room. There was a blank, grey canvas on it. At second glance, the canvas could be seen to be made of glass.

Gus waved Marilyn and Frank towards the chrome and

white vinyl chairs next to the easel. He carefully pushed up the sleeves of the dashiki, then poised his hands over the keyboard as if he were about to play a sonata. Rainbow bulbs glowed in sequence, then blinked out.

'Impressive!' Frank said. 'But how does it work?'

'Negative experiences of our past selves can have devastating influence on who we are in the present life,' Gus explained. 'The way to unlock the potential of the present is to discover who we once were, and heal the wounds suffered by the previous personality.'

'Ah. Then – '

'Rembrandt allows us to make a picture of the offending moment in the past life and, by altering it, replacing it with a more acceptable image, cleanse its power to hurt in the present.'

Two emerald waves oscillated on the computer monitor. Gus watched them intently for a few moments, then typed in a command. Numbers scrolled up the side of the screen. He sat back and folded his arms. Slowly, an image coalesced on the glass canvas.

'Gee!' Marilyn gasped, leaning forward.

The colourful scene showed a well-endowed blonde in a low-cut nightgown reclining against a satin pillow, a rich portrait in light and shadow. In one hand she held a bottle of pills. Behind her, a man could be seen apparently just turning to leave the room.

'There *you* are on that fateful day, Marilyn. With your friend.'

Marilyn began to sob. 'I never knew my parents! I lived at the orphanage or with foster parents. Nobody ever really cared about me. Not even Bobby or Jack or – '

'Yes, well. That was only one version of your past life,' Gus said sternly. 'All things are possible in the Cosmic Record that we tap into.' He turned to the visitor. 'What we've been creating here, in all these sessions, is a more acceptable past life for Marilyn to live with in this one. Rembrandt has done its work with this portrait of how things were. Now, *she* must make it what it should have been. She must make the last, most significant change.'

'What's that?' She snagged a tissue from a box on a nearby table and sniffled into it. Blonde hair straggled forward over her pudgy face.

'We've been over this already, Marilyn! See your friend? You decided his approval would have made all the difference.'

Gus held out a long thin brush with a glowing cluster of glass fibres on one end. Hesitantly Marilyn pointed it towards the scene on the liquid crystal screen.

'Go ahead,' Gus said. 'Turn Jim around. Paint his arms enfolding you. Heal the wounds suffered by your past self.'

'Jack,' she said through the sniffles. 'Not Jim. Jack.'

As the brush hovered over the screen, one arm of the man faded and disappeared. Then as Marilyn's brush strokes became more determined, the arm re-appeared over the woman's shoulder, the fingers giving her an approving squeeze. The expression on the man's face changed, too. A smile replaced the air of distance he'd been wearing. Now the portrait showed a book in the woman's fingers instead of the pill bottle.

When it was complete, Marilyn set the brush down. She stepped back and looked at the picture, her mouth slack-jawed.

'Are you satisfied with it?'

She nodded. 'It looks real, Gus.'

'It *is* real, my dear!'

'Fascinating chiaroscuro,' Frank murmured. 'I can see why you named it Rembrandt.'

Gus turned to the keyboard. 'We'll freeze the picture for you, capturing the past as it should have been – thanks to modern technology.'

'So in this revised version of history she doesn't commit suicide,' Frank said. 'But now what?'

Marilyn spun lightly away from the easel, diamonds bouncing. Her face seemed to have dropped several years' worth of worry-lines. She gave Frank a radiant smile.

'Jack respected my brain. He really did!' she said in a bright voice. 'He expected such great things of me.'

'Really? And will you achieve them now?'

'Oh yes! I'm going to write a book about my experiences.'

'Here.' Gus disconnected the electronic canvas and took it off the easel. He handed it to Marilyn.

'You designed your own software, of course?' Frank said. Gus smiled. 'Trade secrets, my journalistic friend!'

Marilyn clutched the painting to her breast, then planted a kiss on the therapist's cheek. 'It's fab, Gus! Thank you!'

'Now that we've healed this wound you've been dragging around from your past life as Marilyn, you can go on to success in this one.'

'I think I'll use the name I was given in this life again, you know?'

'A wise decision.' Gus nodded soberly.

'You can call me Brenda now.'

'Wonderful! Will you stay for refreshments, Brenda? I'll have Luz bring coffee and cakes.'

'Gee! I have to watch my weight.' She blew another kiss and danced out of the room.

'You don't really expect me to believe that painting a picture of someone's imagined past life actually changes their present?' Frank said, setting down his coffee cup so Luz could refill it.

'You saw what you saw,' Gus said. He stuffed another honey cake into his mouth. 'Past life therapy always leaves me starving!'

'And she actually believes she was once Marilyn Monroe?'

The therapist sat cross-legged, an orange-robed guru on a white vinyl couch. 'A person's past is just one interpretation of complex cosmic events. Out of the billions of memory fragments from this present life – some real, some not so real, some entirely imaginary – all stored in our brains, we make a selection which we call our past. And sometimes the result is a destructive influence on present behaviour. The analyst's job is to help the analysand arrive at the right selection, to yield a truth that is palatable, a truth that supports a healthy life in the present. Every psychotherapist attempts to do that. Even Freud understood it!'

'Spare me the pyschobabble,' Frank said.

Gus bristled. 'My concern is to make things better! If bad experiences in this life affect us, why not experiences in *past* lives?'

'This is all very subjective.'

'Exactly! So in my therapy we subjectively select not the *true* but the *optimum* imagery and proceed from there.'

'Hmm.'

'The client just has to exercise caution visualizing the past he wishes to change.'

The phone rang and Gus picked it up. 'Ah yes, Cleo my dear! And how was the Nile trip? Really? Too bad. Yes. Yes. We have an appointment for tomorrow. Toodleoo!' He turned back to Frank. 'Charming woman, truly charming. But very indecisive. Can't decide whether she wants Rembrandt to paint Caesar or Antony for her.'

'So?'

'Oh, she'll keep coming in.' Gus replaced the phone and took another cake.

'Aren't you a trifle expensive?'

Gus disdained to answer.

'I'm still sceptical,' Frank said. 'After all – Cleopatra, Marilyn Monroe? Do you really expect me to believe this?'

'It's what the clients believe that matters,' Gus said. He glared up at Frank. 'Who did you say you were? You look mighty familiar.'

'I have one of those universal faces.'

'Are you from the *New York Times*? They don't understand alternative science on the east coast!'

'Let's say I'm a freelance.' Frank was silent for a moment. Then he asked, 'And the results you get?'

'The results are always good.'

'Does the cure stick?'

'You can check my references.'

'I know you have a lot of rich satisfied clients, and a healthy stock portfolio as a result.'

'What of it?'

'Certainly no one values anything they don't pay through the nose for.'

'I've been over this again and again for the AMA and the FDA and the Better Business Bureau. I'm perfectly clean.'

The phone rang again. Gus nodded at Frank before he answered. 'Well hello, my friend! What? Of course we're making progress. Any day now we'll have your troublesome previous self identified. Just keep on – What's that? Well, certainly narrowing the field to early nineteenth-century generals was a big step forward! Hmm. No, I don't think anyone else has claimed to be – Certainly. Talk to my secretary about an appointment. I'll transfer you. Au revoir!'

'I think you're a charlatan, a trickster,' Frank said, as Gus hung up the phone.

'High-tech wizard, perhaps. But I object to being called a charlatan by people who don't take the time to understand my theories or my methods.'

'You claim to be achieving results that elude traditional psychiatry.'

'They don't have Rembrandt – my patented, computerized canvas. It's the old truth about a picture being worth a thousand words. Especially a picture of your past that you alter to fit your present needs.'

'Faith healing?' Frank suggested. 'Don't get me wrong, Gus. I believe in the powers of the mind, too.'

'You're oversimplifying my therapy.'

Frank persisted. 'But belief does have something to do with it?'

'Show me a cure – mental or physical – that doesn't work better if the patient believes in it. That's been true since Hippocrates wrote his oath. What I've done is add modern technology.'

'A wonderfully potent combination, faith, science and money,' Frank agreed. 'You really seem to do something – whatever it is – for these wackos that come to you thinking they were Caesar and Cleopatra.'

'Of course I do something for them! I change destructive

images of the past into constructive ones. Look here! I'm
not going to waste my valuable time – '

'What about the dangerous ones, the ones who think they
were Genghis Khan or Hitler?'

'I've had three Jack the Rippers, if that's what you mean.'
Gus lifted one arm and patted the bulge that was revealed
under his dashiki. 'My trusty little forty-five keeps things
friendly.'

Frank stood by the glass wall, idly gazing at the cloud-
wreathed peak of the mountain. 'Perhaps we could help
each other.'

'What could you do for me? Write me up in the popular
press as some kind of New Age freak?' Gus snorted. 'I
don't need that kind of fame.'

'I'd better admit I'm not a journalist. That was Marilyn's
– Brenda's – idea.'

'Well then – ' Gus began angrily.

'But I do have something to offer.' Frank turned a chair
around and straddled it, facing the therapist. 'I can make
you wealthy, Gus. More than you ever dreamed. I have a
proposition.'

'You call me a fraud and a charlatan, and yet you want
to work with me?'

Frank shook his head. 'I think you're on to something
bigger than you realize. I want a chance to benefit from
your invention. I want to re-do my own past, just as you
advertise.'

'And who do you think you were? Never mind! I'm not
going to take you on anyway.'

'Not a past life,' Frank said. 'This one.'

'Out of the question!'

'How much do you want? You can name your own fee.'
He laid a credit card edged in genuine 24-carat gold on the
glass coffee table in front of the therapist.

'Money!' Gus's fingers twitched several times, but he
made no move to touch Frank's credit card. 'There's more
to life than money.'

'Notice the Swiss bank?' Frank slid the card a little closer.
'I have unlimited credit on that card. Go ahead. Check up

on it. Unlimited. Think about that, Gus. You could buy yourself everything you've ever dreamed of. Not tempted? All right. You could buy respectability in the medical community. You could command the AMA's admiration.'

'Who gives a flying fuck about the damned AMA?'

'A man of discernment!' Frank said. 'Well then. What do you want? The Nobel Prize? How about that for *real* recognition?'

'Ridiculous! You can't – '

'It could be arranged,' Frank said. 'There are ways.'

Gus took a deep breath before replying. 'Rembrandt only makes pictures of past lives.'

'Past lives – the past of this life – what's the difference?'

Gus took a handkerchief out of a pocket in the dashiki and wiped sweat off his brow. 'It takes months to achieve the results you witnessed here this morning.'

'I don't need months. Just today.' Frank pushed the card until it lay almost under the therapist's fingers.

Gus's eyes were watering. 'Just today, he says, just today! What do you think I am, some kind of magician?'

'What I think is, you're a clever man, Gus, with an invention that's bigger than you know: half real science, half hocus pocus.'

Gus gazed thoughtfully at the man in the black track suit. 'Somehow you don't seem the type I usually get. Why should I bother with you?'

Frank smiled mischievously. 'I thought perhaps you might be intrigued when you heard who I am.'

The therapist frowned. 'You do look awfully familiar. But even if I were to accept you, it's difficult to identify the absolutely appropriate key image, the one on which everything else depends. It took Brenda weeks to see her problem crystallized on the night she committed suicide as Marilyn Monroe.'

'I know the exact moment.'

Gus thought that over in silence. Then he picked up the gold-edged credit card. He stared at it as if he were memorizing the account numbers.

'I'm not guaranteeing anything.'

'Of course.'
'And you're perfectly clear what you want?'
'Justice,' Frank said.

'You understand I'm not in the vengeance business.' Gus took an impression from the gold card. 'I may work on the frontiers of established medicine, and I'm certainly not averse to making money! But I do subscribe to the Hippocratic oath. Only beneficial treatments according to my abilities and judgement, et cetera, et cetera.'

Frank snatched the card impatiently out of Gus's fingers and slipped it into a pocket in his track suit. He lay on the white couch near the computer as the therapist adjusted something like an astronaut's helmet with wires over his head. Outside the picture window, the afternoon had clouded over and threatened more snow.

'What's the helmet for?'

'Magnetic resonance imaging picks up the signals from your brain. You don't need any artistic skill. When you tell me what someone or something from your past was like, Rembrandt constructs a visual analogue of it from your memory. Just like the original painter, my Rembrandt captures the subtleties of psychology.'

'When one person changes his reality, other people's gets changed too, doesn't it?'

Gus stopped, electrical leads in one hand.

'Okay, okay,' Frank said cheerfully. 'I was only thinking out loud.'

'You get a new chance,' Gus said. 'And in some ways, by reacting to the new you, so does everybody around you.'

The therapist seated himself in front of the computer console. 'Now, we don't have time for mistakes or evasions. I need to get as much data as possible for Rembrandt to work with. I want you to think about my questions and answer them as thoroughly as you can.'

'Fire away.'

'What's the earliest memory you have of your mother?'

'I don't have *any* memories of my mother.'

'Your father, then?'

'A big man,' Frank said. 'Old, even when I was growing up – beard and all that. Stern. Playful when the mood took him. Absolutely always right. I adored him. And I hated his guts.'

'Typical,' Gus commented. 'Very Freudian. Rembrandt's getting some good images on that already. What about family?'

'Lots of brothers. Mike was the oldest. I came next. Several after that. I forget most of their names.'

'How – '

'We were an extended family.'

'Oh.' Gus added more commands to the computer, watched the images forming and dissolving on the small monitor, made some minor adjustments. 'Your father looks like a real authority figure. No wonder you were ambivalent about him! Tell me about your home life.'

'Every day the same: perfect. Dad and Big Brother Mike taking care of things for us younger ones. It was paradise, I tell you.'

'Then I fail to see – '

'Who can live in paradise? I screwed up. I challenged the old man. Wounded his pride. Did I say he was unforgiving? There was a big family row. Some of the younger ones sided with me. Mike – who I adored! – sided with Dad. Dad demanded I apologize. I refused. Dad kicked me out. And Gabe – ' Frank was unable to continue for a few moments. Then he said, 'It's been hell.'

'You poor devil,' Gus commented.

'If I could get back . . .'

The therapist gazed thoughtfully at his client for a moment. 'You want to go home again? You're sure? Back to that time when everything was perfect?'

'Something like that.'

'*Something* won't do! We're working with a computer here. You have to be as precise as you possibly can.'

'Yes, then.'

The therapist leaned over to thumb a switch on one side of the computer. 'Southern-looking place, isn't it?'

'With a few eastern touches.'

'Check the screen,' Gus instructed.

Frank removed the helmet and turned to the easel. A family portrait filled the liquid crystal screen: father and sons standing stiffly on the porch of a rather elaborate family estate, all white marble columns and trailing vines. The physical textures, the play of light and shade were astonishing. To one side, a dark little figure in overalls and straw hat slunk away downhill in shadows.

'Interesting,' Gus said. 'A truly archetypal image.'

'All those years ago. That's how it started.'

'But now we're going to change things. Take up the light brush.'

Frank reached for the brush, then hesitated again. Outside the window, evening shadows crept up the mountains. Far below, Palm Springs scorched the desert with neon light. A fighter plane taking off from March Air Force Base roared across the darkening sky.

'What're you waiting for?' Gus turned on a lamp. 'Paint yourself in the middle of the family group again. It'll be as if all those years of separation had never happened.'

'I haven't been perfectly honest with you,' Frank said.

'Not important now! Correct the picture.'

'I don't think you realize who I am.'

Gus gazed at him calmly. 'Even if you're Old Nick himself, you aren't powerful enough to change your own reality by yourself, are you?'

'It's not as if I haven't tried long enough. But computer technology augments the mind's inherent powers. Even a superior mind like mine! I've had to wait for your invention. Tell me, doesn't that possibility worry you, that I might *really* be Satan?'

Gus sighed. 'Do hurry and alter the picture. It's almost suppertime.'

As if she'd been listening behind the door, Luz came silently into the room carrying a tray full of tacos and bottles of Mexican beer. She set them down on the glass table, lit another lamp. Outside the window, a coyote howled. Luz withdrew.

'I owe it you to tell you this,' Frank said, dabbing tentatively at a corner of the canvas with the light brush. 'If I paint myself in the middle of the picture, between Dad and Mike, things are going to change.'

Gus munched on a taco. 'That's the whole idea.'

'My actions here will change the world. You may not like the result.'

'I hope you won't be disappointed when it doesn't happen quite like that? Here, you might as well help yourself to some food. At least have a beer.'

'You're a fraud, Gus.' Frank touched the electronic canvas again; colour bloomed under the brush. 'A small-time magician. Yet I believe your machine works – in spite of you.'

'Physician. Magician. What difference does it make to you, Fred?'

'It's Frank. But Dad used to call me Bub.' He carefully daubed the screen with coloured light. 'Everything you see around you that's bad in this world has been caused by my feud with my father.'

'Classic paranoia,' Gus mumbled, his mouth full of taco.

'I really am the devil, you see.'

'And you're the third one of those I've had, too!'

'I've been wasting my time all these centuries trying to change things *now*. But I finally figured it out. If I change the past and get back *inside*, where the real power is, can you imagine what'll happen? Devastating!' He grinned at the therapist. 'Everything I always wanted. And your Rembrandt holds the key.'

Gus took a swig of beer. 'You're planning a palace coup against God?'

'Mock if you want. I've had a long time to think how I might've handled things if I hadn't been kicked out.'

'Are you certain you haven't overlooked anything?' Gus said, setting the beer glass down. 'You need to be very careful about a thing like this.'

'Wonderful,' Frank said sarcastically. 'Contraindications from a fraud!'

'And a devil who thinks he's finally outsmarted God.'

Frank made several swift passes with the light brush. 'There.'

Gus leaned forward to see the picture Frank had made. Seated in rocking chairs on the front porch of the large, white-columned southern-looking mansion, Dad and the boys listened to a banjo player. Frank was recognizable on Dad's left side, surreptitiously sipping whisky.

'Yahoo!' Frank tossed the light brush up into the air. '*Now* you'll see a difference!'

'You're quite an artist, Fred,' Gus commented. 'But don't say I didn't try to warn you. There was a real flaw in your thinking.'

Frank was already running out the door. Then he stopped abruptly.

Outside, the snow sparkled like a field of diamonds, yet the air was warm and pure and smog-free as the first day of creation. The soft perfume of exotic blossoms drifted over the snow. A mountain lion strolled past the ashram side by side with a young California big-horn.

'I'd forgotten that reference,' Gus said.

'Wait a minute.' Frank stared down at the valley where the lights of Palm Springs were going out. Over to the south, a lake was replacing the former Air Force runways. 'This is some kind of trick, isn't it?'

Gus shrugged. 'You wanted to go home. That's what you got.'

An odd, whickering sound came to them over the snow.

'Damn,' Frank said. 'Well, at least I know a lot more now than I did way back then! I'm just going to have to – '

He broke off.

Something huge flapped towards them over the peak of San Jacinto Mountain. Giant white wings turned silver in the moonlight.

'What in hell?' Frank whispered.

As the bird drew closer, they could see what appeared to be the tip of an olive twig drooping out of its enormous beak.

'Nice touch,' Gus said.

'If He thinks he's going to smooth everything over by going smarmy on me – ' Frank said belligerently.

'A new beginning,' Gus reminded him. 'For Him, too.'

The dove – which was about the size of an elephant – hovered just above Frank's head.

'Come to take me home, have you?' Frank asked.

The dove opened its beak. The olive twig began to grow out towards Frank – a twig, a branch, then a whole fistful of branches, then a bush. And as it grew, it twisted upon itself, adding spines and brambles till it resembled a tangle of barbed wire.

'What?' Frank said. 'No! You don't mean – '

He screamed as the razor-sharp convolutions of the bush slid over his head and shoulders, enmeshing him.

'Oh my.' Gus shook his head. 'Apparently Rembrandt works better than I thought.'

'How can this be happening?' Frank yelled, as the bird lumbered to take off again with its cargo. 'This isn't how I wanted to do it!'

'I guess He's had time to think how to do things differently, too,' Gus suggested.

The dove flapped ponderously up into a sky filled with a blue jewel of a moon. Frank's screams died slowly away.

Gus turned back to his ashram which seemed to be paling a little around the edges. He stared at it thoughtfully for a moment.

'Oh well. I never was particularly happy with that design.'

He went back inside.

Things continued to get better.

Sheila Finch was born and raised in London. After doing graduate work in linguistics and medieval literature at Indiana University, she moved to California where she teaches science fiction and creative writing at El Camino College. Finch has published three science fiction novels, *Infinity's Web*, *Triad*, and *The Garden of the Shaped*. Two more in the Shaper series will appear in 1989. She has also published science fiction and fantasy stories, including appearances in *Amazing, Asimov's, Fantasy and*

Science Fiction and *Fantasy Book*, as well as in original anthologies. She has three daughters and one granddaughter.

CHAPTER THREE

THE HORSE OF IRON AND HOW WE CAN KNOW IT AND BE CHANGED BY IT FOREVER

M John Harrison

There are many who consider Tarot readings (and probably Tarot stories) an insult, or even a perversion. For them the cards describe the path to personal enlightenment, and should only be used for instruction and meditation. But if a pack of cards can lead us to mystical revelations, why not some other set of coded information? For instance, a railroad timetable. . . . M John Harrison keeps a notebook at all times. In it he writes down overheard bits of conversation, street notices, and so on. The idea for this story, he tells us, came to him partly from seeing that wonderful sign on the train between Wakefield and Huddersfield.

Recently I switched on in the middle of a television arts programme. Two men were moulding in brass something which looked at first sight like the stripped carcass of a turkey, that exact, sharp-edged cage of bone which reveals itself so thoroughly through all the strips and flaps of flesh after Christmas dinner. It turned out, though, to be something less interesting, a classical figurine, a Poseidon or Prometheus which systematically lost its magic as the layers of casting plaster were knocked off carefully with the back of an axe. This was so essentially disappointing – a striptease through which, by removing veils of strangeness and alien signification, the sculptor revealed a value ordinary and easily understood – that to replace it I turned off the TV and imagined this:

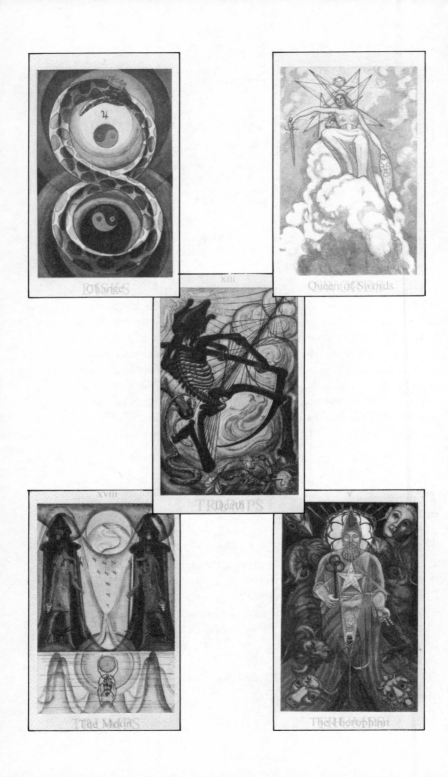

TrUMPS

The Magus

The Hanged Man

The Lovers

The Chariot

Another foundry, somewhere in the night, somewhere in history, in which something like a horse's skull (not a horse's *head*; a skull, which looks nothing like a horse at all, but like an enormous curved shears, or a bone beak whose two halves meet only at the tip, a wicked, intelligent-looking purposeless thing which cannot speak) came out of the mould, and all the founders were immediately executed to keep the secret. They had known all along this would happen to them. These men were the great craftsmen and engineers of their day. They could have looked for more from life. Yet they crammed down their fear, and got on with the work, and afterwards made no attempt to escape.

This was how I learned the secret of the horse, which I now give here, after first folding it across itself like a slip of paper, in a further intricating gesture.

1 *The Fool.*

A young man, in whose dark hair a single strand of grey has recently appeared, decides to set out on a series of excursions suggested by the fall of the cards.

Complex rules will determine the direction of each journey. For instance, the suit being Wands, he will only go north if the journey is to take place in the second half of the year; or if the next card turned up is a Knight.

Equally intricate rules, whose algebraic clauses and counter-clauses he intuits with each new cast of the cards, cover the choice of south, west and east; of destination; even of the clothes he will wear; but he will always travel by train. This decision is based on the relationship he has identified between the flutter of cards falling in a quiet cold room and the flutter of changing destinations on the mechanical indicator boards at railway stations. This similarity rests, he is willing to admit, on a metaphor: for while the fall of the cards is – or seems – random, the sequence of destinations is – or seems – controlled.

To represent himself in this affair, the young man – or Ephebe – has chosen the Fool. This card, therefore, will never turn up. He has subtracted it from the deck and keeps it beside him; each afternoon, as the light goes out of the room, it seems to fluoresce up at him from the table or the arm of his chair, more an event than a picture. We move forward through time by the deeply undercutting action of Desire. As the Fool steps continually off his cliff and into space, so the Ephebe is always a presence attempting to fill the absence that has brought him forth. He is a wave tumbling constantly forward into each new moment, and his journeys are thus in every sense a trip. By following the journeys as they fall out, he believes, he will open for himself a fifth direction; and to help identify it he will bring back from each journey an object. These objects or *données* will eventually comprise both a 'compass' and a set of instructions for its use.

All the Ephebe's journeys begin from London.

2 The Magus, representing Heterodox Skills.

Some are no more than commuter trips, on trains with automatic sliding doors and the interior design of buses. They arrive at the platform loaded with well-groomed, purposive people who seem prosperous but new to it: clerks and estate agents already a bit pouchy in the face, doing all they can with a shirt and a tie and a padded shoulder to pass themselves off as dangerous, successful accountants from the City – men and women in their early twenties who pride themselves on looking like self-satisfied bullies.

Trains like this run hourly between Harrow and Euston, through a station called Kilburn High Road, the high walls of which are covered with the most beautiful graffiti. They are not scrawls whose content – 'LUFC wankers die tomorrow', 'No brains rule' – and context are their only significance, but explosions of red and purple and green done with great deliberation and exuberance, shapes like fireworks going off, shapes that bulge like damp tropical fruit, with an effect of glistening surfaces. They are names – 'Eddie', 'Daggo', 'Mince' – but names which have been transformed from sign or label into illustration: *pictures* of names. After them everything else looks dull, the high brick walls of the next station – South Hampstead – resembling the walls of some great windowless linear prison. The children who do this call it 'bombing'; they bomb their personalities on to the walls.

When the train stops at Kilburn High Road the doors slide open as if it is waiting for someone and after a long time an old man gets on and goes to an empty seat. His overcoat is belted but he has no shirt on, so you can see clearly the mass of springy yellowish-white hairs between his withered old pectoral muscles. A rank smell comes up from him. As soon as the doors close, he rolls a cigarette and smokes it with relish, smiling and nodding around at the other passengers. The men stare at their polished shoes. The women draw away and look angrily at one another as he pulls back his cuff to consult his watch. This grand gesture reveals the word FUGA tattooed inside his grimy wrist. 'No one dare remind him,' the Ephebe muses, 'that this is a No Smoking carriage.' And then: 'We should live our lives the way those children sign themselves, bombing our names on to the prison walls inside our heads.'

From this, his first excursion, he brings back a flattened cigarette stub, porous and stained brown at the end where the old man has held it gently between his lips.

3 The Hanged Man, representing 'the descent of light into darkness in order to redeem it'; in its female aspect, 'the Sophia of Valentinus'.

New trains run on the line between Wakefield and Huddersfield. Inside them, next to every door, is a sign which reads: PRESS WHEN ILLUMINATED TO OPEN. Illuminati everywhere should know about this sign. Between Wakefield and Huddersfield illumination is likely to come as a corollary of the abandoned factories visible from the train; the rubbish that clogs the shallow river; the dour failed lives in the houses beyond. What is the Ephebe to do on receiving it? Press the button and jump out of the train?

In the overheated carriages of the 22.01 his journey pulls out like chewing gum; then snaps.

At Dewsbury a tired-looking woman gets up to leave the train. Round her neck she is wearing five or six gold chains, each bearing either her initial or her Christian name. They cling and spill between the tendons of her neck like a delicate gold net. She stands in front of the doors, which will not open for her. The sign is illuminated but she has not noticed it. Soon the train will pull away again and she will still be on it. She looks around with growing agitation.

'I can't just work these doors out. Can you?'

The Ephebe would like to be able to reply, 'What you call yourself, who you claim yourself to be by putting on all your necklaces, is not as important as the act itself.' That gesture, of netting or fixing, he believes, is what actually identifies her. He would like to be able to explain, 'People love you for the identity in the act, an identity so frail they must constantly help affirm it.' But all he actually says is, 'I think you have to press the button.'

At this the train gives a lurch, as if it has lost its patience.

From this journey the Ephebe brings back an item of personalized jewellery in the form of the name SOPHIA. The Aeon called Sophia, Valentinus reminds us, astonished to find herself separate from the Good, mistook for its light the tawdry, bluish flicker of the created world, and flung herself towards it. By desiring God so strongly she fell away from Him and into the city of Alexandria, where she still redeems herself daily as a prostitute. (In some versions of her agony, Sophia *becomes* the city, and as library, language, labyrinth, is thus the instrument of Mankind's redemption. In others, rather than falling away from the Father, she denies herself to Him in reprisal for some never-defined unkindness to His children.)

4 *The Lovers, representing 'Alchemical Marriage' and the Concordance of Opposites.*

Now the Ephebe lives along the line.

His journeys divide themselves between those on routes

he has never travelled in his life – such as the one that worms its way, stopping at every station from Shotton on round the coast, from Crewe to Bangor; and those he already knows by heart, so that he can recognize every power pylon, sub-station or battery-hen house between, say, London St Pancras and Sheffield Central.

He delights in the surprises of an unknown line.

Suddenly the sea is racing along by his shoulder, light spattering off it like frying fat. Later the train crawls past container depots, and a tank farm lit up mysteriously in the night. The guard announces, 'Once again lays'n'gem I do apologize your late arrival and inconvenience cause,' and the Ephebe wakes next morning in the Rose & Crown; where like some travelling salesman he feels obliged to guzzle bacon, eggs, sausage and hot tea while he looks speculatively out at the wet provincial street.

As a result of one of these journeys he drifts into a tranced, sensual affair with a young woman a little older than himself who runs her mother's boarding house. In the mornings she serves breakfast to the guests, while he lies in bed imagining the men as they watch her moving about the room with her tray. Though she has already brought him his own breakfast in bed, kissed him, watched him eat it with a kind of unfashionable pride in his appetite, the Ephebe sometimes finds himself envying them what he thinks of as an intensely *formal* experience of her. They see her only once or twice a year, at the beginning and end of a day. Some of them try to look down her blouse as she puts the crockery on the table; others are content to talk to her about the weather; yet others are hypnotized by the quick deftness of her hands as she lays out knife, fork and serviette, or calmed by the smell of her body beneath the smell of her perfume.

When he tries to explain this to her she laughs and tells him, 'You're so greedy!'

This goes some way towards understanding though perhaps not far enough. Increasingly, after she has taken away his breakfast tray, the Ephebe catches himself staring up through the attic skylight at the heavy white clouds, wondering if he can disguise himself and, like some boy out of a medieval poem, appear one morning among the commercial travellers at the breakfast table to observe her unobserved; and from this journey he brings back only the sound of her voice as she urges him, 'Fuck me, fuck me,' in the night.

5 *The Chariot, representing Self Expression.*

All journeys are enchanted.

It isn't so much that the landscape distracts you, as that something about the motion of the train – something about the very idea of constant, rushing, forward movement – makes you restless and slow to settle to anything. You read a few pages of a book and look out at some swans on a canal. A newspaper opened suddenly just down the carriage sounds like rain spattering on the window. Another chapter and you make your way down to the buffet or the lavatory. Between each event a reverie pours itself, as seamless as Golden Syrup, as smooth as the motion of the train. You wonder what the weather will be like in Leeds or Newcastle, turn to *The Independent* to find out, read, 'The world economy is likely to remain subdued.'

Looking up from these words to a landscape of hedges and ponds, copses and little embankments, the Ephebe sees with amazement a strange vehicle bounding along beside the railway line.

In a long, complex frame of metal tubing, suspended on four tractor wheels, are cradled: an engine wrapped round with copper pipes and sheaves of old electrical wiring; clusters of what seem to be household butane gas bottles; and, well to the rear, the padded seat of some old-fashioned military jet, into which is strapped a man. Gouts of earth and water spray up from its enormous wheels. From time to time this whole machine seems to be consumed by a kind of radiant discharge, through which its driver or pilot can be seen helplessly or furiously waving his arms.

Is he a prisoner of his vehicle? Or does he prefer to drive on the edge of disaster like this? He is a wasted old man. When it can be seen, his face runs the gamut of expression, wild with fear one moment, laughing with excitement the next. His long grey hair blows back in the slipstream. His lips contort. He has fastened himself into a tight brown leather suit along the arms and legs of which run clusters of neoprene tubing. Out of these at intervals erupt thick coloured fluids, which splatter over his chest or into his eyes. Though he blinks furiously, he suffers the indignity without harm; but wherever the machine is touched it blackens and smokes briefly, and lightning writhes along its chassis members.

One huge wheel flies off suddenly into the air. The old man claps his hands to his face. At that moment the train enters a tunnel, and the Ephebe can see only himself, reflected in the window.

If the appearance of the machine has filled him with astonishment, its disappearance leaves him with a curious mixture of elation and anger he can neither understand nor resolve. By the time he is able to unclench his hands and wipe his forehead, the train has left the tunnel for open ploughland across which spills a tranquil evening light. Wrestling desperately with one another, the old man and his machine have passed back into the dimension from which they came, where they leap and bucket and belly their way forever through rural England, scattering clods of earth, steam, small bushes and dead animals. But in the palm of the Ephebe's hand remains a small intricately machined metal item, melted at one end to slag.

This he brings home with him. For months it remains warm to the touch, as if it had only lately been thrown out of the hearth of the heart.

6 *The Two of Discs, representing Change.*

Some journeys encourage a different kind of fantasy.

In his journal the Ephebe records:

For some time I was enchanted by a tiny station called Long Eaton on the main line between Derby and Loughborough. Here, two slatted wooden platforms surrounded by larch, pine and variegated holly gave the air of a rural halt at once bijou and mysterious: the last place you would expect an Inter City turbine to stop. Sitting in the train, you had no idea what sort of landscape lay behind the woods. The wind rushed through them, so that you thought of yourself as being on some sandy eminence away from which spread an intimately folded arrangement of orchards and lanes, of broad heathland stretching off to other hills. Afternoon light enamelled the leaves of the holly. Owls and wood pigeons moved amid the branches. Everything was possible in the country – or garden – beyond.

Then the light passed, the wind dropped and the train began to move again; you saw that the trees were dusty and birdlimed, and that they had hidden only housing estates, allotments, and a light engineering plant. A fat woman with a hyperactive child came into the carriage, sneezed in your face. 'Just sit down,' she warned the child. Instead it stared defiantly into her eyes for a moment then wandered off to make noises with the automatic door.

Despite this I always looked forward to Long Eaton, as if I hoped each time that the enchantment would be maintained. Then one day I glimpsed, fleetingly, through the windows of a train speeding in the opposite direction, a station called Haywards Heath (it was on the line between London and Brighton), and realized immediately that both it and Long Eaton were references to a lost type, that intimate little station of middle-class children's fiction forty years ago. Conifers and sandy soil; foxes and owls and stolen ponies; gorse and gypsy caravans in a rough field; then some mystery about a pile of railway sleepers near the tracks, shiny with rain in the green light at the edge of the woods.

The Ephebe has recognized his mistake. But is he cured of it? Or does he still hope that one day he will abandon his life as it now is, some freak fall of the cards throwing him into another one in which he gets down from a train at just such a fictional station without even a suitcase and walks towards some granite tor steeped in evening light? Whatever the answer to this question, he brings back from a subsequent journey a children's novel called *Island of Adventure* – though to give him credit he does not actually read it.

7 The Queen of Swords. 'We are the words; we are the music; we are the thing itself.'

Long journeys encourage the Ephebe to read and write; but they also outline the great gap between the lived and the written. Under a railway bridge at night, in Glasgow perhaps, he finds himself staring into the window of Apollo Video Supplies. There on a large screen, the following video clip repeats itself endlessly and silently to the drunks who stagger past:

In front of an Asian boy who watches captivated, a sword is beaten into existence out of the sparks of the anvil. The boy's father lies dead. The boy will grow up to be a Ninja fighter, and avenge him. His eyes are huge now as he discerns his uncertain yet triumphant future in the steel. The sparks stream past.

Exactly what you would expect, thinks the Ephebe, and indeed this boy is only a cliché; but look up from the screen and you can see the orange sparks fly out of it and down the road, where amid the dancing hailstones they light up in other dreary shopfronts something more than 'Winter Woollens – Reduced'.

Language is a scandal because it can make connections like these. Stories pass the experienced world back and forth between them as a metaphor, until it is worn out. Only then do we realize that meaning is an *act*. We must repossess it, instant to instant in our lives.

8 Death. Everything opens to contain its opposite.

Whenever the Ephebe looks up there is something new in the landscape – gorse spilling down the side of a steep little hill with a farm on top; factory chimneys dissolving in a blaze of sun he can't bear to look at; a clear night somewhere up north, with contrails drawn across Orion and the Dog – but eventually journeys like this must become tiring. The clean yellow front of an Inter City train, rushing towards the platform in the sunlight, no longer fills him with excitement. He's slept in too many overheated rooms, under thick continental quilts; eaten in too many station cafés; awaited too many connections. He is losing faith in the insights he had, the relationships he formed.

All he remembers about the city he's in is a display of popular wedding stationery – twenty per cent off – which, as he walked past it, seemed for a moment to merge indistinguishably with the cigarette ends, burger cartons and supermarket receipts on the pavement: so that for a moment everything became illegible to him, because the floor of the display window and the street, the inside and the outside, were only extensions of each other. He yawns and stares in the mirror. Behind him his bag is packed.

Later, the 17.18 Sheffield/ St Pancras is delayed by repair works along the line, then again by a fault in one of its power cars. It's Sunday. The Ephebe dozes and then wakes up abruptly. The train isn't moving and he has no idea where he is. He looks for lights or signs in the night: only dark fields. He has no watch – it was broken in Edinburgh – and the only one he can see belongs to a woman sitting across the aisle. Made of plastic, this has a dial transparent to its own works, greenish flickering cogs in the complexity of which your eye loses the position of the hands.

The Ephebe falls asleep again for a moment, dreams briefly of the old man and his strange energetic machine, racing alongside the train but this time looking in, then wakes suddenly in the horrified knowledge that he has cried out in his sleep and the whole carriage has heard him. He has become someone who makes noises in his sleep on the London express: a worn-out middle-aged man with bad teeth and a cloth briefcase, his head resting uncomfortably in the corner between the seat-back and the window.

From this journey, though, he brings back a memory of his childhood in Warwickshire.

One July morning, sitting hypnotized by the sound and weight of the river in Stoneleigh Park, he watched the hot sunlight spilling and foaming off the weir until he could no longer separate the look of the water from its strange, powerful, almost yeasty smell. Most of the objects of his childhood, he remembers, were transfigured in this way for him; and he notes in his journal that night:

Little earthy lanes and banks become secret entryways into the warm fields and bemused emotional states of childhood, when in a kind of excited fatigue you watch your own hand come closer and closer to the dry grey wood of an old gate, and find yourself unable for a second to context the one by the other or find a single context – unless it is something as huge and general as 'the world' – which will accept both. In the end you are able to understand only the intense *existence*, the photographic actuality of such objects. In that kind of childhood everything is fused into the light like flowers fused into a glass paperweight. At first I thought this light was in itself a fusing-together of other states or qualities which I could only vaguely label – 'self awareness', 'growing sexual curiosity', 'the unconditional trances of narcissism'. Now I see that the child is contrived wholly of the things he has already experienced: a spiderweb in the grass; a jet flying overhead; a cocoon of cuckoo-spit; the flare of light off the windscreen of a designer car. These elements are reassembled as a way of looking at other things. It was this continual fusing and re-fusing – this infolding – of experience which I perceived as a light bathing the landscape.

What we call 'meaning' is not what the light discovers, because what it discovers is itself. Now cast by the adult on new objects, it is valuable only for its very act of illumination. *Perception* is meaning. Meaning is an act.

9 *The Moon, representing 'the state of impure horror'; human faculties reach their limit and collapse before the Inward Light.*

As soon as the journeys are over, the cards can be laid to rest.

The Ephebe waits in the taxi-rank outside Charing Cross Station after his last trip. A short, badly dressed woman of about twenty-five or thirty is walking up and down the station forecourt shouting, 'You bloody piece of paper, you bloody piece of paper,' at a letter she holds in her right hand. Her face is red with effort, her hair straggles down around it. A maroon wool coat like a carpet compresses her fat breasts. 'You *bloody* piece of paper!' Eventually she varies the emphasis on this accusation until it has illuminated briefly every word; as if trying for the feel of some final, indisputable delivery. Her sense of drama, the transparency of her emotion (whether it is unaffected misery or something more complex and theatrical declaring itself) leaves him unnerved.

No one else seems bothered. Out on the Strand the taxis continue to drive homicidally at one another. The people waiting for them laugh and talk about the price of things. But as his cab arrives, and he sees the light dancing in the raindrops on its bonnet, the Ephebe cannot repress a shudder. Later, when he tries to recall the incident, he will be able to fasten only on the minor details – the minicab touts, for instance, mooching up and down the queue pleading in soft voice, 'Any long jobs?' while the woman stares down at her bit of paper like Ellen Terry as Joan of Arc and rubs her free hand in the food stains down the front of her coat.

'You bloody piece of *paper!*'

That afternoon he sits by the downstairs front window of his small house, looking out into the street. Rain drips steadily on the window sill. 'This drip, which is sometimes doubled, sometimes trebled, syncopated,' he once wrote to a friend, 'is all that is most monotonous about London residential streets.'

In fact it is a street he rather likes: in summer all rain and sunshine and every minute the most surprising and confusing changes of light.

Over the road from the Ephebe's window two beautifully trimmed bushes stand out against a brick wall. He has no idea what they are. The word 'buddleia' comes to mind when he looks at them; but they are evidently conifers. Under certain lights, especially in the mornings – 'When the world looks promising again despite what we know about it' – the brick takes on an old warm red colour. The wall itself seems to recede a little, as if the street had widened, and at the same time it becomes taller and longer. At that, the bushes no longer seem like bushes at all. Rather

than being in front of the wall, they define two arch-like
spaces *in* it. It is an illusion: but suddenly the Ephebe seems
to be looking through two arches at a hedge some way
behind the wall. The effect of this is of a glimpse into the
well-matured garden of some great house near Warwick or
Leamington, and it always delights him.

Tired out now by his journeys, unable to convince himself of the need to unpack his case, unsure of the success of
his experiment, he makes himself a cup of coffee, then
another. The room behind him is dim and quiet, full of
second-hand furniture.

On a little veneered table he has arranged the incomplete
Tarot, the Fool which represents himself, and the objects
of his search – a flattened cigarette end stained with nicotine
and spittle; an item of personalized jewellery in the form
of the name SOPHIA; the vulnerable but determined whisper
of a woman approaching her climax in the middle of the
night; a small, intricately machined metal object, melted at
one end; the children's novel *Island of Adventure*; particles
of sleet billowing down an empty pavement; a page from
his journal – though he cannot yet bring himself to do
anything with them. Instead, he finds himself watching the
school children running up and down the street. At half
past four there is an increase in traffic. The rush hour has
begun.

About fifteen minutes later the woman he watched this
morning outside Charing Cross Station waddles into view
from the junction with Harrow Road, crosses on to the
opposite pavement, and, going through one of the 'arches'
in the wall, disappears from view. Sunlight splashes the
pavement. Rain falls through it like a shower of sparks.
Without thinking, the Ephebe leaves his house and rushes
after her. The 'arch' is closing again even as he passes it. He
has the sense of penetrating some material halfway between
wood and stone, then something which is neither, something membraneous which clings for a moment round his
face.

Now he is in the garden. Paths race out everywhere in
front of him, across great lawns, between high topiary

hedges, over patios paved black and white like chessboards surrounded by grey stone urns and leaden statuary. In this confused, ideal moment, the Ephebe believes he may go anywhere. With a shout of elation he attempts to fall forward instantly and endlessly in all possible directions; only to find to his dismay that in the very exercise of this privilege he has selected one of them.

The house, in all respects the same as his own, is empty.

Though the carpets have been removed, odd items of furniture remain – a small inlaid table, an old-fashioned brass fender with grotesque mouldings, an ironing board folded up in a corner – as if some tenant is still in transit.

He sees the woman he has been pursuing, standing quite still in her maroon coat staring out of a bay window in an upstairs room; he sees her through the open door, lumpen and heavy, from the landing at the top of the stairs. Light pours round her thickened, monolithic silhouette, transfiguring the bare floor of the room, illuminating where it spills out on to the landing rolls of dust beneath creampainted skirting boards. He knows that if he was able to enter the room and look over her shoulder now, he would not see North London or his own house. The light fixes him, photographic, frozen; it is the same hot, silvery light which falls on the dense trees on the other side of the valley, giving them the look of giant mosses, thick clumps and curtains of moss of the sort that drips down the ornamental waterfalls in old gardens.

'All the things it might be,' a voice says clearly. 'The one thing it is.'

At this a white bird flies past the three panes of the bay window, its shadow flickering between elongated bars of light over the walls of the room: entering the first pane from the left and leaving from the right, it crosses the third in the same direction, only then flying across the central pane from right to left, after which it vanishes.

'The one thing it is.'

The Ephebe knows that he must cross the doorway of this room. He must pass through the moment he finds himself in. Before he can do this, though, the woman must turn towards him, so that he sees balanced on her shoulders the skull of a horse. It is not a horse's *head*, but a skull, which looks nothing like a horse at all; and out of this enormous curved shears, this wicked bone beak whose two halves meet only at the tip, will come words. 'You bloody piece of paper,' she must admonish him. Only then will he be able to pass.

'You bloody written thing.'

10 The Hierophant, representing 'occult force, voluntarily evoked'.

The journeys are over.

The Ephebe, having returned to the front room of his own house and made himself another cup of coffee, has arranged on the veneered table – alongside the incomplete Tarot, the Fool which represents himself, and the objects of his search already noted – a further nine cards. For each card of the original spread, we discover, he drew an alternative which has remained unconsulted until now.

These blind or uncommunicating cards provoke completely different interpretations of his journeys, and of their 'meaning' for him and for us. For instance, as an alternative card to the Chariot he drew the Aeon ('God has deconstructed the Old Universe and has learned too much to be able to build another'). Had he looked out of the opposite window of the railway carriage that day, he would have seen only a toddler with a string of snot at its nose, pedalling its plastic tricycle through the weeds, the heaps of dried mud and discarded plasterboard in the back garden of a newly completed council house in the Midlands. To simulate speed, the child kicks out violently with its little legs, while from its open mouth comes a constant high-pitched imitation of the roar of a jet fighter overhead – 'Nnnnneeaaaa!'

Here are the alternative cards he drew, in order:

The Nine of Discs; the Six of Wands; the Four of Swords; the Aeon; the Ten of Discs; the Ace of Swords; the Devil;

the Princess of Wands; Fortune. He is left only with the card he chose to represent himself. This was the Knight of Swords. As he turns it up, the Fool, which it replaces, charred and curled as if by some great heat or light, vanishes in incense smoke! He hears the horse repeat gently, 'All the things it might have been.'

Initiated now, the Ephebe smiles thoughtfully. Next to the Lovers he places the Four of Swords. He remembers the young woman whispering, 'Fuck me, fuck me,' in the night. What would he have seen if he had turned his head away from her then and looked into the quiet darkness of their upstairs room? The journeys are over. They have just begun.

M John Harrison was born in Warwickshire in 1945 and began writing in 1962. His first work was published in science fiction magazines in the mid-to-late sixties. Some years later he became interested in the central paradox of the Tarot, which is where the accidental collides with the inevitable, and used it to generate both symbols and structures in his *Viriconium* stories. He lives between London and Yorkshire, balanced on the knife edge that separates the random from the determined.

CHAPTER FOUR

THE GODDESS OF THE LAND

Caitlín Matthews

It was 31 July – Lammas Eve; in Irish, the Feast of Lughnasadh. I had been researching various fragmentary mythological themes in order to finish my book, *Arthur and the Sovereignty of Britain*, and I'd reached a dead-end. I particularly needed to know more about the Irish god, Lugh's, foster-mother – Tailtiu. Textual evidence could take me no further. I reached for my Tarot pack and, almost facetiously, asked it to tell me more about this lost story. I shuffled and cut the cards for a long time, feeling sleepy. Then I turned the ten cards over and was astounded to find I had drawn no less than seven major arcana cards – a sure sign, in a normal reading, that the querent could expect a great cosmic movement in their life.

I had hit the main lode of the myth and the story was already writing itself in my head before I could grab pen and paper. In the story which follows, I have not attempted to give any great overlay of authentic Irish texts; indeed I have taken a few liberties with existent mythic traditions. I have left the characters' names in Irish, but a rough guide to their pronunciation follows:

Tailtiu = Teltie   Eochaid = Yochy

Scal Balbh = Scolbav   Lugh = Lookh

In the times beyond the times that were, when Ireland was yet unsettled by mortal race, lived Tailtiu and her kind. She was of the undying race, which people now call Faerie. In those days the sky was closer to the earth and when night fell, the heavens were clear and bright, unclouded so that one might walk by the light of the stars. Ireland was covered with forests abounding in wild beasts, none of whom feared the Faerie kind.

Now Tailtiu loved to walk the groves of ancient trees and gaze into the waters of a crystal well by the light of the

THE WORLD.

JUSTICE.

THE TOWER.

JUDGEMENT.

stars. One night, following her custom, she sat gazing into the well when she saw reflected there the Seven Sisters, which we call the Pleiades. With wondering eyes she saw that each star had become a beautiful maiden. Six were dressed in milky white robes with fillets of star jewels netted about their long hair, but one held a phial of starlight in her lap.

'Tailtiu,' she said, 'we have waited long for this night when we should be reflected in these waters, for we are your sisters, kinswomen beyond the earth, and in all the turnings of the heavens we have felt your yearning, for we know your heart.'

Now Tailtiu had always yearned for companions to share her delights: the deep-tracked forests, the birds, beasts and fish, the wonders of the night. For she was not like the rest of Faerie kind in her desire to live closer to the living land. Her family had come to Ireland in crystal boats across the seas to the West and were as likely to return there, but not Tailtiu.

The star-sister said, 'Take up the vessels at your feet and draw up the waters of the well.' And she poured the phial of starlight into the crystal waters of the well. Tailtiu reached for the two jugs which stood always ready to quench the thirst of whoever might pass by.

'With this water,' said the star-sister, 'you may cause companions to visit these shores and many new things will be seen in your land. Because of your great love you will be known as Mistress of all growing things, and Mother of the land.'

Tailtiu scooped up the liquid starlight in one of the jugs, transferring it from one vessel to another as she thought upon what might come to pass. Following the bidding of her heart, she poured one jug upon the ground of the grove and the other back into the waters of the well in thankfulness. Now the waters reflected only the starlit sky.

She returned home and fell asleep. In the morning she did not need to return to the grove to see whether her actions had borne fruit. All about her the land was flourishing with new life. By pouring out the star-waters upon the land, the whole earth was burgeoning. New kinds of beasts and birds came to her wondering touch. She was happy beyond measure that the land of her dwelling should be enriched.

The time had come for her people to return to the blessed islands in the Western seas but Tailtiu refused to leave the home that she loved. She had made a garden out of wilderness; the birds, beasts and fishes answered to her calling; even the living rock and the rich earth responded to her touch, and no place was desolate since she came to tend it. But though she would be entirely alone, she refused to leave Ireland and watched sadly as the crystal boats sailed beyond the dip of the sun. One gift her people gave her before they left Ireland's shores. It was given at the bidding of great Danu, mother of Faerie kind, she who saw into ages to come. It was a stone of great power, hewn from the Lands in the West, beyond the Four Cities, and none might step upon that stone but he or she became as the Faerie kind, but only in so far as his or her nature might be enhanced: its property was to increase whatever was put upon it.

Many years passed, though these were like so many days to Tailtiu. She went about the land, tending it, making it grow ever more lovely and more fertile. One day she stood gazing out across the Eastern sea when she saw a great number of boats upon the waves. She watched as they drew nearer and nearer and saw that there were people upon their decks. Her heart beat faster, for her desire was granted. Just as the magic of the star-waters had made the land fertile, so, too, the waters she had poured into the pool of vision had wrought their work. The waters teemed with vessels full of people with whom she might share the land.

But every time the ships tried to land upon Ireland's shores they were washed back beyond the ninth wave. A tall warrior stood in the prow of the first ship and with him his poet. The warrior was handsome and fair, not at all like Tailtiu's kind who were dark and bird-boned, and her body yearned for him. The poet was like her own kindred, short and dark, but with secret eyes. But Tailtiu's sight was filled with the tall, golden warrior. The poet spoke to him and then turned to Tailtiu.

'Woman on the shore, it has been revealed to me that it is by your will that we are come hither to your land but the sea holds us back. Speak words of welcome and we shall be able to land.'

Tailtiu called back, and her voice fell gently upon the ears of all in the boats, so that they were filled with wonder, for it seemed the very earth had spoken and it was a voice of comfort and peace.

The tall warrior stirred and stared fixedly at the slender woman with the voice of wonder, and, forgetting what was proper for a king, replied himself, 'It is Eochaid, King of the Fir Bolg.'

'Then Eochaid and his people are welcome to these shores and to the heart of Tailtiu,' she answered.

Eochaid and his people came ashore. They had never seen such a fertile land before and were glad that they had chosen to accompany their king on his dangerous voyage. For Eochaid had had a dream in which he had been taken to this land and in that dream he had seen a dark and beautiful queen. Although he should have married a woman of his own kind, he had yearned for the dream woman and would have none but she. His wise men and his poet had agreed that this was a true dream and so the voyage was made without map or compass, with only Eochaid to guide the mariners.

Eochaid and his people were of mortal kind, but though some were awed and others greedy, all received Tailtiu's loving welcome, and none more so than Eochaid himself. They were soon married and though Tailtiu's people told many stories of the dangers of mixing their blood with mortal stock yet she was glad to be loved by Eochaid. He seemed to be the best of men. His judgements were wise and discerning, his decisions perceptive and orderly. Tailtiu was glad to share her land with her new companions. Soon Eochaid's people spread out through the island and settled. They knew how to harvest the riches of the earth and how to herd the beasts which wandered freely.

It was with sorrow that Tailtiu saw so many beasts enslaved or hunted, but so many people must live somehow, but it was the way with mortals that they ate flesh. Years passed and the people spread further into the island. There was less land for more people. Some muttered about unfair portions and others blamed Tailtiu whom they feared because of her Otherworldly blood. She and Eochaid had no children and there was murmuring that their king should have chosen a mortal princess, not one of Faerie kind, forgetting entirely that it was due to Tailtiu that they lived in Ireland at all. Some went to Eochaid's poet and asked him to influence the king.

The poet was trained in many arts, both mortal and Otherworldly, for he was partly of Faerie stock, though immortal blood did him no good, for he was a man proud. He was called Scal Balbh and was *tanaiste*, or successor to Eochaid, who was his half-brother. He divined that Tailtiu was the cause of the land's fertility and that, moreover, she kept hidden the Stone of Increase, which all druids and men of wisdom had heard of.

'King and brother,' he said to Eochaid, 'your reign is wise and just, yet the land does not prosper as it ought. You are childless and the people murmur about enchantment. Your wife is of Faerie kind and may be barren. It is known to me that she has the powers of increase: speak to her and bid her use her magic arts to benefit the land, if she will not use them on her own behalf.'

Eochaid loved his wife dearly and forbore to ask her, but Scal Balbh's crooked words entered his heart and eventually he begged Tailtiu to help him. It was Tailtiu's first understanding of the nature of mortal kind and she was troubled. She fled to the grove of the well to seek advice from her star-sisters but, as she gazed on the waters, the evening sky was overcast as it had never been until Eochaid's people came. She lamented that Eochaid seemed to love her no more and her tears fell into the well. The surface of the well cleared and there were her star-sisters shimmering upon the waters. She with the blue cloak looked with pity upon her earthly sister.

'Because you gave back freely of our gift, we freely give to you the gift of sight. Look within the waters, follow your heart and do not look for wisdom in the affairs of mortal kind.'

The waters shimmered and cleared, showing a crescent moon which waxed to the full, though no moon shone over Tailtiu's head. From its heart a spark flew into the heavens and whirled to form a sparkling sun. It shone upon the land of Ireland and from its centre stepped a young boy with fair hair and he rode upon a moon-mare with joy. The heaviness of Tailtiu's heart lifted at this prophetic vision and she understood what she must do. Resolutely, she returned to Eochaid.

'There is no magic, as your people call it,' she told her husband. 'I am of Faerie but I am like your people in that what I love flourishes.'

Eochaid folded her to his breast, 'I did not think otherwise, but my brother has spoken of the Stone of Increase. . . .'

'I have never had need of it,' said Tailtiu, 'but it was given to me by my mother against some great need and that time has not come.' And because Eochaid would not compel her, Scal Balbh gave secret orders to the men in his pay. They seized the king and murdered him while he was out hunting. Scal Balbh gave out that Eochaid had died on the tusks of a wild boar, but Tailtiu knew that none of the beasts would have scathed her husband, and she feared the evil of mortal kind while she wept for Eochaid.

He had not been buried a week when they came for her and married her to Scal Balbh, Eochaid's *tanaiste*, for, though he was his brother's legal successor, Scal Balbh knew that he needed Tailtiu to complete his plan. She lay with him unwillingly and was unable to conceal from him the hiding place of the Stone of Increase. He soon took charge of this hallowed relic of the Blessed Lands and stood upon it when he was made king. The Stone of Increase was neither good nor evil; it merely increased whatever was laid upon it. So, because Scal Balbh was at heart a man of blood and violence, though he followed the high calling of a poet, he became bloodier and more violent.

He compelled Tailtiu to go about the land, to make the land ever more fertile. In this he was wise, for he knew that he himself did not have the power of love. Escorted by armed guards, Tailtiu went about the land: she would bless the ground, set the first seed in the furrow; she laid her hands on fruit trees and on the bellies of beasts with young that they might bear twins. And wherever she went, the land grew fair and fruitful. But though she went about tirelessly, still Scal Balbh's people were unsatisfied. There was not sufficient land to grow enough crops, so numerous had they become. Nothing would serve but that Tailtiu clear the land of trees with her own hands, and plant crops in the clearings.

Sick at heart, Tailtiu suffered herself to be yoked to chains and driven to tear down the forests which had given her such joy. She was chained to gangs of slaves raided from distant shores, people as sick and sorry as herself. And though she grew big with child, Scal Balbh did not relent, but humiliated her further, lodging her with slaves, tearing away all shreds of her former queenship, for he now possessed the Stone of Increase and no longer needed her help.

Within the forests there was one great tree, an ash, which was Tailtiu's special tree. Where once vast forests of oak, birch and pine grew, there was an empty plain, all save for this one ash tree which none could uproot, though men with axes tried to hack it down. They harnessed Tailtiu and her companions to a chain and tied it about the mighty trunk, lashing her back with whips, to bring it down. As the tree toppled, so Tailtiu felt the first rending pangs of childbirth and, though women were speedily brought, she died delivering her child – a boy whom she named Lugh.

Scal Balbh gave orders that the child be given to a wet-nurse and bade his men bury Tailtiu's body under a mound of the earth which she herself had helped to heap up from the clearing of the forests. There she was interred and there forgotten for many years.

✳

Lugh grew up to be a fine carefree youth who delighted in the wide plains and hills of his country, and in the beasts, birds and fishes which populated its lands and rivers. He grew up ignorant of his mother and her shameful death, for Scal Balbh ordered everyone to silence on this matter.

Now his counsellors muttered together about the boy for it was uncertain whose child Lugh was – Eochaid's or Scal Balbh's, since his mother gave birth to him nine months after Eochaid's death. Scal Balbh had married again – a woman of foreign race, a princess of mortal kind – and she had her own designs about the succession. All that anyone could say with right was that Lugh was Tailtiu's son.

Scal Balbh knew by his arts that Lugh was Eochaid's son. He disliked the way in which the boy favoured all alike with his open, frank demeanour, rightly fearing how things would be if the boy ever found out the manner of his mother's death. He ordered that Lugh be sent into fostering with an old, pensioned-off huntsman on the borders of what remained of the great forest. In this way Scal Balbh showed that, though he forbore to kill the lad, Lugh was no longer considered of royal stock.

Lugh was too young to realize the implications of his exile, indeed he was glad to learn about the nature of the beasts and their relationship to the land and the seasons. The old huntsman was stern but kindly, and he saw to it that, although Lugh learned many things considered unsuitable for a lad of noble stock, he also inculcated in Tailtiu's son a love of justice and discerning wisdom.

The time came for Lugh's manhood test which all young men endured. His foster-father judged that Lugh should spend the night in the forest, finding food, shelter and other provision for himself. Although Lugh was well versed in the lore of the forester, this was no mean testing for, since Tailtiu's death, many animals were now quite wild and likely to harm an unprotected wayfarer alone in the forest. The old huntsman reckoned that Lugh would find adventures there to test his wits and hunting skills.

And so Lugh set off in high spirits, walking the woodland paths with joy, for he was his mother's son after all. He struck off across the forest in search of game and spent the day hunting and assessing his surroundings. Towards evening he had still not found a place to shelter and it was by chance that he discovered a secret clearing which was perfect. In its centre was a well of sweet water and a lone ash sapling beside it. He was thirsty and leant down to drink, unshouldering his kill. He was surprised to see a reflection over his shoulder of a beautiful dark woman with a careworn face. Turning, he found no one behind him. Wondering he knelt and tasted the waters of the well again. Immediately he grew sleepy and, with his head resting against the ash sapling, he fell asleep and dreamed a strange dream.

The woman whose reflection he had seen came bearing three golden cups – one of milk, one of wine, and one infused from some dark herb which made the liquid black.

'These cups are all yours, my son: the milk of fostering, the royal wine of Kingship, and the drink of forgetfulness, by which you may be brought into the inner kingdom of your mother's kindred when your reign is done.

'For you are Lugh, the son of Tailtiu of the Blessed Islands and of Eochaid the Fair, from the lands over the Eastern seas.'

And she related to him her story, for it was none other than Tailtiu who had appeared to Lugh. As he listened, he grew hot with anger at his mother's suffering and his stepfather's cruelty. He was glad that Scal Balbh was not his father after all, for now he might lawfully kill him.

Tailtiu said, 'Although you never drank from my breast, yet you have been laid at the breasts of a lowly slave who shared my toil; though you have not drunk the red cup of lordship, yet it will be given you to drink, for your reign will be long and just. It will be many years before you come to drink the dark cup of forgetfulness whereby you will forget mortality and be restored to your mother's kind. I bid you now, chop down the ash tree behind you and make yourself a spear. When I was dying I had in my hand an ash-key which the winds blew to this place where I knew you would come. Make the spear from its wood. Strike fearlessly so that I may be avenged. All manner of helpers will come to assist you in ridding the land of Scal Balbh's iniquity. I bid you only be gentle to the innocent beasts of this land, merciful to the innocent, generous to the poor and a father to the land under your rule.'

Tailtiu faded from his sight and in her place sat a beautiful but stern woman whose hair was bound by a fillet of gold, with a star-crystal upon her brow. She carried a bright sword and a pair of balances such as are used to measure precious metals.

'Lugh, King of Ireland, Tailtiu's son, I am your mother's sister from the star kingdom. I give into your keeping this sword of light, wrought of star-metal. It will never fail you in combat, but it is the sword of justice so you should never strike without just cause. I give you also this scale, for by it you may measure the just portion of every man and woman in the times to come.'

Lugh awoke suddenly. It was still night and the stars were reflected in the quiet waters of the well. He looked into its dark depths and saw there reflected the Pleiades. He knew, by their rising, that winter sowing would soon be near, just as country people know today. Beside the well he found two old jugs discarded in the long ferns. He dipped one into the well, and the waters seemed made of starlight, like the woman in his dream. He poured the contents of one jug into the other, watching the sparkling liquid as it passed from vessel to vessel. And in his hands the two jugs fused together to form a double cup of crystal. The star-woman was once more reflected in the well, but this time Lugh was awake.

'This cup has two gifts. If you pour from the darker end, the land will dry up. If you pour from the other lighter end it will be made fertile. We give this cup into your keeping until your purpose is achieved. Use it carefully.'

Lugh wonderingly touched the crystal cup. Looking down beside him he saw the starry sword and the scales and he recalled his dream. Following his mother's advice, he fashioned himself a spear from the ash sapling, thinking all the while of Tailtiu's sufferings. He handled it appraisingly: it was an unyielding spear, straight as his mother's back, and he resolved to plunge it into the heart of Scal Balbh.

He returned to his foster-father who waited anxiously, though he took care to express unconcern when Lugh appeared. The lad was a boy no longer, that was clear. He walked with a sure foot and a purposeful look was in his eye. He bore weapons and gifts of strange power which no common boy might have won in his manhood testing. Lugh burned to tell the old huntsman what had happened, but he could not conceal his anger that everyone had kept silence about Tailtiu.

'Many people knew and loved her,' said the old man, 'and we grieved for her sufferings, for she was of Faerie kind. But we were few and too weak to help her. It is our shame that we flourish because of her torments, eating the bread which she blessed, drinking the milk which her labour provided. But now you are a man among men, you are free to act as you will.'

'Then,' said Lugh, 'let all people remember my mother and grieve for her,' and he poured the crystal cup upon the ground with the dark end towards the earth. A thin, bitter draught soaked into the ground which caused Ireland to become a wasteland. No crops grew, the harvest was ruined, beasts were barren and the rivers began to dry up. There was no creature which did not suffer hunger and thirst. People murmured and remembered Tailtiu and her blessing of fertility with fondness and they began to speak out against Scal Balbh.

The sun did not shine and the sky grew dark with storm so that Scal Balbh and his queen and their counsellors fled their palace and took shelter in a great tower which housed the riches of the land. Scal Balbh set his guards about it and used his arts to protect the tower from attack. Inside he and his queen wanted for nothing, for he used the Stone of Increase to multiply food and drink.

Meanwhile there was great suffering across the land. Lugh grieved that the innocent beasts and people oppressed by Scal Balbh were in want, but he hardened in his resolve.

Many people flocked to his side, and beasts and birds, hitherto wild and unbiddable, became his messengers and helpers: the otter in the river, the salmon of the lake, the eagle of the mountain, the ox upon the plain summoned together the people of Ireland to help Lugh in his endeavour. But though he attempted to take the tower by force of arms, he was unable to succeed because of Scal Balbh's enchantments. The people still starved and he did not know what to do; though he had weapons of great power, it seemed they were of no avail and Lugh began to lose heart. He had sworn not to restore the land until Scal Balbh had been dealt with and he would not break his oath.

One night, overcast and gloomy, he was near despair. There were no stars and no moon to be seen, nor did anyone dare kindle a flame, for Lugh and his people were encamped on the plain near Scal Balbh's tower. He drew out the sword of light to give some glimmer to his men. The sword was strangely light to hold and it seemed to increase in radiance when he thought about his mother. He thought back to the night of manhood testing and wondered about his ability to become a king. As though in reproof to these doubts, a sliver of moon showed through the clouds. Its beams made a path between earth and sky and from the moon stepped a magnificent white mare. She cantered down the moon-track and with her teeth she pulled his sleeve.

Lugh knew that his mother's people had sent the mare to help him. Mounting upon her, he snatched up his spear and balances and together they were riding into the air towards the tower. The mare struck her hooves sharply against its stones and Lugh, understanding her meaning, struck the tower with his sword of light. The sky was illuminated with wheeling sparks as the star-metal bit into the dark stones. Scal Balbh's magic was no match for such powerful weapons.

The tower was breached and Lugh leapt down the stairs into the hall where Scal Balbh and his court sat feasting on the rich fare they kept hoarded there. Scal Balbh did not expect attack from above and he had set no guards, but those who were in the hall fell back before Lugh's approach, none could withstand the bright strokes of his sword.

Taking his spear in hand, Lugh raised it, aiming it at Scal Balbh's heart, where he cowered on his throne, king no more. With one thrust, the ash-spear penetrated the poet-king's breast. His eyes widened and he wailed, 'Tailtiu's curse!', and plunged headlong from the window to the plain below.

The queen and her children were brought before Lugh who judged the queen with his scale. One by one, he picked the gems from her wrist, brow, breast and fingers, and laid them in one half of the scale. In the other pan he placed a loaf of bread and a cup of water. The jewels were by far the heavier.

'These precious things were bought by the labour of my mother and of the peoples your husband enslaved to work the land my mother cleared. As you have not sought the death of any by your hand, I give you life; yet you are not worthy of such royal state as this. You shall draw water and knead dough in the kneading trough for the rest of your life. Your children are guiltless and I shall send them into the keeping of honest folk who will give them all that they need.'

The queen disdained to beg for mercy. 'Rather than such a life as that I choose Scal Balbh's way,' and she cast herself from the window before any could stop her. Each of the counsellors who had schemed Tailtiu's death was given a similar choice: death or servitude.

Then all the people of Ireland came to Lugh and begged him to assume the kingship. But he said, 'I will do that, but first every creature and being in Ireland must assemble at the mound where Tailtiu is buried.'

The day was dark and the land dry and bitter when at last all were assembled. The animals raised their thirsty throats and the people stretched out their hands to Lugh for mercy. But it was not until the tears of the people had watered the plain that Lugh took up the crystal cup and poured from the lighter end the bright draught of healing. As the liquid fell to the ground, the earth was speedily

renewed. Men, women and children knelt with cow, stag
and goat as the thirst-quenching waters rose in the dried-
up river beds. And as they drank, their hearts were glad-
dened and the terror of the time faded from their minds.
The sky cleared, rain fell and the land was cleansed of
sorrow.

Lugh took the spear of vengeance and plunged it into the
earth of Tailtiu's mound where it rooted, becoming a
mighty ash tree and, though the land all about was fruitful
once more, nothing ever grew in its shade; it became the
centre of a great plain of assembly for all the tribes of
Ireland.

Then Lugh caused the Stone of Increase to be brought to
the mound. It was carried on the back of the moon-mare,
for no man wished to touch it, and she was harnessed by
the birds of the air. Lugh took it and laid it on the plain.
In the sight of all the people he stood upon it to be invested
as king. And if he was wise beforehand he was twice as
discerning afterwards. As he stood there it seemed that he
was in communion with the lands of the West, the undying
plains of wonder where the dead are alive, and where the
Faerie race spend their lives in feasting and song. He saw
coming towards him from that land his mother and she bore
the red cup of lordship which makes a king. It is not known
what passed between them at that time, for that is a mystery.
But to this day when kings stand or sit upon that stone,
poets call it the Wedding Feast of the King with the land.

After he had been proclaimed by the people, Lugh spoke:
'Let there be peace upon all people. From this day, every
year on my mother's death-day we will hold sacred games
in her honour. And because all past deeds are to be forgotten, let there be no sorrow but mirth and feasting. Let there
be sport and contests for the young men, and games for the
children, and stories for old folk, and let men and women
come together in love. For the land is fruitful again and
harvest time is a time for rejoicing. Justice will be given
freely to all and the bounty of the harvest will be distributed
to the needy.'

But Lugh did not forget that the year's harvest had been

wasted by the cup of cursing. He caused the food and drink which had been hoarded in Scal Balbh's tower to be brought to the plain of assembly and there he laid it upon the Stone of Increase until there were supplies to last for a whole year. He gave to each according to his or her need, and the people blessed Tailtiu's son. He reigned long and wisely, returning at last to his mother's kind when the time came.

He kept the sword of light and the scales of justice in remembrance of the star-kindred, and he rode the moon-mare whenever he made a circuit of the land. No better king was there ever in the history of Ireland. But the cup which blessed and cursed he returned to the well and there he smashed it on the stones. As the crystal pieces flew apart he saw, lying at his feet, only two ancient earthenware jugs with which once Tailtiu had brought mortal kind to Ireland. The other gifts of power passed into the keeping of wise men and women who, whether Faerie or mortal, guard yet these Hallows of the land. But whenever kings or queens have need of their power they must seek long and hard before they are able to use them, for they belong to the Goddess of the Land and can only be wielded by the wise and just ruler.

And this is why we keep the memory of Tailtiu at Lughnasadh or Lammas to this very day. In the house in which this story is told there will be no lack of good things. If it be told at a wedding, that couple shall not separate without conceiving a child. On all who hear this tale, the blessing of Sovereignty, who is the Goddess of the Land.

Caitlín Matthews is a writer active within the Western Esoteric Tradition, about which she co-wrote a two-volume history *The Western Way* with John Matthews, her partner in the mythic and Arthurian fields. With him she has designed *The Arthurian Tarot*. Her other books include *Mabon and the Mysteries of Britain* and *Arthur and the Sovereignty of Britain* – a two-volume study of the *Mabinogion* – and *The Elements of Celtic Tradition*. She is co-editor, with Prudence Jones, of *Voices from the Circle*. She spends a lot of time in the Celtic fifth and sixth centuries, an era which she is currently reconstructing for a series of forthcoming novels. She has lectured in Britain, Europe and America, but, as a poet, singer, and harpist, her lectures nearly always turn into storytelling and workshop.

CHAPTER FIVE

THE SHIP OF NIGHT

Cherry Gilchris

This story progresses from reality to manifest archetype into dream
in a simple yet subtle way. The Tarot is a mirror in which the archetypes are reflected and though not everyone uses this method of
interior vision, most people remember their dreams. The ship of night
is that very barque which pulls up every night at our bedside. The
images of the day mix and mingle with the heightened reality of
dreamscape producing the archetypes which people our sleeping
consciousness. In Cherry Gilchrist's dream story, the little foxes are
not allowed to spoil the vines for too many nights.

You won't believe me, but it was in fact Friday the thirteenth when I laid out these cards. Friday 13 May, at
10.30 a.m., to be exact. I rose from my chair purposefully
to fetch my pack. The dog looked at me warily; perhaps I
was about to do some singing practice, which she loathed.
She slunk out of the room to be on the safe side. Five cards,
the rules said. I shuffled them, and shuffled again. Five to
be drawn: one for me, three for the story, and one, perhaps,
for you, the reader. Out they came. Temperance * Justice
– Death – The Moon * Strength. Well, how corny can you
get? Friday the thirteenth and a central triad like that. Surely
there was an element of mockery here. Should I start again.
  Wait. A little whisper of realization ruffled the back of
my neck. This was a story that had already been told, a
situation that had just unfolded. The lion with open jaw,
held by the lady, the two dogs baying at the moon – this
was the tale of the foxes and me, a little saga that had been
under way for several days now. Ah, but then it won't
count, will it, because I'm supposed to be creating something new? But I'll start to relate it anyway, because the

cards seem to be issuing a kind of demand that I gather the threads together, look for its essence. And it's also true, isn't it, that every little story is part of a greater one? Perhaps I might get a glimpse of this if I follow what is in front of me.

This foxy tale is no saga of country life. I live, in fact, in the heart of the city, the centre just a few minutes walk away down steep stone steps. But it is quiet here. Our little area is old, eighteenth century, with walled gardens and cobbled streets, laid out where there were once orchards and pleasant pastures for the inhabitants of the smoky city below to stroll on a summer's evening. There are still mulberry trees, fig trees, and an old sacred spring at the back of someone's house. Not that the foxes are left over from those balmy days of pre-urban living. No, they've crept back along the railway tracks, the river banks, the old gullies and conduits that run forgotten under busy streets. Opportunists to the last, they scavenge for their food and live under garden sheds. I didn't know about them when we first moved here, not too long ago, but I soon found out.

At first I was enchanted with this secret city wildlife. I loved the thought that, come the night, another form of life was taking over. While we humans lay cosily in bed, wild beasts came out, mated, fed, played, but in the morning were gone, leaving little trace of their presence. So little, in fact, that much of the population round here still does not know that they exist. It is a little like those tales you read as a child, where there is a fairy market at night, where shadowy, moonbeam creatures sell their miniature treasures in a world which is like the one you know, but infinitely more magical. If you could only wake up at the right time, you could step into that elusive world and take part in it. . . .

I suppose, with the foxes, it was as if this started to happen. And, like those reckless mortals in legend who venture out to join in with fairy dancing, commerce, revels or anything else, I found out that it was not quite so delightful as I had expected. There was a price to pay for going into the world of night.

Just recently, a family of cubs had been born close by. I didn't know they were there until the time came for them to be taken out by their mother for night romps and education in the gentle art of pillage and theft. The first crisis came when she abandoned one of them in our garden. I heard this terrible, desperate calling, which shattered my dreams and roused me from my bed. It's strange, isn't it, that universal cry of help from the young? Whether it's a bird out of the nest or a child lost in a supermarket, the tone is the same. There's an insistency, an urgency that you recognize, which goes straight to the centre of your being and tugs at you.

I got up, and looked out of the window. Dawn was sullenly approaching, and I had to concentrate my vision to see anything in the cold, smoky grey light. Finally I could make out a vixen in next door's garden, moving low and rapidly with a cub close behind her, while in ours another cub raced up and down, unable to climb the high stone wall that separated him from his mother. She would come back and rescue him, I thought, and left them to it.

But the next night, soon after it grew dark, the cries began again. They sounded a little like a dog, or, to be more precise, like a Jack Russell terrier with a sore throat. They had a strange, husky penetration, though, like one of those alarm calls in your sleep, a voice that breaks into the comfortable unfolding of your current dream and rouses you, calling your name, perhaps, or speaking just one word that resonates through your body from top to toe. It was terrible. The cub called, cried and wailed the whole night through. It went through every range of emotion, uncannily human in its piteous calling. At times it became exhausted, and could only give faint, despairing groans. At others it worked itself up to a pitch of hysteria and grief which would have torn at the stoniest heart. I felt there was nothing I could do, not at this point anyway. I had to give the mother a chance to find it and take it back. Even if it was starving, what could I do if I did retrieve it? I couldn't take over from the mother, I couldn't rear a cub. I had to leave it to its fate. If it had to die, then so it must be.

Well, the following night, I couldn't stand it any longer. Maybe I could catch it, and maybe, if I put it over the wall into next door's garden, it could find its way back to the earth, even at the risk of its mother rejecting it. Out of bed, slippers and dressing gown on, dog safely shut up and torch in hand, I went out to see what I could do. As soon as it heard any movement outside, of course, it became absolutely quiet and still, so I think it was my determination to put a stop to this suffering (for both of us) that allowed me finally to track it down in a corner of the garden, crouching under some old planks. I picked it up by the scruff of the neck, as one would a puppy, although it looked more like a small piglet with its long nose. We had a good look at one another, the cub pissed itself with fright, and then I took it to the wall where I could just reach high enough to put it on the top and give it a gentle push off the other side. Back I went to bed, and sleep – glorious, undisturbed sleep.

So, my mission successfully accomplished, I went about in a sentimental haze for a few days. There was no more noise, and I was convinced I had saved the cub from death, from perishing miserably. But this was not to last. Come twilight one evening, I heard the dreaded 'Yap, yap, yap' again. I suppose if you're a doctor, and you work hard to set a nasty break in a patient's leg, only to have him come back a couple of months later with the other one broken, you'd be bound to be less sympathetic. 'Not you again!' It detracted from my sense of achievement, too – why must the creature be so stupid? Only in the morning was I prepared to make another effort, motivated more by loss of sleep than anything else. I found the cub in a little hole that it had dug for itself in the vegetable garden; just big enough to hide in, for as I peered into the dark space two glowing, cross eyes looked out at me.

I guess it was not sensible to plunge my bare hand in and grab it. In retrospect, it was really very stupid. Its teeth, needle-sharp, went straight to the bone. With my free hand, I prised open its jaws, and it promptly grabbed that one instead. Two hands savaged. When I managed to get a grip on it, I chucked it over the wall with no more ado, and went inside to plaster my wounds with remedies.

At midnight, under a full moon, just below the bedroom window, it started up again. It was then that the penny dropped. This wasn't an abandoned cub. This was a deliberately dumped cub. After all, it hadn't starved, had it, despite several nights of misery on its own? So it must be able to feed itself. It had been able to start digging a hole, hadn't it? So it could dig a bit deeper and make a proper earth. Plainly, its mother had been going round doing the neighbourhood drop: 'You stay here, Charlie; this garden's for you, Flossie, I'm leaving you here.' And so on, and so on. What I had thought were the death cries were in fact those of a creature having to face a new life. And I, like a fool, had tried to return it to its old life. Well, as we all know, that never works, does it?

The final ridiculous scene was about to unfold. I can't help but go back to the analogy of dreams, where an epic that starts off with deep emotion and cosmic overtones ends up in absurdity. I was very tired – it had been a trying day. All I wanted to do was sleep. The yelps I could cope with, but suddenly there were loud scrabbling noises close to the house, followed by 'splish, splosh' sounds. Up, open the window, and all was revealed. The cub had climbed up the water butt and fallen in. I admit I must have stood there for several minutes, wondering if this was the answer to my prayers. But the thought of fishing a drowned cub out of a barrel of dirty water in the morning was far, far worse. . . .

Quickly dressed, cursing loudly, I went out. I would have laughed if I hadn't been so angry. The cub's snout was stuck bravely up into the air, and with his two front paws he paddled frantically to try and keep afloat. I put on leather gardening gloves this time; I wasn't going to be caught twice. Even in its desperate plight, it still tried to bite me. It is true that Nature has no gratitude; why should it? But then I wasn't going to have much sympathy either. I found a plastic washing-up bowl and heaved out one black, stinking, slimy fox cub onto the grass. It glared at me angrily and scuttled away into the bushes where I left it to recover.

You think I'm making this up, but no, I couldn't. My inventive powers don't run to this kind of absurd scenario – I always try to pitch my imaginings on a grander scale. But when I had drawn the cards and found the story of the foxes written plain there, it niggled away at my mind, and I wondered if I could use it as a key to something with a bit more depth. Nothing came; I tried this idea and that, but they all fizzled out. Come night-time again, I was wide awake, restless, unable to let go and relax. Perhaps a walk through the late-night city would help – it would prove some sort of a distraction, at least.

I clattered down the familiar stone steps, holding the old metal handrail since they are pitted and tricky to negotiate in the uneven light of the street lamps, which are picturesque, but ineffective, like something out of Dickens. At the bottom, I struck off into the city, through the commercial quarter where once merchants had traded cargoes of cloth, sugar, slaves even, down to the docks from whence their riches came. I am always attracted to water, especially to water where there is the coming and going of boats. It's a long time now since these docks have been used extensively for trade, but they have plenty of life. There are now marinas for private boats, smart waterfront cafés and new housing developments along the old quays, and the docks themselves are an intricate network of waterways, through routes and blind alleys winding away into the lesser-known quarters of the city.

I'm not sure what I had in mind to do, but when I saw the boat pulled up I had no second thoughts. 'Moonlight cruise', the board announced. Hadn't heard of such a thing before, but then it was the tourist season, and all sorts of novelties were on offer. 'One and a half hours – see the city by night. £2 only.' A dozen or so people were on board already, and the captain stood by the gangplank ready to welcome any hesitant participant.

'Coming?' he asked cheerfully. He was a big man, with a florid face but a curiously sardonic, thin-lipped smile. 'You won't regret it. Not long to wait, we're off in five minutes.'

I took my place at the prow of the boat, where I found myself sitting next to a stout middle-aged lady in a buttoned-up navy mackintosh.

We chatted in a quiet, comfortable way. She was a warden, she explained, in an old people's home, and had to work some very awkward shifts. She'd taken the cruise before, and it covered those difficult in-between hours very nicely, particularly when she was transferring from day to late-night shift, and needed something to keep her going until she started work.

'There's one or two other regulars here,' she said, nodding over at the other side, to a hunched-up man in black, who sat fingering a straggly grey beard. Next to him a young couple sank blissfully into each other's arms. To my unspoken question she replied, 'Once you've seen it by night, you want to do it again. What you see by day seems rather tame by comparison.'

The boat was filling up now, with some twenty to thirty passengers. The captain decided that this was enough, and turned on the engines; with that quiet *chug chug chug* noise we left our moorings and set off through the docks. Little flickers of light caught on the rippling, slapping water, and indeed the water was brighter than the surroundings, for we quickly left the populated quayside and turned off through waterways flanked with heavily built warehouses and derelict yards. Where there were windows, they were barred, and where there were boundary walls, they were topped with barbed wire. On the paths which ran by the water, once unloading bays, I could make out grass and weeds, and it looked as though this part of the city had been deserted for a hundred years.

In fact, said our captain, a cynical and amusing commentator, it still had life in the day, and might in time have more. The usual planning disputes were raging between industrialists, conservationists, and city council officials.

'I've no time for age for its own sake,' said Rita (my companion) darkly, which I thought was strange, given her profession.

'If you look over to your right,' said our gallant captain,

'you will see that Webber's Bank has won its appeal to re-build, and that demolition is already in progress.' All eyes turned to gaze upon a half-torn-down building which looked, in this dim light, like something out of a craggy Romantic landscape.

But as we turned the corner by the side of it, this image was rudely shattered by the rubbish that we encountered. In the water itself, bits and pieces bobbed up and down – plastic sacks, old bottles, screwed-up paper bags. On the edge, where we could now see behind the ruined façade, were dusty piles of bricks and rubble, and perhaps twisted pieces of iron and broken planks, though it was hard to make anything out clearly. The female lover gave a little scream: 'Aah! Rats! I saw them move!' But, before anyone on the boat could react, came the sound of a sniggering, husky laugh from the darkness of the shore. We all turned sharply, and as the boat slid gently past, I could make out the stooped figure of a man, raggedly dressed, looking towards us with a mocking grin before bending back to his task. A sack lay near him amidst the rubbish, and with a long pole he turned over the piles around him, picking over the debris and putting choice finds into his sack. The captain waved to him as we passed; he was obviously a familiar character in these parts.

Now we passed into a kind of leafy tunnel. I had lost track of direction, and could only guess vaguely what part of the city we were in, but I reckoned that we were still fairly central, and that somewhere above us busy roads stretched away, and that the people who frequented them probably had little knowledge of what went on in these watery depths below. I think the trees were willows; it was hard to see, but I detected a gentle brushing of the water with their drooping branches. The tow path was grassy now, and the captain told us stories of how the barges came into the city from the furthest parts of the country, patient horses plodding, dreaming of a full nose-bag at the end of the day, brown, monkey-faced bargemen with robust wives, washing strung out along the bow, and a couple of kids playing with broken pottery shards picked up as treas-

ures along the way. It was as if the waterways themselves
had not forgotten, and here, submerged below street level,
there was nothing to interrupt the old dream that resounded
day after day.

There was a child on board now; probably about six or
seven, leaning against his mother and curled up into sleep,
thumb in mouth. She smiled when she saw me looking. 'It's
his birthday,' she said. 'He was determined to stay up and
see it in at midnight; he loves to try and stay awake. I
promised him he could come, even though I knew he
wouldn't manage it. I'll tell him in the morning that he did
the whole trip. It'll make him happy.'

Most of the company were lost in their own thoughts,
or, in the case of the lovers, in each other. The bearded
man that I had noticed at the start of the voyage seemed
restless though, muttering to himself and looking anxiously
at a tattered paperback book that he held. Perhaps it was
just a collection of pages, because I couldn't see any cover,
only torn pages which he thumbed feverishly, as if he were
trying to find and then memorize his favourite poems. But
there was no hint of enjoyment in his face, only a driven,
haunted look.

'You say he comes here often?' I asked Rita, as discreetly
as I could.

She nodded. 'Yes, a few times.'

'For pleasure, do you think?'

She shrugged, in a dismissive kind of way. 'Perhaps.'

'I wonder if he has a home to go to? But then I suppose
if he was a down-and-out, he wouldn't have the money to
come.' She clearly did not want to follow this up, and I
stayed silent, ashamed of passing comments on my fellow
passengers of which she clearly disapproved. 'Do you enjoy
your work?' I asked her, in a feeble attempt to remedy the
situation.

She smiled at me unexpectedly, a warm, beaming smile.
'Oh yes. Oh very much. Old people are so rewarding. Very
special. They are the perfection of a whole life-time. Unless
you can understand that, you don't know them at all.'

By now, we were floating down a broad stretch of water, at ground level.

'This is the main waterway out of the city,' the captain announced. 'The motorway of dockland. We shall be going a little further. And here we're taking a swing to the left, to avoid the weir. All marked out and perfectly safe, even at night.'

I could hear the rushing of the river weir. I suppose we must have emerged from the completely artificial canal and dock network into a natural but structured watercourse. A wire rope and a string of fluorescent flags showed up on the right, and the boat veered away from them. But just as we turned, there was a movement from the other side of the boat. The hunched man's mutterings had grown fiercer. He stood up, and, in the space of what cannot have been more than a few seconds, hurled his book, then his overcoat, and then himself into the water. I gasped, and stood up to cry out, then found myself yanked firmly back to my seat, with a warm hand pressed heavily over my mouth. I struggled, but Rita held me firm.

'Be quiet!' she hissed.

I looked around, and up at the captain, but he and Rita were already exchanging glances. He raised an eyebrow to her, and she nodded with assurance. Satisfied, he straightened the boat into her new course, and delivered a few more comments into the microphone about features of the landscape. I couldn't believe it. And none of the other passengers seemed to have noticed. The lovers, who had sat next to the man, were by now at the whispering, tickling and giggling stage of their embraces. Everyone else looked vacant, as if the slow flow of water had glazed over their minds and eyes.

I turned sharply to Rita. 'Why don't we stop? Why don't we rescue him?' Not that I could see him any more – he was gone with barely a splash, swallowed up by the racing waters that swept down in torrents to the river below.

She pulled out a package from her brown plastic shopping bag and calmly unwrapped a selection of sandwiches. 'Eat one, my dear. The egg ones are nicest – the ham wasn't up to much today.' Almost hypnotized by her assurance, I took one.

When she saw that I had bitten into it, she said, 'It was his time, dear. The way he wanted to go.'

'What do you mean?'

She sighed. 'For a writer,' (had I told her that?) 'you don't look very far, do you? When one of my gentlemen, or ladies, is ready to go and I am as sure as I can be that the time has come, then I will be there to see them off.'

'You mean – suicide?'

'Not exactly. Oh no, I wouldn't hold with that. That's a war against yourself, isn't it. No, those who know that their life is drawing to a close. And that's the greatest perfection, you know. And quite natural, too. You look at animals – they know when it's time. Well then. Some of my clients don't want to catch lingering illnesses and have doctors prodding them and all their relatives weeping over them. How would you like to die like that, in a home or a hospital? Not much, I expect. Not a pleasant last memory to take with you, is it? So I make sure they can get out and about, and find it as they want it. By water this time. He loved the sea, that one. . . . Used to be a writer, once, like you. . . . Took him several trips before he felt familiar with this place and knew just where he wanted to go.'

I made as if to get up and look over the side of the boat, but she pulled me back. 'Don't be foolish, dear. That's one thing you must never do, try and follow them – they'll go clean and quiet if you let them.'

I was shaking. 'I've witnessed a death, then. Something I haven't seen before. I might have seen more – I might have learnt more.'

Rita shook her head kindly. 'That's not the way to know more, half going with them. That's the way to do yourself a mischief, and maybe them, too. There's plenty more to learn and to see if you'll be patient.'

I was thoroughly jolted now. Was this a sleeping world, or a waking one! Was it night or day? What did she and the captain know that I didn't . . . ? We were approaching a barrier. Heavy, steel doors loomed up before us in the

water, dark water slapping against them as the boat dropped
speed and came to a pause at the place where they blocked
our way, tightly closed. On a short quayside to our left, a
little cottage snuggled into the high guarding walls around,
and one light still burned in a small upstairs window.

The captain whistled, then called, 'Diz! Diz! Open up!
– Short for Disraeli,' he told the now stirring passengers,
provoking a few titters of disbelief.

We could hear the sound of footsteps in the cottage, then
a few grumbling noises as the front door was unbolted and
opened. A dark, squat little man moved out towards us.
Though his movements were slow, I sensed tremendous
physical power in his presence, something of the wrestler's
strength in his body.

'Come on, Diz. You're supposed to have had these open
for us.'

'You'll have to pay.'

'You must be joking! We're regulars.'

'Everyone has to pay. Double rates at night.'

'They're always like this,' Rita told me. 'He'll have to
pay, he always does in the end.'

'Extra levy, I'm afraid,' said the captain. 'Fifty pence
each.'

There was some complaining, but he was firm. No, it
wasn't on a per boat basis, but was per head. And yes, the
child too, even if he was under sixteen and asleep. He was
sorry, but there it was. As I turned towards the moonlight
to see the contents of my purse better, the coins that I was
taking hold of slipped from my fingers and fell into the
water. By this time, the great steel doors were opening,
making surprisingly little noise, and the boat was sliding
gently through into a dark stretch of water beyond. The
captain's mate came towards me with his leather bag to
collect my fare.

'I'm sorry, I've just lost my money overboard. I haven't
any more.'

He shrugged, and grinned unpleasantly. His teeth were
yellow and pointed, and he reminded me, for the first time

since I had stepped onto the boat, of the foxes at home. 'Well, you'll have to get out, won't you.'

I looked at him in disbelief. 'You've got to be joking.'

'Oh no, far from it. Them as doesn't pay gets off. We don't wait, and we don't accept any debts. Out.' He jerked a thumb towards the bank and nodded at the captain, who steered in closer to the shore.

I glanced around, but no one seemed interested in my plight, any more than they were in the man who had jumped overboard. Rita had disappeared, too. I would have shouted, I think, but before I had a chance to do so I found that I was being heaved ashore by the captain and his evil-mouthed assistant. It could have been funny, or at any rate, ridiculous, but it wasn't.

And then the boat was gone, and I was standing on a narrow path, with nothing but darkness ahead and steel doors, firmly closed again, behind me. Then I really did shout. I bawled, and hollered. Surely the gate-keeper would hear me and come out. But he didn't. I began to grow hysterical, I am ashamed to admit, and was beating my fists against the metal, making a noise fit to wake the dead, when I felt a quiet tap on my shoulder. I spun round. It was Rita.

'Well, dear, you're one of the lucky ones, aren't you?' She seemed amused.

'What do you mean?'

'I'm sure you didn't really want to go any further, did you? Wouldn't you rather be getting home now?' And indeed, I suddenly realized that I was dead tired and would like nothing better than to be back in bed. 'I always get out around here myself. It's not so much fun further on.' Her tone somehow gave me the impression that this was a great understatement.

'How do we get out?'

She gestured. 'Put your hand over there, to the right. You'll find a little metal ring that hangs loose. It's set into a lion's head, actually – very pretty, if you could see it by daylight. Reminds me a little of Venice. Lions everywhere there. Just feel for it, and turn it very gently.'

I could feel the lion's head all right, and the metal teeth

and jaws that I had to reach into to grasp the ring. I did as
she said; the ring turned, and a small inner door set into
the great doors swung open. We stepped through it, back
onto the little terrace in front of the cottage. There were no
lights at the windows now.

'What do we do now? It must be miles back. And I'm
not sure I could find the way.'

'Oh, nothing to worry about. Just take that path up there
–' she pointed to a narrow track that I hadn't noticed before,
leading up steeply behind the cottage. 'It's a bit of a scramble, but you'll come onto the road, and there'll be a bus
along shortly.'

'I've no money.'

'There are free late-night buses.' She chuckled. 'Part of
the council's attempts to make life safer at night. They never
think whom they might attract onto the buses this way.
But you'll be all right.'

'Are you coming, too?' I asked.

'No, I've my own way back. I'm due to start work soon,
not too far from here. Well, it's been pleasant meeting you.'

'Perhaps we'll meet again sometime.'

She smiled. 'I wouldn't count on it. Night encounters,
you know, quickly forgotten. I expect you'll sleep well
enough tonight, though. Pleasant dreams!'

And then she was gone, still clutching her plastic shopping bag, marching briskly away in her sensible shoes and
stockings as the darkness quickly swallowed her up. I was
alone, completely alone for the first time since I had stepped
onto the boat. Was it really only an hour or so ago?

I took the path she indicated, and scrambled up to the
top. Although bushes scratched at my clothes, and the earth
was dusty and slippery, I made it without mishap. On the
level high above the water, which was now well out of
sight, I came out suddenly into urban life again. The track
emerged between two houses, and in front of me was a
main road, still lit, with a few late-night dog-walkers about
and a bus stop close to hand. The shop windows, garishly
illuminated and full of electrical goods, cheap clothes and

furnishings, looked unreal. Was this the everyday city I was so familiar with?

I did not have to wait long, although it was no ordinary bus that turned up. 'Party Special', its indicator proclaimed. Not, it appeared, a party as in an outing, but as in party – good time and knees up. The driver stopped for me. He was merry, but sober, which was more than could be said for some of his passengers.

'Welcome aboard, madam! Seats for singles on your left, couples on the right, dancing in the middle, bar at the rear. No charge, you're welcome.'

The inside was decorated with balloons, and twirled silver festoons, and all around a couple of dozen partymakers were obviously having a wonderful time. Music blared out, and the standard of dress was more like a trendy disco than a city transport bus. A young man, a little drunk, but good-humoured, tried to pull me into a dance. I resisted, feeling boringly sober and out of place in my trousers and warm sweater. Then – oh, what the hell – I thought, and let him lead me into some kind of exuberant dance. I let the rhythm of the music sweep through me. It had been a crazy enough night – let it become a little crazier. At the end of the number he put his arm around me, and grinned.

'City centre,' called the driver. 'Your stop, madam. It's been a pleasure having you aboard. Mind how you go.'

Five more minutes, and I was home. The city looked quiet, unperturbed, nothing different from usual. What had I expected? There was no noise from the garden either. Rita was right; bed was very welcome. Just before I drifted off, just as the images started to flow, I seemed to see her face bending over me, and heard her voice saying:

'Drops, dear. Little drops. That's what a really satisfying dream is like, isn't it – the kind that tells you everything without needing to go through it all.'

Yes, I thought, that's what I would hope for now. If she bade me sleep well, I certainly did.

Cherry Gilchrist was born in 1949. She gained a degree in English and

Anthropology at Cambridge University and began a varied career which has centred chiefly around publishing and music. She has had twelve books published including titles on alchemy, divination, astrology and the feminine archetype, reflecting her deep interest in symbolism and esoteric philosophy. This short story is her first published work of fiction – an area which she would like to develop in the future. Cherry is a qualified astrologer and has given many talks on this and related topics often in connection with the Saros and Nine Ladies Organizations. She is also the general editor of the *Compass of Mind* series. As a singer, Cherry Gilchrist specializes in the Baroque and Renaissance repertoire, and gives concerts with the professional West Country ensemble, Arcadia. She also works as a freelance soloist and as a singing teacher. She is at present researching the connections between alchemy and Baroque music.

CHAPTER SIX

THE PERSISTENCE OF FALSE MEMORY

Robert Irwin

When Cardinal Moderatio set out to encounter the mystic philosopher, Ramón Lull, he hoped to find the ultimate weapon in the war against heresy. Lull's theatre of memory is a well-organized, regimented system for storing all events, persons, objects and concepts. Yet, if this ultimate weapon is so potent then how come Lull himself has lost the key to certain parts of it?

Historically, Lull was an unusual blend of mystic and hermeticist, ardently devoted to the conversion of Moslems and Jews to Christianity. His *Ars Combinandi* made use of cabalistic permutations of letters, figures and symbols and was to have served as the great tool of mass conversion.

Were it not a precious thing, that you could so read in one book all that which in all other books (which heretofore have been, and are now, and hereafter shall come out) hath been and is and shall be learned and found out of them?

In the summer of 1311, a little before the opening of the Council of Vienne, Cardinal Moderatio took ship for Palma. He had been summoned, yes summoned, by the Majorcan philosopher hermit, Ramón Lull. Lull's message had been delivered to Moderatio in Brescia by a mendicant friar. In his letter, Lull wrote (somewhat obscurely) of a new device which would infallibly rescue the Saracens from their heretical errors and thereby hasten the Second Coming of the Redeemer which all men must await with great impatience. Moderatio had wondered queasily what this

device could be. It was perhaps merely a new refutation of the Koran? But it might be something bolder. Perhaps a design for a mighty dam which would divert the Nile from Mahometan Egypt and take its life-giving waters through Christian Abyssinia? Or perhaps a devious scheme for training French prostitutes in Christian theology and then sending them out east to be the concubines of sultans, whereupon the wily handmaidens, once brought to bed, would easily be able to convert their benighted masters? Moderatio had listened to many such schemes in the past and had rejected them. But study of Lull's letter had persuaded him that something was being promised or, it might be, threatened; something that was less easy to understand and therefore less easy to reject. The quotation in Lull's letter seemed familiar to Moderatio, but he could not quite place it. Was it perhaps from one of Lull's own works, the *Fama Fraternitatis*? *De Modo Auditu Angeli*?

Disembarking at Palma, Moderatio spent the night in the little port as a guest of the Aragonese seneschal. That evening, while the Cardinal and the seneschal dined, the Cardinal's servants were busy hiring mules and collecting provisions for the following day's excursion. Beyond expressing the opinion that Majorca's most famous citizen could not survive many more winters, there was nothing that the seneschal could tell the Cardinal about Lull's activities in his mountain hermitage. In the morning the mule train set out to bring the Cardinal and his party to the foot of Mount Randa. Moderatio left his attendants encamped on the lower slopes of the mountain, where the olive groves give way to fir trees. He proceeded alone and on foot through a woodland path to the hermitage on the crest. It was sultry and the sweat came up on the Cardinal's cheeks in perfectly formed tear drops. Lull's refuge was a small house of cracked stonework. A solitary pine had struggled up through the dry earth in front of the door. A horn was chained to one of its branches. Moderatio put the horn to his lips and blew. Even while the sound of the horn was echoing round the hillside, Ramón Lull, *Doctor Invincibilis*, appeared at the door. He wore a turban in the Byzantine mode and a crimson robe decorated with gouts of flame. Curving Turkish slippers pointed out from beneath the robe. As soon as he saw the Cardinal, Lull closed his eyes. Then, after a long pause, he pronounced the words,

'Cardinal Moderatio. Welcome.'

There were no further courtesies. Lull stood filling the doorway of the hermitage and made no move to usher him in.

'Why have you come?' the old man wanted to know.

'I received your letter.'

'You received my letter, but did you understand it?'

Moderatio realized that he was being addressed as if he was a schoolboy, but he took it calmly enough.

'You wrote of a book which is all books. I believe that you mean by that the Bible. You also referred to Angelic Keys and to images that are too horrid ever to be forgotten and finally you seemed to promise a device which will convert the Saracens. It is this last that I have come to see and, if I am allowed, I hope to make favourable report of it to the Pope.'

'You have not understood my message.'

'Then there is no scheme for converting the Saracens.'

'There is and you shall see it before you leave. But you must see it with the eyes of understanding and there is much you do not understand. Indeed, I should say that you have not understood anything.' Lull paused. 'Have you ever studied the Art of Memory?'

The Cardinal shook his head. 'My masters in Paris did not consider it necessary, and besides my memory is serviceable enough. . . .'

Lull interrupted, 'Then your masters in Paris did you a bad turn. The Art of Memory is. . . . Do you know what the Art of Memory is? It is the most powerful weapon in the arsenal of Christendom and it is one of which the Caliph and his Mahometan doctors know nothing.'

The old man stood swaying in the doorway. 'There are mighty powers in the properly trained Christian mind. I see that it will be necessary to give you a demonstration.

But first, let me try you with this. How do I know that your name is Moderatio and that you are a cardinal?'

The Cardinal reflected cautiously. One thing they had taught him in Paris was to distrust deceptively simple questions. All the same, how should Lull not know who he was? They had first met five years ago in Gaeta, then on two other occasions in Padua. Then, most recently, Lull had written to him and now here he was in response to the letter. Who should Cardinal Moderatio be, if not Cardinal Moderatio? But properly cautious, he made no reply, only shrugged his shoulders.

Lull continued, 'I am an old man, very nearly three times your age. I have seen popes, kings, cardinals, princes, deacons, barons, chaplains, merchants and all manner of folk come and go in my life. No untrained natural memory could possibly hold such a mass of stuff and not lose most of it.' Lull tapped his forehead. 'But I have hollowed out chambers in my head and made its wild garden into an artificial memory of awesome power. I have made chambers in my skull, and in each chamber there are niches, in each niche there are memory images. You, for instance, when I want to remember you . . .' (And here the Cardinal gained the impression that Lull did not often want to remember him,) '. . . you are found in the one-hundred-and-eighty-fourth chamber of the Palace of Memory, in the sixth niche. Because you are a virtuous cardinal, I have visualized you as a cardinal virtue, a winged angel. Because you are thirty-three years old, which is the age at which Christ died (a very good age to die by the way), I visualize a crucifix at your feet. Because you are an Italian, I picture strands of spaghetti instead of hair springing from your head. Finally, because Moderatio is an anagram of "I Dream Too", I picture the whole in a dream cloud issuing out of my head. It is simple and it tells me all I need to know about you.'

The Cardinal was very polite and said nothing, but Lull sensed the doubt in the young man's mind. 'That is only the beginning of it. Come inside.'

And the old man took him by the hand and drew him into the hermitage. Moderatio felt the old man's hand trembling at his wrist, but when he looked down at the gnarled hand he perceived that what he had first taken for senile tremblings was in reality something fiercer and more vital. It was as if some powerful spirit shook and writhed under the philosopher's skin.

The hermitage's interior was cool and dimly lit. Books and charts were strewn all round the room. There was no furniture, only a straw mattress and something humped in the centre of the room covered by a large piece of tarpaulin.

'Pick a book. Pick any book,' the old man urged. 'Take a book from anywhere in the room, open it at random. Tell me what chapter you have opened it at, and I shall tell what is in that chapter word for word and letter for letter.'

Moderatio walked over to a pile of books in the corner and then hesitated. Surely this seeking out of texts at a hazard smacked a little of the *Sortes Virgilianae*, the reprehensible practice of bibliomancy? Besides, the books were all so strange. The *Turba Philosophorum*, the *Tractate Middoth*, al-Hazred's *Necromicon*. He picked up a book, let it fall open and then closed it hastily. The page was full of minutely detailed diagrams of women's internal organs, cut open and displayed under unfamiliar constellations of stars. Besides, the text was in cipher. He picked another work whose title at least was familiar to him.

'*Picatrix*, part four, chapter twenty-three.'

With his eyes closed and his arms tight by his sides. Ramón Lull began to recite, ' "The adept should know that he is embarked on the highest of all branches of knowledge. For he will learn that he is a man and that man is a world in miniature or an abridgement of the whole. It is for this reason that his skull is shaped like the heaven above him and there is nothing under the heavens that a man's intellect is not capable of encompassing. But before proceeding any further the adept should be warned also of certain pitfalls and snares which if not detected will lead infallibly to. . . ." and so on and so on.' Lull opened his eyes. 'Have you heard enough? I can remember every word that is on that page. What is more I can tell you which letters were written in black ink and which in red. Are you not impressed?'

'Goodness, yes. This is something marvellous,' said the Cardinal politely. But he wondered privately how this was going to convert the Saracens? The Caliph was hardly going to be converted by an aged hermit's demonstration of how he could remember the Caliph's name.

Lull laughed drily. 'But that is nothing, absolutely nothing. I should not have called you here from Naples just for that. Now I shall show you something truly marvellous.'

And with that the old man stooped and set to tugging at the tarpaulin. The Cardinal tried to help but was waved away. Then the Cardinal did indeed marvel. He could put no name to the thing that was revealed and lay gleaming in the dim light. It was like the skeleton of a brass sphere set in an oaken table. Or it was a little like an orrery. Or a planispheric astrolabe. Or, perhaps, an armillary sphere. But it was not very like anything the Cardinal had ever seen before. He fluttered his hands over it, not quite daring to touch it.

'What is it?'

'It is the engine that will convert the Saracens and the Jews. It is the answer to everything. It is my *Ars Combinandi* machine. It is the embodiment of every book that has been written or shall be written. I myself, who have written so many books, will write no more, for the *Ars Combinandi* knows all and can be made to reveal all.'

The Cardinal looked at the device more closely. It was indeed a work of extraordinary artifice. Two sets of nine great brass rings, calibrated in Latin letters and Arabic numerals, hung suspended within one another, connected only by sliding pivots, encircling a central sphere in three segments. The whole was encompassed by a raised wooden rim on which were incised the signs of the zodiac and to this a sliding silver pointer was attached. The pointer in turn was connected by an elegant series of gears to a large spindle which held the outermost of the sets of brass rings in place.

'His Holiness will be most pleased to see this! What does it do? Will it tell the time?'

'It tell us what Time is,' replied Lull grandly. 'You may converse with it if you wish.'

The Cardinal raised his hand and said 'Hello' very tentatively. The machine did not reply.

Lull, who had not noticed, went on talking. 'It is the outward embodiment of my work on the Art of Memory. It is an artificial memory. All of human knowledge is stored in abstract here. The central sphere is divided into three parts, signifying the three active capacities of Will, Intellection and Sense. The innermost of the two constellations of rings corresponds to the Nine Names of God, and the outermost set of rings corresponds to the nine levels of existence from the Divine to the Inorganic. So it is that we have three and nine and nine variables and, if we add this moving arrow here, the *quaestor* or investigator, we have twenty-two variables in all. The resulting sum is two to the power of twenty-two minus one which comes to four million, one hundred and ninety-four thousand, three hundred and three. As you know, that is the number of all the separate things which exist in the universe. I presume your masters in Paris taught you that? Every particular thing in the world can be located by correct manipulation and combination of the wheels. Yet even this is not all, for the *Ars Combinandi* engine's memory is not a passive one. It is potentially active knowledge and mobile, for by correct manipulation of the rings and by movement of the *quaestor* it can produce syllogisms, calculate men's fortunes and refute heresies. All done by concrete logic! Now, if you will give me a question I will set the machine to answer it for you.'

The Cardinal thought wildly. O machine, are you happy in your work? Will it rain tomorrow? Are cats more intelligent than dogs? Yet he did not wish to appear light-minded.

So in the end, 'Ask of it is there a God?'

Lull set to work adjusting the rings until they were in an alignment that satisfied him. Then he moved the *quaestor* to a predetermined position. Then the rings began to spin and the sphere to revolve and now the *quaestor* on the rim began to move with them. At last it came to rest on a coded set of symbols.

Lull brought his code book over to the machine. Together he and the Cardinal ran eyes and fingers down the columns of enciphered entries. At last they had the machine's answer. 'NOT YET!'

* * *

The four modes of Intellection (Identity, Negation, Reciprocity and Inversion) cross-correlated with the three active powers of the intellect and those cross-correlations in turn to be considered in the light of the notations generated by the powers of the twenty-two letters of the cabbalistic alphabet. A single summation of the essences and qualities produced in such a computation ought to have been possible. Long chains of abstract thought snaked through the skull.

Lull lay on his straw mattress in agony of mind. The Cardinal had said nothing before politely bidding farewell and commencing his descent down the mountain. There had been no need. Both men now knew that the *Ars Combinandi* machine could never be shown to the Pope. It was certainly heretical. I'll consign the devilish thing to the flames, Lull thought. And I'll burn my books. Books, ciphers, elements, syllogisms, everything that boiled in his head now seemed to him like an awful fever, a sickness from which it would be difficult ever to recover. I am dying of abstractions, he thought. I am petrified. A stone is to be classified as inorganic. It partakes of the quality of lithicity. Because it is cold and dry, its governing astral influences are. . . . Stop. Stop. He now thought that he would like to see an actual pebble and to smell the distinctive smell that wet stone gives off in sunlight. He would like. . . . What would he like? He thought that he would like to return to the world as it was when he was younger and its outlines were cleaner and sharper and the light was brighter. The time when he perceived things as they were, unmediated by grey thought. He would like to look on a human being and touch flesh.

There had been a girl, he remembered. He could not remember her name. They had been lying together in an orchard on the outskirts of Palma, just off the road that goes out along the coast. His hand had been on her thigh. There was a patch of blue which must have been her skirt, though he could remember nothing more of her dress. She was laughing and he was laughing. But he remembered that moment for one reason only, for it was the beginning of his new life, the last laughing gasp of his old sinful self and the commencement of the career of the *Doctor Invincibilis*. For at that moment, sensing the presence of someone else in the orchard, he had suddenly looked up from the laughing girl and, in great amazement, beheld the Christ in a vision hovering over them in the orchard, suspended from the Tree of Adam on which he was crucified. Lull cried out and repented. From that moment on he had shunned women and all earthly things, cared only for God, and worked on his philosophy. As for her, the girl whose name he could not remember, doubtless she had married and grown old and ugly, bearing children. It would be pointless now to seek her out. It was even likely that she (but her name?) existed now only as a collection of greening bones in a field.

Lost memories often return unbidden to men and women in their dotage. That is well known. (Though nothing ever came unbidden to Lull's memory.) Nothing, once seen or heard, can ever be destroyed, is ever truly lost. The memory has it somewhere. One only needs to find the path. Now, it was strange that he, the master of the *Ars Memorandi*, could not remember her name or even her face. He lay there concentrating. At last he remembered what it was that he had forgotten that he had remembered to forget. In the early days of his study of the mnemonic craft, he had trained himself to remember all the scenes and acquaintances of his youth in every minute visual detail. Those friends who were virtuous and those scenes which were edifying he could recall almost instantly. They had their fixed locations in the open parts of the Palace of Memory. But he recalled now that he gathered memories of every incident which was shameful, every scene of temptation and every loose-living companion of his youth and consigned them to a tower in a rarely visited corner of the Palace of Memory and having done so he had locked the door of the tower and never since gone near it.

So it was certain that the girl was in the tower, preserved in all her youth and beauty, every inch of her flesh and every pore of her skin, every eyelash in place and untouched by time. She would be perfectly preserved – like a homunculus in a jar of oil, or rose petals pressed between the pages of a forgotten book, or love letters preserved in a sealed casket. But to enter the tower, to summon up her memory, it would be like raising the dead, a sinful resurrection. Lull played with the temptation, played and succumbed. After all, there could be no danger in it, for he was now very old and schooled in all the disciplines that Christian living has to offer. It could do nothing but good now to contemplate the follies of youth in the light of experience. He felt an obscure excitement.

A few minutes later he closed his eyes and began to concentrate. He was entering the Palace of Memory. The ground plan of the Palace was modelled on the Pope's Palace in Avignon, the largest building Lull had ever seen. He paused at an alcove in the first vestibule. In it an Ass faced a Rhinoceros and an Ichneumon fly hovered in the space between them. Then he smiled. AIR, the first of the four elements. Sure enough in the next alcove he found WATER, a Warthog pursued by an Alchemist bearing a Turnip on which stood an Earwig Rampant. Similarly vivid memory images filled the alcoves assigned to EARTH and FIRE. The main audience hall, much used in Lull's daily calculations, was crowded with rioting imagery. An Orator, a Juniper Tree and a Pack of Hounds marked out the path of an Aristotelian Syllogism. A Winged Egg . . . an Elephant bearing an Obelisk . . . a Peacock . . . a Tinker, a Tailor, a Soldier and a Sailor all playing at Cards . . . a Gangrenous Lamb . . . a Swing supporting a Minstrel in Flames. No time to decode all this now. The hermit hurried through the audience hall and out through the door behind the throne.

Locating the locked tower was a lengthy business. From time to time he had to stand and refamiliarize himself with the Palace he had created. But once located, a simple trick of the memory sufficed to open the locked door. Stella was lodged on the top floor of the Tower. (Yes, he had remembered her name as soon as he was through the door.) With mounting excitement the hermit ascended the stairs. The stairway was crowded and Lull noticed that he was sweating. Dissipated friends from his past filled the stairway and sought to detain him, but he paid them no attention.

At last he had the door of her chamber open. The tiny room was mostly filled by a blazing star which hovered in the centre and cast its rays over the strange objects which, ranked in their tens and hundreds, covered the floor and walls – an anchor attached to severed hands, a Judas tree growing upside down, a row of false teeth carved in wood, a man with a noose round his neck waiting to be hanged, a mossy pentacle. . . . Lull set to work sorting through the apparent clutter. Swiftly he solved scores of complicated anagrams and acrostics, decoded a beguiling rebus and finally translated the star into Stella.

Its light was snuffed out and Stella undulated before him in the twilight. Her dress was blue, but covered in a pattern of pomegranates. He had not remembered that.

Lull contemplated her with delight. What a woman! What is woman? In the hierarchies of existence woman is, like man, located between the Angelic and the Bestial. Yet there are certain essential qualities which distinguish her from man. First the Feminine Principle is a passive one. Secondly, the astral influence governing *femininitas* is that of Venus, which is warm and moist. The correspondent in the cabbalistic letter system is *Gimel*, for that also is warm and moist, but it is *Gimel* in its passive aspect only, as may be plainly seen from the function of *Gimel* in its active masculine role within the Tree of Sephiroth. But there are also the qualities of fruition and parturition to be considered in their various aspects. . . .

Then Stella spoke. 'It is terribly hot in here. Do you mind if I loosen my bodice?'

'It will be hotter in hell,' muttered the philosopher abstractedly.

Robert Irwin has spent most of his life asleep and dreaming. In his waking hours he has written three novels, *The Arabian Nightmare*, *The Limits of Vision*, and *The Mysteries of Algiers*, plus one history book, *The Middle East in the Middle Ages*.

CHAPTER SEVEN

AS IT FLOWS TO THE SEA . . .

Storm Constantine

Though the Tarot images belong to the European Renaissance we can find their equivalents in any time and place. Just as we now find Mayan Tarots, and Viking Tarots, and Tibetan Buddhist Tarots (several of those), there are now three or four science fiction Tarots. Storm Constantine's comedy of manners uses the modern Magickal Tarot to bring us crooked deals on faraway planets. If many of the stories in this book contain a Tarot-reader as a character, 'As It Flows To The Sea . . .' has something more unusual – a store-front alchemist, expert in poisons and illicit transmutations.

Sabriel Leaves left the club by a back door. 'I have lost before,' he thought, shrugging himself further into his coat. 'It is nothing. People have lost more than I did.' He found that such reassurances meant very little in the face of the enormous financial squashing he'd just received. What made it worse was that the grin he'd had to face across the table belonged to his erstwhile partner, Gustav Mealie. Mealie's rings had glittered with appalling smugness as he'd scooped the credit shards over to his already handsome pile of winnings. Outside, the air was humid and thick, the town lit by the glow of an immense, vapid moon. Sabriel Leaves decided he disliked this world, a revelation made all the more depressing since he now owned no funds with which to leave it.

Cambium Delta should never have been colonized, he decided. It appeared to offer very little; its fields and forests were grey and ragged, unpleasant to all five senses, and its animal life was colourless and hairless and invariably toxic. The planet's only attribute was its situation in the galaxy; men had turned it into a sprawling space-port of several,

linked townships. When he'd arrived, Sabriel had thought the stark, industrial buildings had possessed a weird kind of beauty, now he saw them as temporary, off-centre, heartless. He'd been under the impression that he had to meet his partner, Mealie, to discuss business – they'd owned a thriving, inter-planetary export company, dealing in cheap, local trinkets that could be sold for scandalous amounts once shipped half-way across the galaxy. Mealie had given no intimation of what was to come. Sabriel had walked into the crowded, low-ceilinged bar, smiled and sauntered to the table where he could see Gustav Mealie sitting with a couple of tarnished-looking females. It was only after two bottles of liquor and the first game of fayning that Mealie had announced he was breaking the partnership up. Sabriel had been careless; he hadn't covered himself. He'd let Gustav handle all the business side and had no way of proving whether Mealie's claims that the last shipment had gone down in flames over Tatarka was true or not. Mealie said they were ruined, although his smile and his jewellery spoke otherwise. 'So what do I do?' Sabriel had asked, a question which served as a dessert to a host of others, which had begun with, 'What money do we have left?'

'Do, my friend?' Mealie's large handsome face shrank back from a toothy smile. 'Why, you have half of what was left in our account. Start anew – as I shall.'

Sabriel had demanded why Mealie wanted to end their partnership. After all, it had worked very well; he doing the planet-hopping searching for merchandise, while Gustav sat on Croon Cree looking after the administration side. Sabriel could not see why Mealie should want to change that. Mealie's eyes had swivelled away from Sabriel's as he answered. He spoke vaguely of new interests, new fields, a desire for independence. In truth, Sabriel thought, he must have had a better offer from somewhere. 'We might as well enjoy ourselves while we're here,' Mealie had added, shuffling fayn discs with unsettling, professional ease. The liquor had numbed Sabriel's common sense. He agreed – and lost, crushingly.

'How could I have been so stupid?' he wondered, rhetor-

ically, as he scuffed the metallic streets. Mealie knew Sabriel's weaknesses and had efficiently exploited them. It had
been a blend of pride and defiance that had kept him playing, round after round. He remembered the feverish cer-
tainty that he would win soon; after half of his funds had
slipped towards Mealie's pile, there was no going back. Of
course, the situation was not as bad as it seemed. Sabriel
still had reserves in private accounts on Croon Cree and
Zanzibar Cloud, which meant that once he was home he
could survive until he'd sorted himself out, but that did not
answer the immediate problem of how to get home. He'd
trusted Mealie too much and had neglected to memorize his
credit codes. Mealie had always handled everything to do
with finance. Sabriel had never even booked his own cruiser
seats. At best, he could only work here in Euterpiax until
he had enough to place an interplanetary call so that his
friends on Croon Cree could forward him a ticket home or
the funds to purchase one.

Sabriel crept into the flimsy hostelry where Mealie had
booked him a room for the night; it was a gaudy and
unwelcoming place. He felt as if destitution was a word
printed indelibly all over him and shied from the furtive
vision that greeted him from mirrors on the wall in the
reception area. He looked like a kicked rodent and the
receptionist raised her eyebrows at him in distaste. 'Damn
the guts of Gustav Mealie!' he thought as he scurried to his
room. Inside, an intense and pungent humidity hung in the
air. Sabriel dimmed the lights as best he could, tore off his
clothes and took a shower. Over the hiss of water, he
could hear forlorn sounds coming from the town centre;
honkings, mechanical groans and the sighs of listless craft
sweeping drunkenly into the dark sky. Still wet, he lay on
the bed trying to ignore his reflection in the mirrored ceiling. He looked as if he had just been brought back from
the dead. Memories of happier days on far worlds flitted
provocatively through his mind. He dismissed them with
colourful curses. If he'd had any sense he'd have made
provisions to gain access to the business account, he would

have salted money away as insurance against a situation
such as this. Gustav Mealie had come out on top. He'd
discarded Sabriel without a thought. No doubt he was
moving on to better things in which Sabriel had no place.
Sabriel guessed there was a lot more to Mealie than he knew
about.

Burdened with a depressive gloom by such thoughts, Sabriel
Leaves writhed and grunted into a shallow sleep, only to
be abruptly roused several hours later by the piercing whine
of the hostel's intercom system. He waved his hand in front
of the answer panel next to the bed and mumbled, 'Yes?'

'There is somebody in reception to see you, Mr Mealie,'
a nasal female voice replied. Sabriel paused. He choked off
the retort that he was not Mr Mealie.

'Ask them to come up in a few minutes, will you?'

'Of course.' The connection was broken. Sabriel heaved
himself off the bed and rubbed his face briskly. A visitor
for Gustav? Here? Obviously, when the room had been
booked, Mealie's assistant must have used the wrong name.
A happy oversight. For reasons unknown, Sabriel felt an
inexplicable elation at the event.

Shortly, a small, elegantly attired gentleman named
Caspar Soames presented himself at Sabriel's door. Sabriel
had activated the air-freshening system in the room, dressed
himself in clean clothes and had slicked back his dark hair
with water. Now, he felt more capable of dealing with the
situation. Caspar Soames strutted into the room, making
genuflections of greeting that hailed from some little-known
culture. Sabriel responded languidly.

'I had problems locating you, Mr Mealie,' Soames said
in a reedy voice. 'I seem to recall you were to leave a
message as to your whereabouts at Spaceport Delph.'

'I regret the inconvenience,' Sabriel replied. 'Still you are
here now.' His mind was tumbling over itself wondering
how to conduct this interview. Clearly Soames had not met
Gustav in the flesh before. Was this the new business partner? It seemed likely. Sabriel thought it too good an opportunity to miss.

'I had to ask Information to look for your name on the hostel reservation lists,' Soames was saying. 'They weren't too happy about it. It was costly.' Lucky that this place was fortunately placed alphabetically, Sabriel thought, otherwise Mr Soames might have gone straight to Gustav.

'My office will reimburse your expenses,' he said. 'Take a seat. Would you like a drink?'

The small man pursed his lips and shook his head. 'I anticipate only staying here a moment or two. I have little time to spare, as I'm sure you appreciate . . . in *my* line of business.' He grinned in a particularly unpleasant, fleshless way.

Sabriel inclined his head. 'Naturally.' He hoped that Soames would introduce the subject of the meeting and played for time by mixing himself a complicated cocktail from the room's portabar.

'All I require from you at this stage is the deposit we talked about,' Soames said, sniffing.

'My office will arrange it.'

Soames made an exasperated sound. 'Have you forgotten already? I stipulated cash for this venture.'

Sabriel was glad he had his back to the man. Cash? What an outmoded concept. He smiled. What on earth was Gustav getting mixed up in?

'Forgive me,' he said. 'I've been working too hard recently. Facts escape me. A keepsake from a childhood illness whose symptoms included a fever to the brain.'

Mr Soames clutched his throat with one hand. 'How unfortunate.' He looked suspicious. 'I hope this disability will not affect our transactions.'

Sabriel shook his head. 'Unlikely. You have proof as to my success. Surely that reassures you.'

Soames shrugged. 'You have a partner,' he said. 'Even though my investigations as to your financial position produced sound results, it is still possible that Mr Leaves was the mastermind behind your schemes. I'm still perplexed as to why you wish to exclude him from this business. He seems trustworthy.'

'You do not know him,' Sabriel replied, which he felt
was how Gustav would have responded to such a remark.

'True. Anyway, I have the sample you requested. Do
you wish to try it now?'

'Er. . . .'

'It is fine quality psychedrine, refined by the thought
processes and essential juices of Tellagoona maidens,
pounded with piquant oils and sieved by the white hands
of exquisite blind eunuchs of Shar C'mui. . . .'

Sabriel turned his back again while his features wrestled
with expressions of shock, disbelief and, regrettably, sheer
fright. Psychedrine was possibly one of the few narcotics
which various authorities still tried to ban the use of. Therefore, it was an extremely desirable and costly item. It wasn't
so much that the effects of psychedrine were dangerous or
addictive, but rather that the method of refining it was
questionable to say the least. Its components included the
essences Soames had mentioned – that alone meant natives
of Tellagoona had to be farmed and butchered to obtain
them – and there were also the rumoured elements of live
foetus marrow and animal remains. Only a fanatical enthusi-
ast of unexplored experiences could possibly wish to try
such a drug. Sabriel was sure it would even taste of blood
and suffering. He'd always suspected Gustav of being totally amoral as well as hard, selfish and cunning. Now his
suspicions had been confirmed. The penalties for being discovered possessing psychedrine were so harsh, anyone
caught doing so could expect never to see the light of day
again. The benefits of dealing in it successfully were similarly extreme. Gustav could look forward to lifelong afflu-
ence on the strength of a single deal, Sabriel was sure.

'Well, Mr Mealie?' Soames's voice compelled Sabriel to
turn around. He took the small silver box which Soames
offered him and opened it. A delicious scent invaded the
room as he did so, casting back the curtains of Cambium
Delta stink. It smelled of breathing flowers, erotic dreams
and half-glimpsed visions of unimaginable, heart-breaking
beauty. Sabriel quickly closed the box. The temptation was
great. He noticed Caspar Soames raise a smirking eyebrow.

'Take it, Mr Mealie. Lie down upon your bed and drop a single pinch upon each open eye. You haven't tried it before, I can tell. Anyone who has would never hesitate.'

'Rather early in the day for such delights, isn't it?'

Soames laughed. 'As you wish. It doesn't matter. All I'm doing is selling the stuff. What you do with it after that is your business.' He stood up. 'Now, the thirty thousand standard credits, if you please, then we may discuss how to conclude our business.'

'We shall have to meet later,' Sabriel said quickly. 'There are certain details that have to be finalized.'

Soames made an irritated sound. 'I object to having my time wasted. How much later? I had hoped to be off this charmless chunk of rock by tonight.'

'I will meet you for lunch in the Dry Dog. It's a quaint establishment not far from here. Allow me to apologize for this inconvenience, but I'm afraid it's unavoidable.'

'Very well, but I shan't wait long.'

'Thank you. May I keep the sample?'

Soames was already at the door. 'Of course.' He nodded abruptly and left.

Sabriel sat down on the bed, holding the psychedrine box in his hands and stared at it unblinkingly. What now? Several courses of action presented themselves. By now, Gustav Mealie must be wondering where Caspar Soames had got to and very shortly would no doubt begin investigations of his own as to his whereabouts. It was a tricky situation. Sabriel called reception and asked them to put a call through to Gustav Mealie at his hostel. 'Tell him that a Mr Soames will be meeting him for lunch at the Dry Dog after being unavoidably detained elsewhere,' he said, and then lay back on the bed to think. After a while, he got up and left the hostel. Within half an hour he was knocking on Gustav Mealie's door.

Mealie did not look overjoyed to see him. 'Yes, what is it?' he said irritably, his face foamy with depilatory cream. 'I thought we'd concluded our business last night.'

'Last night, you filled me with drink, delivered the news you hoped would destroy me and cheated me of my half of our earnings.'

'My dear Sabriel,' Gustav blustered. 'I most certainly did not cheat you. As I recall, you have never been a particularly adept fayning player.' He grinned in a manner intended to placate. 'Come now, we all need to diversify occasionally. I enjoyed our partnership, Sabriel, but feel that I've gained all I can from it.' He batted Sabriel's arm with a comradely fist. 'How about I reimburse you what you lost at fayning last night?'

Sabriel took a step back. 'Forgive me for saying this, Gustav, but I can't help suspecting that I'm owed rather more than what you took from me last night.'

'What can you possibly mean by that?'

'Don't bother to look aghast, Gustav. I expect I've been used and deserve to have been simply because of my own ingenuous stupidity. However, I think it's only fair that you allow me to examine the ledgers back on Croon Cree so that I may be assured of your honesty.'

Gustav Mealie gave a flippant shrug. 'If it will mean anything to you, Sabriel, go ahead. I assure you I spoke the truth last night. Nearly all we had was wrapped up in that root-carving delivery from Pazhin. I was as shocked as you were.'

Sabriel's heart sank. Gustav's relaxed pose obviously meant the ledgers were works of fiction and all funds were distributed into different areas. So much for that plan. He sighed. 'Very well, I accept your offer of returning what I lost last night. It grieves me to sink so low but I have little desire to stay here for much longer.'

Mealie laughed heartily. 'That's my lad, Sabriel. Take things in good grace. Here!' He tossed a couple of credit tokens at Sabriel which were taken from a heap of such tokens on the bedside table. Sabriel pocketed them and then hesitated. 'Was there something else?' Mealie asked, impatience beginning to tinge his voice again.

'I can't think of anything.'

'Good. Please excuse me, Sabriel. I have a luncheon appointment.'

Sabriel left the room, feeling he'd missed some opportunity, but couldn't work out what or why. His fingers ran over the smooth edges of the silver box in his jacket pocket.

Disconsolately, he roamed the streets of Euterpiax. Perhaps something would come to him. He believed in the power of coincidence, that same power which had brought Caspar Soames to his hotel room. He was continually conscious of the box in his pocket, aware of a faint but insistent aroma that escaped the confines of the silver seal. Far from hinting at luscious visions, it only reminded Sabriel of news reports he'd heard about atrocities glimpsed on Tellagoona; the coppery clouds above the psychedrine plants, the corrals of listless, hopeless essence donors for whom salvation could only ever be the kiss of the draining spikes, the inevitable dark. Sabriel could not decide how to utilize the knowledge he now possessed. Gustav Mealie deserved a slap from the hand of Justice, but Sabriel was unsure of the manner in which it should be delivered. Above him, a grim, metallic sky boiled above the saurian outline of the town. He felt dwarfed by the looming buildings pressing down on either side of the black street. People hurried past, all busy, all engaged upon pressing tasks of their own. Not many folk were penniless in Euterpiax; it was a waterhole for the affluent, on their way to more picturesque worlds at the rim of the galaxy. Sabriel sighed. Now he wandered down a bleak, cornerless lane named, incongruously, Shadow's Curl. On either side identical doorways, flanked by single, scratched plastic windows, offered access to the booths within. An alley of alchemists, lank-witches and scryers. Sabriel gazed half-heartedly into the bescarved, betasselled and beribboned windows. Perhaps he should seek the advice of one of the diviners to be found within. An advertisement in one of the windows wiped the sardonic smile from his lips. 'Learn the Secrets of the Universe's Poisons' it declaimed boldly, and underneath, 'For a mere dinkin, step within and Clytie Tredway will teach a Secret'. Sabriel smiled again. How quaint. What had really caught his eye, however, was the legend beneath this information: 'Psychedrine – learn how the dreams become nightmares with no waking; Loquatim – nervousness banished to the point of complete insensitivity', and so on. Apparently Clytie Tredway knew how to mutate benign or harmless substances into lethal or debilitating toxins; interesting. Sabriel Leaves lifted aside the door curtain and stepped within. He found a gaunt, dishevelled creature sitting at a velvet-draped table on which stood a box of coins, a murky glass half-filled with tea-coloured liquid, and a much-thumbed pamphlet. The woman looked up and said, 'What's your business, mister? A faithless lover, a brutish parent, careless friends. . . .'

Sabriel sat down opposite her. 'None of those. A fiendish business partner.' He removed the silver box from his pocket, opened it, and put it on the table between them. 'This is psychedrine,' he said. Clytie Tredway shut her mouth with a snap. Her eyes narrowed as the unmistakable, seductive scent of psychedrine investigated the sordid corners of her booth.

'Well, sir. . . .'

'Tell me what you can do with that.'

'It is a rare thing, mister, a rare thing. I've never handled it.' She could not keep her eyes off the box. Sabriel winced at the hungry gleam she could not conceal.

'Oddly enough, you claim to have knowledge of its transmutations, or perhaps you didn't write your own sign out there.'

Clytie Tredway pulled herself together. 'My predecessor had worked with the stuff a couple of times,' she said, with a sniff, and began to thumb through the pamphlet. 'Ah, yes . . . well, this is interesting.'

'How interesting?'

'Well, according to the words of Dame Merdice, president of our guild, psychedrine has only to be immersed in the simple beverage, ermola, to become an intoxicant of the most alarming nature.'

'Please explain.'

'I hardly can. Cavortions, madness, euphoria, manic glee, occasional violence, delusions, speaking in tongues – these are only a few of the possible symptoms. All the more sinister because whatever peculiarities manifest in the victim take at least twelve hours to develop, so that a poisoner can be off and away before he . . . or she . . . is suspected of crime. The effects are irreversible.'

'I see. Are these widely known facts?'

'Psychedrine itself is hardly a widely known fact, sir. I admit that the sole reason for it being mentioned on my placard is to whet people's interests. Psychedrine is a legend, a dream drug. I had never expected to come across it.' She eyed the box once more with a furtive, half-guilty glance.

'How much of the stuff is needed to . . .'

Clytie Tredway obviously did not care to hear whatever indelicacies Sabriel might come out with. She essayed to maintain a certain dignity about her work.

'Two good-sized pinches, according to Dame Merdice's pamphlet. You have enough psychedrine there to send a good portion of Euterpiax insane.'

'That is not my intention,' Sabriel said drily. 'Madam Tredway, I have no dinkins – only credit tokens of disproportionately high amounts. Will you accept half of this psychedrine in payment for what you've told me?'

She shrugged. 'You must be mad, but I am definitely sane. Of course, I accept it.'

Sabriel hovered cautiously around the entrance to the Dry Dog for at least half an hour. He investigated several shops in the area, emerging each time to eye the unimposing façade of the place where Gustav Mealie and Caspar Soames were destined to meet. He wondered if they would actually make contact successfully, still unsure of whatever action he would take himself. Eventually, he saw Mealie striding purposefully down the street, his air that of a man about to be offered vast wealth. Sabriel ground his teeth. He experienced irritation, anger and then calmed himself to a steely resolve. Sabriel waited five minutes before following Mealie into the inn. Mealie went directly to the bar, swaggering

and preening at the bored woman serving behind it. Sabriel
waited until he'd bought himself a drink and settled himself
comfortably in a window-seat, before sauntering casually
to the bar himself. Mealie must have noticed him instantly.
A quick glance over his shoulder assured Sabriel of the
poisonous, dark, rodent expression he had expected to find.

'What do you want of me now?' Mealie asked Sabriel as
he sat down.

'Do I understand I am not welcome?' Sabriel shook his
head and smiled ruefully.

'I'm expecting someone. I have business to conduct;
important business.'

'Don't worry, I'll be gone before your new partner
arrives. Can't we share a last drink together?'

Mealie rolled his eyes. 'Sabriel, you sound like a spurned
female. Have I misunderstood the nature of our partnership
all these years?'

'I don't mean to sound bitter. You are right. I went to
have my fortune read today and was told it was time my
circumstances underwent a drastic change. Perhaps you
have done me a good turn, Gustav.'

Mealie made an irritated sound. He looked uncomfortable. Sabriel took some moments to savour the situation,
sipping from his glass and gazing carelessly round the bar.
Small bursts of fidgeting began to escape Mealie's suave
restraints. Eventually he said, 'Sabriel, did you follow me
here?'

'Perhaps.'

Mealie rolled his eyes. 'Oh, for God's sake! What do you
want? Can't you leave me alone. I don't need haunting.
Your behaviour is most unhealthy!'

'I had a visitor earlier today.'

'Really!' Mealie turned to look out of the window, cran-
ing his neck to peer up and down the street.

'Yes. It was somebody who expected to find you. A Mr
Soames.' Sabriel put his glass down on the table carefully.
Mealie gently eased himself back against the seat and narrowed his eyes. For once, he was quite at a loss for what
to say. 'I didn't enlighten him as to my identity and the

poor man spent several minutes trying to exact a rather large sum of money out of me.'

'Sabriel, enough of this clever word-play. If you have a point to make, make it.'

'I suppose you think I will try to blackmail you.'

'By that, I expect you are intimating you know something of the nature of my business with Soames.'

'I know that it is a risky, immoral but highly lucrative venture. How much do you know about what you're becoming involved in?'

Mealie sighed. 'Sabriel, it is not your affair. Our partnership is dissolved. If you have some wild plan concerning betraying me to certain authorities . . .'

Sabriel interrupted. 'I am offended. Do you really think I would do that?'

Mealie took a nervous sip of his drink. 'Many people might, even those you were not feeling hard done by, bearing in mind the nature of the commodity. I am not a fool, Sabriel.'

'If all goes well, you will be a very rich man, Gustav.'

Mealie waved this aside. 'What did you say to Soames?'

'He is under the impression that he will be meeting me here so that I may give him the money for the deposit on the merchandise.'

'And I presume you want to stay here to keep your appointment, only using my income and my goodwill to conclude your business? Am I to understand that you are forcing me to continue our partnership, Sabriel?'

'You give in easily, Gustav.'

Mealie smiled and made a careless gesture with his hand. 'You have outwitted me, Sabriel.' He eyes did not smile. Sabriel could see his own death waiting in that blank gaze. He was not deceived. Mealie laughed loudly. 'Young scamp!' he said. Sabriel was given a vision of a damp, dark alley, a hired assassin, a tidy extinction.

'We are still partners, then?' he asked.

'How could I ever think of losing such a resourceful fellow?'

'How indeed. Allow me to purchase us some refreshment. I owe you that at least.'

'Thank you.'

Some minutes later, Sabriel returned from the bar. Mealie still grinned at him in a manner designed to be comradely but which appeared almost insane; a veritable rictus of a grin. 'Isn't that Mr Soames coming in at the door?' Sabriel said. 'We shall have to tell him of my little deception. Let's just call it a wise precaution, shall we?'

'As you wish, Sabriel. You'd better beckon him over; it's your face he'll recognize.'

Sabriel nodded. He raised the china cup he held in his hand. 'To our success, Gustav! Finish your ermola. Perhaps Mr Soames can be persuaded to furnish us with something stronger.' Mealie smiled and drained the cup.

Storm Constantine is an occasional Erisian, whose interest in the Tarot and connected studies precede this lifetime. She is the author of the Wraethu trilogy: *The Enchantments of Flesh and Spirit, The Bewitchments of Love and Hate* and *The Fulfilments of Fate and Desire.* With the assistance of the visionary group, Thirteenth Key, Storm intends to extend her creative talents beyond writing, into music and video. She lives in the Midlands of England and shares her house with a vortex of chaos.

CHAPTER EIGHT

HANGING THE FOOL

Michael Moorcock

The prolific Michael Moorcock has written in more genres than many
writers have written books. His popular fantasy novels include a series
named for the Swords cards in the Tarot. Rather than sword and
sorcery, however, the current tale explores a territory Mike has
recently added to his imaginative map: the pre-World-War-II deca-
dence of the international rich. In this darkly comic story we learn a
new and horrible method for creating a Tarot card.

1 The Hermit.

His wife, he said, had negro blood. 'It makes her volatile,
like Pushkin.'

Watching him later, as he played the table, I saw him
show panic twice. He recovered himself rapidly on both
occasions. He would tap his wedding ring sharply with his
right index finger. His hands were long, not particularly
thin, and as tawny as the rest of him – a lion, lazy and
cruel, quick as a dagger. 'Lord, lord,' he would say as his
wife made her appearance every evening just before dinner,
'she is magnificent!' And he would dart towards her, eager
to show her off. Her name was Marianne Max and she loved
him in her careless way, though I thought it more a mother's
affection, for she was at least ten years his senior.

He would escort her into the dining room and afterwards
would never gamble. Together they would stroll for a while
along the promenade. Frequently I saw them silhouetted
with the palms and cedars, talking and sometimes embracing
before returning to the hotel and the suite permanently
booked to them. The Hotel Cumberland was older than
most and cared more for pleasing its regular customers than

THE HERMIT.

ACE of WANDS.

THE HIGH PRIESTESS

THE LOVERS.

PAGE of WANDS.

QUEEN of PENTACLES

WHEEL of FORTUNE.

JUSTICE.

attracting the new money which had come to St Crim; it was a little run down but maintained its elegance, its superiority over more modern buildings, especially those revivalist deco monstrosities which had risen across the bay on the French side, upon the remains of the old Ashkanasdi mansion, where the so-called Orient Express brought rich Americans in large numbers.

I had been spending the summer with my ex-wife, who had a villa just above the town, in the pine woods. Every evening I would go down to dine at the hotel and perhaps indulge in a little baccarat.

De Passoni was the chief reason for the regularity of my visits. The man was so supremely unselfconscious, so unguarded, few would have believed him a convicted murderer, escaped from the notorious Chatuz Fortress outside Buenos Aires some years earlier. There was no sign that he feared recognition or recapture. He appeared to live entirely for the day. And there was, of course, no deportation treaty between Argentina and St Crim.

I had not by the middle of the season found any means of approaching him, however. Every time I tried I had been rebuffed. His wife was equally impossible to engage in anything but light conversation.

She was the Countess Max, one of the oldest titles in Wäldenstein. Her first husband, Freddie Max, had been killed during the Siege, leading a cavalry charge against the Prussians across the ruins of the St Maria and St Maria Cathedral. She had remarried after a year, regaining her estates by her alliance with Prince Osbert, the new prime minister. He had died of influenza in 1912, whereupon she had appeared openly with de Passoni, who was already her lover, until the scandal had forced them to St Crim where they now lived in unofficial exile.

De Passoni had his own money, from his father's locomotive works, and it was this he gambled. He took nothing from her. Neither did she expect him to take anything. Residents of the Hotel Cumberland said they were a bloodless pair. I thought otherwise.

2 The Nine of Pentacles.

When I came home from North Africa, the following
spring, my ex-wife told me that the couple had disappeared
from the Hotel Cumberland, although their suite was still
booked and paid for. There was a rumour that they were
in the hills outside Florence and that the Italian police were
resisting an attempt to extradite him. His father had investments in Milan and considerable influence with the authorities. My ex-wife became vague when I asked her for more
details, a sure sign that she possessed a secret which she
hoped would add to her power.

While she was in her private sitting room taking a telephone call my ex-wife's companion approached me that
evening. The woman, Pia, knew through a friend of hers
that Countess Max had been seen in Florence and then in
Genoa. There was talk of her having brought and equipped
a steam yacht. De Passoni had not been with her.

I asked Pia, who disliked me, why they should have left
St Crim. She did not know. She shrugged. 'Perhaps they
were bored.'

Returning, my ex-wife had laughed at this and then
grown mysterious; my sign for leaving them.

I borrowed her horse and rode down to the cliffs above
Daker's Cove. The Englishman's great Gothic house was a
shell now, washed by the sea he had attempted to divert.
Its granite walls were almost entirely intact and the towers
showed well above the water line even at high tide, when
waves washed foam in and out of the tall windows, but the
great weather vane in the shape of a praying mantis had
broken off at last and lay half-buried in the sand of the
cove. Daker himself had returned to England and built
himself a castle somewhere in the Yorkshire Dales. He lived
there the year round, I heard, a disappointed recluse. The
remains of his great garden were as beautiful as ever. I
rode the chestnut down overgrown paths. Rhododendrons,
peonies, lilac and great foxgloves filled the beds, and the
whole of the ground was pale blue with masses of forget-
me-nots, the remaining memories of England.

What had he learned, I wondered, from all his experience? Perhaps nothing. This was often the fate of those who attempted to impose their own reality upon a resisting and even antagonistic world. It was both a failure of imagination and of spirit. One died frustrated. I had known so many politicians who had ended their days in bitterness. The interpreter, the analyst, the celebrant, however, rarely knew the same pain, especially in old age. Neither, I thought, was that the destiny of those whose politics sought to adjust genuine social ills, who responded to the realities of others' suffering.

The paths joined at an abandoned fountain, a copy of the Kassophasos Aphrodite. Even though she was half-obscured by a wild clematis which clambered over her torso and shoulders like a cloak, she retained her air of serene wisdom. I reined in my horse and dismounted.

Struck by her similarity to the Countess Max, I wondered if I, in my turn, were not imposing my own fancy on the reality.

3 *The Ace of Wands.*

I had returned to Paris for a few days. My investments there were under attack from some manipulations on the Bourse which it soon emerged were fraudulent. By careful covering I was able not only to counter the threat and recover my capital, but make a handsome and honest profit from those whose actions might well have caused me considerable financial embarrassment.

Hearing I was at my house my friend Frere came to see me. He had a message from my father to say that he had been taken ill and was in Lucerne to recover. My own business was over. I went immediately to Switzerland to find my father in reasonable health and breathing almost normally. He was working on his book again, a catalogue of the important buildings destroyed in France and Belgium during the Great War. It was to be his acknowledgement, he said, to an irrecoverable moment in our history, when peace had seemed a natural condition of civilized mankind.

My father asked me to visit my brother at our estates. I had not been to Bek since the last family gathering immediately following the Armistice. Uncle Ricky was long since gone to Italy, obsessed as usual, with a woman, but my brother Ulrich, whom we called Billy, was running the place very well. He was most like my father, more prepared than I to accept such rural responsibilities.

When I left Lucerne the summer had come. Mountains were brilliant with wild flowers and the lake shone with the tranquillity of steel. The train wound down to the French border first and then travelled across to Germany. I changed in Nuremberg, which always reminded me of a gigantic toy, like the one made by the Elastolin firm, with its red castle and walls, its neat cobbles and markets, the epitome of a Bavarian's dream of his perfect past. I had a light lunch at the excellent station restaurant and was disturbed only once, by a gang of men, evidently ex-soldiers, who marched in military style through the lanes shouting of revenge against the French. I found this singularly disturbing and was glad to get on the train which took me to Bek's timeless woods and towers, her deep, lush fields, so like the country-side of Oxfordshire which I had explored while at Balliol before the War.

Billy met me himself, in a dogcart, having received my telegram that morning. 'You've been in Africa, I gather?' He looked me over. 'You'll be black as an Abyssinian, at this rate!' He was curious about my mining interests in Morocco and Algeria, my relations with the French.

Since I had taken French citizenship, I explained, I had had no trouble. But I was disturbed by the Rif and Bedouin rebels who seemed to me to be growing in strength and numbers. I suspected German interests of supplying them with weapons. Billy said he knew little of international politics. All he hoped was that the Russians would continue fighting amongst themselves until Bolsheviks, Whites, Anarchists, Greens, and whoever else there were, had all wiped one another out.

I had less unsophisticated views, I said. But I laughed. Ivy-covered Bek came in sight at last. I sighed.

'Are you ever homesick?' Billy asked as he guided the dogcart up the drive.

'For which home?' I was amused.

4 *The High Priestess.*

From Marseilles I took the train down the coast. The sun had turned the olive trees and vines to an astonishing sharpness and the white limestone glared so fiercely that it became for a while unbearable. The sea lacked the Atlantic's profundity but was a flat, uncompromising blue, merging with a sky growing hotter and deeper in colour with every passing hour until by three o'clock I drew the blinds and sat back in my compartment to read.

I determined not to go to Cassis where Lorna Maddox, the American, had told me she would wait until she returned to Boston in September.

I had met her at dinner when I visited Lord St Odhran at the opening of the grouse season, the previous summer. She had told an extraordinary story about her own sister receiving in the post a piece of human skin, about the size of a sheet of quarto writing paper, on which had been tattooed an elaborate and, she said, quite beautiful picture. 'It was the Wheel of Fortune, including all the various fabulous beasts. In brilliant colours. Do you know the Tarot?'

I did not, but afterwards, in London, I purchased a pack from a shop near the British Museum. I was curious.

Lorna's sister had no idea of the sender, nor of the significance of such a grotesque gift.

I discovered that the card indicated Luck and Success.

For at least a week, whenever I had time on my hands, I would lay out sets of cards according to the instructions in the book I had bought at the same time. I attempted to tell my own fortune and that of my family. I recall that even my Uncle Ricky had 'Safety' as his final card. But I made no notes of my readings and forgot them, though I still kept the pack in my luggage when I travelled.

'She was told by the police that the tattoo was quite

recent,' Lorna had said. 'And that if the owner were still alive she would have a trace of the design still, on her flesh. The ink, apparently, goes down to the bone. The theory was that she had regretted having the thing made and had it removed by surgery only a month or so after it had been done.'

'You're sure it was a woman's skin?' I had been surprised.

'The police were pretty certain.'

'What did your sister do with the thing?' St Odhran had asked.

'The police held it for a while. Then they returned it to her. There was no evidence of foul play, you see. My brother wanted it. It fascinated him. I believe she gave it to him.'

I knew her brother. His name was Jack Hoffner and he often visited St Crim. I had no great liking for him. He was a bad loser at the tables and was reputed to be a cruel womanizer. Possibly the piece of skin had belonged to some deserted paramour. Had she sent it to Hoffner's sister as an act of revenge?

5 *The Nine of Wands.*

It was raining by the time I reached St Crim. Huge drops of water fell from the oaks and beeches on to tall irises and there was a sound like the clicking of mandibles. Mist gathered on the warm grass as my car drove from the station up the winding road to the white house with its gleaming red roof and English chimneys. The scent of gardenias in the rain was almost overwhelming. I found that I was suddenly depressed and looking back through the rain saw the sea bright with sunlight, for the cloud was already passing.

Pia waited for me on the steps, her hair caught in some multi-coloured gypsy scarf. 'She's not here. But she'll be back.' Pia signed for a servant to take my bags from the car. 'She told me you were coming.'

'She said nothing of leaving.'

'It happened suddenly. A relative, I gather.'

'Her aunt?'

'Possibly.' Pia's tone had become almost savage and it was clear she had no intention of telling me anything else.

It had always been my habit not to enquire into my ex-wife's life but I guessed she had gone somewhere with a lover and that this was disturbing Pia unduly. As a rule she kept better control of herself.

My room was ready for me. As soon as I had bathed and dressed I took the car back to the Cumberland. Almost the first person I saw as I stepped through the revolving door into the foyer was the Countess Max who acknowledged my greeting with a warmer than usual smile. Her husband came hurrying from the elevator and shook hands with me. His palm was moist and cool. He seemed frightened, though he quickly masked his expression and his face grew relaxed as he asked after mutual friends.

'I heard you had gone to Genoa to buy a boat!' I said.

'Oh, these rumours!' Countess Max began to move away on de Passoni's arm. And she laughed. It was a wonderful sound.

I followed them into the dining room. They sat together near the open French doors, looking out to the harbour where a slender steam yacht was moored, together with several other large vessels chiefly the property of visitors. I was on the far side of the room and a party of Italians came in, obscuring my view, but it seemed to me that the couple talked anxiously while preserving a good appearance. They left early, after a main course they had scarcely started. About half-an-hour later, as I stood smoking on the balcony, I saw a motor launch leaving a trail of white on the glassy water of the harbour. It had begun to rain again.

6 *The Lovers.*

By the following Sunday I suspected some radical alteration in the familiar routine of life at St Crim. My ex-wife had not yet returned and it was impossible for me to ignore the gossip that she had gone to Tangier with Jack Hoffner. Further rumours, of them disappearing into the interior wearing Arab dress, I discounted. If every European said to be disguised as a Tuareg was actually in the Maghreb then I doubted if there were a single tribe not wholly Caucasian and at least ninety per cent female!

However, I began to feel some concern when, after a month, nothing had been heard from them while the *Shaharazaad*, the steam yacht owned by Countess Max, was reported to have docked in El Jadida, a small, predominantly Jewish port south of Casablanca. They had radio equipment aboard.

I took to laying out my Tarot pack with the Hermit as Significator. I constantly drew the Ten of Swords, the Ace of Wands and Justice, always for the future but the order frequently changed so that although sadness, pain and affliction lay forever in my future they were not always the finale to my life. The other card drawn regularly for the future was the Lovers.

We turn to such methods when the world becomes overly mysterious to us and our normal methods of interpretation fail.

I told myself that my obsession with the Tarot was wholesome enough. At least it lacked the spurious authenticity of psychoanalysis. That particular modern fad seemed no more than a pseudo-scientific form of Theosophy, itself pseudo-religious: an answer to the impact of the twentieth century which enabled us to maintain the attitudes and convictions of nineteenth-century Vienna. Every one I knew was presently playing at it. I refused to join in. Certain insights had been made by the psychoanalystic fraternity, but these had been elevated to the level of divine revelation and an entire mystical literature derived from them. I was as astonished by society's acceptance of these soothsayers as I was by the Dark Age rituals in St Crim's rather martial sub-Byzantine cathedral. At least these had the excuse of habit. Doctor Freud was a habit I did not wish to acquire.

I remained at St Crim until early September when I received a letter from my ex-wife. She was recovering from typhus in a hospital run by the White Sisters in Tangier. She was alone and had no friends there. She asked me to cable funds to the British Embassy or have my agent help her. There was no mention of Jack Hoffner or de Passoni and the Countess Max.

I chose one card at random from my pack. It was the Wheel of Fortune. I went down to the hotel and telephoned my friend Vronsky. That afternoon his Van Berkel seaplane landed in the harbour and after a light supper we took off for North Africa, via Valencia and Gibraltar.

The machine was a monoplane of the latest type and was built to race. There was barely room for a small valise and myself. Vronsky's slightly bloated, boyish face grinned at me from the rear cockpit, his goggles giving him the appearance of a depraved marmoset. Since the Bolshevik counter-revolution Vronsky had determined to live life to the absolute, convinced that he had little time before someone assassinated him. He was a distant cousin of the Tsar.

The plane banked once over St Crim, her wooded hills and pale villas, the delicate stone and iron of her harbour and promenade, the mock-Baroque of her hotels. It would only be a matter of seven years before, fearing the political situation in Italy, she gave up her independence to France.

The plane's motion, though fluid, filled me with a slight feeling of nausea, but this was quickly forgotten as my attention was drawn to the beauty of the landscape below. I longed to own a machine again. It had been three years since I had crashed and been captured by the Hungarians, happily only a matter of weeks before the end of the War. My wife, a German national, had been able to divorce me on the grounds that I was a traitor, though I had possessed French citizenship since 1910.

Gradually the familiar euphoria returned and I determined, next time I was in the Hague, to order a new machine.

After refuelling stops we were in sight of Tangier within a few hours. As always, the shores of Africa filled me with excitement. I knew how difficult, once one set foot on that continent, it was to leave.

7 *The Page of Wands.*

The Convent of the White Sisters was close to the British
Consulate, across from the main gate to the Grand Socco,
an unremarkable piece of architecture by Arab standards,
though I was told the mosque on the far side was impressive.
Apart from the usual mixture of mules and donkeys, bicy-
cles, rickshaws, the occasional motor car and members of
almost every Berber and Arab tribe, there was an unusually
large presence of soldiers, chiefly of the Spanish Foreign
Legion. Vronsky spoke to a tall man he recognized from
before the War. The exchange was in Russian, which I
understood badly. There had been some sort of uprising in
a village on the outskirts of the city, to do with a group of
Rif who had come in to trade. The uprising was not, as it
had first seemed, political.

'A blood feud,' Vronsky informed me as we crossed the
square from the shade of the great palms, 'but they're not
complaining. It brought them in from the desert and now
they have a day's unexpected leave. They are going in there'
– he pointed through the gate – 'for the Ouled Näil. For
the women.' And he shuddered.

We knocked on a rather nondescript iron door and were
greeted by a small black nun who addressed me in trilling,
birdlike French which I found attractive. Since they did not
accept divorce, I simply told her I was visiting my wife and
she became excited.

'You got the letter? How did you arrive so soon?'

'Our aeroplane is in the harbour.' I lifted my flying
helmet.

She made some reference to the miraculous and clapped
her little hands. She asked us to wait but Vronsky said he
had some business in the new town and arranged to meet
me at the Café Stern in three hours. If I was delayed I
would send a message.

The little negress returned with a tall olive-skinned old
woman who introduced herself as the Mother Superior. I
asked after my wife.

'She is well. Physically, she's almost fully recovered. You

are Monsieur von Bek? She described you to me. You'll forgive me. She was anxious that it should only be you.'

The nun led me down whitewashed corridors smelling of vinegar and disinfectant until we entered a sunny courtyard which contained a blue mosaic fountain, two Arab workmen repairing one of the columns and, in a deck chair reading a book, my ex-wife. She wore a plain lawn dress and a simple straw cloche. She was terribly pale and her eyes still seemed to contain traces of fever.

'Bertie.' She put down her book, her expression one of enormous relief. 'I hadn't expected you to come. At least, I'd hoped – ' She shrugged, and bending I kissed her cheek.

'Vronsky brought me in his plane. I got your letter this morning. You should have cabled.'

Her look of gratitude was almost embarrassing.

'What happened to Hoffner?' I asked. I sat on the parapet of the fountain.

'Jack's . . .' She paused. 'Jack left me in Foum al-Hassan, when I became ill. He took the map and went on.'

'Map?' She assumed I knew more than I did.

'It was supposed to lead to a Roman treasure – or rather a Carthaginian treasure captured by the Romans. Everything seemed to be going well after we picked up the trail in Volubilis. Then Michael de Passoni and Countess Max came on the scene. God knows how they found us. The whole business went sour.'

'Where did Hoffner come by a map?'

'His sister gave it to him. That awful tattoo.'

'A treasure map? The Wheel of Fortune?'

'Apparently.' The memory appeared to have exhausted her. She stretched out her arms. 'I'm so glad you're here. I prayed for you to come. I've been an absolute ass, darling.'

'You were always romantic. Have you ever thought of writing novels? You'd make a fortune.'

On impulse I moved into her embrace.

8 *The Queen of Pentacles.*

I remained at St Crim for several months while my wife grew stronger, though her mental condition fluctuated considerably. Her nightmares were terrifying even to me and she refused to tell me what they involved.

We were both curious for news of Jack Hoffner and when his sister arrived at the Cumberland for a few days I went down to see her. My visits to the town had been rare. In the evenings my wife and I played cards. Sometimes we read each other's Tarot. We became quite expert.

Lorna Maddox believed that her brother was dead. 'He hadn't the courage for any prolonged adventure – and North Africa sounds dangerous. I've never been there. Someone killed him, probably, for that map. Do you really think it was sent by a deserted mistress?'

'Perhaps by the one who actually inscribed the tattoo.'

'Or the person who commissioned it? I mean, other than the recipient, as it were?'

'Do you know more about this now?' I asked. We sat indoors looking through closed windows at the balcony and the bay beyond.

'I'm not sure,' she said. 'I think Michael de Passoni had it done.'

'To his victim?'

'Yes. To a victim.'

'He's murdered more than once?'

'I would guess so. I heard all this from Margery Graeme who had quite a long affair with him. She's terrified of him. He threatened to kill her.'

'Why would he have told her such secrets?' A waiter came to take our orders and there was a long pause before she could speak again.

She had magnificent blue eyes in a large, gentle face. She wore her hair down in a girlish, rather old-fashioned style identified with pre-War Bohemia. When she bent towards me I could feel her warmth and remembered how attractive I had found her when we had met in Scotland.

'Margery discovered some papers. Some designs. And a

set of Tarot cards with the Wheel of Fortune removed. The addresses of several tattooists in Marseilles were there. And the piece of skin, you know, came from there. At least the postmark on the envelope was Cassis.'

'Everyone goes to Cassis.' I was aware of the inanity of my remark which had to do, I was sure, with my wish to reject her information, not because it seemed untrue but because it seemed likely. I was beginning to fear a moral dilemma where previously I had known only curiosity.

9 *The Wheel of Fortune.*

Business at last forced me to return to Paris. Dining at Lipp's in St Germain on the first evening of my arrival I was disturbed to see the Countess Max. De Passoni was not with her. Instead she was in the company of a dark man who was either Levantine or Maghrebi. He was strikingly handsome and wore his evening clothes with the easy familiarity which identified him, as we used to say, as some sort of gentleman.

Countess Max recognized me at once and could do nothing but acknowledge me. When I crossed to greet her she reluctantly introduced me to her companion. 'Do you know Moulay Abul Hammoud?'

'Enchanted, monsieur,' he said in the soft, vibrant voice I associated always with the desert. 'We have already met briefly, I believe.'

Now that we stood face to face I remembered him from a Legation reception in Algiers before the War. He had been educated at Eton but was the religious leader of the majority of clans in the Southern and pre-Sahara. Without his control the clans would have been disunited and warring not only amongst themselves but making desultory raids on the authorities. Moulay Abul Hammoud not only kept order in large parts of the Maghreb but also maintained enormous political power, for upon his orders the desert Berbers as well as large numbers of urban Arabs, could forget all differences and unite to attack the French or Spanish.

It was commonly agreed that Moulay Abul was only awaiting the appropriate moment, while the benefits of colonial occupation outweighed the ills, before declaring the renewed independence of the Saharan kingdoms. His influence was also recognized by the British who acknowledged his growing power in North India and also in their own Middle Eastern interests.

'I'm honoured to meet you again, sir.' I was impressed by him and shared a respect many had expressed before me. 'Are you in Paris officially?'

'Oh, merely a vacation.' He smiled at the Countess Max. She looked darker, even more exotic than when I had last seen her.

'Moulay Abul was of great service to me,' she murmured, 'in Morocco.'

'My wife has only recently returned. I believe you met her there. With Jack Hoffner?'

The countess resumed her familiar detached mask, but in spite of seeming ill-mannered I continued. 'Have you heard anything of Hoffner? He was meant to have disappeared in Morocco or Algeria.'

Moulay Abul interrupted quickly and with considerable grace. 'Mr Hoffner was unfortunately captured by hostile Tuaregs in Mauretania. He was eventually killed. Also captured, I believe, was the poor countess's husband. The authorities know, but it has not been thought wise to inform the Press until we have satisfactory identification.'

'You have some?'

'Very little. A certain map that we know was in Hoffner's possession.'

It seemed to me that the Countess Max tried to warn him to silence. Unconsciously the Moulay had told me more than he realized. I bowed and returned to my table.

It seemed clear that Hoffner and de Passoni had failed in their adventure and had died in pursuit of the treasure. Possibly Moulay Abul and Countess Max had betrayed them and the treasure was in their hands. More likely the answer was subtler and less melodramatic.

I was certain, however, that Moulay Abul and the Countess Max were lovers.

10 *The Ten of Swords.*

The tragedy eventually reached the Press. By coincidence I was in Casablanca when the news appeared and while the local journals, subject to a certain discretion, not to say censorship, were rather matter-of-fact in their reporting, the French and English papers were delighted with the story and made everything they could of it, especially since de Passoni was already a convicted murderer and Hoffner had a warrant for fraud against him issued in Berlin at the time of his disappearance.

The Countess Max emerged more or less with her honour intact. The Press preferred to characterize her as an innocent heroine, while my wife was not mentioned at all. Moulay Abul remained a shadowy but more or less benign figure, for the story had been given a Kipling touch by the time the writers had licked it into a shape acceptable to a wide public.

The opinion was that de Passoni and Hoffner had duped the Countess Max, getting her to buy the steam yacht they needed to transport the treasure back to Europe as soon as it was in their possession. The map, drawn on the skin of a long-dead Roman legionary, had become the conventional object of boys' adventure fiction and we learned how the two adventurers had dressed as Bedouin and ridden into the Sahara in search of a lost city built by Carthaginians who had fled conquering Rome. More in fact was made of the mythical city than the map, which suited Hoffner's family, who had feared the sensational use journalists would have made of the bizarre actuality.

I was invited to dinner by General Fromental and his wife and should have refused had not I heard that Moulay Abul was also going to be present.

By chance it was a relatively intimate affair at one of those pompous provincial mansions the French liked to build for themselves in imitation of an aristocracy already

considered impossibly vulgar by the rest of Europe. My
fellow guests were largely of advanced years and interested
neither in myself nor the Moulay, who seemed glad of my
company, perhaps because we shared secrets in common.

When we stood together smoking on the terrace, looking
out at palms and poplars, still a dark green against the deep
blue of the sky, and listening to the night birds calling, to
the insects and the occasional barking of a wild dog, I asked
after the Countess Max.

'I gather she's in excellent health,' he said. He smiled at
me, as if permitting me a glimpse of his inner thoughts.
'We were not lovers, you know. I am unable to contemplate
adultery.'

The significance of his remark completely escaped me. 'I
have always been fascinated by her,' I told him. 'We were
frequently in St Crim at the same time. She and de Passoni
lived there for a while.'

'So I understand. The yacht is moored there now, is it
not?'

'I hadn't heard.'

'Yes. Recently. She had expressed some notion of returning to Wäldenstein but the situation there is not happy.
And she is a cold-natured woman needing the sun. You've
a relative there, I believe.'

'An ex-wife. You know her?'

'Oh, yes. Slightly. My other great vice is that I have
difficulty in lying.' He laughed and I was disarmed. 'I make
up for this disability by the possession of a subtle mind
which appreciates all the degrees and shades of truth.
Hoffner deserted her in Foum al-Hassan. I was lucky
enough to play some small part in getting her back to
Tangier. One should not involve women in these affairs,
don't you think?'

'I rather understood they involved themselves.'

'Indeed. A passion for excitement has overwhelmed
Western females since the dying down of war. It seems to
have infected them more than the men.'

'Oh, our women have always had more courage, by and

large. And more imagination. Indeed, one scarcely exists without the other.'

'They do define each other, I'd agree.'

He seemed to like me as much as I liked him. Our companionship was comfortable as we stood together in the warm air of the garden.

'I'm afraid my wife mentioned nothing of your help,' I told him.

'She knew nothing of it. That man Hoffner? What do you think of him?'

'A blackguard.'

'Yes.' He was relieved and spoke almost as if to someone else. 'A coward. A jackal. He had a family.'

'Two sisters living. I know one of them slightly.'

'Ah, then you've heard of the map?'

'The one you mentioned in Paris? Yes, I know of it. I don't think his sister recognized it for a map.'

'Metaphysically, perhaps, only?' His humour had taken a different colour. 'Oh, yes, there is a map involved in many versions of that design. I thought that was common knowledge.'

'You're familiar with the Tarot?'

'With arcana in general.' He shrugged almost in apology. 'I suppose it's in the nature of my calling to be interested in such things. Hoffner's death was no more unpleasant than any he would have visited on – on me, for instance.' He turned away to look up at the moon. 'I believe they flayed him.'

'So he's definitely dead. You saw the corpse?'

'Not the corpse exactly.' Moulay Abul blew smoke out at the sky. It moved like an escaped ifrit in the air and fled into invisible realms. 'Just the pelt.'

11 Justice.

My return to St Crim was in the saddest possible circumstances, in response to a telegram telling me that my wife was dead. When I arrived at the house Pia handed me a sealed envelope addressed to me in my wife's writing.

'You know she killed herself?' The voice was neutral, the eyes desolate.

I had feared this but had not dared to consider it. 'Do you know why?'

'It was to do with Hoffner. Something that happened to her in Africa. You know how she was.'

We went down to the kitchens where Pia made coffee. The servants were all gone, apart from the cook, who was visiting her sister in Monaco. The woman and her husband who had kept the house for her had found her body.

'She cut her wrists in the swimming pool. She used Hoffner's razor.'

'You don't know why? I mean – there wasn't anything she discovered? About Hoffner, for instance?'

'No. Why, did you hear something?'

I shook my head but she had guessed I was lying. Handing me the coffee cup she said slowly: 'Do you think she knew what was going on? With Hoffner and de Passoni?'

'She told you?'

'The Countess Max stayed with us for several days. She went down to the hotel. She plans to remain there until the funeral. Hoffner's sister is there, too. A bit of a reunion.'

'You think my wife was guilty? That she had a hand in whatever happened in Morocco?'

'She knew Hoffner was involved in every sort of beastly crime and that half the Berlin underworld was after him – not to mention the New York police and the French Secret Service. He betrayed men as well as women. She told me he was threatening her but I think she loved him. Some bad chemistry, perhaps. He excited her, at least. The Countess Max, on the other hand, was thoroughly terrified of him. He had a hold over her husband, you know.'

'So he forced them into his adventure?'

'Apparently. They needed a boat.'

I found that I could not bear to open the envelope my wife had left for me and walked instead down to the Hotel Cumberland where I found Lorna Maddox and Countess Max taking tea together in the cool of the salon. They both wore half-mourning in honour of my wife and greeted me with sincerity when I presented myself, asking me to join them.

'It must have been frightful for you,' said Lorna Maddox, 'the news. We were appalled.'

'Her nerves were terribly bad.' The Countess Max remained distant, though less evasive, less cool. 'I thought she was brave. To go inland with the men like that. I refused, you know.'

'But you believed the map?'

'I had no reason to doubt. Jack was completely convinced. The woman – the woman on whom it had been inscribed was – well, you know, of very good family over there. She was no more than a girl. The secret was passed from mother to daughter, apparently. God knows where Jack heard the story originally, but he made it his business to find her.'

'And seduce her,' said Lorna in a small, chilling voice.

'He was proud of that. I gather it was something of a challenge.' The Countess Max raised china to her lips.

'Surely he didn't – he couldn't . . . ?' I was glad to accept the chair Lorna Maddox offered me.

'Take the skin?' she said. 'Oh, no. That was sent to my sister by the girl's uncle, I gather. There was for a while some suspicion of a blood feud between her family and mine.'

'Moulay Abul put a stop to that.' The Countess was approving. 'Without his interference things might have become considerably worse.' She frowned. 'Though poor Michael's not entirely convinced of that.'

I was shocked. 'Your husband's still alive? I understood that he had died in North Africa.'

'Moulay Abul saved him also. Through his influence he was given up to the French police and is now at sea, escorted back to Buenos Aires by two Sûreté sergeants. He was relieved at first. . . .'

'He'd heard what happened to Hoffner?'

She stared directly back into my eyes. 'He saw it.'

Although it was not yet five I ordered a cognac from their waiter. I marvelled at the self-control of such women.

It was still impossible to guess their real feelings – one towards her brother, the other towards her husband.

There was little more to say.

'The matter's been resolved in the best possible way.' Lorna Maddox sighed and picked up a delicate cup. She glanced at me almost in amusement. 'You are very upset. I'm sorry. We were fond of your wife. But she would encourage men to such extremes, don't you think?'

I returned to the house and opened the packet, expecting some explanation of my wife's part in the affair. But she had written nothing.

The envelope contained a folded section of almost transparent skin on which had been tattooed a Wheel of Fortune. It had been wrapped around the Tarot card representing Justice. There was also a visiting card bearing the printed name of Moulay Abul Hammoud and on the reverse, in clear script, a few words – 'With my compliments. I believe this is morally, madame, your property.'

The note was, of course, unsigned.

Michael Moorcock was born in 1939. He was a professional writer and editor by the age of 16. He has edited *Tarzan Adventures* (1957); *Sexton Blake Library* (1959) and *New Worlds* (1964). He has two daughters and one son, and is presently married to Linda Steele. His awards include BSFA, World Fantasy, John W Campbell, August Derleth, Nebula, Guardian Fiction Prize, et cetera. Books include *Behold the Man*, the Jerry Cornelius Quartet, the Eternal Champion series, *Dancers at the End of Time*, *Breakfast in the Ruins*, *Gloriana*, *The Brothel in Rosenbrasse*, *Byzantium Endures*, *The Laughter of Carthage*, *The City in the Autumn Stars*, *Mother London*, also various record albums, anthologies, et cetera. He travels regularly and extensively in Europe, America, North Africa and the Middle East. He has recently finished a new Elric novel and is working on the third Pyat novel, *Jerusalem Commands*.

CHAPTER NINE

THE EMIGRATION

Josephine Saxton

The fascination of creating stories with the Tarot is the intersection of a writer's concerns with the demands laid out in the order of the pictures. Probably no one but Josephine Saxton could have looked at this sequence and come up with her vivid and picaresque tale, with its swings between apocalypse and delight, liberation and tragedy. And yet, when we read it and look back at the pictures we can see how the direction of the story, and many of its incidents, were simply out of her hands. In a note with the story, Josephine wrote that she hadn't planned to write science fiction. The cards made the decision for her.

Filling in the documentation on the screen was a nightmare. Every time Mama had a line filled in with the name and date of birth of one of us, either she would go and press the wrong key and cancel it again, or the baby would stagger up and do that or worse with its sticky little hand. Once, Mama had been at it for about three hours when she suddenly yanked the disc out and hurled it across the room, tears of frustration pouring down her thin white face. I recall she put her hands up to cover the shame of her loss of control and we all looked the other way until she'd got herself in hand. But all eight of us understood the frustrations of the Linker, because it was so demanding for details, and they were all on other discs and, even when you came up with the right info, the Linker would ask you to wait, Processing In Progress, oh sure. And then when it whistled you had to run to it in case it went off again, sometimes it was hours. We had to fill in every detail, not only superficial things like dates of birth, height, weight, but chromosome band codes, hourly blood sugar averages

THE STAR

THE HANGED MAN

THE POPE

THE WORLD

THE HIGH PRIESTESS

THE SUN

THE TOWER OF DESTRUCTION

over the previous six months, all kinds of madness that still didn't say who you were. So we kept our mouths shut, our fingers crossed, and looked away while Mama struggled with her tears. Not that there was anywhere to look in a room just big enough for us to lie down in, stacked up in the fold-down bunks, and for the Linker and two doors; one to the water room and one to the outside, a double door that, of course.

But that was not the whole of the problem, because we had been discussing it all for weeks before we even put in an application to get permission to put in a real application, and once the documentation began there was even more argument. After all, once you'd been shipped out to some-where the back of some place light years away, you couldn't ever come back. You had to be either very positive about it all, or very negative, which is to say that you couldn't stand the life on Earth another minute, and anything had got to be better. Mama was of the second group, she was going off her head.

I was of the first kind, but at that time I was only fourteen and arrogant with it. I knew that when my time came to be interviewed for Motherhood, I was going to make a mess of it intentionally. At school there were rumours of some stuff you could take which wrecked the pictures of your chromes without actually making you feel ill or doing any permanent harm. I hadn't thought it through, obviously; I thought I preferred the life of a lower class slave, which was likely what I would otherwise have got. But I wanted to do something with my life; I thought I would handle myself a lot better than our Mama. I wasn't going to spend the rest of my life indoors in a cell with a group of children, communicating with the rest of the world mainly through the screen. I wanted a better life, I wanted to emigrate, I wanted what they showed us in the commercials. But Mama said it was all a government con and it would be just as vile out there as it was in Leamington. She said she'd lived long enough to get the feel of a line being handed, and those ads were just too good to be true.

'When they get you out there, Mary,' she had told me,

'they won't be giving you a room all to yourself, and nice
work outdoors and fancy places to have leisure in; they'll
probably give you a pick and shovel and send you off down
a uranium mine or some such, and you'll never see a tree
again no more than you do here. They need slaves on those
new planets, I don't doubt, or they just want to clear us
off here where we're taking up too much of the space.
And besides, you know nobody ever leaves Leamington.
Everybody says that, once you are settled here, it isn't a
bit of good trying to move. Something always calls you
back to it, from anywhere you can think of to name.'

But that was on her bad days. In another mood she was
almost like a different woman. She'd curl up on a bunk and
invent stories about a new world, where you didn't have to
have double doors, and where you could walk about in the
daytime with hardly any clothes on, picking real fruit off
real growing outdoor trees, like in olden times. We all
listened and loved it, but even we thought that was fantasy.
No government ever gave anything away free yet, so why
start now? We weren't totally loony, but we did still want
to emigrate. Wherever it was, it had to be better than where
we were then.

Leamington Spa back in 2027 must have been one of the
most overcrowded towns in the Midlands. After the waters
began to rise but the hills were radioactive, everybody came
to the lower-lying areas inland, and forced their way into
anywhere they could set up a camp or get a room. All those
lovely old Victorian terrace houses had people camping in
the gardens, both back and front, after all the rooms were
filled up. Birmingham had gone, so had Coventry, and we
had been unofficially requisitioned. Mama said it would
always be like that, because nobody could ever get away,
although wherever there was to go was full up, as far as we
knew. But that was just the flooding, when London got
drowned along with a few other important places, and we
had yet to face the sun. When the ozone layer lost its
tension and flew off altogether, what land was left above
the waters just burned up straight away along with those
people who'd been out for the three days it took to disap-

pear. Not that there were many deaths at first, it was all the cancers which began to appear on people.

Anyway, I'm depressing you with history; I can't help it sometimes, when I start thinking how our family might all have stayed together if only we had stuck it out.

I recall her filling in the documentation and having a hell of a time with it. Our room was so cramped, eight of us in it, with just the water room, where we bathed and cooked. The other facilities were shared. It was a beautiful old building overlooking a green and the river Leam. It had once been a one-family house but at the time I'm thinking of there would have been about seventy-five people living in it. I wish I was there now, even with so little water. Here, you have a two-gallon ration all to yourself every day, but then, we were lucky if we had that much for the whole lot of us. Once a week they'd turn the shower on for about twenty minutes and all this warm dirty water would come after the warning on the screen, so we'd all strip off and take turns to have a wash down, but there were rows if somebody took too long, and whoever went last didn't get their share. I remember once being last and getting nothing but a wetting and I had to wait another whole week, and I spent the whole of that week cultivating hatred for the rest of them who didn't smell as bad as I did. You never got to like your own smelly greasy state, or at least I didn't. Something in me just knew that there was a way to be that felt good, and I used to imagine silky skin, clean cotton clothes, a breeze blowing around and just the sheer delight of being clean and outdoors and not dying of it.

And I got all that and more, here on Sethun, a dot in some place called The Diamond Galaxy. We all got that and more. I didn't see any of my sisters or Mama after landing; they separated us in Immigration. Word has it that Mama committed suicide. She'd managed to lie about her age in order to get here and she was past childbearing, so perhaps they found her out and she was given the choice of either returning to Earth, or going down the mines. My heart bleeds to think of her fate here, and after she'd got a taste of clean air and fresh food. Actually it isn't fresh, it comes light years on a ship, but they are so good at faking freshness you could fool me.

I would love it here if there was only us, but Mama was right. We were spun a line by the government, and we were sent here as slaves. I long for home, Leamington Spa, even though you couldn't go out except in a full suit, and with all the other hardships and the horrible overcrowding. At least they are all women. Here, there are men. They own the planet, and we are their slaves. And all of us on Earth had been brought up to believe they were extinct, and there they all were, large as life and twice as nasty as even we had been taught. They weren't all men from Earth, I discovered later, but they weren't much different the way they behaved. Although, so far, this place isn't threatened by nuclear holocaust and plagues because of them and their wars and the stupid way they used scientific discoveries. For a woman though, this place is just ruined, that's all. Men! Well, it is incredible I know. It is a nightmare, and I think I'll never get over the shock of seeing them that first day out of Immigration.

I was all alone with my pack of personal belongings, having just realized that I'd been separated from my family on purpose. It hadn't really sunk in that I wouldn't see any of my sisters again, or Mama.

I was almost fifteen and as strong as an ox; I was fanatic about going to the gym at that time, and even on the poor diet I'd managed to get some solid muscle on me. And I stood there in this great hall, echoing music everywhere, little shops full of things to read and eat, people rushing around in nice clothes, it should have been wonderful, but more than half of those people were unmistakably men.

I'd never seen one before. It was horrifying. There's something about them that is quite eerie, I think; they sort of look at you as if you are a plate of food; they actually lick their lips, some of them, and a look comes into their eyes which makes my blood run cold. They don't touch you, of course, because rape is maximum penalty and using another man's woman also, but you have to submit to your employer. I didn't know any of that as I stood there with my pack like an outcast. I just started shaking, thinking about AIDS and pregnancy and all kinds of other diseases too, come to that, plus pain and humiliation; I think it was the worst few minutes of my life. You can get used to anything, or at least find ways of living with it.

Rohan may think I live with him, but I don't. I live inside my head, in a place I've invented, and whenever he comes too close I just go there.

It must have been so easy for Mama, having her first children. Back on Earth you just had a very simple operation to get pregnant, and all the assurance that the child would be in perfect health and, of course, a girl. There hadn't been any men on Earth for a long time, just sperm banks, enough to sort out all the best and to last for thousands of years. Mama had too many babies, of course, but that was her beautiful chromosomes, each one perfect. Some women couldn't have any babies at all, but at least we never had anyone born who wasn't perfect. Nothing was left to chance. Here, your child can be anything, anything at all, although it isn't that common actually, to have bad problems. But it is disgustingly primitive to leave everything to chance, totally irresponsible, I think. And all women here think so too, but this makes no difference to reality.

There were some women who banded together and started organizing petitions, and they all died, just like that. It was passed off as a coincidence, and there's no Ombudsman here! This has happened more than once. We're expendable you see, there's plenty more where we came from.

So there I was in shock at several painful traumas all on one day, watching these *men* walking about everywhere, just like in the nursery stories. I recalled one of my favourites which Mama used to tell us: '. . . and the Princess and the Frog heaved and heaved on the Magic Rock, and finally managed to hurl it over the balcony onto the great hall full of suitors, and the Magic Rock exploded and burned them all up to a cinder, and the two friends lived happily ever after.'

If I had a Magic Rock I'd see that it crisped up as many

men as possible all in one go; I'd probably choose a darts match or something like that where they all gather together, no women allowed. I have all kinds of fantasies about how to get rid of the men, and about how lovely this world would be without them. Of course, they managed to get rid of themselves back on Earth, didn't they? During the height of the AIDS epidemic, when they finally got a vaccine, but it turned out to be sexually selective. A man discovered that, too – he would have got the Nobel Prize for both Medicine and Peace, but they don't award posthumously. Instead they have a plaque in Westminster Abbey, with some poem a woman wrote about how he had served humanity, most of all by his error.

At first I was terrified I was pregnant, but I later found out that the men have to take a pill until they have permission to breed. They actually do what they do for relief and their own pleasure. It doesn't take long, that's one good thing, and another is that the diseases do seem to have been wiped out, everybody is screened frequently. Homosexuality is also maximum penalty; I suppose that's why they use us such a lot even though most of them would prefer each other. Another thing Mama was right about is that the work is hard here. I do ten hours a day on a building site. They chose me for that because of my strength, but I have the advantage because my strength is increasing, and, someday, if it comes to it, I might just use that strength for tearing off Rohan's stupid empty ugly drivelling head.

Now you might be wondering if there is anything good and hopeful in my life at all, and I can tell you that there is.

It is the place I float off to when the going gets too tough. It is a wonderful place, and I am not alone there. I have made friends here amongst the women I work alongside, and when I got to trust some of them sufficiently to talk about private things, I told them about my secret Inlife. To my surprise, almost every one of those women also had an Inlife; they all had invented another reality to live in, alongside or behind of this one, which unless you are a robot is hardly worth hanging around for. The truly wonderful thing about Inlife is that every woman seems to go to more or less the same place.

The first one I discovered with an Inlife very like my own was Annie, a big heft of a laughing white woman with emotional strength to match her muscle. While we were running up and down ladders with hods of bricks or laying cement we got to talking when the overseer wasn't near, and we eventually got around to exchanging pictures from Inlife. It got so eerie after a while, and we even described people we had met there and were sure they must be the same.

'It wouldn't surprise me if I met you there one day,' I said to Annie, and she replied, 'Well, why not? Let's work on it some and see if we can't do just that.' I couldn't think how it might be done, but she could.

'Well, you know how we've invented the place; I see it as a planet totally free of human males, therefore it is peaceful, free of war, pain, crime, prisons, pollution, cruelty, murder and rape and all the whole horror of male domination. I also like to get creative on the landscape and the villages and the weather and so on. And then when people started appearing, if I wanted to meet a certain person again I just *willed* it, and with practice it happened. I reckon it can't be that hard to kind of call one another when we're in there; say I called you, you'd hear me in your mind and float off for a spell. Say you'll try it?' Of course I would try it, and I did, and it worked. Immediately.

We soon became skilled at some really intense imagination work, people with minds and brains and hearts who are treated like unfeeling robots do get good at that kind of thing. I guess it must be a trick that slaves and prisoners throughout history must have tried, maybe with success. Maybe there's a ghost Inworld where they all live still, all the executed and tortured to death. That's a sentimental idea but I defend it on the grounds of kind ideas being a lot better than cruel ones. So in a way those bloody old bossmen have done us a favour. It wasn't long before we had around a hundred women inhabiting the same Inlife together, and every day the place became more real. And it is a good place.

The very air is relaxing, you don't have to be on your guard even for a moment. Everybody and everything is to be trusted, so there is no worry. There's universal good health because we don't kill animals for food, and the vegetable foods are grown organically, there isn't even one poisonous *man*-made substance in the place. There's plenty of space so there'll never be any need to quarrel over territory, or food, and especially not over each other, because women by themselves just don't have that possessive and aggressive thing that men are in the grip of; we share more easily it seems. Back in Leamington I recall there used to be quarrelling over love but I now think that was conditioning, sort of copying ingrained patterns left over from when there were men, and women belonged to them. Nobody belongs to anybody in the Inlife place, so passion flares up and is glorious, but tends to run its course and turn into long friendship. We have a common aim and purpose too, so ill-feeling doesn't seep into things like it does on the building sites or in the houses.

We work hard, as hard as we do on Sethun, but it's not slavery. There's fields to be tended, orchards to be planted, irrigation channels to be dug and houses to be built. It is happy work though, we sing for joy not just to get a rhythm going or to irritate the overseer. We don't have overseers, we just get on with it. We have created a good climate with the rainfall mostly at night, and inhabited it with harmless animals and plantlife, no poisons, thorns, killing teeth. I suppose I'm describing a sort of paradise, but it isn't for fools, it is real, as real to me as here on this vile bloody planet of Sethun, the world of men. I know that Earth and Sethun would be like our Inworld if it wasn't for men and the way they run things.

So that is what it is like, a lovely place, with a small community of pioneer women and all the world before us. You could say that at last I have emigrated. I only wish that Mama and my sisters could join us. I wish it constantly, I am working on it. Someday maybe I shall look up from planting corn and see Mama walking towards me, all upright and shining clean in a nice dress, with a smile on her face. Maybe. Why not? Inlife is where anything can happen.

Inlife is also where things can happen *from*. This part of it all began not long ago. A woman called Amy thought it up. Her idea, which we are all now working on, is this. Given that we managed to get Inlife into a reality while we were still bodily on Sethun, can we not now imagine things for Sethun from Inlife? When we are all there, which is easy to arrange at night because we only need to think towards each other now to get a message around in a matter of minutes, could we not have a meditation session with pre-arranged ideas, and transfer them? I can hardly convey how exciting this is to me. Because if we can, it means, doesn't it, that Inlife is really a solid place, that we are travelling there not just in our imaginations, but in another dimension.

And it might be happening already, because one of our first projects was to make some of the men less selfish and greedy. I thought that would be far too difficult for a beginning, but it seems there were occasional signs of success. For example, one evening mealtime, I was kneeling with the dishes while Rohan ate his fill. It is a very big fill, too, for somebody who does hardly any physical work. He has a pot belly and double chins, and the grease sticks to his whiskers. He usually says little; maybe he complains, sometimes he grunts a compliment, telling me to remember how to cook a certain sauce, or else. Mostly he doesn't even look at me, I'm hardly there for him as a person. So I was incredulous when he suddenly made eye contact, and then held out a piece of pork in his fingers.

'Here, have a bit to eat while you're waiting your turn. You must get hungry kneeling there waiting after you've cooked it and all.' This is of course unheard of, for a man to be at all sharing with a woman, and especially, most especially, for him even to think for a moment about her needs in any respect at all. I just stared at him and shook my head. I thought it was some sort of game where if I took the meat he'd have an excuse to beat me, not that he needs an excuse but for a laugh he thinks up 'reasons'.

'Eat, woman, don't dare refuse,' he snarled, angry that the first kind thought he'd ever cast towards a female had met with a rebuff! I took it, eyes down, thanked him, and tried to eat. But I couldn't, because most of my mind was in Inlife, and, there, we don't eat meat. I knew that the pork had been factory-farmed in very cruel ways, the sows chained to the floor and the piglets toothless so as not to hurt their teats, and the teeth had been yanked out by a man with pliers. The scream of piglets having their teeth pulled is a scream of pure agony, and the grunts of misery from a sow who just wants to turn over or walk around should be enough to put anyone off pork forever. I could hardly chew it even though it was delicious with marination and good hot roasting. The incident just sort of petered out, it led to no more talk, and when he'd finished his meal he waddled off to his chair for a rest while I picked at the rice and vegetables. I'd been starving and would usually have eaten quite well from what was left. But some connection had been made between Inlife and the 'reality'. Rohan's consciousness had been touched.

But not very much, he was just as bad as ever later on. Other women reported success too, but marginal. The great thing was that such a manoeuvre was possible at all. What came out of subsequent talks, both at work and in the Inlife, was that most women weren't sure they wanted 'humanized' men around after all, they much preferred to have as little to do with them as possible, and leave them to be whatever they were on their own despoiled territory. It had gone that far. Being a slave *can* be a kind of freedom, as Japanese women discovered in historic times. It was not ideal, but Inworld compensated for everything. It was all we had, and we worked to make it good.

But like many creations out of the imagination, it took on a life of its own. Our Inworld may be about to change completely.

We had agreed in an almost implicit way that our Inlife include no childbirth. There is plenty of that on Sethun in the households of those men who get permission and who have a woman in reasonable health. They organize it thus to regulate the population, so I understand, and so far I'm glad to say the question has not arisen for me. Even though Inworld is real enough, we never needed to create our own population. There will always be women who hear of us and want to join. New people come often. They are distinguished by the way they walk around as if drugged, smiles on their faces and amazement in every line of their bodies. It is good to see them. Strangely, none of them arrive pregnant, because even those who are pregnant on Sethun, always arrive completely themselves, without child, on Inworld. It is truly another dimension, a different life of freedom and choice and relaxation and without tribulations and pain. Marvellous things happen.

Not long ago two of my sisters arrived, and I can hardly tell about the joy it gave us all to be reunited. The knowledge had spread a long way in a short time, that there was escape to be made from the men of Sethun. My sisters had been taken far away, but, of course, Inworld is only a willed thought from wherever you happen to be. I welcomed them, and we wondered about the rest of our family, but there was no word except the sad news that the rumour I'd heard about Mama was true. Jean and Milly told me about their horrible husbands and I told them about mine, and because of where we were we laughed about it, for at that time it belonged to the hell of Sethun and not the heaven of Inworld. Neither of them had any children either, although Milly wanted some. She always had, even back on Earth in Leamington. She'd always been more help to our burdened Mama than the rest of us. But she, too, wanted to go back to Leamington, where the getting of a baby was without the nastiness. But we all knew we'd never get back there in any reality, for once a slave always a slave, and anyone caught attempting to escape is murdered immediately. They paid good money for us to the government of Earth, although of course we didn't know that at the time. Many of the men of Sethun, Milly said, had originally come from a planet where all the women were struck barren by a virus, which had been intended as a weapon of war. It seems to me that everywhere in the Universe is vile except for our Inworld.

And even that is under threat. Something very inexplicable is happening to Inlife.

A woman here gave birth. She was pregnant here but on Sethun she was not. It is a mystery. At first when we got to know, it was thought by many that the event was connected with our trying to influence the men of Sethun some time before. Some people said that we had created a hole in the fabric of our reality by connecting the opposite way, and that somehow an event which was not meant to be in our scheme of things had slipped through. One woman suggested that the pregnant woman, called Nancy, should not come to Inworld any more, but she was soon put right by a chorus of voices and was sorry to have been so mean. Nancy herself said she had no idea how it had happened. It was, as far as we knew, parthenogenetic. But I am a practical woman, and so are my sisters, and we thought that Nancy was telling a lie, and that one of us, here on Inworld, is not a woman at all. We thought a man was amongst us, the father of the coming child.

I looked at all my women friends and wondered, is it you, are you the man who somehow invaded our wavelength and our world, and brought sexual duplicity and childbirth into our lovely part-time home? Is it you, I thought, looking at some strong-looking woman with a long stride? I hate such thoughts, such doubts, such worry. It is as if a cloud had crossed our skies and was getting darker and lower, threatening our peace and quiet. Who was the traitor who first told a man of Inlife? And why would she do such a thing? We all asked such questions, but still there is the question of the baby.

The baby. When it was born, I heard its crying in the house across the green, its wailing rent the air and brought women out from all around, some smiling, some weeping, but not one without a reaction of some kind. And I? I could not keep away. I had to run across the green, almost against my will, to see the baby, to know for certain. When I got to the door there were two women in attendance.

They told me that everything was fine, no problems, and, yes, I could have a glimpse of the infant. Nancy was sitting up in bed with a smile on her face, clutching him to her breast.

'Isn't he beautiful?' she said, answering my burning question which I could never have asked for fear of upsetting her. I gazed down at him, and the most wonderful feelings stopped my heart, a lovely ache filled my breast.

He *is* beautiful. He stopped suckling and his little shiny mouth seemed to smile, and his tiny perfect little hands clutched at her shirt. He made a little sound and opened his eyes for a moment. He looked at me and I gave a cry of delight, for you can see the consciousness in there, shining innocently out of the darkest blue. This was the first time I had seen a baby and wanted to hold it, for on Sethun, the few I'd seen I avoided, as we all do, for they come from pain and hate, it always seemed to me. Not this one, it never could have arisen from anything but love. This baby is an additional joy in our marvellous Inworld, the first to be born, and with an aura of being special therefore. And he is a terrible threat to all we have so far made.

But it is such a lovely threat, a threat to break your heart and then mend it again, to warm your mind and shed light, only making stronger our desire to protect all living creatures, and continue a world which is not a vale of tears.

'Yes, Nancy, he is really beautiful. Have you thought of a name yet?' A boy's name.

'Not yet.' Someone came up behind me and she said, 'Perhaps you'll call him after the father?'

'Hush now,' said one of the women attending, 'she must not be upset.' But you couldn't have upset Nancy at that time, she just smiled, secure with her secret, which she divulged. 'He doesn't have a father, I can tell you all now. I could not before in case you all persuaded me to cast him out before he arrived. I *willed* myself to have a baby, I am both mother and father to him. The only thing I forgot to will was the sex, for I never thought of it, us having no males at all. And to me, our perfect Inworld is not perfect if I do not have the freedom to realize this dream.' She looked at her baby, and she stroked his head with such gentle tenderness, and I knew that our world had changed forever.

Perhaps it will be all right. Perhaps it is the only time it will happen. Maybe this is not real at all, maybe Inlife is all a figment and there is not a heavenly place to live, no peace and quiet, nothing but dreams.

All these thoughts tumble about in my disturbed mind as I thank Nancy and walk out, stunned, onto the sunlit green where lots of women are now gathered. And among them my sister, Milly, who has gone pale with longing.

'Oh Mary, that lucky woman,' she whispers, looking at me with eyes all soft. I know how she feels.

'Do you not think that all of us could have children here, if we wanted to? Do you think we all ought to talk about that? I'm sure I'm not the only one to feel like this.' Her hand clutched her belly as if she was starving. It is a completely atavistic thing which has got hold of her, it is like a madness the way it has consumed her in so short a time.

'Do you want to be like our Mama, worn out and with nothing in her life but motherhood?'

'Of course not; it wouldn't be like that, here. We need have only one or two, we won't have men telling us whether we can breed or not, and there's so much space here, and it is a healthy place too, I can imagine children *running* on this green, playing out of doors in a way we never could.' I can clearly see her face shining with a fanatical light, possessed by desire and idealism. And by ancient biology.

'But Milly, that baby is male. He will grow up to be a man. What then?' Nothing deters her.

'But he will be brought up in this place by women, we can train him to be good and not to create misery, show him how to love and not to dominate, not to be greedy for territory, not to. . . .'

'Mama told us, remember, that when there were men on Earth, women always thought they could change men. And they could not.' And she had an answer for that, too.

'But that was on Earth, that was Mama talking in our tiny home in Leamington, and it was history, Mary, history. This is Inworld, everything here is different, because we made it like it is.' So there was nothing more to be said, it would be a waste of breath. Milly tells me that she thinks she is pregnant, an Inlife child, and that she doesn't mind if it is a boy or a girl. Well, I mind. Because in fourteen or so years we shall be seeing our first men emerge, and we shall be indulgent and proud and forgiving. They will begin to take all the best of everything for themselves.

It was truly a dreamworld after all, it seems to me. I have another dream. I want to go home. To Leamington. I want to rebuild that world, to reclaim the land, purify the air, replace the ozone canopy, organize a really new place for people to live, in peace and plenty forever. Leamington calls me back, it is like I was told, you can never really leave it, not forever. I have no idea how I could escape from Rohan and leave Sethun, but I know that if I keep the dream and the wish alive, someday it will happen, just like Inworld happened. I don't want to have an Inlife any more, it means nothing to me now. All the women there are getting pregnant, not caring if it is girl or boy, blithely and surely destroying that perfect dimension in which good life has thrived.

The beautiful baby calls me too, but I am not going to make a girl to be made wretched by a man; all that must stop, somewhere, somehow. I am working on a dream of home.

Josephine Saxton There is no suitable explanation of me in under a hundred words.

CHAPTER TEN

CAVE PIRATES OF THE HOLLOW EARTH

Peter Lamborn Wilson

The cosmologies of the esoteric mind lend coherence to a chaotic
universe, but once out of adolescence the anarchy of youth is soon
forgotten and conventional world-order sets in. The untrammelled
haunts of the underworld where boys are free to roam, unconfined
by school, grown-ups and convention, are to be found in the pages
of *Cave Pirates of the Hollow Earth*, which Jascon reads secretly under
his desk. It is the compelling picture of the magician on the front of
the book, which, Tarot-like, leads him into a world where magic and
derring-do are the order of the day. Fantasy is far and away more
exciting than reality, though the two may have closer correlations
than Jascon first thought.

I

The cover of the book shows a small band of boy pirates,
their long hair tied back in red or black bandanas. Gold
hoop-rings pierce their earlobes. Barbaric jewels (obviously
stolen) decorate their necks, wrists, ankles and fingers. They
wear bright-coloured rags and sashes round their waists, or
torn velvet vests – but their arms, legs and feet go bare.

By their faces and postures you can see that the boys are
frightened but angry. They brandish short swords with
wavy curved blades.

Their enemy, apparently a sorcerer in a night-blue robe
sewn with cabbalistic signs, planets and stars, stands on a
rock ledge with his arms outstretched. His hands are clawed
and pointed in some mystic gesture, and from his fingers
an electric-blue ray shines like a sparkling laser. The ray

The Magus of Power

strikes the ground near the boys' feet and causes a little explosion, a shower of pebbles. Behind the sorcerer's beard you can detect an amused smile.

The scene takes place against the background of a vast cavern with tunnels leading off into gloom and blackness, the lofty ceiling dripping with stalactites, the floor bristling with stalagmites tall as petrified trees.

At the top of the picture appears the title of the book, cleverly drawn so that it seems carved in the rock vault above the boys' heads: *Cave Pirates of the Hollow Earth*. All the colours are bright as candy, but the printing is a bit crude; in a few places the inks have run and bled into each other slightly.

Very very carefully Jascon slips the book out of his bag and hides it inside the open schooltext on his desk. Slyly he glances around the study-hall to see if anyone has noticed – but everyone's eyes look glazed with early morning boredom, noses down, pencils scritch-scratching, chairs occasionally creaking – and the Preceptor (a mouldy young man with a laughable moustache) appears to have fallen already into a light hypnotic trance.

Good.

Jascon spends several minutes simply admiring the cover. He paid for the book with his own credits, and he's not about to spoil his pleasure by rushing into it.

At last the walls of the schoolroom have faded out of his sight; nothing remains but the mysterious picture. He opens the book and begins to read.

II

The story opens at the camp of the boy pirates, deep and far back in the unexplored and unmapped caves of Gondwana, which (as everyone knows) is another name for the Hollow Earth under the continent of Antarctica.

A river runs through their cave, black and deep and transparent. When you swim in it, phosphorescent bubbles trail from your arms and legs like strings of opals, moonstones and pearls.

On the bank of the river you can see their boat, called a pirogue, a long narrow flat canoe painted shiny black, with places for six pairs of rowers. The oars also serve as poles, for skimming over shallow water, and as weapons. The boat's prow is carved like a snake's head, and its two eyes serve as lanterns. The stern mounts a rudder in the shape of a fish-tail.

The pirogue has a name, but the name is not painted on the bow. In fact, no one knows the boat's name except the pirate-chief, Vathael, because an enemy who discovered the boat's name could work magic against it and ruin its luck – or so the pirates believe.

The boys make their camp with a few ragged tents and lean-to huts on a beach of polished black crystal sand. Around their fire lurks a shadowy forest of giant mushrooms and huge shelf-fungus growing from the stalagmites, white giant ferns and tangled creeping vines hung with feathery moss, pale fleshy orchids and clumps of glowing lichen. Fire-flies and little birds that shine like hot coals flicker and streak through the jungle of dim shade.

As for the boys themselves, you can tell they're all true Troglodytes or 'Trogs', descendants of the aboriginal cave-dwellers, by their skin so white and pale, and by their huge eyes which have no colour but the black of full-dilated pupils, like chips of polished obsidian set in globes of milk – and by their long silky hair, the strange colour of garnets dipped in coal-black ink. Judging by the cover illustration they're all about twelve or thirteen (the same age as Jascon, the reader).

What do they do all day in that land of perpetual twilight? Fishing for eels with long bamboo poles; gathering mushrooms or peaches in the forest; hunting for marmosets or russet voles; trapping land-crabs. . . . Finding enough to eat (and more than enough) is so easy in the deep caves, you might wonder why they bother with piracy at all.

In their spare time – which is most of the time – they swim in the river or play in the woods. They sleep whenever they're tired and wake up when they feel like it. In fact, they have no clear idea about time at all. Sometimes they squabble about whose turn it is to do the laundry or wash the dishes, and end by deciding to put everything off and be dirty, lazy and comfortable. But they take good care of the pirogue. They spend hours and hours sharpening their swords and the edges of their oars.

No school. No family. No church. No job. And if by chance this perfect life should ever be threatened by even a vague hint of dullness – of *too much* perfection – then they pack up and go roving, and see what they can see.

So one day Radjah, the chief's best friend and first mate, returned from a scouting expedition in great excitement. He told the others he'd spied a water-caravan, at least a dozen gondolas laden with goods and passengers, camping on the edge of the Miasma, obviously headed for Port Terror.

'A whole *caravan*? You expect us to hit an entire armed and guarded caravan?' asked one of the boys.

The others all eyed each other uneasily. Even Vathael looked doubtful. No one spoke up.

But then, 'Well . . . I suppose we might think of *something*. . . .' said Sardono. He was the shaman of the group, a witch-boy who'd learned a bit of magic from his grandmother before running away from home. 'Vathael,' he went on, 'why don't you go take a look at this caravan yourself? Meanwhile . . . I have an idea.'

With a mysterious smile, Sardono turned and trotted briskly off into the forest where he disappeared from sight.

Radjah sighed. 'That lunatic! Do you think he's just showing off again, or . . . ?'

'Well,' said the chief, 'I don't suppose it would hurt to just go have a look, eh?'

III

At this point, Jascon has left the study-hall and is sitting in his first class of the morning. Despite the greater risk involved, however, he's still buried in *Cave Pirates of the Hollow Earth*, hidden on his lap. In one small corner of his mind he's praying the teacher will forget his existence and ignore him – but the rest of his consciousness is absorbed in the story, and the teacher's voice is reduced to a distant drone wordless as the buzzing of a fly.

IV

Vathael the pirate captain and his first mate Radjah have climbed a giant fern and are spying from this perch on the caravan. Six great gondolas (not a dozen!) are beached, and six tents have been pitched against the possibility of rain (for the Hollow Earth is so vast it contains its own weather). Not far away lies the Miasma, a great swamp where – for some unknown reason – luminiferous lichen and moss will not grow, so that the marshes remain plunged in eternal darkness.

At once the boys notice the presence of armed guards, mercenaries hired to protect rich travellers. Each of these roughnecks carries a real pistol, each worth ten times its weight in gold. Radjah suggests giving up and hightailing for home, but Vathael hisses, 'Ssshh!', and takes from his pouch an ancient pair of opera glasses.

Scanning the camp carefully he notices one of the tents, the largest and grandest, lit from within by oil lamps. The tent-flaps are open; focusing the glasses, Vathael makes out the pavilion's interior.

A man with a beard – perhaps a merchant? – is seated at a little table, just now in the process of unlocking a metal chest. He reaches in and fills his hand with something. A gloating expression seems to cross his face. He lifts a fistful of whatever-it-is, and laughs. He opens his fingers and sparks fall back into the box . . . brightly coloured sparks . . . jewels!

Vathael whispers this news in his friend's ear. What a fantastic haul it would make! Yes, but . . . thirteen boys with swords against maybe thirty grown murderers with guns? Impossible.

Unless, of course, Sardono can come up with a really powerful spell.

'I doubt it, chief.'

'Me too,' Vathael agrees unhappily.

Less than an hour later, back at their own camp, they find the shaman squatting in front of the fire, grinding something in a crude rock mortar. He's wearing a kerchief tied over his nose and mouth.

'Careful! Don't get too close,' he warns them with muffled voice.

Vathael notices a basket of blue mushrooms, glowing faintly like little night-lights. 'What are they? What are you up to?'

'Something better than magic,' says Sardono smugly. 'I've had my eye on a clump of these for a long long time. . . .'

'Well? So?'

'It's called Sleep Dust.'

'What? Never heard of it. What does it do?'

'I'll show you. Shan, come here!' Sardono orders his little brother. 'Do you volunteer for an experiment? I promise it won't hurt you.'

Shan objects. Sardono offers him his second-best skinning knife and a pound of sugar. Shan agrees.

Taking a pinch of blue powder from the mortar, the witch-boy blows it into Shan's face. The little boy screws up his nose as if to sneeze, then collapses into a dead faint, curls up and begins to snore.

'Sleep Dust,' says Sardono with a maddeningly superior smile.

'. . . A*ha*!' Vathael and Radjah exclaim together.

And they smile, too.

Sleeping Shan they left behind, with two of the other youngest boys to guard the pirogue, and set out through the forest on foot. They arrived at the merchants' camp about midnight.

At the caravan site they found all quiet, everyone asleep except for five sentries seated round a burned-to-ashes fire, and passing a bottle. How convenient.

Sardono crept as close as he dared, then stuffed a charge of powder into a long bamboo blow-pipe, and *huffed* it towards the guards. Within a minute all of them toppled over as if they'd been clubbed.

He then made a round of all the tents, blowing pipes of Sleep Dust into each of them.

'Good work,' Vathael whispered. 'Now, all of you, ransack the tents and take everything of value. Be sure to get *all* the guns! Sardono, you and me and Radjah will have a look at the big tent. . . .'

'There's no need to whisper!' crowed the shaman. 'They're all conked out and hibernating!'

'Shut up! Quiet, you fool. . . .'

'What, still nervous, captain? I assure you . . .'

'Keep your voice down. Something's not quite right.'

Stealthily they tiptoed towards the pavilion. All was silent, all was dark. But suddenly –

With a loud *Ka-poof* the whole tent seemed to explode with a burst, and the silk flew up into the air like a startled bird.

Where the tent had vanished stood a man, the man with the beard, fully dressed in an ankle-length robe of midnight blue and silver stars. In one hand he held a rod of green glass, and on his shoulder perched a baby pterodactyl with devilish crimson eyes.

The pirates stood there petrified and gawking.

The man smiled.

'So,' he said pleasantly, 'planning to murder us all in our sleep?'

V

'Jascon! JASCON? Are you asleep, boy?'

The class tittered.

'No, ma'am.'

'Answer the question!'

'Umm . . . would you mind repeating the question?'

The teacher assumed a martyred expression. Then, 'Krill,' she said in threatening tone.

'Ah . . . krill . . . ,' Jascon answered, '. . . major source of . . . that is, they're like tiny shrimp . . . millions of

them, in clouds . . . whales used to eat them. So . . . pro-
cessed into paste, with vitamins and stuff added . . . and,
uh, annual production [mumble mumble] million tons . . .
uh. . . .'

'Thank you, that will be quite enough. One demerit. . . .'
She pencilled a mark in a ledger open on her desk. 'That
makes *nine* against you, this week alone.'

As the woman turned back to the wallscreen and reached
for the keyboard to continue her lecture, Jascon mouthed a
rude word and made a rude gesture, though no one noticed.
Then . . . his attention faded from the classroom again,
back to the world of pirates.

VI

The rest of the crew were running off into the woods,
scurrying in terror at the sight of the sorcerer – but the
captain, the first mate and the wizard-boy were pinned by
the man's gaze – or else foolhardy enough to stand their
ground.

'Certainly not!' said Vathael. 'We came to steal your
jewels, not kill you. We're not *ghouls*, y'know. But
now . . . we may have to change our plans.'

He drew his sword and stepped forward. Radjah did the
same, though his hand trembled; Sardono simply stood
rooted to the spot as if magnetized.

The man's smile grew even warmer. 'Hoping to bluff
your way out, eh? Well, I must say I admire your
spirit. . . .'

Vathael raised his sword *en garde* and inched forward
another step.

'But,' said the sorcerer, 'I think you'll have to change
your plans yet again.' Casually he raised the green rod – or
was it a wand? – and pointed it at the motionless Sardono.
An emerald ray flashed from its tip and hit the shaman in
the heart; a green halo fizzed around his body – *snap*! –
and in his place a green lizard (about twelve inches from
snout to tailtip) lay stunned on the ground.

'Holy shit of the Goddess,' muttered Radjah. His courage

failed him; dropping his sword he whirled round to flee –
but a second bolt of green lightning hit him between the
shoulderblades. He, too, lit up like a lantern of jade and
was transformed in the blink of an eye.

Now there were two lizards.

At this point Vathael lost his temper. 'Dammit! That's
not *fair!*' Raising his sword above his head, he charged
forward blindly – and of course a split second later, there
were *three* lizards.

Reaching into a heap of baggage the chuckling sorcerer
produced a fine large cage of gold. Then, at his leisure, he
strolled about picking up the half-conscious lizards by their
tails and dropping them into this elegant prison.

'Please accept my hospitality,' he said. Then he locked
the gilt bars with a tiny gold key – which he swallowed.

VII

The school cafeteria, enormous and windowless, rang with
soprano voices and clanked with silverware. Jascon sat by
himself, so he could eat and read at the same time. By
coincidence today's main dish was a soup made of krill
paste and hydroponic vegetables, smelly but tasteless. . . .
Not a very *big* coincidence, however, since krill appeared
on the menu several times a week. Prison food, thought
Jascon. They serve us prison food.

No sooner had he opened *Cave Pirates* than a classmate
sat down next to him and began to chatter away about
something. Jascon eyed him with distaste.

'. . . so we got a new holo-vid, the latest model, you
should see the tank, it's about THIS big, the colours are
amazing, what's your favourite show? I like all the police
shows, wouldn't it be great to be a cop? *Zzzaappp! Br-br-
br-br-br!*'

The disgusting kid, imitating lasers and machineguns, was
spitting krill all over the table in a fine spray of soup.
'Right? Right? I'd love to be a cop, wouldn't you?'

'No,' said Jascon. 'I'm going to be a criminal when I
grow up.'

'It cost over five thousand credits, but we got a rebate.'

'Big fucking deal,' Jascon muttered, and buried his nose in his book.

VIII

The sorcerer seems to have some secret and perhaps occult reason for keeping the three lizard-boys captive. Perhaps he intends to boil them up as part of some spell? If so, he gives no indication of his plan. But when he looks at them a gleam comes into his eyes.

Next day the rest of the caravaneers wake up with headaches, and scold the guards for drinking on the job. 'We might have been robbed!' says one of the merchants.

After breakfast they break camp and stow everything in the gondolas. No one notices that the sorcerer has acquired a cageful of lizards overnight, and of course the boys are unable to call out for help.

A black-and-white picture in the book shows the lizards, large iguana-style creatures with big skin frills like paper fans around their necks. They each have three eyes, and a tongue with a triple fork. According to the text, their skin is dry, smooth and green as seaweed, with various streaks of jewel-colours, seashell-colours, kaleidoscope-colours – extremely handsome. The third eye allows them to see behind their own skulls, and the three-pronged tongue is actually a 'nose' which literally tastes the air for thousands of different scents.

The sorcerer stows the golden cage under a seat in his gondola, where they can see very little (even with their third eyes) and smell only the odour of old boat. The caravan sets out into the Miasma. 'Nothing much to see anyway,' the man whispers to them. 'It's dark as the inside of your heads!'

The prisoners could communicate with each other only by sign-language, and even that method proved frustrating (lizards aren't very good at self expression). Under the seat with only blackness before their eyes they soon got over being scared and simply felt bored.

That night at the next camp (much deeper into the lightless Miasma) the sorcerer set their cage down near the campfire, where they enjoyed the heat like true cold-blooded reptiles. Of course, they weren't *really* lizards, but only boys who *looked like* lizards. Nevertheless, the shape of your body has a lot of influence on your state of mind: if you believe you're twelve inches long and green, sooner or later you begin to behave in a reptilian manner.

A great many insects, attracted to the campfire, began crawling or flying near their cage. Some even blundered between the bars. For a while the boys resisted the temptation with feelings of disgust. But they were famished, and the bugs actually smelled good. Finally Radjah broke down and ate one. Clearly he liked it, since he immediately caught another with his long tongue and gobbled it up. . . . So Vathael and Sardono imitated him. They discovered that insects taste delicious to lizards' palates – each one different, but all crisp and sort of buttery.

Seven times the caravan moved on, and seven times pitched camp, ate and slept. At the end of that time they reached the far side of the Miasma (luckily without meeting any giant Caveworms) and came again into a region of light.

'So, my young saurian friends – have a view of your new homeland,' said the sorcerer, holding the cage aloft in one hand and gesturing with the other.

All three eyes wide open, tongues flickering to sample the breeze, the boys peered through the bars of their cage at a wide wide landscape. The cavern appeared so vast they couldn't make out the ends of it, and so lofty it seemed to have a sky rather than a roof. The floor of the cave was covered with a broad shallow lake, miles across. Cathedral-sized stalagmites rose out of the water like rough cone-shaped islands. Some were broken off into weird shapes, others were covered with ferns, bamboo and orchids, like mossy sugarloaves or pyramids with green fur.

Mist lay in long streamers and rolled in vague fogbanks;

the stalagmite-islands thrust themselves out of the wispy stuff like thoughts rising out of a clouded mind.

In the distance they could just make out the rest of the caravan floating away, small as dragonflies on the calm lake's surface, poling for the far end of the cavern and the brawling frontier town of Port Terror, a smugglers' paradise still several days' journey away.

The sorcerer stood on a small dock, his luggage heaped around him. Behind him (as the boys could see without moving their heads) lay an island, or rather a tower, or rather a stalagmite hollowed out (lamps burning at the windows) into five storeys of rooms. The rock, dull red-ochre, was alive with flowers and mushrooms. From a distance, with its shades drawn, the tower would appear simply as one of hundreds of similar islands.

'Yes, you can see we're all alone, out here in the sticks,' said the magician. He turned and carried them up rock-cut mossy steps to the tower's door, an upside-down V-shaped slit in the stone, fringed with ferns.

'This is my elaboratory. I'll just hang your cage here in the window, where you can snap up the moths and fireflies, and admire the scenery. I'll chain the pterodactyl to his perch so he won't bother you. Now if you'll excuse me, I have much to do and no one to help me. . . .'

The man moved away into the gloom of the room, but then turned back. He smiled, making a little apologetic gesture with one hand. 'I'd prefer you as guests rather than, well, prisoners. But consider this: you tangled with me of your own free will, and now you're suffering the consequences. But who knows what will happen next?' He laughed. 'I almost never use my powers to look into the future. I like to be surprised.'

He turned again and made his way through a jumble of furniture and alchemical equipment – flasks, retorts, athanors, alembics, ambixes and stills, crocks of dried herbs and crushed jewels, a bulky oven with many metal doors of different sizes, stuffed animals, skulls, heaps of cobwebbed books. . . . As he began clambering up a wooden ladder he called back, 'Anyway – it's not so bad, being a lizard, eh?'

And with another pleasant laugh he faded upwards into shadow and vanished into darkness, leaving the pirates to their slow reptilian meditations.

IX

Recess.

Hundreds of children running and playing, their shrill voices echoing off the dome overhead.

Jascon is talking with a boy called Melvill. Jascon doesn't really like the kid, who's something of a bully and a patriotic bore – but Melvill is rich, and has lots of pulp literature to trade.

'You got *Red Witch of Old Gondwana*?'

'Yeah.'

'I'll give you . . . how about an original number one of *Doktor Deth*?'

'Nah. I got that.'

'Okay, what about a complete set of *Captain Riptide*?'

'Nah. I got that, too. I want credits.'

'I'll give you *this*, after I finish reading it.' Jascon held up his copy of *Cave Pirates*.

'Shit, I got that one, too. I got everything.'

'Isn't it *great*?'

'What, *Cave Pirates*? Nah, I didn't like it.'

'Why not?'

'It's about Trogs.'

'So?'

'So my dad says Trogs are an inferior race. Savages. Welfare bums. Mutants.'

'Oh yeah? Well, your dad is an inferior asshole. That's . . . that's *racism*. The Trogs were here first, and. . . .'

'Oh, you got me scared now. Look, I'm shaking. I know why you're such a Trog-lover, Jascon. You probably got mutant blood yourself.'

'Screw you.'

'Let's see your webbed feet!'

'You want to see my foot, bend over, condom-face!'

'Hey everybody! Jascon's a *half-breed*!'

Furious, Jascon turned and stalked away across the playground.

So what if I am a half-breed, he thought. I'm *proud* of my Trog blood. And some day . . . some day . . .

Jascon didn't finish the thought. Instead, he plopped down on a bench, opened his book, and escaped back into fantasy.

X

All night the boys worked on one gold bar of the cage, chewing it with weak little lizard teeth. Luckily it turned out to be solid gold, softest of all metals, and by morning they'd made some progress.

Next day they saw the sorcerer several times, rummaging for something in the heaps of bizarre apparatus of the elaboratory, or else drifting in and out the door on unknown errands. Aside from a bit of goodnatured teasing, he said nothing to them all day, and failed to notice the half-chewed-through bar.

That afternoon he began drinking mushroom wine. Every time he passed by, the boys saw a flagon in his hand and smelled a musty smell. By bedtime the sorcerer seemed rather woozy. The ladder gave him a good deal of trouble, and his footsteps overhead made a staggering pattern across the ceiling.

Soon loud snores filtered down into the elaboratory. The lizards went to work and quickly finished gnawing through the bar. Together they bent it with their snouts, until one by one they managed to slip through the gap to freedom.

Radjah and Sardono made signs urging an immediate escape. But Vathael had other plans. He didn't intend to remain a reptile all his life!

He began to scout around the room, looking for something, and the others had to follow whether they liked it or not.

Lizards can climb anywhere. Not an hour had passed, when Vathael suddenly found the Book. By lucky chance

it lay open to just the right page: 'A Spell For The Trans-
formation of Any Victim Unto the Semblance of a Saurian'.

The magician had called them 'saurians', no doubt a fancy
word for lizards. Eagerly Vathael searched the text for a
counter-spell to undo the hex and change 'the Victim' back
into a human being. Several heavy vellum pages had to be
turned somehow, but at last he found it. How simple! All
they had to do was bathe themselves in brandy, plain simple
brandy!

And there, by another lucky chance, stood a bottle of
brandy! – on the edge of the desk, just in the right position
to be toppled over and smashed to bits on the stone floor.
It took mighty effort and much time, but at last they
succeeded.

Quickly (the noise might wake the wizard!) they
scampered down the table-leg and rolled over and over in
the puddle of potent-smelling alcohol.

And at once . . . found themselves *boys* again, naked, cut
and bleeding from the shattered glass, wet and reeking of
distilled grape.

In a panic, without a word, they picked themselves up
and raced for the door.

It wasn't there!

Somehow the mouth of the cave had closed its lips. Terrified, they turned back to the window, only to find it, too,
(like an eyelid) sealed up tight. They were trapped.

'What'll we do *now*?'

Upstairs they could hear the magician, still snoring away
like a crocodile.

'Vathael, you're the captain. Think of something!'

'Radjah, scout up some rope. Sardono, get that *Book of
Spells* and see if you can find anything useful. We'll *force*
him to let us go.'

Minutes later, they're creeping up the ladder to the second
storey. There they find themselves in a bedroom, hung with
old tapestries and lined with old carpets. By the guttering
light of candles they see the bearded man, his robes in

disarray, sprawled out on a velvet couch. Quickly they tie him down with the ropes.

With shaky voice, Sardono reads aloud from the Book a 'Domination Spell, Guaranteed To Make the Victim Your Willing Slave'.

Then Vathael tugs at the man's sleeve . . . then slaps him a few times, till he yawns and blinks and comes to his senses.

'Aha,' he says. 'You've done very well indeed, and in such a short time! I knew you lads had nerve, but now I see you are cunning as well. This is splendid! Perhaps I could persuade you to stay on as my guests? Perhaps even as my apprentices? Hard work at times, but interesting and well-paid. You see . . .'

'That's enough! We've put you under a Spell of Domination. You must obey us. Tell us how to open the door!'

'Domination, eh? How quaint.' The man smiles affectionately at Vathael. 'I like your spirit, captain.'

Angrily the boy grabs a letter-opener from the table next to the sorcerer's bed, and points it at the man's neck. 'Tell me! or else you'll be sorry. . . .'

'My little pirate, don't be foolish. I'm offering you an education, adventure and wealth. Why not at least think about it?' The man gazes into Vathael's eyes.

'Stop trying to hypnotize me!' Vathael pinks the wizard's throat with the knife, and a tiny drop of blood appears.

'Ouch! My, my, ruthless as well as cunning, aren't you?'

'VATHAEL! LOOK OUT!'

Sardono and Radjah both tackle their leader at once, yanking him backwards, and the three of them topple onto the floor in a heap. Vathael sees that the ropes binding their 'victim' have transformed themselves into giant snakes, which are now writhing and hissing and threatening to strike out at them with long curved poisonous fangs!

And then . . .

XI

. . . the bell rang for History class.

Interrupted at this thrilling moment in his reading, Jascon was naturally unable to concentrate on the day's lesson. Ordinarily he found History *almost* interesting, and the teacher the least disgusting of the school's faculty.

Today's lecture concerned the founding of Little America, 'our great nation'. Some 223 years ago, scientists in Antarctica were investigating something called a missing ozone hole, when their calculations led them to discover a seemingly endless network of caverns beneath the ice, so extensive and deep they called it the Hollow Earth.

Their scientific station, 'Little America', was moved underground. Soon many pioneers flocked to the South Pole to settle in the caves, warmed by hot springs and lit by eerie fluorescent fungi. 'Our City began to grow. But imagine our ancestors' amazement when they discovered that the Hollow Earth was *already inhabited. . . .'*

Well, I've heard all this about a million times before, thought Jascon. I think I'll just keep on reading my book. . . .

XII

. . . And he read on and on, all through History class, and all through Religion class as well. Jascon hated Religion, and he *despised* the teacher, a dried-up loose-lipped ass, too stupid and mean even to be a real minister. It was dangerous to read *Cave Pirates* in Religion class, but Jascon took the risk.

'The Preacher' (as the children called him) burbled on about all his favourite things, the American God and the Un-American Satan, about how Little America had to pick up the Torch dropped so long ago by Big America, how we must keep the Faith. How our duty lies in Obedience, Cleanliness, Honesty, Hard Work, Prayer and Purity. How we must guard against evil thoughts of sensuality, and help each other overcome doubt and sin. . . .

. . . In short: the usual boring old crap.

XIII

'. . . So you see,' the wizard was saying, 'I must confess I arranged the whole thing as a kind of test. That is, I hadn't *planned* on capturing three pirates and turning them into lizards. But once I'd done so, I began to wonder if I could solve this problem in such a way that *all of us* would gain rather than lose. I needed to know if you were as clever and bold as you seemed to be. I decided to leave a few clues around, like the open Book and the bottle, and discover if you had the imagination to make use of them.'

'But . . . why didn't the Spell of Domination work?'

'Oh, it did – at least, a little,' answered the man with a smile. 'Why do you think I'm offering you a reward now, instead of, well, instead of losing my temper – as I might well have done? Eh? Yes, you've won me over, Vathael.'

'What kind of "reward"?'

'I'm so glad you've decided to listen to reason. Let me pour you something to drink, something sweet (don't worry, no magical elixirs, I promise) – and we should clean up your little wounds from the brandy bottle. I'll see to all that, and, while you relax, I'll explain my proposition.

'First, I'd like you to stay here for a while as my guests. I could teach you some valuable tricks, even in a few days – martial arts, magical defences, that sort of thing. You'd find it all useful, even if you don't want to accept the job offer.'

'What job?'

'Once I've prepared you and given you a few . . . things that might come in handy, I'd like to hire you to go on a journey for me. At the end of the journey, I want you to steal something, and then bring it back to me.'

'Well . . . this is getting interesting. But tell me: why don't you go and steal this whatever-it-is yourself? Why hire three kids to do it for you?'

'A fair question. The answer is . . . hmm . . . wait a minute.' Frowning, the wizard gestured at the wall, and at once a window popped open in the solid stone. The man leaned out and sniffed the air. Still frowning, he returned and sat down again.

'Thought I heard something,' he explained. 'Yes . . . the answer to your question is this: the object we're discussing is owned by another sorcerer. Unlike me, this fellow is most unpleasant – actually a sort of black magician. Of course, that's only *my* opinion. But it is true that he killed someone to get hold of this object, and since then he's put it to very bad uses – very nasty indeed. I'd like to rescue the object, but this man knows me too well. He'd *feel* me coming, and he'd think of some way to stop me.

'You, however, are unknown to him. Even if he notices you, he'll see only three lost children. He'll use only the simplest and most primitive defences against you, thinking he can beat you easily. But I can *predict* what all those defences will be, and I can *prepare* you to slip through every trap. Before he knows what's happening, you'll have the . . . the object – and once you have the object, *it* will protect you.'

'Hmm. This begins to sound pretty good. Maybe even fun. But . . . just what exactly *is* this object?'

'I'd prefer not to discuss that now. You'll know before you leave here, I promise.'

'All right – but I've got one more question. Who is this evil magician? Where? And . . .'

'Vathael, it would be better not to talk about him too much. In fact . . .'

Suddenly Sardono let out a shriek of fright. 'Ah-h-h! *What is that?*'

He pointed to the window, which the sorcerer had forgotten to close. On the sill perched an enormous bird – a crow, it seemed, but at least fifty pounds in weight, white as a corpse, with two shiny silver eyes.

'Oh shit,' muttered the sorcerer to himself.

The crow opened its beak and cawed:

'*You! Mentioned! My! Master's! Name!*'

'I never did, you stinking vulture! Did I, boys? Did I?'

'Uh . . . no . . . No! He never mentioned any name . . .
that is . . . ,' Vathael stuttered.
'You! THOUGHT! His! Name!'
The sorcerer was fumbling in the folds of his robe. . . .
'I! Will! Tell! Him!'
'You flying sack of worms,' yelled the wizard, whipping
a glass wand out of some inside pocket, 'You'll never

XIV

'Jascon! What is that you're reading?'
'N . . . nothing, sir. . . .'
'Don't lie to me. Let me see what you were reading so
avidly while the rest of the class was *praying*. Hold it
up! . . . Aha! I knew it! Give it here! Let me have a look
at this . . . So, just as I suspected. *Pulp*! Escapist fantasy
trash! Immoral, nearly pornographic! Haven't I warned you
about the dangers of such garbage? Haven't I, class? Eh?
Eh?'
'Yessir,' answered some repulsive toad.
'So! This is what we do with immoral literature! We . . .
tear . . . it . . . to . . . *shreds*! Later on, I will *burn* it. But
you? What shall we do about you, Jascon? First, I shall
notify the Principal, and your family, that you will be
suspended from school for one day.'
'Lucky bastard,' muttered someone – but the Preacher
didn't hear it. His blubbery lips were flecked with spit.
Jascon felt like throwing up.
'And since you like pulp literature so much, to keep busy
you'll write me a five-hundred word essay on the subject.
Call it . . . let's see . . . call it "Satan's Propaganda". Yes!'
The Preacher was pleased with his own creativity. He
smiled. 'And remember: if I am not pleased with your little
essay, I can recommend that you be treated *chemically* by
the School Psychologist. Disturbed children can be *cured*,
you know. Do you understand? Good. Class dismissed.'

XV

School has ended for the day. Shaken and furious, Jascon sets out for home.

As he walks through the streets of Little America's 'downtown', he sees everything through a haze of angry tears. The monorails and moving sidewalks are peopled with blurred figures, many of them in uniforms. The escalators and elevators are jammed with ant-like busy humans; none of them seem real.

Metal girders and plastic walls in bright artificial colours. Cramped claustrophobic corridors and ramps. Overhead, 'uptown', stacks of condos are piled up in geometric pyramids – and above them, vast plastic domes protect the City from the steamy wet weather of the deep caves. Everything closed in, thought Jascon, like a huge jail.

By the time Jascon reached the edge of his own neighbourhood, he'd calmed down a bit. He'd decided to *steal* another copy of *Cave Pirates*. The decision made him feel somewhat less humiliated. With a sigh, he looked around him.

Old depressing run-down pre-fab suburban streets. Beggars, and vendors selling fried paste or used shoes. Hydroponic sheds and abandoned warehouses. Stacks of housing for the poor, with laundry flapping limply from the balconies.

At the corner of Erebus Avenue and 201st Street, Jascon sees the old Trog fortuneteller. He's noticed the man before but never paid him any attention. For some reason today he takes a second glance.

Ragged and dirty, black patch over one eye, toothless and grizzled, the old faker squats before a blanket with a few jars and cans of dried mushrooms and herbs. The bottom of a broken beer bottle serves him for an incense-burner, and some strange-smelling weed is smouldering on the glowing charcoal.

The fortuneteller has laid out a hand of playing cards, bent and greasy, in a diamond-shaped pattern on the blanket. One of the cards catches Jascon's eye – a crude picture of a boy holding a cup.

He looks up and finds the ancient tribesman grinning at him, as if sharing some secret joke.

Blushing and upset, Jascon retreats.

Mentally he compares this trickster to the unnamed sorcerer in *Cave Pirates*, and admits to himself that real Trogs are not nearly as romantic as the pulp variety.

But then . . . what if? What if that fraud actually *knows* something? Would I dare to speak with him? Should I? Would he ask for credits?

Home at last, Jascon finds that his mother has already been informed of his punishment, and is seething with anger at him. Jascon lives alone with his mother, who is in fact one-quarter Trog. She's out of work, (female troubles), drinks too much, and sometimes entertains gentlemen callers. She sends him to his room without supper.

Angry again, and bored because he has nothing to read, Jascon lies on his bed and daydreams rather than do his homework.

In the other room he can hear his mother watching the 'tube' – not a holovid with colour tank, but an outdated black-and-white stereopticon. The news comes on, and the announcer says something about 'another bandit outrage in the Outback. . . .'

All at once, Jascon feels a fever of excitement. 'Bandits' might be the same as 'pirates'! For the first time it occurs to him that *out there*, in the 'Outback', in the deep and distant caves of Antarctica where no one from Little America likes to go – there might be *real* adventure.

He thinks again of the old Trog fortuneteller, and makes up his mind to speak with him, no matter how embarrassing. A busy day tomorrow! Steal a book . . . and talk with a magician!

Later that night he sneaks out of his room and finds his mother – as usual – fast asleep in front of the vid, still glowing with midnight test-patterns. He steals some algae-bread and soy-cheese from the kitchenette, and goes up onto the roof of his building.

The working-class neighbourhood lies outside the City domes, on the edge of a two-mile-wide polluted lake. Jascon can see it from the roof: lined with factories rather than magic islands. He surveys the lakeshore with a little pair of toy binoculars, just like the ones Vathael used to spy on the wizard's camp.

Focusing even farther out, he sees the Trog slums on the other side of the stinking lake, dark, miserable and silent. Even farther yet, too far to see clearly, there are cave-mouths, gaping great holes leading away into the endless mazes of Gondwana, the Hollow Earth.

Jascon has always feared this scene. He's never wanted to think about the *real* Caves, the infinite dark dank fateful tunnels beneath the Ice, beneath the City, beneath the World.

Instead, he's buried himself in dreams.

But now the sight of the unknown thrills him. Now he begins to wonder if the real world might be as interesting – or even *more* interesting – than the world of his books.

Besides, he thinks, my life here is a mess anyway. I wish I never had to spend another minute in that scumbucket of a school.

A light rain begins to fall, cooling his bare skin.

He dares to wonder . . . and wonders at his own daring. Should he run away from home? . . . and head for the deep caves?

Peter Lamborn Wilson has published extensively in comparative religion, art history, Sufi studies, Persian translation and poetry as well as journalism and other forms of hackwork – but he's just getting under weigh in SF. A story appeared in *The Third Interzone Anthology* (and has been translated into French and Japanese); another in the forthcoming Subgenius SF-theme anthology *3-Fisted Tales of 'Bob'*; others in zines such as *new Pathways, Edge Detector, Live From the Stagger Café*, et cetera. He is editing (with Rudy Rucker and Robert Anton Wilson) a huge SF anthology for *Semiotext(e)* magazine in New York. His SF novel *Hunter's Moon* remains unsold. Hint, hint . . .

CHAPTER ELEVEN

THE TENTH MUSE

John Matthews

This story is an attempt to say something about what happens when the impossible is made real; and when the laws of the universe, most of them invented by people who wanted to explain things they did not understand, are broken.

Though the world of Draconia and its petty troubles is left behind by Middleman and Bettina, the other world to which they escape holds other challenges. The Tarot pack from which this story derives includes in its fifty cards, the liberal arts, the planets, the Christian virtues and the orders of humankind, as well as the nine muses and Apollo. If you want to find out who the tenth muse might be then you must read on, because her omission from the canonical lists seems to have been an oversight.

It is said that there are nine circles or spheres which surround the world, which is naturally at the centre of all Creation. Each has a name and a meaning, each is ruled by a goddess or a god, and each follows its own implicit laws. It is also said that people of singular race live upon the surface of each sphere, walking and talking in the firmament above us. Some hold them to be inferior, others, superior, and there is much debate in the halls of wisdom regarding these and other matters. Yet none knows for certain, and if there be such folk, then they are most assuredly strange and given to pursuits such as we of Earth would find wholly repugnant, and quite foreign to our way of thinking. Suffice it, therefore, to say, that whilst we may speculate upon the existence of these supernal realms, they are as petty and lacking in meaning as are those idle folk who profess to tell the future in the stars, or prophesy events to come with cards.

The Book of Blech, Hygestus Prognosticator

Middleman used to hear voices. Or rather, *a* voice. It wasn't something he talked about of course – on Draconia such things were frowned upon, if they were believed at all, which more often than not they weren't. Apart from which he could never really remember what the voice said to him – only that sometimes it was there, inside his head, speaking quietly about one thing or the other, perhaps answering a question.

That was something else Middleman did that he kept quiet about – he thought deep, questioning thoughts. In his line of work – he was a letter-carver working mostly on tomb-stones or monuments to the mighty dead – there was plenty of time to think, even though it *was* discouraged on Draconia.

On this occasion – the one I'm going to tell you about – Middleman was thinking about the girl he loved. Her name was Bettina and Middleman loved her with all his heart and soul. Which was unfortunate, because there was no way that he could ever have got to do more than think about her, were it not for an extraordinary chain of events.

Bettina (who was, by the way, a talented musician, dancer and singer) came of a good Draconian family. Her parents, Trebuschino and Olinka, were both extremely rich, as well as extremely miserly. They held on to their money as though they expected to wake up one morning and find that everything they possessed had vanished in the night through some mysterious agency – perhaps from one of the lower spheres – and they would no more have considered Middleman as a prospective son-in-law than they would have considered giving away all they possessed.

Their miserliness was outmatched by only two other people on the whole of Draconia – Duke Tollicos and his wife Udoxia, who were not only extremely wealthy, but also greedy, lustful, avaricious, gluttonous and sybaritic – in short, all the worst aspects of Draconian nature.

The trouble began for Trebuschino and Olinka (or more particularly for Middleman and Bettina) when Tollicos happened to catch sight of the girl in the street. Of course he immediately wanted her, and having sent spies to discover

·C· GRAMMATICA XXI ·ZI·

·D· ·TERPSICORE· XIII· ·13·

·E· ·DOXE· VII· ·7·

all they could about her and her family, he went to see
Trebuschino and demanded to know how much he would
take for his daughter's 'services'.

This put Trebuschino in a quandary. On the one hand
he wanted Tollicos's money very much; on the other he
was, in his own way, genuinely fond of his child. The idea
of her lovely pink-and-white flesh being pawed over by
Tollicos filled him with disgust. But he was also afraid of
the Duke, who could, without difficulty, ruin him. So he
asked for time to consider what sum he might require and
went to talk to Olinka.

She, in turn, was horrified; though there was a gleam in her
eye as she mentally calculated how much they might screw
out of the Duke. They were still deliberating when they
received a visit from the Duchess Udoxia. She was a large,
well-built woman in her forties, who had a habit of stroking
her belly as she talked in a manner which was somehow
both suggestive and repulsive. She wasted no time in coming
to the point, which was that she knew what Tollicos – 'That
rancid pig!' – was about, and demanded to know how much
he had offered for 'that twig of a child'.

Trebuschino managed to stammer out that no price had
as yet been agreed on. Whereat the Duchess laughed heartily
and made the couple promise to ask for more than even
Tollicos would pay.

'Why does she care?' demanded Trebuschino, when the
Duchess had swept out again. 'Everyone knows they both
carry on like this.'

'Never mind why,' said Olinka. 'The question is, what
are we going to do?'

'We must get her away – far away – so that the Duke can
never find her.'

'But if we do that he will crush us. We might – lose
everything.'

'If we don't, then *she* will crush us. And what she leaves
undone he will finish. We can't win.'

A large tear welled in the eye of Olinka. It followed an

unaccustomed course down one furrowed cheek. 'Then –
what are we going to do?'

'Middleman.'

'What, that horrid letter-carver who's always hanging
about trying to see our dear Bettina?'

'Just so. He thinks he wants to marry her. Well, let him
have her. He may be a low-born jackanapes, but it's better
for him to have her than Tollicos. If we pay him a little . . .'

'A very little. . . .'

'. . . Enough to get him away. At least he'll care for her.'

So it was that an astonished Middleman received an urgent
summons to the house of Trebuschino and Olinka, where
he received an amazing offer – that he should run away
with Bettina, marry her if he wished, *and* get paid – if not
handsomely, at least well – for doing so.

Middleman thought quickly, then asked, quite plainly,
what the reason was for this sudden change in his fortunes.

Trebuschino answered just as shortly, 'You've no need
to know the reason – just see that you get far enough away
so that no one from around here is likely to catch up with
you.'

Middleman wondered briefly who 'no one' might be, but
refrained from asking. He looked at Trebuschino and
Olinka and said, 'All right. I'll do it. Providing Bettina
agrees.'

Since there was small likelihood of their daughter not
agreeing, Trebuschino and Olinka allowed smiles to relax
the tension in their faces and the bargain was struck.
Middleman did not volunteer where he intended taking
Bettina – indeed he could not since as yet he had no idea –
nor did her parents demand that he tell them.

In the end, it was the girl herself who decided their route
and so precipitated their great adventure.

Bettina, of whom we have heard much but know little,
was more than merely a pretty face. She was, as remarked,
a talented musician, besides which, she also had a head on
her shoulders. It so happened that she had, quite by chance,
overheard the discussion of her fate between Tollicos and
her father. She had never really doubted that Trebuschino

would refuse, but it came as a delicious surprise when they put their plan regarding Middleman to her. It was, of course, an ideal solution to her, and she lost no time in agreeing. She was married to Middleman in a terribly quiet ceremony by an ancient priest who could scarcely mumble the words past his toothless gums, and only a day later the couple left the city and headed out into the country.

They took with them enough money – painfully counted out by Trebuschino – to pay their way all round Draconia if need be, and to set up house wherever they chose. That 'wherever' was finally decided by Bettina herself.

After less than a day on the road she told Middleman the reason for her parents' sudden change of heart, and added her own thoughts on the matter, together with their solution.

'No matter how far we go, Tollicos is bound to catch up with us sooner or later. I don't care what father and mother think – he's going to see through the whole thing. And if by chance he doesn't, they will certainly say you ran off with me. What else can they say? So, we must get right away. Not just anywhere in Draconia, but – onto another sphere.'

'Another sphere!' Middleman trembled at the mere thought. People might not even have letter-cutters in the lower worlds. As for the higher – one just did not go there unless invited. Then he thought some more and realized they really did not have any choice. If they were going to escape Tollicos, or worse, Udoxia, they had to go somewhere no one would follow. Getting off one sphere onto another was not so difficult, probably because no one in their right mind ever wanted to do it. All one had to do – which Bettina and Middleman did – was go to any one of a dozen places where the worlds were more or less permanently aligned, and let oneself down from one to the other.

In this case they found a large iron bucket on a kind of pulley attachment, which had presumably been left there by another mad Draconian, and having checked that it was securely fastened to a great rock which arched out into

space, Bettina and Middleman climbed into the bucket and
began to lower themselves down.

Once over the edge they were in shadow. Above them
they could see the massive, endless-seeming underside of
the Draconian sphere; below were nothing but fat clouds,
greyness and a darkly spinning vortex of light and shadow
which seemed to indicate the next level.

Unfortunately, before they were more than half way, and
still suspended between the worlds, the rope to which their
conveyance was attached gave way and they began to plum-
met down at great speed.

Air rushed past them with a shriek; lights danced and
swung on every side. Middleman clutched Bettina and had
no time to think anything except, 'This is it. The end.' But
in this he was mistaken.

The bucket landed softly, with a great plop, in what was
evidently a huge pile of dung – from what animal they could
not tell, but there was no mistaking it. They clambered out
and staggered away as fast as they could.

The place in which they found themselves was not at all
what they had been lead to expect. No one on Draconia
did much in the way of speculation about the lower or
higher spheres – they had no call to do so. Theories which
existed were not current, therefore, but dated back to much
earlier times. The most popular claimed that all the lower
worlds were denser than the upper levels, and that any life
forms dwelling there must consequently be squat and ugly:
trees or bushes stunted, flowers short of stem, animals thick
legged, humans (if you could so call them) squat and probably hairy. The air, too, must be considered as polluted,
and it was probably very hot, since the sun, moon and stars
fixed to the bottom of each sphere must be much closer to
the surface than on Draconia, which only had the higher
(therefore loftier) spheres above it.

Whatever expectations Middleman and Bettina may have
had were shattered at once by the world in which they had
landed. It was certainly greener than Draconia, and there
were perhaps some different kinds of trees, but in almost
every other respect things were the same. The same roads

meandered between green hills; the same small houses
dotted the landscapes; the same birds (more or less) sang in
the heavens; and what looked like an identical sun (beginning to set) shone down out of a familiar blue sky.

Indeed, so alike was the place to which they had come
that for a moment Middleman wondered if he had not fallen
asleep and dreamed the whole descent. Then, as they made
their way over a field of long grass, Bettina pulled at his
arm and pointed to where a figure could be seen advancing
towards them.

It seemed woman-shaped, though dressed in a strange
close-fitting costume which enclosed both limbs and trunk.
On its head was a wide-brimmed hat which shaded its eyes
and made it impossible to see the face beneath at all clearly.
However she (for it most assuredly was a she) seemed in
no way threatening, and the hand she extended was clearly
in greeting.

'Hello, you must be the newcomers. Glad to meet you.
Name's Sportinoza. Welcome to Bidewell.'

'Er . . . thank you. I'm Middleman and this is my – wife,
Bettina.'

'Hello to you both. Didn't know you were bringing your
wife. Still you are both welcome, of course. Good. Well, I
expect you'd like to settle in. The Contest does begin
tomorrow after all. First come, first light, eh?' Chattering
on, she lead the way across the field to a gate beyond which
was a large house with a gabled roof and several chimneys
from which smoke rose lazily into the evening air.

Middleman had no idea what anything the woman had
said to them meant, but he was anxious not to betray the
fact that they were from another sphere, since one could
not tell if the natives were friendly or not, despite appearances. So he said nothing beyond an occasional 'yes' and
'no'.

They were shown into a bright, airy room in which, once
alone, they discussed the situation in lowered voices.

It was evident that Sportinoza had mistaken them for
another couple, and that she expected Middleman to take
part in some kind of contest, though whether of strength

or skill they could not say. Whatever it was, Middleman decided he would just have to try and bluff his way through. 'Somehow or other I have the strangest feeling this was meant to happen. Though I don't know how, or why.'

They were woken next morning by a smiling Sportinoza, who offered to escort them to the Contest. With no idea what to expect the two Draconians followed her, chattering all the way about the weather and the excellent turn-out of people. Long before they arrived at the site they could hear what sounded like a large crowd. They arrived at last at a natural bowl-shaped amphitheatre, around which were set a number of massive upright stones. Each was gaily painted a different colour and decorated with spirals and zigzags. Only one was plain, a huge black basalt pillar more than twice the height of a man, which looked oddly forbidding, perhaps because it was the only one with no one standing before it. The rest had a collection of assorted people gathered about each of them. All were gaily dressed and none of them squat or hairy. They were talking, or rather shouting, at the tops of their voices. Straining to hear something which would offer him a clue to what was going on Middleman could pick out only a few phrases from the babble. He heard '. . . far outclasses yours.' 'Such imagination!' 'There's no doubt Mossdene can do better than anything Skilla can come up with,' and a number of 'Wills' and 'Won'ts', 'Cans' and 'Can'ts' bandied about between the supporters.

As they hesitated at the edge of the crowd Middleman and Bettina saw that there were ten of the huge stones, and that in front of each one was a chair set up facing it. In each of these the contestants sat, silent and concentrated. The rest of the noisy crowd thronged on all sides, or went in and out of some brightly coloured tents set up close by. Judging by the merry sounds within, some kind of alcohol was being served there.

The only stone which did not have anyone sitting in its chair was the undecorated black pillar, and after a moment's hesitation Middleman lead Bettina over to it and looked up at its massive face.

It was, he now saw, carved all over with a faint tracery of intricate spirals and interconnected lines. Something about it made him shudder, and he was about to turn away to join one of the other groups, when he realized a hush had fallen and that everyone was staring at him.

Then Sportinoza thrust her way through the crowd. Her normally smiling countenance was downcast. 'You are quite certain this is what you want?' she asked. 'I mean, it's not too late to withdraw.'

Something in Middleman wanted very much to say that he had made a mistake and to ask what was going on; but the feeling that 'all this was meant to happen' was still with him, so instead he smiled at Sportinoza and said simply, 'No, this is where we will stay.' He wasn't really sure why he said this; in fact, the moment the words were out he wished them unsaid, but by then it was already too late. Sportinoza turned to face the crowd with hands on hips and said loudly, 'There's no need to stare. This gentleman has chosen to represent the tenth Muse as is his right.'

Middleman felt Bettina's hand on his arm. 'But there is no tenth Muse,' she whispered. 'Not unless these – these people have invented one.' She added, not without reason, 'Middleman, I'm afraid.'

'So am I,' he admitted. 'But I don't see what we can do.'

'We have to try something,' said Bettina. 'Wait here!'

Before Middleman could say or do anything to prevent her, Bettina hurried after the retreating figure of Sportinoza. When she caught her up, Bettina called, 'Wait! Can I speak to you a moment, please?'

Sportinoza turned her friendly countenance to the younger woman. 'Of course, dear. Can't spare long, though. Contest begins in a few minutes.'

'About that,' Bettina said. 'I know it sounds silly, but there's been a mistake.'

'Mistake, dear? What's that?'

'It's just that, well – Middleman and I aren't from around here. We just happened to arrive at this moment, but we don't really know what's happening.'

Sportinoza looked taken aback. 'You mean you didn't

come for the Contest at all . . . ? But we were expecting you . . . !' Then, as light dawned, she became anxious. 'Then your man didn't mean to chose the Black Stone at all? Dear me!'

'What's going to happen?' demanded Bettina. 'Please tell me.'

'Well . . . , you really don't know? About the Contest, I mean? Oh dear . . . ! Well, every year people come from all over Astronica to meet and hold this contest in the name of the Muses.'

'Calliope, Urania, Terpsichore, Erato, Polyhymnia, Thalia, Melpomene, Euterpe, Clio,' listed Bettina.

'Yes. And Her we don't name. The one your Middleman has chosen.'

'What does he have to do in the Contest?'

'Fancy not knowing that! You must come from a very distant part of Astronica. But it's very simple. Each of the contestants has to think a Perfect Thought. It goes into the pillar and is recorded there. Then the Muses judge and the winner gets a prize.'

'The Muses themselves are judges?' exclaimed Bettina. 'You mean they actually appear?'

'Well, of course! How else could they do the judging? – Oh, sometimes they send a messenger. Once Apollo himself came instead of Erato, but that's never happened since.' She gave Bettina a curious stare. 'You really don't know anything about it, do you?'

'Thank you,' Bettina said hurriedly. 'You've really been a great help.' Before Sportinoza could say anything more she hurried back to Middleman and told him what she had found out.

He brightened visibly. 'That's wonderful. Now I know what to do, it won't be half as difficult. Thinking is something I do rather well,' he added, with a certain shy pride. 'The only problem is, we don't know who this tenth Muse is, or why no one else seems to want to represent her.'

'Look,' Bettina interrupted, 'it looks as though someone is going to make an announcement. Maybe you'll be able to work it out from what he says.'

A large, expansive figure had emerged from one of the bright tents and there were calls for silence. The newcomer, a man with a red face and a very loud voice, began to announce. 'The great Contest for the favour of the Muses. Give your support now for Terabinth, representing Clio, Muse of History; Mossdene, representing Polyhymnia, Muse of Heroic Songs; Johnstondi, representing Thalia, Muse of Comedy . . .'

The voice boomed on, but Middleman was scarcely listening. He was thinking furiously, 'However did I get myself into this?' and wondering how he was going to carry off what seemed to be required of him, and what would happen if he failed. Then he heard his own name.

'. . . and finally Middleman, representing the Nameless One – the Muse of Death.'

The word sank into Middleman's brain like a hot knife into soft wood. 'Death'. And he had chosen her. Well, it was too late to do anything now. Too late to withdraw. Too late to wish himself back on Draconia, where thinking got you a bad reputation. He stared at the stone in front of him and wondered rather foolishly what to do. As silence fell he stole a surreptitious glance at the other contestants. All of them had their eyes tight shut. Hopefully Middleman closed his. Nothing happened. Then a cool voice sounded in his head, which seemed strangely familiar.

'You are the first mortal on any of the ten spheres to choose me in a thousand years. You have pleased me greatly, Middleman. Listen, and I will tell you what to do. But I cannot help you make the Perfect Thought. That you must do for yourself.'

Middleman's eyes snapped open, but there was no sign of the speaker. Yet there was no doubt – the voice was one he had heard often on Draconia while he worked on memorials for the departed. He closed his eyes again and tried to form a thought. 'What must I do?'

'Let your mind be blank. Focus on the stone. Then, when you are ready, offer your Perfect Thought to the stone. It will be recorded there for all to see and judgement will be

made by my sisters. But hurry, you have only a short time
left.'

Middleman struggled to obey, without success; then suddenly his mind cleared, the ordering of his thoughts began
to flow again as they had always done at home on Draconia.
He set himself to think, not of Death as it was portrayed
in all the worlds, as a terrible spectre; but rather as a friend.
He thought of the voice he had heard so often, and with
that there came a picture, a woman's face of great and
disturbing beauty, strong and noble and fearful at once, but
with a deep sorrow underlying it that touched Middleman
at the greatest depth of his being.

Slowly he opened his eyes, and there, mirrored on the
black stone, which seemed now to be touched with silver,
was the face he had envisioned. He heard a gasp from beside
him and turned to where Bettina stood, staring with sudden
tears in her eyes at the stone. 'She is so beautiful. How
could we have not seen this before?'

'Easy enough in a world without a tenth Muse,' he murmured, feeling suddenly weak. He looked towards the other
contenders and saw that on each of their stones stood out
a brilliant, coruscating image, representing the Goddess of
their choice. Each one was extraordinary, a masterpiece, he
saw at a glance. By their side his own imaged thought
looked poor and drab.

A sudden shimmering in the air betokened the arrival of
the Goddesses – among them one who wore a grey cloak
with the hood pulled up to hide her face. They stood together in the centre of the bowl, a brightly glimmering group
whom Middleman found it difficult to see or to look at
directly. Presently, she of the cloak approached him
directly; with her came a goddess of surpassing beauty and
delicacy whom Middleman somehow knew to be Melpomene, the Muse of Tragedy.

Middleman bowed his head at their approach and when
he lifted it again he found himself looking into a pair of
level grey eyes which he knew saw everything. The rest of
the face remained in shadow. The voice he remembered in
his mind said, 'You have made an image of me that will

change the thoughts of all people towards Death. Yes, it is a fearful thing, yet from my presence comes much that my sisters cannot give. Desire to overcome, to cajole or supplicate Death has inspired many great works of men – much poetry, many dreams and works of art that give hope. Where death itself seems ugly, I can make it beautiful. No one may see me directly, until their time comes. But you have made a face for me that will be theirs for all time. For that I, and my sisters, thank you and declare you the winner of this Contest.'

On all sides there were cries of 'Middleman! Middleman!' Bettina was hugging him. Sportinoza was beaming. Then the Goddesses were gone and only Middleman heard the voice in his mind that said, 'I can offer you no reward for what you have done, nothing beyond the approbation of your fellow mortals. Yet I promise you that your life will be blessed and that you will always have time to think.'

And thus it was that Middleman became famous. He and Bettina settled upon the second sphere of creation known as Astronica, where they lived a long and happy life and had a large family. Middleman taught letter-cutting and Bettina the arts of music and dance. And sometimes Middleman talked of his perfect thought and what it meant to him and others. And when it was time for him to die, it is told that the Goddess herself came, and that she pushed back the hood of her cloak and allowed him to see her at last, unveiled.

John Matthews As well as numerous non-fiction books on the Arthurian and Celtic myth-cycles, he has published a number of short stories which derive their energy from this same source. An accomplished lecturer and storyteller, he is currently at work on an SF trilogy *The Emperor of Paradise* (written with his wife Caitlín Matthews) and a massive Arthurian novel on which he has been working for over twenty years. When not working on a new book he divides his time between visiting ancient sacred sites in Britain and watching old *Star Trek* movies.

CHAPTER TWELVE

THE WIND BOX

Scott Bradfield

Nowhere has the Tarot become more popular than in California, capital of the New Age. Scott Bradfield's wildly imagined comedy spins off from the cards to penetrate the terrors behind Los Angeles sunshine and optimism. What really causes earthquakes? Could it be longing? Scott's story is one of several to include a Tarot-reader as a minor character, as if the cards wish to honour their representatives.

Sometimes he stood baffled by white sunlight and just watched cars go by. Bright convertibles, battered Fords and Chevrolets, roaring buses, long smooth white limousines with dark windows. The heat seemed to pull at him, like the flashing sunlight off chrome and windshields, like his sense of great quakes and tremblers stirring dreamlessly awake in the deep earth beneath his feet. Obdurate mountains grew down there, massive and subcrustal seas and continents. That was the first thing he noticed about Southern California: the sea of movement embedded in it. For the first few days he slept in his car on Mulholland Drive, but eventually he found a mouldering bungalow studio apartment off Vineland Avenue in Burbank, and a large unsprung stuffed chair in an abandoned lot nearby. He purchased a curiously stained mattress from the local Salvation Army and transported it home in a neglected shopping cart. Large dense men with rough menacing beards, sun-stained leather jackets and reflecting mirrored sunglasses intensely disregarded him as they kicked their motorcycle ignitions with spurred black boots. Sometimes at night he would sit on his front porch in his tattered green lawn chair and just watch the planes descending overhead,

218

THE FOOL.

DEATH.

THE TOWER.

THE DEVIL.

their flashing green and blue lights casting pale watery shadows through the high buzzing power lines. He could hear the power lines when he slept; they invested everything, even his dreams, with a cool staticky mist. It was the only coolness he knew that summer.

The heat woke him every morning at 6 a.m. He fixed instant coffee, Cocoa Puffs, Potato Stix with ketchup, hearing the blare of televisions converge in the littered courtyard. The screeching of cartoon automobiles, the abrupt explosions of animated cats, a deep-throated, impossibly voiced villain crying again and again, 'Destroy the transformers! Destroy the transformers!' He sat at his wobbly table in the muggy kitchenette, gazing out the window at refuse in the courtyard and mangy, addled cats dozing underneath a tyreless Ford Rambler. Unravelling truck retreads lay strewn about, fragments of irreparable furniture, unidentifiable hunks of metal, a sun-bleached stray number 12 billiard ball, and everywhere thousands of crushed and decomposing cigarette butts like gravel at the bottom of a tropical fish tank. There were times when it seemed to him the entire world had ended. There were other times when he just wished it would.

Vast rolling geothermal plates slipped and heaved, buildings toppled, freeway off-ramps collapsed. Earthquakes crashed through the valley like benedictions; the planet's thin mantle abrupted and fell, swallowing entire cities. In his dreams everything was destroyed. There was only the hot amber sand again, the primordial Santa Ana winds turning through everything. Sometimes he lay in bed for hours, feeling drained of energy, as if in his dreams of destruction things had actually collapsed inside of him. Later he would sit on his porch glancing through secondhand men's magazines he had purchased at Phil's Paperback Exchange on Ventura Boulevard, the perennial television playing from the neighbouring bungalow into the otherwise abandoned courtyard like some unscathed bit of technology after the soft, impactless explosion of a neutron bomb. In the bungalow across from his, a woman with a brittle voice and pale dry hands would occasionally prise open her kitchen's dusty venetian blinds and gaze at him for a while, her television mindlessly promoting cereals and deodorants to the courtyard's stunned and diarrhoeic cats.

'What are you doing?' she asked one day. He could glimpse only smoky dust swirling behind her cracked blinds.

'Nothing,' he said.

'Are you the man that drives the bus? Do you drive the yellow bus?'

He thought for a moment. 'I don't think so,' he said.

A chattering pneumatic hammer started up miles away. 'I just want you to know, then,' she said after a while. 'I just want you to know that we all think you're doing a very good job.'

'The mind has special powers all its own,' Victory told him, sitting with him during her breaks at the Golden Pancake Coffee Shop on Lankershim Boulevard and smoking Tareytons. 'I believe that very strongly. I don't think you can ever get to know me really well unless you understand I happen to be a very mind-oriented sort of person. A lot of people aren't mind-oriented sorts of persons at all. A lot of people just think money matters, or having a nice car.' She never really looked at him, but rather out the window at the flashing sun. A painting on the coffee-shop window depicted a fat jolly chef staggering underneath a platter of enormous pancakes and syrup. 'That's why I came to LA, you see. Because LA is the land of the next great superrace. There's a conjunction of planetary currents and influences here which are very powerful. That's why Aimée Semple McPherson came here. That's why Krishnamurti came here.'

He drank his coffee and thought about enormous pterodactyls carrying people off in their bloody talons, withering droughts, vast clouds of hazardous waste settling over the city like a bird on its nest. And earthquakes. Sudden, impossible, perfectly enunciated earthquakes. They didn't speak to his mind, but to his bones. It was like the articles

in supermarket tabloids about mothers psychically contacted by their unborn children. Unborn children wanted
to tell you things. They wanted to prepare you for their
imminent arrival.

Victory lit another Tareyton. 'You're a very good listener,' she told him after a while. 'Men are never usually
very good listeners, you know.'

Victory's real name was Eleanor Davenport, and her
father was a fundamentalist minister in Austin, Texas.
'Being raised by fundamentalists can be a very wearying
experience,' Victory told him. 'There's no room for growth
when you've got a big helmet on your head. Ever since I
came to California I feel as if I have won the most important
battle of my life, and nobody can ever tell me how to think
or behave ever again. That's why I changed my name when
I came here. To Victory.'

Victory had been living in Burbank for two years, sharing
a two bedroom block-style apartment with a legally blind
Tarot-reader who went by the name of Governor Pearl.
'She has taken the name Governor Pearl because it combines
traditional masculine ideas with traditional feminine ideas,
thus helping create entirely new patterns of socially accepted
feminine behaviour. A person's name is very important
since it tells people who you really are inside. Otherwise
you're just like everybody else. You're just a Mary, or a
Jane, or a Bill. Basically I guess you could say Governor
Pearl's a very thoughtful, caring sort of person who's hardly
ever home, but pays half the rent anyway.' David never
met Governor Pearl, but a few times Victory pointed her
out to him as she drove past the diner in her long white '55
Thunderbird convertible, manoeuvring slowly through the
crowded street-traffic, her guide dog Jeff panting beside her
in the passenger seat. Governor Pearl wore dark sunglasses,
and had a long gaunt face with close-cropped hair. 'She's
not really completely blind,' Victory said. 'She can still
make out general shapes and things.'

Usually they spent the night together at his place, lying
naked and pale on the sweating mattress, gazing absently at
the thin gauze curtains as if expecting, at any moment, some

indication of a breeze. Victory loved to talk, and even when she didn't have anything to say she had numerous questions to ask.

'Do you ever think of spiritual things, David?'

'I don't know. I guess so.' He could still hear motorcycles echoing in the courtyard, tearing and shaking at things like tremblers beneath the world's floor.

'Like what sort of spiritual things, David? Do you ever wonder about your rightful place in the universe? Do you ever wonder why you were born, and what your purpose in life is? Do you believe there are spiritual beings who have come from millions of years in our future to determine our lives and thoughts, residing underneath our world because they fear our violence and narrow-minded hypocrisy? Or do you believe we all have free will, and that each of us is a God of his or her own private universe, the universe of the self? In our private universes we live forever. Nothing restrains us in the universe of our minds, because that is the real universe, and this one that we think is real is just a prison where we go when we want to punish ourselves. Do you ever think about things like that, David? Is that why you're so quiet all the time? Have you ever read Jung? Or Gurdjieff? Have you ever been to a phrenologist? Do you believe in phrenology?'

Sometimes David grew dizzy and disoriented by Victory's questions. They seemed to multiply in the tiny hot bungalow like strange misshapen insects with hard chitinous bodies and jewelled glistening wings. They fluttered and banged against the naked overhead light bulb; they crawled into your clothes and sheets and facial hair. He developed a flickering migraine, and thought as hard as he could. 'I don't know,' he said finally. 'I don't know if I've thought about that stuff or not.'

Victory was convinced David should meet her Spiritual Work Group counsellor, who owned a house in Sherman Oaks. The house was filled with paperback books on tidy mahogany shelves, energy crystals, pyramid tents and totems, and original native American religious artefacts stored behind polished glass-panelled cabinets. 'It's like a museum, kind of,' Victory said. 'It's like a museum of higher thought.' She pulled her battered Toyota Corolla up onto the slender kerb. 'He's giving one of his famous High Energy Workshops today. People come from all over the world to attend them. But he's graciously agreed to meet us both afterwards for a short while.'

'Intellectual abilities are not something to be taken lightly,' Dr Simonson said, drinking Orange Pekoe tea from a large ceramic mug. The mug was imprinted with a blazing red and amber mandala. 'With knowledge comes great responsibility, and I don't mean responsibility to mere mankind, for we share our universe with creatures of many different species. There are creatures on Rigel–7, for example, who breathe pure methane. They have evolved many thousands of years beyond our puny race. Because they dispensed with violence long ago, they no longer possess hands or feet. They make love by means of pure meditation. Often lovers are together for thousands of years without ever meeting face to face, without ever knowing what each other looks like.' They were sitting in the large ornate living room which was crowded with more bookshelves, enormous foetal stone sculptures, and an intricate stereo system with thousands of records filed in varnished oak cabinets. The room felt infinitely heavy, David thought. It felt like massive tectonic plates jostling underneath continents, oceans, gravity. David thought he felt something shifting in all that buried weight, tearing. He placed his hands under his knees.

'Ideas belong to the entire universe, David. That's all I'm saying.' Meanwhile, David tried to envision the ruptured walls of Atlantis, the ocean pouring through and pounding everything to bits. Enormous cyclopean squid pulled away, pumping like hearts. Strange convoluted creatures with bloated, symmetrical features. Vast green plains of algae and rocks, dark intricate caverns filled with unglimpsed and impossible life-forms. Nobody could hear or see anything down there. You could only feel it, that sudden *beat* of the sea. The super race, with their nightmarish faces and inflated, brainy skulls, had long anticipated everything, even their own destruction. The world of the mind goes on forever, they thought. And the world of the mind is all that matters.

David felt a sudden, weightless sense of relief rise in his chest as he considered the earth's doomed secrets. Then, after a moment, the plates in the cupboards began to rattle. The large bay windows chattered faintly in their frames like whirring insects. Victory clasped shut her purse.

'Don't worry,' Dr Simonson said. 'It's just a little trembler. We get them all the time.'

After the destruction of Atlantis the sea looked exactly the same. A few jostling whitecaps, waves. Gulls screeched and wheeled, clouds drifted overhead. On the ocean's surface it was as if nothing had happened.

'Earthquakes are very important psychic occurrences, you know,' Dr Simonson said. 'Earthquakes help the world breathe. They adjust the world's psychic energy so everything can flow smoothly again through our eternal minds.'

'This is the guest room,' Dr Simonson said. 'This is my office. That's an original Dali, a Braque, a Chagall. Great art gives us knowledge of the soul. This is my Marvel Comics collection. This is my science fiction room. My girl comes in four times a week and cleans everything, even the windows. Here's where I keep my pinball machines, video games, hot tub. All of these bay windows – I had them recently installed myself. I commissioned a semi-Olympic-sized swimming pool for the yard. I'm going to tear down the garage and the guest bathroom and build a tower, which I will fill with my metaphysical library, my Indian and East African religious statues, and a massive, a really humongous Dolby sound system. When I play Strauss, it'll sound like a football stadium. It'll sound like the entire place is lifting off into outer space.' By this time they were back in the living room and Dr Simonson was offering them Ginseng tea, Chinese almond cookies and Hershey's Chocolate Kisses.

'When I came to LA in 1972, I had nothing,' Dr Simon-

son said. 'I was driving a '63 Chevy Nova. It had three bald
tyres and no brakes. If I wanted to stop, I had to downshift
into low, then pull out the emergency brake. I was drinking
two quarts of Albertson's Whiskey a day. I was going
nowhere fast. I was going to hell in a handcart. Then I met
a girl on the beach at Venice and told her about my dream.
I dreamed of an institute that wasn't an institute. I dreamed
of a corporation that wasn't a corporation. I dreamed of a
radical organization which wouldn't get into any trouble. I
dreamed of a group of people sharing their noblest thoughts
and ambitions. I dreamed of all this.' He gestured abstractly
with his teacup. The bay windows, library, contracted
swimming pool. The San Fernando Valley lay spread out
in the distance, dully glittering like an enormous transistor
component. 'Her father was Andrew McLanahan, senior
Vice-President of the Fluor Corporation, and she had a
trust fund she wanted to do some good with. She believed
in my dream. As a result, my dream became a reality.' He
poured more tea, gazing absently out the sparkling bay
window. The entire Valley was bleached with smog, as if
everything in the world was fading into whiteness around
them, everything except for this room. Everything except
for the statues and books and records and shelves. Everything except for Dr Simonson and the Worldwide Institute
of Higher Learning, Ltd.

Some nights he took long walks through Burbank, Van
Nuys, Encino, even White Oak, trying to recall his life
before LA. It was all very cold and indistinct, as if it weren't
really his life at all but just some movie he had seen years
ago on TV. He saw himself sitting in the back yards of
strange houses. The houses were owned by men and women
named Nancy and Bob, Dawn and Phil, April and James.
Sometimes he sat in their cool beige living rooms and
awaited their questions. 'Do you like it here in Lompoc?
Do you miss your friends? Would you like bologna and
cheese, or ham salad? Do you like your room? Do you
have any hobbies? Do you ever like to read a good book?'
Then the men would take him into the garage to see their

power drills, shortwave radios, miniature trains. He liked
to watch the trains go round and round on the hissing track,
and sometimes the men said, 'You can stay and watch for
a while, but don't touch anything. We'll call you when
dinner's ready.' And then leave him in the dark garage to
watch the trains run round. He was afraid he might touch
something by accident. Then the entire plyboard frame,
plastic trees and houses, tracks and cars and station houses
would all fall crashing senselessly to the concrete floors. He
knew he shouldn't touch anything. Maybe he shouldn't
even look. Whenever things were broken or missing, they
always asked him first. Trevor and Sally, Alex and Mary-
Ann. They were always looking at him as if they could see
broken or stolen valuables reflected in his eyes. That's why
he preferred to sit alone in back yards where there wasn't
anything valuable he could damage or destroy. If he sat
very quietly, the women wouldn't ask him any questions,
or make him any more sandwiches. If he sat very quietly
they might forget he was even there at all, as if he were the
brick barbecue, the high tessellated bird bath, the thorny
rose bushes bound to thin green bamboo poles. There were
Indians he had read about who could sit so still you couldn't
see them, even if they were right in front of you. He would
hold his hands clasped in his lap, and open them slightly
from time to time, careful not to let too much air out.
When he clasped his hands together they formed a wind
box, and you could hear the wind if you held your ear
close. He liked to hear the wind and keep it safe there in
his hands, where it wouldn't disturb anyone, or attract any
attention. An old woman had taught him the trick in one
of the first houses where he had lived. The woman had
made liverwurst and cheese sandwiches. Tomato soup.
Chex Party Mix. He couldn't remember her face any more,
but he could still remember the liverwurst and cheese sandwiches, tomato soup, and Chex Party Mix.

Victory gave him Gibran's *The Prophet*. She gave him Tol-
kien's *The Fellowship of the Ring*. She gave him numerous
paperback novels by Philip K Dick. The books had broken

spines and were thumb-soiled. Their lurid covers depicted robots, embattled space ships, babies drifting through space. 'Philip K Dick is the greatest American writer of our century,' Victory said. 'He was the only great writer to understand what a big and amazing place our universe is, as big and amazing as the darkest places of our own minds.' Twice each week she brought him to her Spiritual Work Group at Dr Simonson's house where he was encouraged to share his latest 'ideas'.

'Always remember,' Dr Simonson urged them, solemnly igniting Sandalwood incense and pouring the inexhaustible Ginseng tea, 'all ideas are good. No ideas are bad. There are half-formed ideas and undeveloped ideas. There are ideas which you don't understand, or which don't make you comfortable. But remember. We are a collective human enterprise of this Planet Earth, competing in the universe of love for greater knowledge, more perfect comprehension and truer love. Even as we speak, our thoughts and ideas are being projected into the living rooms of Tau Ceti and the Omar Asteroid Belt. In Tibet, men of vast religious wisdom have ingested hallucinogenics in order to mentally transport themselves here to Sherman Oaks and thus monitor our secret progress through the world of intellect. Would you like to start, David? Since you're our new member, would you like to give us a little information about your intellectual life?'

He wanted to say yes. He wanted to tell them about the destruction of Atlantis and the imminent destruction of LA. He wanted to tell them about the wind box, the smooth taut skin between Victory's shoulder blades, the white moon pulling every evening at the deep earth. But all he could say was, 'I don't know. I don't think so.' He couldn't even look them in the eye when he said it. He looked instead at his hands folded in his lap. The wind in the box. The wind didn't move if you held it very carefully. 'I guess I can't really think of anything,' he said.

Some nights, at home in bed, Victory tried to draw him out.

'You have to learn to share, David. I don't mean this as an insult, but when you don't share your secrets, you're acting like a very selfish individual. What would the world be like, David, if nobody ever shared their feelings with anybody? It would be a pretty cold place, wouldn't it, David? Don't you think it would be a pretty cold world we lived in?'

'I guess so,' he said. He thought it might be like Antarctica, covered with ice. You could wear heavy clothes in Antarctica like a disguise. He thought he wouldn't mind living in Antarctica.

'Tell me, David. Tell me how you feel.'

'I don't know.'

'Of course you know, David. How do you feel? How do you feel about me?'

'I like you, I guess.'

'You *like* me? You *guess*?'

He thought for a moment, watching his Marlboro smoulder in the glass tray. He picked it up. He shrugged. 'I guess I love you. Is that what you mean?'

One evening after work Victory brought home a Feel Wheel in a large cardboard box. It was packaged like a board game, and contained a cloth sheet partitioned like a dartboard. In each vari-coloured segment was stencilled a different human emotion. Love. Sadness. Hate. Sorrow. Rage. Embarrassment. In the middle of the design, where the bull's eye would have been, it said, 'I need to be left alone.' Victory handed him a red plastic checker.

'Now put the red checker on the emotion you feel most,' she told him. 'Only you can't put it on the centre one this time, because, see, I already put my blue one there.'

They smoked some marijuana. David felt cool and blurred. The deep earth seemed very close and compact.

'So why do you feel rage, David? Why do you feel so much rage all the time?'

'I don't know.'

'What does it feel like, David? How do you feel when you feel rage?'

'It's like steam in a kettle,' he said. 'It's like water in a

garden hose.' As he began to talk he grew slightly disoriented. He felt as if he were fading away. As if the ground
underneath his feet was slipping, slipping. 'Sometimes I
even travel down there, you know. I move among plates of
stone and basalt, past sunken lakes of oil and natural gas.
The stones are etched with skeletons of prehistoric dino-
saurs and men. Enormous fish with teeth and tiny, atro-
phied arms.' As he talked, he tried to recall the silence
which had resided in his bungalow before Victory. He felt
as if that silence were being threatened by the pressure
gathering along this deep earth's trembling faults and fissures. 'Trilobites like intricate snowflakes, enormous plugs
of lava, brilliant veins of gold and silver, and then this
terrific pressure just building. I can feel it in my neck, my
back, my teeth. I get these sinus headaches. I'm afraid to
move or touch anything, because I know I have to be
careful, I have to be careful with other people's things. And
then other times, you know, I *want* to reach out. I *want*
to give it a little push.' A sudden, weightless sensation filled
his chest and sinuses like a gasp of helium. He felt slightly
panicked, as if he had been discovered in some embarrassing
act by strange people who would post him off to other,
stranger houses. Then he heard the dishes rattle in the kitchenette. An aluminium pot clattered onto the floor.

'Did you feel that?' Victory asked. She was leaning back,
her eyes dilated and stunned as if by one of her own insights.

'It's like a dead ocean down there,' David told her. 'It's
like Atlantis. There are entire planets down there that have
been buried for millions of years. Sometimes they just need
a little push. Sometimes they just need you to notice they
exist.'

The next night after one of his longest walks he could feel
the muscles taut and alert in the backs of his legs. He
stopped at Seven-Eleven for orange juice and Kit Kats, and
arrived home around 10 p.m. to find Dr Simonson in the
kitchen washing an Underdog coffee cup in the cracked
sink. Victory was on the floor leaning back against enormous frayed pillows reading a paperback copy of Jung's

Man and His Symbols. The third person in the room was a man. He was sitting on the sofa. He was tall and gaunt, with large thick-rimmed glasses. He held a large gunmetal black box in his lap. He didn't look up when David entered the door. He seemed to be thinking about something.

The tiny cap fitted neatly over David's head and was attached by coiled wires to the black box.

'Alpha waves record the mind's mental activity,' Dr Simonson told him. 'The Alpha wave is the dominant strain in intellectual thought. William Burroughs knows about it. Timothy Leary knows about it. The world's greatest advances were not pioneered by scientists, but by artists. Galileo, for example, was not an astronomer, but a poet of abstract space. Don't be afraid, David. There's really absolutely nothing to be afraid of.'

The thin man adjusted dials on the gunmetal box. Then he attached another thin wire to David's wrist with a velcro band.

'We are all poets of infinite space,' Dr Simonson said, holding his warm teacup between his hands. 'We all deserve worlds as beautiful as the worlds we live inside.'

Sometimes they sat for hours in David's apartment while the gunmetal black box emitted its endless ribbons of tape. David felt very uninvolved with the entire process, smoking cigarettes and gazing aimlessly through the books and magazines Victory brought him while Dr Simonson discoursed about civilization.

'Every individual has a certain skill or talent,' he said, slicing Gruyère cheese and attaching the fragments to whole-wheat crackers. 'Every individual has certain responsibilities to mankind as a whole. Some men are strong, or beautiful, or know how to fix an automobile. Some are good at maths, or sculpture, or computer programming. But some men have special skills which you don't come across so often. These men are the guiding forces of civilization. Everybody in the world is equally important, David, but these men I'm talking about are really important.'

Sometimes, gazing at the smoky television screen, David

let his mind descend into the notched and convoluted maze of the deep earth. The dead planets were still there. The patient faces of special people and super advanced races. They all kept very quiet now that Dr Simonson was listening. They, too, heard the whirring of Dr Simonson's machine, and Dr Simonson's voice conferring with the thin man.

'What were the readings like?'

'I can't tell.'

'Did you check them against the seismograph?'

'Well, there's correspondences, I guess. But we haven't had any strong variations. We need a couple of good jolts first.'

They were looking for something. Sometimes it seemed as if they were looking for something inside David.

'David?'

'Yes.'

'How do you feel?'

'Okay.'

'A few days ago, when you were with Victory. How did that happen? What did you do?'

'I don't know.' David had made one firm resolution. From now on he wasn't telling anybody anything.

'What did it feel like?'

'It felt like everything moved suddenly. Everything started shaking.'

Dr Simonson's eyes were very black, David thought. After a while Dr Simonson said, 'I mean in your mind, David. What sort of intellectual focus did you have? Did you hear voices? Did anyone tell you what to do? Was it anybody you recognized?'

David thought for a moment. 'I don't know,' he said. 'I don't think so.'

'It was very, I don't know,' Victory said. 'It was very spiritual. I guess that's all I can say. I could feel the energy emanating from him and I knew he was a very special sort of person. I knew David could destroy everything if he wanted to, but he's far too benevolent and caring a person to do anything like that without a good reason.'

※

At night it seemed as if nothing unusual had ever happened. There was just him and Victory on the warped mattress, listening to cars in the street, with no real memory of Dr Simonson other than the strange strategic shapes of mandalas and pyramids and Navajo totems distributed throughout the musty bungalow. When it was very late David would let himself quietly out of the house and resume his restless walks, feeling all the world's pressure gathering underneath his feet. One night as he was letting himself out he found Dr Simonson sitting on the bungalow porch in the cat-clawed plastic lawn chair. His white penny loafers were propped on the wobbly wooden porch railing, his hands crossed in his lap.

'I'm not really Dr Simonson, David,' Dr Simonson said, turning to look up at him, the glare of streetlamps reflecting off his glasses and transforming them into white expressionless discs. 'Actually, I'm just Dr Simonson's egoic projection. I'm the man Dr Simonson always dreamed of being. Calm, self-assured, loving, immensely intelligent.' He was wearing pleated white cotton slacks and a loose-fitting beige shirt. 'You just go ahead with what you're doing, David. When I'm in this condition, I just like to drift along. You pretend I'm not even here at all. Remember that I'm still asleep in my bed up in Sherman Oaks, okay?'

These were hard desperate days of terrific heat. Temperatures and humidity soared to record levels, and at night David's walks grew longer and more furious, as if he were trying to outdistance himself. Interminable streets with savage impossible names like primal litanies. Lankershim, Tujunga, Sepulveda, Vanowen. He walked for miles and miles, often conspicuously trailed by Dr Simonson who, blocks away, strolled along imperturbably like a white cloud. Sometimes Dr Simonson drove his immaculately buffed El Dorado in the street beside David, playing Strauss's *Der Rosenkavalier* on his compact disc player, his windows rolled down and his convertible top popped back. Sometimes Dr Simonson turned down his music and talked with David.

'You probably don't believe this, David, but I have felt

great anger and resentment in my life, too. I have felt
tremendously violent hatred against the world, have desired
terrible retributions for the many cruel crimes committed
against me. I know I should be more understanding, but
sometimes I'm not; sometimes I'm not very understanding
at all. Just a week ago, for instance, the Internal Revenue
Service froze my corporate accounts. They subpoena-ed
many of my most loyal students, my secretary, my entire
accounting firm. They're trying to declare me a profit-
making institution, rather than a non-profit therapeutic
health maintenance community service, which is of course
what I really am. Sometimes I'd like to let them all have it.
Wouldn't you, David? Wouldn't you like to teach them all a
lesson they'd never forget? All those goddamn bureaucratic
phonies downtown. They're all asking for it, aren't they,
David? They're all asking for one killer jolt, and you're the
one that could do it. Let them die. Let them all be crushed
and die. Then they'd know how it felt, wouldn't they?
Then they'd know how it felt to build something you loved
and have it all torn down around you by greedy vultures.'

The pressure and heat were growing intolerable. David suffered painful sinus congestion, recurring flues, chills and
colds, sudden flashing headaches unrelieved by aspirin or
Tylenol. Tension accumulated in the earth's secret faults
and caverns, the deep earth filling up with resentment, like
some cheated lover. It was all perfectly natural, he thought.
In earthquakes natural terrestrial rhythms emerge from the
earth's heart. Crippled women were known to walk after
earthquakes. Blind men saw. Diseases went into spon-
taneous remission. Some great eternal pulse was always
restored by cataclysm. 'You could let it happen,' Dr Simonson said. His eyes were damp and watery with allergy, his
nose red and chafed by his pocket handkerchief. 'You could
give the world back its heart, its breath, its voice. It's like
cleaning out all the world's hate with vast white rivers of
pure energy.'
    Then one night he destroyed Los Angeles over and over
again in his dreams. Deep subcrustal plains slipped and

heaved, enormous fractural fissures opened across the entire San Fernando Valley, swallowing streets and housing tracts, ripping out interminable colonic streams of plumbing and electrical wires. Gas and water mains burst, filling the air with glistening sprays and white roiling clouds. Subterranean toxic waste containers burst and sprayed. The San Andreas Fault gave a sudden pull, and then, with a long, slow and almost graceful flourish, the great fragile promontory of Los Angeles snapped and slid into the boiling Pacific like a string of pearls down the grate of a sink.

David awoke feeling a strange lapse in his stomach, and then, faintly, what might have been the subsiding aftershocks of an earthquake. He looked around the room, but everything seemed in place. The bungalow was quiet, and the streets outside quiet, too. It was almost eight o'clock. Victory had left for work, and the bathroom was still misty from her shower. David lay half-awake in bed for a while. Something seemed very wrong. He picked up the telephone and heard a dial tone. He turned on the television and saw *AM Los Angeles*. After a while he pulled on his light flannel robe and went out to the porch with a cup of instant coffee.

Outside he couldn't tell if the world had ended or not. Perhaps *AM Los Angeles* was on tape delay in some collapsed Hollywood studio while its actual stars and guests struggled hopelessly underneath fallen girders and masonry. The entire courtyard was littered with wrappers and styrofoam fast food containers blown in by the night's muggy Santa Ana. The front end of the crippled Buick had been dismantled, baring rusted axles and joints, corroded drums and cracked brake shoes. The horizon was cloudy with either smog or the dust of pulverized buildings. He felt deeply exhausted, as if he had been running great distances in his sleep. Gradually he realized that someone was watching him. A large grasshopper whirred and chattered and landed by his feet. He looked up at the blinded window of the neighbouring bungalow.

'Did you feel it?' she asked. 'I was awake all night. I was waiting for it, you see.'

The grasshopper looked at him with glassy eyes.

'It's God's fist coming down,' the woman told him. 'That's where earthquakes come from. From God's fist punishing sinners.'

David found a neglected cigarette and book of matches in his robe's vest pocket. The cigarette was frayed and slightly cracked along the seam. He lit it anyway. The grasshopper took off again and crashed into a nest of discarded Wonderbread wrappers. After a while, the neighbour's television started up, and someone on a morning talk show called it a three point seven, and someone else on the panel said, 'A three point seven? That didn't *feel* like a three point seven, did it? It felt at *least* like a four point *five*. . . .'

David was alone in the house all day, smoking a pack of Marlboros he bought at Seven-Eleven, watching daytime movies and reruns of old sitcoms.

'They've arrested Dr. Simonson,' Victory told him when she got home, breathless, her uniform stained with yellow egg matter and ketchup. 'Tax fraud, David. I have to go up to his house before they've sealed it off and get his papers for him. I can't believe this. I can't believe they're doing all this to a nice man like Dr Simonson.'

The rest of the summer was much like the beginning, leaving David the bungalow to himself. Victory was occupied with work and grand jury proceedings, and then, in early September, Dr Simonson was admitted to the Betty Ford Drug and Alcohol Rehabilitation Center in Palm Springs, where Victory regularly drove herself and other Workshop members to visit him. David found a job pumping gas and tuning automobiles at a local Gulf station, and in the evenings after he returned home he would sit on his porch and breathe the gas fumes from his soiled green uniform. The thin man with the glasses never returned, but the gunmetal black box remained on the plastic coffee table.

A cool sea breeze had begun developing by the time Victory left for Iowa. 'Father mailed me a ticket a few weeks ago, and I didn't know if I wanted to go or not until now. I've been thinking a lot about God and family lately, David. I've been thinking maybe it's all right to rebel when you're young and confused, but that later, when you get older, it's time to settle down and raise children so that you can teach them about God's love. If Dr Simonson or anybody from the Workshop calls, tell them you don't know where I went, okay? I hope you're very happy and find God in your heart too, some day, David. I hope what I'm doing doesn't hurt you.'

It didn't hurt him. The next few weeks were filled with a high overcast, muggy and clinging air, a certain heaviness and density of limb and brain. There were no more discernible tremors, but only a sort of faint and misty anxiety which infiltrated news features, community council hearings and all-talk radio. Most of central Los Angeles was inadequately constructed. People recalled the St Francis Dam in the Santa Clara Valley, built with graft and faulty cement by William Mulholland. Los Angeles was just waiting and vulnerable. It would collapse like matchsticks. The Los Angeles 'natives', however, refused to be intimidated.

'All-Talk Radio. You're on the air.'

'Hello, Linda. This is Danielle in Whittier. I just wanted to say, about all this fright-talk about earthquakes? Well, if you live in the Midwest you've got your tornados. And if you live on the East Coast you've got your flash floods and hurricanes. There are electrical storms in Kansas my boyfriend Gary told me about? He saw this enormous ball of electricity rolling down the freeway and it hit another car and the car exploded? Well, I'm just saying, earthquakes aren't so bad, after all. I mean, they're here and everything, so what can we do, right? Oh, and Linda?'

'Yes, Danielle?'

'Do you really think old Teflon pans could be dangerous for frying foods? My sister Betty gave me her old set, and it *looks* perfectly fine and all. I'm just worried about the kids.'

He never saw Victory again, or Dr Simonson, who was released from Betty Ford Clinic in October and, after an elaborate court trial which lasted nearly two years, acquitted of conspiracy and fraud. After paying a substantial fee to the IRS he reportedly moved to the Bay Area where he

organized the expansion of his Free Spiritual Outgrowth
Clinics into Arizona, Hawaii and, eventually, even South
Korea. Sometimes, in his walks through the Valley, David
noticed Clinics springing up in disused shopping and medi-
cal-dental centres. Lovely blonde girls in overalls gave him
pamphlets as he passed. He never really looked at these
women, though. He preferred to look at the beautiful
women driving by in their cool, expressionless convertibles.

Three summers later he was hitch-hiking home from
work on Ventura Boulevard when Governor Pearl pulled
up and offered him a ride in her white Thunderbird. 'I
enjoy driving at night,' she said, turning to look over both
shoulders. Without sunglasses, her right eye appeared life-
less and dim, her left eye overlarge and milky with glau-
coma. As she pulled slowly away from the kerb a passing
car honked and veered. In the back seat her guide dog lay
unharnessed and senselessly asleep.

'I love to drive in LA,' Governor Pearl said, and offered
him a Coors from a white styrofoam icebox, Winstons, the
electric cigarette lighter. Her right eye, trained on the road,
tilted her head to one side. 'There's probably some chips
or something in there too,' she said, gesturing at the large
brown Seven-Eleven bag cluttered with wrappers, unopened
toilet paper, and a discarded Big Gulp container filled with
dissolving Orange Slush.

They took the Ventura Freeway to Santa Monica, then
the winding and exorbitant Sunset Boulevard back into Hollywood, Silver Lake, Chinatown. 'It's so big,' Governor
Pearl said. 'And filled with so many interesting people. Is
that a stop sign ahead?' They slowed to a stop. It was a
Don't Drive Drunk billboard. They got back on the freeway
and drove until dawn, drinking Coors and smoking marijuana. Around 7 a.m. they stopped for Egg McMuffins
before dropping David off at his home.

After that night, David completely forgot about the deep
earth, Dr Simonson, Victory, the wind box, his many concerned foster mothers and foster fathers. It felt like going
away. It felt like awakening to a new life in a new house
with strange people in it and just going away from all of

them, because it was never a place you belonged anyway. The world was very peaceful after you went away. Everything was new and fresh and clean. Everybody breathed easier, thought more clearly, and lived longer, healthier lives.

In the warm regenerate spring he abandoned everything and moved to the Pacific Northwest, where it rained for him nearly every day.

Scott Bradfield Born in 1955, he received a PhD in American Literature from University of California, Irvine, where he taught for five years. For the past two years he has been living as a freelance writer in London – his stories, essays and reviews appearing regularly in *The Times Literary Supplement*, *The Times Educational Supplement*, *The Listener*, *Omni*, *The Evening Standard*, *Interzone* and *Foundation*, as well as a number of other magazines and newspapers. His first collection of stories, *The Secret Life of Houses* was published in 1988. His first novel, *The History of Luminous Motion*, will be published in 1989 in the US and in the UK.

CHAPTER THIRTEEN

SNAKE DREAMS

Garry Kilworth

People who dislike the occult often point out that the Tarot existed as a game for centuries before Antoine Court de Gébelin declared it the Book of Thoth, the Egyptian book of all knowledge. They are right, of course. But deeper meanings can lie within a game. And are games necessarily trivial? Garry Kilworth's 'Snake Dreams' takes us to the South American rain forest, and the most ancient game of all.

When the Indians found him, the fever was well into its third day. MacAllen was barely conscious, lying half-submerged in a pool of filthy swamp water, the murky liquid threatening to end the fever in a sudden and dramatic way. Insects were using MacAllen as an island, to escape the long tongues of the frogs, and around him the Brazilian forest pulsated and murmured, filling his head with strange, warped visions. That light which did manage to filter through the canopy above was of a greenish, sickly hue, and within it shadows moved back and forth like phantoms on business of little urgency.

He felt drugged, as if his skull were full of some warm, viscous fluid that dulled his thoughts, heavy enough to prevent him from lifting his head. He was sick too, vomiting into the stagnant pool, which attracted other creatures not fastidious about their diet. He felt them slide and crawl over his inert form, their touch tingling his inflamed, sensitive skin.

The Indians lifted him up onto bony, strong shoulders. He could hear their voices, but the chatter seemed distant. His limbs were leaden, hanging heavy: logs on the ends of cords. The dark, sinister scenery around him sometimes

danced with slow, rhythmic movements constrained by a
lethargy of its own. At other times, it pressed against him,
its pressure on his brain threatening to squeeze his skull
until it burst like a rotten fruit.

He remembered taking the company launch up-river for a
quick survey. Somehow he had taken the wrong fork and
had found himself in fast-flowing water, white water. Panic
had set in: he was fearful of piranha, and those giant fossil-
like anacondas that basked on the shore. He made for the
bank, but a submerged log holed the launch just as he
reached it. The rest had been a nightmare: stumbling
through the fly-ridden jungle, trying to find a path; drinking
dirty water; being driven insane by the unremitting noise,
the insects, the clammy prison of leaves; and finally, suc-
cumbing to the chills, the sweats . . .

There were times when he felt he wanted to die. He
wanted the Indians to finish it, there and then: to slit his
throat and so defeat the fever. The peace that would follow
seemed to him then to offer such inviting rewards. Death
was merely a horizon, beyond which lay tranquillity.

'I want to live!' he cried, wondering which was lying, his
soul or his mouth.

'I'm dying,' he croaked to them, but they took no notice.
They continued their monkey chatter, which he often confused with the chatter of the real monkeys overhead, and
found the jungle paths down to the river.

As they carried him within the clammy interior of the
forest, through the tunnels of darkness, past the wooden
pillars that supported the thick, layered roof, he tried to
tell them who he was.

"Gineer,' he murmured thickly, his tongue a lazy, fat
snake curled within his mouth. 'Go' lost. Susan. Mus' tell
Susan, got loss.'

Susan, sweet Susan. Cool, cool Susan.

'Med at company dance,' he told a face near him. 'Nice.
Pretty.' The face grinned at him. 'Engineer,' he said, with
final satisfaction, getting the whole word out clearly.

He lapsed back into silence. Susan danced for him, slowly

and sensuously, moving in and out of the shadows. Her movements became sinuous, serpentine. They danced together, holding each other tightly, squeezing one another gently. Then, afterwards, an old, exciting game. A serious game.

'Hot,' he said. His flesh was baking. The face grinned. 'Hot, man!' he shrieked. He would catch fire from within: smoulder, *burn*. There were drums in his ears, throbbing out a painful rhythm. He thought his skin was splitting down his back and a snake was trying to creep inside him. He hated snakes; loathed them with that unknown fear that grips at the back of the brain, where the irrational lurks. He thrashed, but they held him tightly, dancing with him, as if it were a game. A serious game.

Brown, fast-flowing water slid with a sinuous movement between low banks. His temples pounded as they lay him in a canoe, and his eyes, which seemed to be expanding, were ready to explode. His blood was like boiling mercury in his veins and it seemed that his bones had been wrung, twisted like ropes. MacAllen thought he wanted to die.

The Indians would not let him rest. It seemed that no sooner had he been placed in the canoe than he was lifted out again, hoisted back onto hard, bony shoulders. He had not the strength to remonstrate with them. A sudden chill went through him and made him shudder violently. They almost dropped him, but moments later he was carried safely into the darkness of a grass dwelling.

He was in a hut. The cool, reed-strewn earth was underneath him as the hot flushes flooded back, melting the ice water in his veins. A face was close to his: a beautiful, Indian face. He thought she was going to kiss his cheek, but instead, she whispered close to his ear: urgent, intense words which he did not understand.

'I want to die,' he whispered back, afraid that it was true. Terrified of death, he wanted to be released from the fever, but he did not want to slip away completely. Where would he go? To the bottom of the river? It was important to cling on to the banks, but his fingers felt loose, boneless.

He began to rave as delirium washed over him.

✷

Yellow eye. A distant, wavering yellow eye and the smell
of burning fat. Susan was there, moving dimly in the light
of the yellow eye. High breasts. Taut, coppery skin. No,
not Susan. Someone else. She came to him and smiled down
on him with blinding-white teeth. There were markings on
her face. Susan, mismanaging her cosmetics? No – no –
Susan was blonde. This woman had black hair. Black as
death.

'Small lady,' he said, trying to reach up, and again she
smiled. The rushes of his bed pressed into his back, leaving
it sore and uncomfortable. Why hadn't they used river
sand? Sand was soft, warm and comfortable. He tried to
turn over, but she held him, stopped him from thrashing.
Little, dark lady with the strength of ten men.

As he began to recover, he was aware of the giant length
in the shadows of the corner of the hut. She was detached
from it, yet part of it. She was leaning over him, her cheek
close to, touching, his thigh. There was a thin reed in her
mouth. The sharpened tip of the reed was under his skin,
deep in his artery, and she was blowing gently. He could
feel the fluid entering his system: coolness flowing into the
warm blood. His wandering gaze found the thick, long
form with its penetrating eyes, staring at him from the
darkness on the far side of the hut. His brain reeled.

'What are you doing?' he whispered.

She looked up then, and the other creature which was
part of her, slid over the floor and out of the door of the
hut. It took a very long time for it to go.

She smiled at him. A bloody smile. But a fly was bothering him, insistent demands being made in his ear. He tried
to swat it, failing. He felt weak and helpless. She bent her
head again and the reed pricked his thigh. He kept his eyes
on the door.

'Will it come back?' he said.

During the day, he would walk through the hospital
grounds, sometimes pausing to watch the children of visitors playing in the sandpit. Not far away to the south, the
river up which the launch had brought him slid lazily into

the forest, its long length disappearing into the thick, green folds. To the north, nearer still, the city hummed with mechanical life. The children irritated him, messing around with the sand. When he came out of an evening, they would all be gone.

The hospital were almost ready to release him and he had an interview with the doctor that afternoon. In the cool office, with its air conditioning, he felt out of place.

The doctor had a smooth face, remarkably smooth. His eyes were brown and his hair was slicked back, like someone from a nineteen-thirties' film. He was explaining how MacAllen had been found.

'Some fishermen saw you, lying naked on the river bank – tourist types,' he grimaced a little. 'They brought you up-river in their boat and we took you in. That's as much as we know. Your fever had broken, but you were still in a very bad state.'

'I told you I was treated by the Indians,' said MacAllen.

'Yes. You said that.'

'I want to know what kind of medicine they used on me.'

The doctor shrugged, his small sharp eyes registering discomfort. 'Who knows? They have their own ways. Some of them are quite effective. After all, they've been treating themselves for centuries . . .'

'What I want to know,' cut in MacAllen, 'is what these marks are, on my thigh.'

Again, the shrug. 'They would appear to be needle marks.'

'You mean, they gave me injections?'

'I don't know. As I said, they *look* like needle marks – some sharp instrument.'

MacAllen realized his fingers were restless and he deliberately entwined them to keep them still. His dreams had been bothering him.

'Doctor,' he said, slowly, 'is it possible for the body to receive, say, injections of blood – from another creature?'

The doctor's head went back, sharply, and he glanced towards the window before looking into MacAllen's eyes again.

'Creature?'

'What if – what if one were to introduce snake's blood into a vein? Say, the blood of an anaconda?'

'I would say that the system would reject it. You'd be a very sick man.'

'But if one were already sick?'

The doctor picked up a sheet of paper from his desk top and then replaced it on the same spot, very carefully. He had kind features, but there was something a little brittle in his manner, which might have been a dislike of foreigners, or perhaps awkward patients.

'Are you telling me this is what happened? That they injected you with the blood of an anaconda?'

The words were delivered in a soft tone, but briskly, as if time were of the utmost importance.

MacAllen shook his head.

'I don't know. I was confused. The whole scene was confusing. I tried to communicate with them . . .'

'But surely, they did not understand you? I take it you, ah, raved in English?' There was just a trace of contempt in the doctor's enquiry, but MacAllen ignored this.

'Look, all I want to know is, did they poison my blood?'

An impatient sigh escaped the doctor's lips.

'Mr MacAllen, we've done several blood tests. There is nothing to suggest that any foreign agent exists – the virus, of course . . .' He paused, then said, 'I suggest you try to forget the whole thing. When someone is in a state of high fever, all sorts of delusions occur. As you remarked earlier, things become confused. Dreams begin to merge with reality. You had fever dreams, Mr MacAllen – simply that.'

'Is it that simple?'

The doctor looked up, suddenly, with a sympathetic expression.

'Would you like to see another kind of doctor?'

'You mean a psychiatrist? No – no, I'm not . . . I don't need that kind of treatment.'

'And your fiancée arrives this evening?'

'Susan? Yes, I called her yesterday. She's in Paris, at a conference, but she's taking her private jet across today.'

'She must be a wealthy woman.'

'She is – as well as being my fiancée, she's my boss. She owns the company.'

The doctor looked even more impressed and MacAllen could not help adding, 'Not bad for a lowly engineer, eh?'

He could smell the dampness of her skin: a musky smell that reminded him of a freshly dug claypit. She pressed food between his lips. It tasted gritty, like mashed seeds of some hardy plant, mixed with water. The room still spun occasionally, and he never took his eyes off the door. The snake would come back. He knew it would come back. It belonged there, as much as she did, more than him. *He* was the outsider, not the reptile.

A man came to the door, holding a bunch of fish.

'*Gato*,' he said, holding them up. They flashed silver in the white light from beyond. The man laughed. The girl laughed. MacAllen felt the rush of guilt. He was the man that would rob them of their livelihood. He was going to steal their river. He shrank from the girl's touch. She turned and looked at him curiously. Then her eyes changed. They had gone hard, like flints.

She knows, he thought. *She's read it in my face.*

'I don't want to,' he cried. 'I have to. It's my living – just as fishing is yours. The dam – the river has to have a new course. Nothing I can do will stop that.'

She stroked his head, soothed him, murmuring words that made him feel drowsy. Of course she doesn't know, he thought. How could she know? We don't even understand one another. I'm just being stupid. It's the fever. It's making me . . .

But then he stopped, for he sensed that something had returned to the hut. It had got in without him seeing it: slithered into a corner. He whimpered in fright. The hand stroked him as a trembling fit overtook him, seized control of his muscles. Afterwards he felt weak.

Susan came to his room in the hospital that evening. He was sitting by the window, looking out beyond the gardens at the river, and he had to stay where he was, because *she* was also there. *She* was sharpening the tip of a reed with a small, bright blade. Her soft thick lips closed on the blunt end and she blew through the hollow tube, into the palm of her hand. A downy feather wafted up on her warm breath, into the air. Her lips parted and she smiled, redly.

'Hello, Susan,' he said.

The sharp prick again. Cool fluid. He slapped at the spot and looked down, finding he had swatted a mosquito. A red smear besmirched his leg. He was sweating heavily and his blood was throbbing in his veins. He could hear the thrum of his heart, pumping deep inside him.

'Good journey?'

'Darling, never mind about me. You look *awful*.'

Susan, pale-skinned and soft-eyed, with that bloom on her which reminded him of delicate flowers, closed the door behind her. She moved tentatively to the centre of the room.

'Darling, I want to hug you, but I'm not sure – the illness. Is it all right?'

'Apart from the sallow skin – the dark bags under the eyes, and the loss of weight – I'm fine. You can do what you like with me.'

He trusted his sickness now. He could feel his blood stirring at the closeness of her. Even through the warmth of the evening, the heat of her body came to him. It aroused a new kind of excitement: one he had not experienced before the fever. Through the open window, the scent of exotic, parkland blooms filled the air, mingling with Susan's expensive Parisian perfume, but that was not the cause of his sudden anticipation. He was experiencing a catharsis, finding himself underneath the layers of what he used to be. He felt the surge, the rush of blood.

Susan was regarding him with strange eyes. She looked very vulnerable in her printed cotton frock. She looked fragile. Expensive perfume, but simple, cheap dress. That was Susan. He had always liked that compromise about her. She knew he could not afford costly suits, so she dressed down to him.

He stood up, feeling the soft breeze from the window on the back of his neck. Then he reached out his arms.

She came to him, nestled in the hollow of his shoulder.

'Darling,' she murmured.

His blood was on fire now, burning its own courses through his body, finding new channels. Her hot breath was on his cheek. It came out as a series of quick sighs, close to his ear. He pressed his mouth hard against hers, then his breast against her breast, until he could feel the frantic flutter of her heart, like a trapped, terrified bird, beneath.

She moaned in the back of her throat, then took her mouth from his to say, in a half-playful, half-serious tone, 'Darling – not so tightly. You're squeezing me to death . . .'

His arms felt strong. He watched her eyes open wide and thought they would never stop. Never stop. Never stop. Never stop. *Squeeze*, became *crush*. The sounds coming from her throat were taut and high-pitched, reminding him that they were playing an old game, a serious game, which required furtive movements and frantic responses.

Garry Kilworth began writing in the early 1970s when he won the Gollancz/*Sunday Times* SF Short Story competition. Since then he has had published fifty short stories and nine novels, including *Witchwater Country* and *Cloudrock and the Songbirds of Pain*. Translated into ten languages, he has been shortlisted for literary awards six times, and to date remains a breathless runner-up. As an airforce brat, and later as an airman himself, he lived in the Near East, Middle East, Africa and Asia, including the Maldive Islands. Forthcoming is an epic fable entitled *Abandonati* and a general fiction novel *In the Hollow of the Deep-sea Wave*, accompanied by seven short stories.

CHAPTER FOURTEEN

FALSE PROPHECY

Jacqueline Lichtenberg

Halloween is traditionally the time when the gates of the underworld are open to allow the dead to commune with the living. Gavriella however encounters another kind of underworld when she agrees to read the Tarot at a Halloween party. But when the reality of the moment is overlaid by the reality of the festival, can her divinatory skills be of any help to her? The seer who, like Thomas the Rhymer, has the 'tongue that can never lie' may be acclaimed and fêted, but may also be feared and hated. This love/hate relationship with the client is also the inheritance of the Tarot-reader with the gift of clear vision.

Bringing her Mazda to a stop at the red light, Gavriella Dean peered up at the ancient highway signs overhead barely lit by the street lamps. Route 59 East ahead. Route 9W South to the right.

Yes, this had to be the corner. With New York's crazy right-turn laws, she couldn't figure out if she could turn against the red light or not, so she sat there visualizing the Hanged Man, suppressing a touch of hysteria. She'd never read Tarot in public before, and to start at a Halloween costume party seemed – well, risky.

Thy will be done, she prayed, placing her destiny in the hands of God, and made the turn. Maybe she wouldn't find the house. Then she could just go home.

9W climbed and narrowed to a crumbling, two-way track lined with tumbledown businesses. Then she passed the sign that said THE NYACKS' HISTORICAL PRESERVATION AREA, and suddenly there were gorgeous Victorian homes on either side of the road, with carefully painted gingerbread, turrets, and roofed carriage porches on their sides.

THE HANGED MAN.

THE HERMIT.

THE LOVERS.

Ordinarily, she supposed, this area would be beautiful, especially when lit by the perfect full moon now climbing the sky. But many of the houses were decorated for Halloween, some whimsically, some sinisterly. The animated holos of ghosts, witches, and skeletons got to her, and she resisted closing her eyes as she passed them. But she'd been warned.

She started counting streets and landmarks according to her directions. Before she knew it, the land to her left dropped away and the road became a narrow ledge cut into the hillside, treetops and roof turrets poking up next to her car. Over them, she could see the Hudson river, and beyond, the dense lights of the city.

Dirt driveways snaked up the steep hillside on her right, and twisted down to the houses buried under the trees on her left. Racks of mailboxes were stationed at intervals. Some were decorated with jack-o'-lanterns or ghosts. She almost missed the one she was hunting for – under a holo of a red-eyed vampire bat. But, just beyond it, there was a line of cars drawn up against the cliff, their left tyres barely clear of the white line that edged the roadway. She tucked her Mazda in behind a Lincoln, and doused the lights.

She shouldered her bag, dragged the lace shawl of her makeshift witch's costume around her, and walked back to the stairs up to the house. The narrow stair was cut into the solid rock. There were modern lights along the treads and the banister, but the stairs looked more than a century old.

She put her head down and climbed, praying, *If You're sure this is what You want, okay.* She was visualizing the Hermit, staff and lantern lighting her climb to Wisdom, when feet scuffed to a stop beyond her nose, and a man gasped, 'Oh! Sorry!' and backed up the narrow stair.

Simultaneously, she backed down, barely stifling a yelp, and had to grab the banister. The stair treads were an odd height and worn unevenly. Suddenly, she was falling.

Hands closed over her arms and she was lifted back up the steps and set down on a landing edged with shrubbery on both sides. She'd never been lifted like that before; all hundred and seventy-seven pounds of her five-foot-two body just *moved*. It made her feel like a ballerina, beautiful and graceful, until she heard the man grunt with the effort as if he'd strained himself.

Heart pounding, she looked up at her benefactor, a slender young man in a Dracula costume with a rental tag showing at the collar. In one electric glance, she took in the blood-red satin-lined cape, archaic tuxedo, and pale white makeup on hands and face that was so well done, it didn't look like makeup at all. The moon glancing off his eyes had struck ruby highlights somehow. It absolutely made the outfit. 'Red contacts, right?' she gasped.

He laughed. It was a wonderfully rich sound. 'Right. I'm sorry I startled you. My name is Titus Shiddehara.'

'Gabby. Short for Gavriella. Gavriella Dean.' Her voice was choked and husky, and she thought she might faint.

'Here,' said Titus, drawing her through the bushes, 'come over here and catch your breath. It's still a long climb up to the house and witches shouldn't arrive out of breath.'

Against her better judgement, her feet followed him into the bushes which were so thick with vines that the wall of growth closed up behind her.

But then they were on a moonlit lawn under a gnarled oak that had to be a century old. Behind them, the windows of the house spilled out light, music and shrieks that turned to laughter. Behind the house, the hillside rose steeply, covered with trees and vines. The only exposed spot was a huge rock that stuck out of the hill, forming a kind of overlook. She could just discern the hint of a footpath that disappeared into the undergrowth, probably leading to the rock. She couldn't imagine why anyone would go up there. There was no retaining wall around the edge of the rock.

She surveyed the river and the city beyond. The velvet dark was sprinkled with jewels and presided over by the moon which made golden paths on the river. *Like a Tarot card*.

Titus said with restrained disapproval, 'I have to warn you the entire climb from here up to the house is trapped with fun-house tricks, some pretty realistic ones, too. Brace yourself, and don't get startled like that again.'

She stepped away to get a better look at him. 'You were leaving?' She'd arrived a quarter-hour early.

'I – didn't care for the atmosphere. The whole house is filled with things that pop out of closets or swoop down from the shadows of the high ceilings. And there are a few people doing drugs already.' He flashed her a smile. 'I don't suppose I could offer to take you to a movie, or something?'

He hadn't laid a finger on her since he'd dragged her into the bushes. 'I'm tempted. Doesn't sound like my kind of party, either. But I gave my word. I'm supposed to be reading Tarot to entertain the guests.' Tarot wouldn't work if they were doing drugs already, so she was really tempted.

'Do you read at a lot of parties?'

'No. I'm just doing this as a favour to my boss. I've been reading for other people for about a year, but not at parties.' She pulled the lace shawl up, wishing she'd come in a business suit instead of letting her sister talk her into the costume. At least she'd be warmer.

'Gabby, they've already got a lot of readers. I don't think they'd miss you.'

'Maybe I can get away early. But I really have to do a couple of hours at least. I did promise.'

There was a squirming discomfort in her stomach, a warning she was about to do something she'd regret. She never picked up strange guys. That was how women became police statistics.

But when she'd consulted the cards over coming to this party, the theme that ran through every layout was Hanged Man, Hermit, and Lovers; putting trust in the Higher Powers, following the path to Maturity, and facing temptations, or finding a real inner harmony through relationships. But there'd also been a number of Fives tangled through the whole issue, along with the Nine and Ten of Swords. Whatever was due to happen would hurt a lot. But she'd learned long since that challenges like that led to worthwhile triumphs.

'Well,' allowed Titus, 'in that case, I'll wait.' He guided

her back onto the stairs, warning her of hidden obstacles he'd tripped over when he'd discovered the secluded spot. They went up the long, long stair together, Titus warning her at each trap. She didn't tell him how much she appreciated his help, and then immediately regretted it when he delivered her to the door and vanished into the crowd.

Oddly enough, despite the cobwebs and skeletons decor, Gabby's queasy discomfort vanished also. *That man's the temptation I'm here to resist.* She could already tell that resisting wasn't going to be easy.

The host, the man who had financed her boss's venture into newspaper publishing, was standing in the entry foyer beside a real satin-lined, teak coffin wearing a fabulous Dracula costume, complete with appropriate dentition. But she'd never seen a Dracula with grey hair, spectacles, and an ample waistline before. *Well, why not?*

As she introduced herself, Gabby realized that Titus had lacked the fangs, but their host had omitted the contacts.

She'd been told there was to be a Dracula contest later. There were already ten or fifteen Draculas in the living room behind the man she was facing.

'Ms Dean?'

'Uh – yes sir?' The unmistakable odour of pot wafted through the stage-cobwebs. *Well, if it's just pot . . .*

'Please follow Mr Simon. He'll show you to the room we've prepared for you.' He intoned the words with silken menace, and laughed diabolically, then turned to the couple entering behind Gabby, Dracula-and-nightgowned-victim.

He was really enjoying the act, she realized, as she followed the man in the caterer's outfit. As she saw others wearing identical black jumpsuits with red cummerbunds and carrying white towels over their left arms, passing large trays among the guests, she realized he was a real waiter, not a costumed guest. *I'm way out of my class here*!

Installed in what had been a small bedroom, decorated now as a gypsy tent complete with little round table and crystal ball, she ordered a Virgin Mary, then cleared the crystal ball off the table. It was a real one, probably costing more than she made in a week as a features editor. She put it on the floor in the corner and tucked it behind a fold of the cloth which draped the walls. She discovered a small attic window and grunted it open a crack. The cramped room was already stuffy.

Then she saw the antique china bowl on a side table by the door. A huge sign over it, shaped like a hand raised in benediction, read, CROSS MY PALM WITH SILVER AND I'LL REVEAL YOUR FUTURE.

Oh-my-God!

She yanked the sign off the table so hard the whole table collapsed. She grabbed the bowl just in time, and discovered the table was just a folding cardboard parson's table draped with a round cloth. She set it up again and put the bowl back upside down.

A gypsy woman swirled into the room, beads rattling. Immediately, her hands went out to right the bowl. 'Cheesy little tables. You'd think a place like this could afford better! What happened to your sign?'

'Excuse me?' Gabby had no idea who the woman could be.

'I work next door here. Cynthia. Where's your sign? They did give you one?'

'Uh – look, I don't do this for money. Ever.'

Cynthia's whole demeanour changed. Gabby retreated a bit, sensing she'd offended the woman. Then Cynthia put one arm around her shoulders and said confidentially, 'Look, if you take that attitude, you'll undercut the trade. It makes us all look bad – especially if you're any good. Are you?'

'Well, my clients keep coming back . . .'

'So. You are good. Well. You know, it's all right to take money for a reading if it's the only way you can support yourself – which is the way it is for most of us here. And these kind of people – well. They're not going to listen to free advice. If they have to pay for it, what you tell them will make an impression. You do tell the truth, don't you?'

'Yes,' she answered uncertainly.

'You wouldn't want it ignored just because you sold it cheap?'

'No.'

'So. There. You see? That's settled. Where did you say that sign was?'

'I'll – uh – I'll take care of what needs to be done.' Summoning all the courage she'd ever owned, she ushered the woman out the door. People were milling around in the hall, comparing the readings they'd been given.

Cynthia disappeared into the throng, and Gabby snatched the little table and folded it up, hiding the bowl underneath the heap of material, hoping it would blend into the decor. Then she asked blessing and protection for her working space.

She *wouldn't* take money. She had a job – though she might not have tomorrow morning if she just picked up and left. She was behind in her car payments and had no idea how she'd scrape together next month's rent, but her teachers had warned her repeatedly of the dangers of going commercial.

'Are you reading?'

It was a woman with too much makeup and too little dress covering her hips. But other than that, she looked normal.

'Yes, I was about to start.'

The woman held her drink away and turned to display the red sequinned outfit. 'Like it? I'm the Virgin Victim of Dracula. *His* cape is lined with the same red sequins.'

'Oh. Very impressive.' She wondered how many 'virgin victims' the Draculas had brought. Gabby settled at the round table and spread out her silk reading cloth, then began shuffling her cards. 'Have you ever had a Tarot-reading before?' There was no alcohol on the woman's breath. At least there was a chance this one reading would work.

So the evening began. Before and after each reading, she had to explain that there was no charge, that if the reading proved of value, then the recipient could make a donation to their own favourite charity, but even that wasn't necessary. She got very tired of that speech.

Three clients and an hour later, she had to ask for a NO

SMOKING sign. After that, she fell into the natural trance in which she did her best reading, as the gestalt pattern of each card layout became perfectly clear. Words flowed from her, describing by analogy and anecdote, explaining by parables she originated on the spot, elaborating and embroidering on each card's inner meaning for those who would listen. And a moment after she'd picked up the cards to reshuffle, she had forgotten what she'd said.

The clients made little impression on her. They were patterns in the cards, classic problems in living life, layers and crosscurrents of power struggles in domestic affairs, knotty choices of vocation or job, serious quests for spiritual enlightenment.

At some point, she realized she needed to use two different decks, so she moved onto the floor where she could sit in lotus and spread out the work. Taking the most portentous card from the first layout as significator for a second reading, she used the deck she had drawn and coloured herself for the second reading. Comparing the two readings, she could penetrate the mists of the client's subconscious, and finally understand where the anguish was coming from.

'No, that's not what you want. That's what others want of you. What is it you, yourself, need?'

The client, a young, skinny woman dressed as a Dracula, broke into sobs. 'You're right! My God, you're right!'

Gabby looked up and realized she had a huge audience peering down at them. 'Somebody get a box of tissues.' Then she put her arm around the client and talked her back to composure. It took six tissues. She'd hit a nerve.

The onlookers had been friends of the client, most of them privy to the actual problem. Gabby, herself, didn't know and didn't want to know the personal details. 'It's all right to kibitz, and it's even good to watch if you've never seen this done before. All I can do is describe the general pattern of the seeker's current life crisis. I can't reveal anything really private. I can't foretell the future. I can only describe the decisions already made, and the options currently open. I can't even tell what's the best solution. All I

can do is help you analyse your problem in terms of the
value system inherent in the Tarot.'

'Can I go next?' asked someone.

'Certainly.' It was a young man in a Harlequin suit who
folded his long legs tailor-fashion and sat next to her.

After that, she lost track. The crowd around her never
thinned, and though many broke into astonished sobs
during the readings, there was never a lack of volunteers.
As usual with a group, the readings began to fall into a
pattern echoing the pattern of Hanged Man/Hermit/Lovers
laced with varying combinations of Fives and the themes of
the Nine and Ten of Swords. As the crowd around her had
heard her repeat the instructions to the seeker many times,
she eventually left off announcing them.

It was close to midnight, and she had just organized the
people waiting into a line, promising to get to them in order
when one of the waiters brought her another Virgin Mary
and announced, 'Ms Dean, it's time for your break.' He
raised his voice. 'She's entitled to half an hour now.'

Suddenly, there was a space around her, and contrite
murmurings of how tired she must be. Very quickly, the
room emptied. Actually, she felt no strain. She was, however, stiff from sitting so long, and she discovered she'd
been sitting in the cold draught from the window. It felt
good to get up and move. And then she saw the table by
the door.

The bowl was back in place, and it was half full of
currency. She saw a lot of Tens and Twenties, and even a
few crisp Hundreds. It looked like more than a month's
salary.

What am I going to do? Not even wanting to touch it,
she pushed out into the crowded hall where people were
milling about or waiting in line at the other doors. Some of
the Draculas now wore prize-ribbons pinned to their lapels.

She found the lavatory when someone came out. She
went in, glad that her makeup, wallet and necessaries were
in a leather pouch tied to her waist, part of the medieval
flavour of the witch's costume. Refreshed, she emerged to
find their host was working up and down the hall, making

sure everyone was happy. He seemed to be enjoying himself immensely.

She plastered herself against the wall to let him pass, but he spotted her. 'Ah, Ms Dean, you've become quite a hit!' He reached into his breast pocket and came out with an elegantly printed envelope which he presented to her. 'Your fee. Only a token compared to what you've been collecting.'

Pushing the envelope away, she shook her head. He drew her hand up and curled it around the envelope. It was a thick envelope. 'I'm so grateful to Tom for getting you to come. You're worth more than any of the others. I won't forget the favour.' With a raised eyebrow and a nod, he was gone into the crowd.

Clutching the envelope, stunned, she felt large, strong hands come onto her shoulders, kneading the tension she hadn't realized was there. She stifled a yelp, and spun to find Titus behind her. 'Oh! You shouldn't *do* that!'

'I think you need it. You've been working harder than anyone, and with far better results. Ready to leave yet?'

'Oh, I can't.' *This man is the temptation I have to resist.* But there had never been all that many personable men interested in her.

'Listen, Gabby,' he said leaning over to speak softly into her ear as he worked on her back, 'some people here are dealing. This is a Wall Street crowd, very high class, very elegant, but still, the place could be raided. I don't want to get caught in anything like that and neither do you.'

'Dealing,' she repeated, stricken. She turned and noted inanely that the rental tag was gone from his collar.

She wanted to grab her Tarot bag and go. It was plausible that someone here would be dealing. She'd done many readings indicative of substance abuse. Still, she hadn't seen it with her own eyes, and this man was the temptation she had to resist. He'd certainly found her most sensitive button, too. He was just the sort of man no sane woman would get involved with; so sexy she could hardly resist, so insightful he found her buttons before they'd even had a single date, and so manipulative he'd push those buttons shamelessly. What sort of marriage could that lead to?

Besides, she didn't want to get married. She was a career woman on the way up. Wasn't she?

'Titus,' she said, knowing she should keep it formal but unable to remember his last name, 'I *can't*. I promised at least ten more people.'

'You should make them come to your office.'

'What?'

'Good psychologists don't give away free samples.'

'Oh, no. You've got it all wrong.' She explained she was only a features editor for an advertiser distributed free to home-owners in Bergen County, just across in New Jersey.

He eyed the knot of people beginning to collect outside her door and the fervent, animated discussions developing among them. 'I'd say you're in the wrong line of work.'

'Titus, people always behave this way about the Tarot because the results run so completely counter to everything we think we know about reality. But anyhow, Tarot works. Come on, try it, you'll see.'

This time she took his hand and tugged him through a barrier, not shrubbery but people. It parted before them and closed behind them. As she entered the room, she tossed the envelope into the bowl, noticing that there was as much in there now as there had been when she'd left the room. She realized she'd vaguely hoped somebody would steal it.

The floor had been cleaned up, and her things were set up on the table again. She shrugged. She had, out of habit, put all her cards away and wrapped them, so there was no harm done. Titus went with her as far as the client's seat, but as she moved around the table, he balked.

'No, no. This is ridiculous.'

'Suspend your disbelief,' she suggested.

'I'm an astrophysicist in New York for a convention. This just doesn't fit my concept of reality. Not at all.'

Maybe that's what's so strange about his aura. She realized the queasy feeling was back again. Perhaps it meant he was a heavily repressed psychic, or a deeply disturbed person. There was no denying the rich sexual attraction she felt, but it would be a bad mistake to get involved, especially

knowing how incompatible they were. Besides, if he was
not from around here, she'd never see him again after
tonight. She was glad she'd declined to go out with him.

Then she looked up at him, and he was looking down at
her as if she were beautiful. She had to say something or
she'd seem to be staring. 'Why aren't you wearing a prize
ribbon? You're certainly the best Dracula I've seen.'

She was immediately embarrassed at what her mouth had
said of its own accord, but he responded levelly, 'I didn't
expect to stay for the contest, but I'm glad I did.'

'Oh? why?' She was enjoying just being near him and
despite the cluster of people politely hanging back by the
door, she wanted to prolong the experience.

'I hadn't realized so many more Draculas would turn up.'

It wasn't the flirtatious response she'd expected. 'Are you
a connoisseur of Draculas?'

'No, I was just looking for someone. He hasn't come,
and the atmosphere is even worse now. Are you sure you
wouldn't like to go somewhere for coffee? There's a
Denny's up on Route 59.'

She was ready to go simply because he hadn't invited her
to a bar or a dance hall. *Temptation.* 'Titus, I hate to point
this out, but I'm part of that distasteful atmosphere. I don't
think you'd really care for the company of someone who
interprets the world in terms of occult principles.'

'No, no!' Leaning closer, he said confidentially, 'The
atmosphere I referred to was the alcohol and drugs, and the
people who need that to have fun or make fortunes trading
on others' weaknesses. It is dangerous to stay here.'

'Then I guess you'd better go. I did promise.'

He withdrew. She was overwhelmed with a sudden regret
and had to grit her teeth not to call out to him. He paused
and turned back to her, frowned, then said, 'I'll just watch
you work for a while. Okay?'

He wants to protect me! It wasn't the way most men
reacted to her, and it felt oddly thrilling to be so valued.
But then she took another look at him as he turned to
inspect the crowd. Sideways, he looked like Frank Sinatra
in the oldest movies – so thin a strong wind would blow

him over. Mafia Muscle wouldn't even notice him. But even that cynical observation couldn't erase the thrill warming her inside.

Then a black woman in a diaphanous ghost costume complete with clanking chains came forward. Gabby remembered the costume and began shuffling.

The work picked up as it had left off, and she forgot all about Titus. Occasionally, though, as one client left and another sat down, there would be a break in the wall of bodies through which she glimpsed someone putting money in her bowl. She began to wonder if she could take it all home. Maybe, if it was still there at the end of the evening, that meant she was properly entitled to it. After all, she'd never done so many readings in a row, nor worked so hard at them – nor had she ever been so fiendishly accurate.

She began to enjoy the work in a new way. A peculiar gratification swept through her each time she spread out the cards and drew forth a precise statement of the problem. At some point, the queasiness denoting Titus's presence vanished but she hardly noticed. She'd hit a breakthrough in her skills. For the first time in her life, she felt she was worth any amount of money, praise or respect offered her. And she saw that as she became more accurate, her clients left more money in the bowl. She could see a mound of green paper heaping above the rim.

Aware of the spellbound awe of her audience, she began to strive to increase the effect. Occasionally, now, she began to miss. One client simply could not make sense of what she said, and, with another, she found the cards would not synthesize into a meaning. But even when she had to give up, disappointing a client, others came forward eagerly.

They were on the third box of tissues, and the crowd had thinned, the dull roar of noise from downstairs having abated significantly, when five burly Draculas stalked into the room. Three of them spread out as one approached the empty client's chair. Unobtrusively, people drifted out of the room, but Gabby hardly noticed when the last of them left her alone with the four men.

Through the open window, she heard doors clattering

and cars starting up, people laughing and calling to each
other.

The man before her reached into his breast pocket, fumbling with the ribbon and pendant of a replica of a Royal
Order, and brought out six one-thousand dollar bills. He
placed three of the bills on the table before her. 'It seems
you can actually do this witch stuff. So tell me what's going
to happen at 4 a.m. today, and the other three bills are
yours, too.' He fingered the bills he still held.

*I could be completely out of debt. I could afford to go
back to school.* But she said, 'The Tarot can't predict the
future.'

He leaned closer, looming over her. 'Now you and I
both know that's not true. You've already done it accurately
for several people tonight.' He exuded the same kind of
quiet menace that her boss and other powerful men did. It
didn't mean he was the one who was dealing. It could be
about some insider trading on the Tokyo exchange.

She swallowed hard, her mouth dry. *Suppose I can't do
it? Or suppose I get it all wrong?*

He moved the deck of cards in front of her. 'Do it.'

Hands shaking, she shuffled the cards and set them down
for him to cut, muttering the instructions with her mouth
while her mind was frantically invoking protection. The
familiar routine steadied her hands and the shroud of the
reading trance settled over her. She snapped each card face
up on the table in a Celtic Cross. The pattern coalesced as
crisp and clear as any she'd seen that night.

Devil crossed by the Tower, with the Moon beneath and
the Page of Swords behind.

*He's dealing drugs and there's a spy in his organization
who's set him up. Violence, shocking revelations.*

She exposed the Five Swords above, and Judgement
Reversed in front of him. Nine of Wands Reversed in the
seventh position, Five Pentacles in the eighth, Six Wands
Reversed in the ninth, and in the tenth, World Reversed.

*He fears failure, is beset on all sides, is pitied and hates
it, knows he's beaten. Deep down inside, he wants to be
caught, but is terrified of what will happen then.*

All at once, she realized her mouth had been babbling words, and she clamped it shut as one final word exploded into her consciousness. *Suicide. If he fails, he plans to kill himself!*

She found herself gazing into hard, black eyes set in a face gone suddenly pale beneath a Florida tan.

What did I say aloud? She had no idea.

'Who?' he demanded. 'Who's the police spy?'

Her throat emitted strangled noises.

His hand slapped the table, bouncing the cards. 'Who?'

She forced her eyes back to the cards, expecting the images to be ten disconnected entities devoid of meaning. But the story was still clear. 'A young woman you admire and trust, the one person you'd never suspect.' *Oh, God! Why did I say that?*

He subsided into his chair, shocked wonder suffusing his face. 'Of course! I should have known. All the clues were there and I couldn't see it.' His attention snapped back to the cards. 'What will happen if I just don't show?'

She swallowed and gritted her teeth, wishing desperately for Titus to walk in; then, awash in relief that he wasn't there, she said, 'I don't know. How could I possibly know? I can't foretell the future.' Her voice broke into a squeak.

'*Look* at the cards. Tell me!' He was sweating. When she didn't move, he slapped the second three bills down on top of the first and reached into his breast pocket again to pull forth another three. He waved them at her as if she were an informant holding out for a higher bribe.

She wanted the money. She suddenly realized she'd been wrong all evening. The challenge wasn't to resist Titus. The challenge was to resist abuse of power. Overwhelmed with shame, she recalled the ruddy glow of pride she'd felt when the crowd around her had murmured in awe. And there had been greed, too, as she saw the money being heaped into her bowl.

When she lowered her eyes again, the cards were just bits of coloured paper. It would serve her right if she could never read again. She shook her head. 'I don't know. Nobody can know. If I said something, it would be a lie.' She pushed

the money back across the table at him. 'I was only guessing, and I was probably wrong.'

He sat back and stared at her, stone-faced.

She gave the money another little shove, and began collecting her cards.

On the periphery of her vision, she saw his hand move,
flashing a heavy gold ring and watch. The next moment,
hard hands gripped her wrists and she was yanked to her
feet.

One of the men slammed the door of the room, and,
simultaneously, a hand clamped over her mouth and she
was pinned against a tall, hard body. 'She knows too much!'

'No. She's a charlatan like all the others. She was just
guessing. It's not hard. Most everyone here knew we had
a shipment coming in tonight.'

'Well, if she didn't learn it from her cards, she certainly
knows it all now. We have to make sure of her.'

Gabby's heart slammed against her ribs. She could hardly
breathe, but she prayed with all her might. *Are You really
sure this is what You want? I'm sorry for what I did. I've
learned a lesson. Isn't that enough? Do I have to die, too?*
And aside, in her mind, the thought came, *Oh, Titus!*

'You're right,' said the one she'd been reading for. 'Take
care of it.' He was peering out the little window which had
a view of the steep slope behind the house. 'Up there. See
the rock? Drop her over the edge of that. Get some liquor
into her first. Regrettable accident.' He turned. 'Anybody
seen a phone on this floor?'

He went out and before she knew it, Gabby was wrapped
around and tied securely by her sister's shawl. Somebody's
silk handkerchief was tied around her mouth. That hurt.
Her mouth was already dry, her voice husky with over-
use. But she struggled anyway. She managed to kick the
money bowl over as they dragged her out of the room. It
made a satisfying crash. But nobody came. Nobody noticed
as they carried her down the narrow, twisting back staircase,
and past the dark and deserted kitchen. The fifth man, the
one she'd been reading for, joined them and led the way
out the back door.

Vines and branches slapped her face, cold dew mixing with the hot tears that dripped from her eyes, trailing backwards up her forehead because she was upside down.

She found herself being carried up the steep path she'd spotted from the front garden. Where it passed under the trees, the underbrush had been cut back forming a tunnel. A very dark tunnel. She struggled, hoping the man carrying her would trip and fall. Her moving weight did cause him to stagger. He slung her to the ground and slapped her face. 'Stop it, or we'll all have at you before we dump you.'

She glanced at the leader, who was carrying a large bottle of liquor. He seem disinterested. *Well, it would take up some time. Anything for a reprieve.* It was a nice, logical thought but when the man shouldered her body once more, she couldn't bring herself to further defiance. *What's wrong with me? People* survive *rape*!

Before she could talk herself into it, she was rolled onto a cold, hard surface that was almost smooth. It sloped to one side and she rolled involuntarily, which brought the panorama of the Hudson River into view. There were fewer city lights now, and moonlight was coming from the west. But it was still breathtaking. *Oh, Titus!*

When she looked to see what her captors were doing, she found them passing the bottle. The last one wiped his mouth and let out a gusty sigh. 'Too good to waste on her.'

'Let's get this over with,' said the leader as if he really didn't want to kill her. 'Take the gag off and hold her mouth open.'

One of them moved behind her and propped her up, cutting the gag and tilting her chin back. 'Pour.'

Another man held the neck of the bottle up to her mouth. 'Drink. It'll make this easier on you.'

Liquor gurgled into her mouth. She gathered it in her cheek, and when the man holding her clamped his fingers over her nose, she sprayed the stuff out hard. Even without swallowing it, the fumes triggered a coughing fit.

Someone slapped her face.

'Take it easy,' said the leader. 'We don't want to leave any evidence of a fight. I want this done perfectly.'

The one holding her head shifted his grip and one hand crept down her back towards her buttocks. 'Drink, girl, or you'll get it right in there!'

She yelped and surged away from his stiff finger, glad of the layers of thick skirt she wore.

Both hands came back to her head again. 'Pour!'

Her head was forced back. She saw the five men in vampire costumes silhouetted against the stars as they bent over her. Higher up the sheer mountain, a very large oak leaned out above the rock. There was no wind, but the branches shook as she fastened her eyes on them and tried to pray. *I said do what You will with me. I meant it. Honest.*

Deep in the shadow, there was a figure hanging from the biggest branch. It looked human.

Without warning, the oak heaved and a bloodcurdling scream split the air. The man holding her jerked back, gasping, and the others turned. There above them, blotting out the sky, was a huge bat with red eyes and needle-sharp teeth gleaming in the moonlight. Teeth and talons dripped thick, red blood. As it fell on them, engulfing them in a putrid stench, it screamed again.

She could feel the gust of wind from its powerfully beating wings. The sense of horror that washed through her made her previous terror seem like a silly illusion.

The man behind her dropped her. The liquor bottle fell and broke. The creature screamed again. In a mad scramble, the men ran. And *something* was settling down to eat her.

Without transition it seemed, Titus was bending over her, rubbing her wrists and patting her face. 'Gabby? Gabby, are you all right? Wake up. Come on. You can do it. You only fainted. It's all right now.'

She was untied and Titus's Dracula cape was laid over her like a blanket. 'I must have passed out. You'll never believe what I thought I saw.'

'What did you see?'

'It – ' No, he'd never believe it. *She* didn't believe it. 'Where did you come from?'

'The tree. I jumped down yelling, and those men ran.'

She struggled to sit up. 'Men. It wasn't a nightmare. It

really happened. They were going to kill me. You were right. There were dealers here.' That much was real, but the rest – the whole house had been thick with smoke. God alone knew what sort of mixture she had in her blood by now. Small wonder she'd hallucinated.

'Can you walk, Gabby? We'd better get out of here. They might come back.'

She got up and took off his cape. It was too long. No matter what she did with it, she'd trip on it. 'Come on. My car's out front,' she said, trying to sound brave. She doubted she even sounded sane. *Shock. It's shock.*

He took her hand and led her down the dark, twisting trail as if it were broad daylight.

There were still lights on in the house. 'Titus, I'm not going back for my things. Where's your car?'

'Don't worry about me. Just get yourself out of here.'

They picked their way around the house as quietly as they could, then dashed down the long flights of steps to 9W. Panting, afraid they'd been heard, she paused, one hand groping in her belt pouch for her car keys. 'Titus, how can I thank you for saving my life?'

'By not dying now. Are you sure you can drive?'

She held out the car key. It wasn't shaking. Yet. 'Sure. They didn't get any liquor into me. But what about you?'

He walked her to the Mazda. 'Don't worry about me. Just get yourself away. I have my own transportation.'

As she unlocked the door, he opened it and eased her into the driver's seat. He leaned over and brushed her forehead with his lips. 'Go!' He closed the door quietly.

Feeling beautiful again, she started the motor and eased away from the wall, catching sight of him in her right side mirror. The red-lined cape was billowing in the wind like wings, and a stray bit of moonlight made his eyes glow red. She thought she saw a shimmering aura around him that throbbed with power. It had to be an optical illusion. It wasn't at all like any aura she'd ever seen before.

She shuddered.

Oh, come on! Don't be ridiculous. The combination of

passive drug-smoking with liquor fumes had warped her brain.

'*I jumped down yelling and those men ran.*' Sure. *And if I believe that, I'm crazy, not stoned.* Fifty yards away and picking up speed, she glanced into her rear view mirror again, suddenly unable to understand why she had believed it when he'd said it. Why had she scoffed at the thinness of his profile while forgetting that he'd lifted her up the steps quite easily? And what had he been *doing* in the tree? She was a reporter. She didn't fail to ask obvious questions like that.

She was also not stupid. She couldn't fail to see the obvious answer; he was a real vampire.

Her skin crawled and she clamped her chattering teeth together, determined to get home before she had any kind of reaction. At least she was headed south into New Jersey. She'd pick up Route 4 at the G W Bridge and be home in no time. Then she could shake and cry until dawn.

Vampires disintegrated at dawn and reality returned full force. *That's what I need. A dose of reality.*

Titus was probably the police spy she'd thought was the Page of Swords. That was why he was able to handle those men so well. He was trained for this kind of thing, and he just wanted her out of there so the bust would go down smoothly. She'd see the whole thing on Eye Witness News in the morning.

And she'd never see him or anyone from that party again, including her boss. She'd call in her resignation in the morning, borrow some money from her mother, take off for California.

She clung to that resolution all the way home.

Jacqueline Lichtenberg Born 1942. She won early acclaim in the seventies for her *Star Trek* fan fiction, the Kraith Series which gained her a nomination for the Best Fan Writer Hugo. She is primary author of the paperback, *Star Trek Lives!* as well as the founder of the *Star Trek Welcommittee*. Her second Sime/Gen novel won the 1978 Galaxy Award for spirituality in science fiction. Her other books include *Molt Brother* and *City of a Million Legends*, as well as the *Dushau Trilogy*, the first volume of which won her the 1985 Romantic Times Award for Best Science Fiction Writer. She says, 'I enjoy blending romance with a touch of the occult and a strong science motif, to ask hard questions about life's most basic relationships.' She is past Chair of the Science Fiction Writers of America Speaker's Bureau, and in her spare time, she gives Tarot and writing workshops; attends Star Trek, SF, and esoteric conventions; all while pursuing studies such as vampires, Arthurian legend, Astrology, Cabbalah, *Star Trek*, *Blake's Seven*, and *Doctor Who*.

CHAPTER FIFTEEN

THE DEVIL'S PICTUREBOOK

R J Stewart

When the Tarot – that arch creation of the Devil – becomes an instrument of New Age good will and personal growth, then there's the devil to pay in Hell. In this distorted reflection of consumer society, the Devils PI has a hard job to unruffle his Infernal Master's self-esteem. That cunning little pack of cards may include his Master's portrait and many other hellish devices for subverting and repressing the masses unfortunately striving towards goodness, but it just doesn't have the kick it used to have. Can His Infernal Majesty come up trumps and ruin the day?

The Devil was worried; this was apparent by the frozen lower half of His current body, in use for several timeless durations. Many of the lesser lords and princes of darkness, demons and imps, fiends, incubi and succubi, knew only too well how to read such diabolical body language. They saw, read, and responded by burying themselves in far corners of distant worlds. This infernal exodus left the Devil relatively unattended. Indeed, in royal courtly terms He was virtually alone, having no entity in His presence other than the customary background entertainment of renegade transforming elementals, His personal assistant imp (known as the PI) and various devolving archetypes of corruption.

These few, numbering dozens rather than the usual thousands, were His sole attendants. Their meagre numbers were supplemented only by occasional prurient fantasizing tourists, hurling their imaginations blindly into the infernal dimensions through the use of sexual obsessions, fetishistic masturbation, orgies or psychedelic drugs. But they hardly counted, for while the Devil saw them flutter frail as moths towards His throne, they were not able to see Him . . .

THE DEVIL

THE FOOL

flying blind as they did. No, His only real court consisted of His PI. There was an ancient tradition in the infernal dimensions, ancient even in a realm where time was counted in the lifetimes of galaxies, that the PI to the Arch-fiend was always the least intelligent of imps; it was therefore this creature who completely failed to grasp that ice from the waist down was not, in any way, a promising condition or state of diabolical manifestation. So he chose, of course, to emulate contemporary humanity in his opening mode of speech on that fateful occasion.

'Hi, Boss,' chirped the PI, waving a natty tartan phallus. 'What's with the chilled gonads today?' There was a long long silence, filled with vibrations of devouring emptiness and despair. Many sub-dimensions ceased to exist, and two planets engaged upon a promising long-term war with one another accidentally obliterated their shared sun, spoiling a complex plan of suffering and hatred that had been organically, one might even say holistically, channelling its way out into their societies for several centuries. The PI, blissfully unaware of his high-risk no-gain situation, stuck out his tongue. This lengthy organ terminated in a thick legal-size notepad; the PI unscrewed the tip of his phallus, and manoeuvred it until the ball-point pen concealed within the glans was poised over the first page . . .

'So what's for dictation today, Your Diabolics?' The Devil sighed slightly, and turned His hairy head towards the imp; a vast wind roared through the multitudinous caverns of Hell; a flurry of gaudy hot-air balloons, filled with orgiastic champagne drinkers, was swept away high overhead, vaporizing in the blast. The Devil was 3.333^3 times greater in outer size than His PI, yet paradoxically (for such is the nature of demonic physics) he only appeared to be three times as long, wide, high, or deep. This relative paradoxical appearance included the Iced Parts to which the imp, happily oblivious of offence, had so wittily referred.

'*Tarot*,' murmured the Devil, and even as He spoke the ice crackled and seemed to warp itself further around His muscular firmly sculpted epitome of a male waist. Most of the denizens of Hell had by now fled into very obscure worlds, planes, states, or dimensions indeed. A very large number were holding a party inside a pre-cooked ready-to-microwave TV dinner in New York city, for their knowledge of metaphysics was profound. The frozen tray of non-nutritious colourings, flavourings, additives and starch was close to the current manifest *state* of their Master, yet was so far removed from His actual *awareness*, that the demons partying therein were confident of both safety and privacy. The old purloined-letter trick was a well-established technique in Hell.

'Tarot,' said the Devil again, and the PI licked his penis and dutifully wrote 'R-O-T-A' in large clumsy letters. The Devil laid a black searing claw upon the notepad-tongue, shrivelling it away to ash. The PI scratched his buttocks, having felt some pain.

'Listen and do not take notes,' murmured the Devil. 'We will have instead an on-going psycho-dramatic encounter, a kind of in-depth interaction session to bring to the surface of our co-communication our true understanding and hidden feelings concerning Tarot.' By now even the PI was beginning to feel uneasy, and made a serious attempt to upgrade his conversation.

'But Tarot . . . I thought Tarot was one of our best sales, Boss. I mean it's ubikwy . . . ubiquidy . . . everywhere! It's trendy, it swings, it's bursting at the seams with vagueness, confusion, time- and energy-consuming meaninglessness. So what's wrong with it? It's perfect!'

The Devil relaxed a little, and some of the ice evaporated into super-heated steam, revealing His lean arrogant manly hips. Sometimes, He mused, it was indeed useful to slow One's rate of consciousness to a low level that was not far above that of humanity; hence the invaluable tradition of having a very stupid PI. Maybe the Tarot problem could be solved upon a crude human level rather than upon any abstract metaphysical plane.

'That same perfection, oh insignificant speck of bacteria-infested dung, oh cuddlesome deadly plague, is the problem to which we must address ourselves.' The Devil waited while his PI unravelled this statement. 'Tarot has indeed been very successful,' he continued, after a generous pause, 'it is, as you said, ubiquitous in the human worlds, and in many other worlds also. It spreads, like soft margarine, even as we speak.' The Devil seldom failed to mention soft margarine during one of His elucidatory speeches . . . He considered it to be one of His better inventions.

The PI was beginning to attune to the dynamics of the in-depth encounter now, and with practised ease reformed his shape into that of a human white Anglo-Saxon twentieth-century prime-of-life male. It was one of his favourite short-term forms, and would surely be helpful with this current work situation. With hardly a moment's deliberaton, he chose to be a popular record company director, thus gaining the perfect combination of rapacious greed and vacuous stupidity required by his Master. It felt apt for the moment, seemed intuitively right. 'But if Tarot is so good, Your Nadir-ness, why is it so bad?'

'Because,' whispered the Devil, 'they have been tampering with it.' The word *tampering* had many deep disapproving negative undertones; it was uttered slowly and musically, it resonated of interference, folly, overreaching dangerous insight and terrible, terrible risk on the part of the tamperers. Even as it was whispered towering columns of molten slag showered redly about the Infernal Throne, their fall liberating the half-finished conceptual forms of several electronic labour-saving multi-purpose low-cost energy-conscious designer colour-matched devices that would soon manifest in the human world to wreak their trivializing havoc.

The Devil smiled paternally as the forms floated away, and continued, 'Tarot, as it is understood today, was My personal invention. A truly Diabolical Conception . . . The Devil's Picturebook. For the first few centuries it was designed merely to titillate, to underpin some of My better projects manifested by My operatives within state religions . . . a good little suppressive propagandist toy. Then, of course, it was upgraded to a more potent level for the twentieth century . . . but now . . .' He paused and the ice crackled and howled, freezing almost up to his polished pectorals, masking the view of those excitingly inverted muscles and prominent ribs.

'So let me get this right,' said the PI briskly, crossing his neat tailor-made trouser legs to reveal bright yellow silk socks with cheeky red clock patterns, ostentatiously and artily visible above his hand-made brown leather brogues. 'Tarot has been . . . ah . . . *changed* in some way?'

'Exactly, oh classic stereotype of misplaced mediocrity. That shape does you credit today, little maggot. We might even find you some marginal non-elected role in a Western government; how are you on redundant skills like riding a unicycle while encouraging underlings to collect garbage? Not ready for that one yet? Ah well . . . listen and respond . . . go with your feelings, let your intuitions speak out and your body move with them. The infernal dimensions of consciousness and power originated this mockery of a communicative technique, so let's use it to the fullest. It should put us closely in tune with the type of sham human awareness that we seek to maintain in a state of desirable corruption and bewilderment.

'Now, to business: Tarot was part of My two-pronged attack upon humanity, for whom I have always had an affectionate dislike. High technological progress, or rather an illusion of progress through the domination of pointless technology, was to be fused inseparably with a lowering of the imaginative faculties and an increasing trivialization of general consciousness. Tarot was supposed to be a major tool of the consciousness part of My plan. Indeed, it progressed so well that after the nineteenth century (measuring on that delightful wonderful time scale which has helped us all so much) I stopped deputizing demons to overlook Tarot. The absurd Tarot books and Tarot classes were already starting, and by the middle of the twentieth century Tarot was already so popularized and trivialized that it needed no direct *channelling* (ah how I love that term) from Me at all.'

Here the Devil paused, remembering that in encounter sessions one must be overly demonstrative and superficially caring of one's partners, except when engaged in screaming aggressive egocentric tantrums. The PI opened the top of his neatly barbered curly head and drew out a bright white-and-red vodaphone. His clean pink fingers flurried over the keys and he murmured what sounded like Stock Market jargon into the sanitized mouthpiece.

The Devil nodded in approval at this mockery of a shadow of a fantasy. It told Him, through simple and unmistakable body language, that His assistant was really beginning to address the problem in a meaningful and potentially maturing manner. The Devil began to feel slightly more relaxed; he did so enjoy inter-active psycho-drama wherever and whenever it occurred. Now, however, was the moment of truth that could be withheld no longer. As the vodaphone was returned, and the PI lowered the top of his head deftly back into place, the Devil spoke in His loudest tone yet, marginally above a mellifluous whisper:

'But the ongoing situation has been subtly changed some-how. Humans have been sifting through Tarot, using their regrettably regenerative imaginations for those very pur-poses which we have worked long and hard to eliminate. They have, in fact, started to change it *back*.' This last word was uttered with such potency that far away in a distant democracy a battery of top-secret unverifiable laser-bearing missiles melted to bubbling slag in their underground silo.

The Devil coughed in slight embarrassment, but con-tinued, 'They, or even more infuriatingly someone unname-able working through them or even *with* them, have pen-etrated to the very origin, the heart of Tarot. They have begin to use it for storytelling, for . . . *Creation Myths*.'

These terrible words, spoken at almost normal verbal level, caused the PI to blush a brilliant green over his perfect human complexion, and forced him to cover his ears with his well-manicured fingers. Both Arch- and minor fiend sat in silence for a timeless long and short time while the resonances of that terrible phrase worked their way through the infinite caverns of Hell.

The Devil seemed ready to enter into one of His deep introspective fugues, of the kind that lasted for thousands of solar years and caused many tedious administrative problems in Hell.

The PI spoke up, greatly daring, 'So what do we do, Boss? How do we see our way clear to an on-going operative fully implemented and efficiently staffed non-unionized re-pollution of Tarot? Ah, um, human-wise, if you follow my drift.'

'Well,' murmured the Devil, and with this seed sound, this word of power combining both music and intellect, emotion and higher conceptual form, a huge pit revolved into being directly beneath His throne. The throne floated steadily, and after some furious flickering and sizzling, was lit by hundreds of garish multi-coloured fairy-lights which flashed irregularly on and off, spelling out a series of apparently trivial messages such as 'Happy Christmas' or 'Have a nice day.' The black void simpered and giggled beneath, as it should. No mystery or glory in Hell. The Devil flexed his power-packed biceps, and paused to admire the effect of the lights rippling across his oiled skin. He never tired of reading the blurred reflections of those messages as they flashed backwards upon the surface of his own body. They were the greatest sigils of power available for demonic direct action (also known as DDA)in the human world, and they held untold promise.

'The current situation,' said the Devil, 'is what we might well term delicate. We have a satisfying plethora of trivializers on one hand, yet their excellent work is being undermined by gangs of pernicious creativists and storytellers on the other.' As He spoke the Devil raised first His right hand, then His left, showing where the positive and negative polarities of the situation were symbolically and magically located.

'But pardon me, Sir, if I am out of order here,' said the PI, really beginning to get inside his role. 'Surely we want trivializers, we want variant Tarot decks . . . you know, the New Age and all that sort of thing which we start off every century or so? Surely we need things like the Channellers' Tarot, The Tarot of the Jolly Green Giant, The Cybernetic Engineers' Tarot, the Geneticists' Tarot,

The Computer Programmers' program of Tarot programs for programming PC's . . . the Tarot of the Muppets, Tarot for pleasure and profit at no personal risk, Tarot for holistic baking and knitting, Tarot made easy for the way you live today . . .'

The Devil raised a long gilded fingernail, deeply etched with arcane symbols that held the secret illimitable power of utter meaninglessness in all possible worlds. The PI stopped in mid-flow, and unzipped his trouser fly, pulling out a personal mini-computer. He waited for his Master to speak, and even as the Devil replied, he pressed keys rapidly, and attentively studied the glowing screen.

His Master spoke slowly and almost with emotion: 'Some of these meddlers are even producing amended Tarot packs altering or even altogether removing My Image . . . and that certainly does not help us in any way . . . it's heresy, almost blasphemy.'

The PI pressed *Enter* by a neat little contortion, and spoke up, full of supportive warm vibrant communicative and sympathetic tones. 'I see by these new figures that, despite our very best efforts, we have to admit that some of these anti-demonic variants in modern Tarot are actually approaching a certain degree of usefulness.' The word 'useful' was not spoken often in Hell, at least not unless it was a lie. For a fraction of a nano-second even the Devil was taken aback, then he smiled with one corner of his lower lip.

'You are doing well, little virus. We may make something truly negative out of you yet.'

The PI glowed with inverted pleasure, and almost lost his role-playing shape as a large gilded and tasselled breast thrust its presence through his executive jacket. He pinched it between finger and thumb, and it exploded with a pleasant stench.

The full effect of the Devil's ultra-dynamic body could be seen now, the polychromatic wash of the fairy lights around His throne highlighting every contour of His perfect shape. A shower of laser discs, replete with corrupt data, fell upwards from the void beneath towards the human world; a flock of genetically altered sheep manifested through a distant cavern wall, prior to appearing as the merest hint of a formula in the sleeping brain of an influential bio-chemist. They bleated mournfully before fading, like a clarion announcing the return of Hell to smooth running and abnormal operation. The PI knew that they had groped blindly but successfully towards an on-going, thoroughly creative, totally and warmly human solution to an apparently insurmountable problem.

The knowledge that a conclusion was near, a statement of intent, a summation, made him tremble with expectation. There was only one thing that satisfied him more than encounter therapy, and that was the theory of evolution. Perhaps . . . perhaps that, too, could be worked into the final solution of the Tarot problem. He wriggled with anticipation, and then remembered that all the good supportive healthy signs of infernality would be instantly picked up and recognized by the potentially manipulative hosts in absentia. They would shortly return to the Infernal Throne Chamber, and his moment of personal triumph might yet be snatched from him. He fought hard to retain the human-executive simulacrum which had served him so well. His lightweight tweed suit momentarily turned into pink nylon, while his socks flowed into a muddy swirling pattern that did him no credit at all, and spoke not of unique individuality and success, but of moist hours in greasy launderettes. He gripped hard upon the form, summoning depths of energy previously unavailable to him; there was an inner feeling of tearing, of breakthrough, and he succeeded in reassembling perfectly, even down to his crocodile-leather Filofax.

Even as the PI wrestled his way into a raising of consciousness and groped towards integration, the distant party in New York heard the bleating of genetically altered sheep, and came to a hurried end. A proliferation of admiring demons, demonesses, and powers of darkness rapidly appeared, some still dripping monosodium glutamate, and commenced applauding and smiling around the rim of the great circular pit beneath their Master's throne. But first they uttered the obligatory 'oohs' and 'aahs' at the display of tawdry lights and messages. They waited suavely in postures of approval, as the Devil finally gathered Himself, displaying His muscle groups one by one, to declare a policy, a plan of action.

'Let it be thus,' He said quietly, and the last of the ice vanished, revealing His bulging thighs and firm well-developed calves and ankles. Several demons cuddled and coaxed the smiling PI in a great show of sharingness and supportive empathy; they knew only too well that the ending of the problem could also be his personal conclusion of existence . . . many PIs had been snuffed out at this delicate stage of their careers, right upon the brink of possible promotion and emergence into the highly competitive field of active demonhood. The Devil spoke very gently indeed, and many creatures in that place grew huge flapping ears or extended trumpet-like organs or radar dishes or clusters of sensory receptors, the better to hear Him with. Right up to this moment, the PI was unsure exactly what had been concluded: he replayed the entire conversation seven hundred thousand and ninety-three times at very high speed within his mind, while the Devil uttered the first tonguing sound of the letter T . . . then the realization came to him at last, and his consciousness leapt an entire octave of awareness, scrabbling at last into true demonhood. Meanwhile the Devil had finished uttering the letter T. . . .

'To correct the unrequired human trend of making alterations to My Picturebook, the Tarot, and to fuddle their discomforting tendency towards using Tarot for liberation rather than suppression, we will do the following. . . .' At these words all present gasped or moaned in shock and deeply empathic understanding, then waited, holding their fetid breath in predatory silence as the Devil turned directly to his PI for an answer.

But the PI, already showing distinct signs of changing shape into a regular demon, was well prepared. He smiled coolly, and took a tiny infernal-darkness-powered personalized memo-scriber from his anus. He pressed the *Cue* key and read off suavely and rapidly from the distorted letters that flowed across the purple glowing screen. The hosts leant forward to hear his words, ready for the slightest slip; extra ears appeared on the ends of hands or from under armpits, or replaced eyes and noses; no one wanted to miss even the tiniest resonance or inflection of a syllable that he uttered. His confidence was total, however, for had he not undergone the transformative therapy devised by his Lord and Master? Was he not fully integrated and totally ready to take his place as a meaningful member of society?

'We will use one of our most aged, hallowed and powerful ploys in this campaign. Whereas before this time we have made Tarot disreputable, pseudo-glamorous and trivial, we will now make it respectable!' A thunderous chorus of yells, cheers, screams of Hellish delight reverberated through the lower worlds. The air thickened as the infernal host gathered en masse to hear the final operative details of such a major new venture. Looking sideways at the Devil for approval, merely as a courtly convention, for he knew that he had that approval in full, the PI continued:

'Firstly we will take those Tarot variants which are offensive and counter-productive to our requirements and psychologize them at length until they become meaningless.'

Fanfares of approving mirth.

'Secondly we will initiate in all countries and languages approved authorized diplomas available only through degree-based schools of Tarotology.'

Gasps of awe and delight.

'Thirdly we will institute enforced Tarot therapy worldwide, initially to augment then later totally to replace the use of major tranquillizers.'

Here there was a distinct pause in the collective praise, for had the PI not overstepped his limits? But he was ready, and even as a major Prince of Perdition opened his reptilian mouth to criticize, he continued:

'This replacement will be of great value to us, as our most useful drugs are already falling into disrepute and being rejected, and we must plan for the day when a foolish humanity bans their use altogether . . .' A torrent of hand clapping, foot stomping, and brief but satisfyingly unsatisfying group-interaction copulation.

'Fourthly and finally we will work to have Tarotology taught in all schools and colleges as a compulsory subject, leading to a certificate of mental health. We will have Tarot business studies, Tarot economy, and Tarot politics.' A delighted hush and reverent silence at this last statement. Yes, there was envy, spite, malice, and loathing simmering within that hush . . . but this was Hell, after all, and no one is perfect.

The Devil stepped off His throne, and the fairy lights winked out. He shed His grotesquely over-developed parody of a male body, and resumed his true and immaculate form. Many of His vast host folded their ears over their eyes, not being able to look fully upon He who was cast out of Paradise. The Devil floated in full beauty over the silent waiting void . . . and slowly each and every denizen of Hell felt the deep pulse of His terrible unageing, unchanging and all-pervasive power.

'And when that has been done, no one will doubt or interfere with Tarot for a long long time. When that has been done, no one will dare to suggest that Tarot is not entirely My device, or that it is not truly the Devil's Picture-book,' he murmured softly. A light radiated from him, so powerful that it engulfed them all in darkness. In the deepest shadow, a junior demon, diabolically evolved from the husk of the PI, vomited up a Tarot deck and began to shuffle the cards.

Bob Stewart (R J Stewart) is a Scots author, composer, and musician who lives in England. His professional career spans over twenty years of touring, recording, writing and composing (from his first television performance in 1968). He has twenty-one books in publication worldwide (1989), of both fiction and non-fiction, and his work has been translated into French, Dutch, German and Portuguese. He has also contributed to anthologies, magazines and many arts projects. He is the designer of the *Merlin Tarot*, an original Tarot deck, painted by Miranda Gray, based upon early Merlin legends, Celtic mythology and traditional images. As a composer and musician he has written, directed and recorded five LP records, a series of cassettes, and music and songs for feature films, television, radio and theatre productions. Bob Stewart has also appeared on British, European and American stages, television and radio, as a solo performer and as a presenter of material on myths, legends, and magical traditions.

CHAPTER SIXTEEN

KNOWER OF BIRDS

Rachel Pollack

The cards for this story were drawn by myself, as part of the early stages in creating a whole deck. There were only fourteen cards ready when I decided to use them to create my Tarot tale. Following the method suggested for the book, I made no attempt to think of a story before shuffling the cards. When I saw the Emperor the shape of the story became clear. And yet, there was also a card missing. I still have not drawn the Knower of Birds, though the concept has been part of the plan almost since the beginning. From the other cards it became clear that the Knower belonged here as well. Ultimately, a story makes its own rules.

(Special note: a Sacred Ornithology Prize to anyone who recognizes the species of the two birds who visit Julia's backyard.)

Emperor.

There was once a woman named Julia who travelled to a far city on the shores of the sea. This city was built around a double mountain which hid the inland streets from the water. Every morning, at dawn, fog would gather itself on the bay, and as the day became brighter it also became darker, for the fog would stream inland, dampening the Sun. Steadily it would climb the hill, one street after another, until it reached the top of the double mountain. There it waited, gathering its strength for the plunge down the other side, into the valley.

One day Julia left the home of her friends and walked several blocks up the hill to where she could catch a bus which would take her to a lecture at an aviary on the other side of town. While she waited at the stop the wind began

to rise, and the fog began to push down the mountain. Chilled, Julia stepped back, next to a grey house. Two round pillars of wood framed the doorway. One pillar was painted white, the other dark blue. Julia leaned against the white side, hugging herself against the damp wind. She would have liked to press against the door and let the two pillars shelter her, but it seemed rude. Suppose someone opened the door and she fell inside? Or suppose someone came home and found this shivering woman blocking the entrance? The streets all around her became covered in fog. The wind was picking up, rattling windows and doors, shaking trees in gardens behind the homes. Julia wondered if she should go back to her friends' house. She could still hear traffic but it seemed far away, somewhere on the other side of town. Still, she had promised to go out for the afternoon. Suppose her friends had been looking forward to some privacy? Suppose they were making love, or fighting? And there was a noise that sounded like it might be a bus, a kind of laboured rattle pushing its way up the hill. So she waited, while the mist swallowed the houses at the far end of the street. Ten minutes, fifteen minutes, and the engine sound had long disappeared, drowned out by the wind knocking on the houses.

Julia knew she had better get back to her friends. Whatever they were doing, they'd just have to understand. It wasn't safe.

She stepped into the wind. She could hardly breathe. She turned around, putting her back against it. The wind shoved her forward, and she grabbed a mail box to steady herself. When she stood up again, she discovered she couldn't remember which way she was going, which direction meant home. She looked about, but everything lay hidden, some houses dimly visible, others as if nothing existed there but an empty horizon. Sometimes the fog would shift, and a red or a green house would appear out of nothing, hover in the air, and then vanish again. Julia heard crashing noises, broken glass.

She found her way back to the house with the two pillars. Banging on the door she tried to shout for help, but nothing came out of her. The door stayed closed. Maybe she should break a window. She could always claim the wind had done it. She held up her purse; the black leather would protect her hand. Briefly she stood like that, one hand holding the pillar, the other arm stretched out with the hand under the flap of her bag. And then she lowered her arm, remembering her own pain the time she'd come home to find her apartment broken into. Someone on the street must be home, she told herself. Someone would let her in.

A noise like a shout broke the howl of the wind. Down the block a great mass lifted up into the air. Over Julia's head it spun, an entire house, and then it vanished into the mist.

Half crawling, holding on to trees and signposts, Julia pushed towards the place where the house had risen. She found a hole with jagged edges of wood and pipe. Something lay there in the middle, some kind of lump. As Julia climbed down, the wind began to settle, and the fog to lift. It was only when she was standing in damp dirt that she saw that the lump was a man, asleep. Julia stumbled backwards just as the Sun came through a break in the mist. The tight beam seemed to shine only on the man, leaving the rest of the hole in gloom.

He's probably harmless, Julia thought, probably a drunk. He lay curled up, with the collar of his jacket pulled over most of his face. The jacket looked like half of an old pinstripe suit, the kind of thing he'd have found in the Salvation Army. He wore jeans frayed at the seat, and black basketball shoes. A pair of twisting wires snaked along the ground from the spot in the dirt where his forehead lay. They looked a little like horns, or maybe diagrams of his dreams.

It was probably safe now to climb out, Julia thought. Instead, curiosity took her a step forward. The man sat up so suddenly that Julia gasped. He was very tall, she realized, with a deep chest and wide shoulders. Dust had matted his long hair into a mass of thick vines. His bloodshot eyes seemed almost entirely red, relieved only by the hard black dots in the centre.

In a rasping voice he said, 'What does she want?'

It took a moment for Julia to find her breath. 'I'm sorry,' she said, 'I don't think I know who you mean.'

'Haven't you come from my wife?'

'I'm sorry. I don't know your wife. I just came down here because of the storm.' She became conscious of the Sun shining on her, of sweat on her chest and under her arms, and she wondered if he'd accuse her of lying.

Instead he sat back and let his face fall into his hands. His chest deflated. 'I thought you were her lawyer,' he said. 'I thought you came to tell me her terms.' Julia said nothing. 'I just want her back. Can't she understand that? I didn't mean it. I was just – I just got crazy. Thought I could run everything myself. I was wrong, okay? Okay?'

Julia glanced up at the top of the hole. It was just too high for her to jump out and run away. She said, 'I'm sure your wife will understand. Everybody makes mistakes.'

'Then where is she?' he shouted. 'Look at this mess.' He waved an arm, and Julia didn't know if he meant the cellar or something greater. 'I've done my best, I'm just no good at it. She's the one who always ran everything. I don't even like it. I knew that as soon as she left. As soon as she left. Everyone asking me what to do.' He began to cry.

Julia moved back against the edge of the hole. Somewhere outside she could hear people talking. She took a deep breath in preparation for spinning around and climbing out. As if to copy her, the man breathed in as well, expanding his chest and bringing up his head, like a bull lifting its horns to the Moon. When he wiped the tears from his face some of the dirt came away as well. His skin showed as streaks of dark gold.

'Will you tell her?' he asked.

'Tell her?'

'That I want her back. That I want her to come home. *I* want to come home.'

'I'm sorry,' Julia said. 'I don't know your wife.'

'Then find her!' he boomed. 'Sorry,' he added immediately. 'It's just my old habit. See what happens to me without her?' He smiled suddenly. 'Will you find her?' he asked sweetly. 'Tell her I need her. Tell her we all need her. I've made such a mess of things.' He kept smiling, and staring at her.

'All right,' Julia said. She made a noise. Why did she say that?

'Good,' the man said, as if approving a child. 'Good.' He lay down again on the dirt.

'Wait a moment,' Julia said. 'I can't find your wife. I don't know anything about her. I don't even know her name.' No use. He was already asleep. Gingerly she touched his arm, then gave it a shove. He began to snore, a sound like a distant train.

Using a thick board as a step Julia climbed back up to the street. When she reached the corner the bus came. She ignored it and went down the hill to her friends.

In the house that night, some people came over. Over a half gallon of cheap wine they talked about the storm and the rumours of cars flying through the air, and towers of dirt rising into the sky. After an hour the talk shifted to divorce and child care. A man named Tommy didn't know where he would find the extra support money for back-to-school clothes for his daughter by his second wife. Meanwhile, his first wife had vanished, leaving their retarded twelve-year-old son behind. The boy was now with his grandparents until Tommy could work out how to take care of him. And Tommy himself was demanding that his third wife give some support money for their two-year-old. Leaving the boy with Tommy had given her the chance to pursue her career as a corporate colour consultant.

Julia's friends described their own scattered children and divorces. Margaret, whom Julia had met years ago in a flea market, had a grown-up daughter who'd dropped out of college to travel to Mexico with her alcoholic father. Margaret's current husband, Michael, also had an adult daughter. She was living at home in between lesbian love affairs. Michael's second wife had just thrown out their teenage son, Jack, who belonged to some cult which involved dressing in drag. Drinking glass after glass of wine Margaret com-

plained about the danger Michael's 'perverted' children
posed to Margaret's and Michael's three-year-old son.

As soon as it seemed polite Julia went upstairs to the tiny
bedroom they'd reserved for her among the house's shifting
residents. Despite the warmth she put on a long flannel
nightgown and lay down on top of the covers. Why did
she make that promise? It didn't really count. She didn't
even know the woman's name. Downstairs she could hear
a rough weave of angry voices.

High Priestess.

Julia flew home three days later. Leaving the city the plane
passed over a series of salt flats, large plots of land, each
one a separate colour. The irregular shapes, with black lines
swooping across them, resembled ancient drawings of birds.

When she arrived home her little apartment seemed so
peaceful. She thought how she could sit for days just staring
out the back window at the little pond behind the house.
After unpacking, she sat down to watch the news on television. A food shipment to some starving villagers had
become contaminated with poison gas. A man in New
Jersey had stolen an aeroplane and crashed it into his wife's
house. A woman in prison had died in a hunger strike. Her
daughter claimed the guards had force-fed her and she'd
choked to death. When Julia went to bed that night she
found it hard to breathe. For a while she sat up, reading a
book of cartoons. Finally she was able to sleep.

The next day Julia received a new assignment from her
temp agency. A private library outside of town needed
someone to transfer their card catalogue onto computer.
The library turned out to be mostly occult books: seven-
teenth-century alchemical treatises, rare Tarot decks, diagrams of the human body with strange labels, translations of
Hindu beliefs about the universe, and confusing messages
from groups of dead people. At first the work went slowly.
Julia kept looking around at the floor-to-ceiling cases of
forbidden books. She wanted to run from the house before
priests in huge cowls would raid the library. After a few

days, however, she became fascinated by the descriptions on the cards. The books were so varied, so many different theories. When she thought the owner of the house wouldn't catch her, Julia would search the shelves for some book whose title or description seemed especially enticing. She never really understood any of them. For one thing, most were in foreign languages. And even those in English referred to names and ideas Julia had never heard of. She just liked the feeling they gave her, of life being so much bigger than she'd ever believed.

As she neared the end she tried to work more slowly, doing only a few cards an hour. Finally she couldn't stall any more. She typed in the last entry, about some figure called 'the Horned God', and then she went to Mrs Toth and reported that the catalogue was complete. Mrs Toth invited Julia for tea. Sitting in a large room with bay windows overlooking a garden, the two women talked about computers and the need to be modern. Suddenly, Mrs Toth bowed her head and slipped off a chain from around her neck. The chain held a small silver disc incised with a stick figure of a woman in a long skirt, and a pair of birds around her head. 'This is for you,' she said, and before Julia could say anything the woman had placed it over Julia's head.

When Julia got home that evening she put the disc and chain in her jewellery box. Depressed, she watched television, constantly switching channels to avoid scenes of violence or humiliation. Finally, she went to bed, only to find herself lying awake, exhausted. Every time she began to doze off, she somehow snapped herself back. Abruptly, she got up and put on Mrs Toth's medallion. In bed again, she smiled at herself. Moments later, she fell asleep. She woke up in mid-morning to the sound of birds.

That afternoon Julia went to an occult bookshop. The store was clean and elegant, with the books carefully arranged on shelves and carousels around a central display of jewellery, crystal balls, Tarot cards, and polished rocks. Julia leafed through several books, hoping she didn't look too much like an amateur. It all seemed wrong, somehow. Too modern. Mrs Toth's books were mostly bound in thick covers, with leather tooling. These were all paperbacks, with lurid covers showing women dripping moonlight, or cards fanned out like a carnival trick.

When she left the store she began walking aimlessly, unwilling to go home. On a busy street, a white pigeon flew up at her. Julia gasped and put up her hands. Embarrassed, she looked around to see if anyone was laughing at her. Instead, she noticed an old woman standing on the corner, looking confused. The woman was short and slightly bent over, with brittle grey hair. She wore a black cotton dress and worn-out sandals. She was carrying several shopping bags and a large cardboard box. Every time she picked one up another one fell. The woman seemed to want to cross the street but was frightened of the traffic. Behind her people rushed in and out of department stores. When Julia walked closer she saw the woman was crying, from frustration or fear. 'Do you need help?' Julia asked.

'Yes,' the woman said. 'Oh yes, please.' She looked a little like Mrs Toth, a Mrs Toth without money or a home. Julia picked up the box – it weighed hardly anything – and took one of the bags. With her free hand she held the woman's elbow. It took a while for them to cross the street; the woman walked slowly, and, halfway across, a woman in a silk skirt and running shoes almost knocked them down. They made it across just as the light changed.

'Thank you,' the woman said. Julia felt embarrassed. She wished she could walk away, but didn't want to insult the woman, who seemed to be searching for something in one of the bags. 'Here,' the woman said finally, and held up a filthy brown vial about the size of Julia's little finger. 'This is for you.'

Julia backed away. 'I don't need anything,' she said. 'I mean, thank you, but – '

Following Julia, the woman said, 'My mother always told me to return kindness with kindness.' She slipped the vial into Julia's hand and closed her fingers around it. 'It'll help against the pain.'

'I'm not feeling any pain,' Julia said, but the woman hurried away, moving quickly now despite her packages.

Julia looked at the bottle. She should throw it away, she knew. It was probably filled with germs. Instead, she dropped it into her bag and headed home.

Death.

That evening Julia cut her finger while peeling potatoes. It was only a small cut, it hardly needed the Band-aid she wrapped around it. Through the evening, however, it hurt more and more. She took off the Band-aid and inspected the wound. It didn't look infected. Not even swollen. Around eleven o'clock Julia's finger hurt so much she couldn't even watch television. She just hoped she could go to sleep.

In bed, she slid her hand under the pillow, as if the soft pressure would contain the throbbing. Just before sleep she thought she heard someone singing outside the house – a clear soprano, singing a folk song, or maybe a spiritual. And then she realized, it was only a bird. Strange, she thought, to hear a bird singing at night. Maybe it was an owl. And with that thought, and no sense of passage, Julia emigrated to the Land of Dream.

She was sitting in the kitchen reading one of Mrs Toth's books. Across from her the medallion swung from a peg on the back of a chair. She heard a moaning outside the house and walked out through the kitchen door to see what it was. Instead of the small backyard with the pond and the trees beyond it, she stood on a kind of ledge, with a plain stretching for miles below her. The dirt was cracked, and the few trees were withered. All about she saw people sitting on the ground with their heads in their hands, or else leaning against the trees and staring at the dirt. Many of them appeared scarred or bruised. Julia herself staggered as if someone had beaten her.

The scene changed: a large box sat on the ground, an old wooden box, like an antique toy chest. From inside it Julia heard moans and weeping. A tall man came walking up to the box. Dressed in an old-fashioned tuxedo, top hat, and patent leather shoes, he placed his white gloved hands on the lid. Immediately the sounds stopped. Though he stood

with his back to Julia she could see a corner of his face.
The skin gleamed hard and white, like polished bone.

With a grand gesture the tall man flung open the lid of
the box. Julia heard a great whoosh of air as coloured bits
of paper flew up into the sky. High in the air they changed
to birds, all singing joyfully as they flew in and out of each
other under the sun. Julia's own heart became a bird. At
any moment her weightless body would float away into the
light.

She woke up with the pain worse than ever. If she didn't
look at her finger she could swear it was twice the size of
the others. Julia turned on the reading lamp, and at that
moment she remembered the old woman with her greasy
bottle. She scrambled through her bag until she found it.
She looked doubtfully at it until the pain stabbed her again,
and then she pulled out the cork. A sweet smell floated up
to her, like orange concentrate mixed with mint. Nervously,
she touched the cut fingertip into the vial –

And yelped as the sting hit her like a flash of light.
Without thinking she jabbed the finger into her mouth.

The pain vanished, taking with it a neck pain and a lower
back ache she hadn't even noticed until they left her. She
stood up, grinning, and then laughed. For the first time she
noticed it was dawn. She slipped on her bathrobe and went
out to the backyard.

Knower of Birds.

The sky had that gentle blue of a morning promising a lot
of sunshine. The air was cool, the ground still wet with
dew. Julia shivered slightly and pulled her bathrobe tighter.
She smiled at the trees and the grass. A breeze stirred some
branches, as if the nearest tree was smiling back at her. Julia
laughed, and bounced up and down slightly on her toes.

Two green and red birds with gold beaks landed on a
branch near her. Julia didn't know what kind they were –
she'd never learned to recognize things like birds or flowers
– but she didn't think she'd seen anything like them before.
And indeed, when they started talking to each other, they

were discussing trips across mountains and over the sea. Julia found it so natural to understand them that she didn't even think about it at first, and when she did she wondered why she'd never understood birds before. Probably never took the time to listen, she decided, and then forgot about it as she concentrated on the birds' conversation.

Though she knew the words Julia still found it difficult to follow their rather formal style of speaking, a kind of poetic debate. Also – she didn't know how she knew this, she was certainly no expert – they spoke with an accent, like foreigners.

They were discussing what they called 'two-legged mating problems'. After a while Julia realized this meant human relationships. They didn't seem to think too much of human customs. When they had told stories of romantic love and rejection from different countries, they began talking of someone they called 'the master of rage and pain'. This man had lived with a woman who ran a farm or a business or some kind of organization. One day the husband threw her out, taking over the business himself. But where everything had gone so well with the two of them, it all became a disaster when the man tried to do it alone. And now that he wanted her back, he didn't know where to find her. The birds seemed to find this funny, repeating it several times.

'Where does she rest?' one asked, and the other answered, 'On the glass mountain. Where the three stone rivers meet.' And with that, they launched themselves into the sky. Only when they were fading from sight did Julia realize they had been talking about the man she'd met during the storm. For the first time in weeks she remembered her promise to find the man's wife. 'Wait a minute,' she called. 'Come back. How do I find this mountain? Where do I find the three rivers?' If the birds heard her they paid no attention. They vanished among rows of TV satellite dishes growing on the rooftops like mushrooms on the floor of a forest.

Seeker.

Back in the house Julia sat down at the kitchen table. Three rivers. Didn't the Mississippi have branches? Tributaries, that was the word. Tributes brought to the king. As far as she could remember, they didn't all meet in the same place. And she'd never heard of any glass mountains. Anyway, the rivers could be anywhere. The birds were so well-travelled.

Julia walked into the living room, her bathrobe flapping behind her. Mixed in with some magazines under the television she kept an atlas. She checked the Mississippi, the Nile, the Amazon, the Congo, the Danube, the Don, and then leafed through the maps at random. Now and then she found some likely intersection, but never a mountain right at that location.

She dropped the book on the rug. They didn't just say a mountain, they said a *glass* mountain. And stone rivers. What was that supposed to mean? Maybe they meant lava flows. And a volcano. Didn't lava become like glass? She remembered reading about Aztecs and glass knives harder than steel. The atlas told her nothing.

The next morning Julia went to all the different bookshops she knew, looking for studies of volcanoes. Finally she went to the State University and asked to see a professor of geology. The graduate assistant who spoke to her smirked when she asked if he would describe a volcano as a 'glass mountain'. He laughed out loud when she asked about the meeting of 'stone rivers'.

Outside the building Julia thought to herself, it's not fair. How was she supposed to know what a couple of birds meant? Why couldn't they be more explicit? And anyway, how was she supposed to climb the glass mountain? 'It's easy for them,' she said out loud. 'They just have to flap their silly little wings.'

On the way back to her car Julia passed a storefront appealing for help for abused children. There were pictures of kids with broken bones, burnt faces – Julia felt faint. Leaning against a tree, she stared up at the sky. Why do we do these things? she wondered. What's wrong with us?

It was like – like something got broken, or misconnected. Above her a trio of birds glided on invisible currents. 'Help us,' Julia whispered. 'Please.'

A series of loops and swirls brought one of the birds – a gull, she thought – down to rest on the hood of Julia's car. When Julia ran up to it, the bird flapped its wings to rise into the air a few inches, and then plopped down onto the metal. 'Oh,' Julia said. 'I'm sorry about what I said. I was just upset.'

'Follow,' the bird commanded. It circled over her car until she manoeuvred out of the parking spot and then it began leading her down the street. Around corners and into the centre of town they travelled, with the bird resting on the roof of the car whenever Julia had to stop for a light. Through town, through rush-hour traffic jams (where Julia worried that the gull would get impatient and strand her), over to the edge of the city, where the city street met the old state highway and Interstate 85. And at that point, on a fence surrounding the construction site for an office building, the bird came to a rest.

Julia jerked the car to a stop and got out, only to have the bird take off again, climbing so quickly Julia couldn't think of chasing it. She looked around, wanting to cry. In front of her the sign proclaimed the glory the new building would bring to the city. Beyond it rose a ziggurat of blue glass. Julia remembered the local news station describing it as a 'model of post-modernism'. She turned away, looking at the highway. Three roads. Concrete. Stone –

With a shout she turned back to stare at the skyscraper. The glass mountain. At the top the afternoon Sun lit up a row of glass triangles in different colours. On top of each one she saw a speck, a bird, a congress of birds.

Gift of Rivers.

Unfinished, the building stood unguarded as well. Julia discovered a hole in the fence just big enough for her to squeeze through. Inside, she found a single elevator working to carry her up the central shaft, and at the top an open doorway to the roof.

The roof was much bigger than it looked from the street, the glass pyramids higher and more translucent. The afternoon light passing through them made the flat rooftop a quilt of blended colours. Still brighter, however, were the birds. All sizes and all shapes, some with long necks and huge wings, others so small two or three might have fit in Julia's palm. A few circled round their miniature peaks, as if too high strung to sit still. Most simply perched, their claws scratching the glass. 'Hello,' Julia said softly, and a great flood of welcome crashed over her, from chirps and whistles to deep croaks. Julia laughed and clapped her hands.

Three loud claps answered her from behind. Julia jumped and turned around. An old woman stood near the edge of the roof. She wore a long green dress with short sleeves and a hem that was coming unravelled. The dress hung loosely on her thin body. Instead of having wrinkles, the woman's face was smooth, almost polished, as if everything extreme had worn away with time. Her fine hair moved continually in the wind. A trick of the Sun, or maybe the light filtered through the triangles, gave the hair a quality of shifting colours, gold mixed with brown, red, even green.

Julia shook her head slightly. She'd never expected the woman to be so old. She remembered an aunt who'd married a younger man and how everyone had gossiped about them. Without thinking, she glanced down at the silver medallion hanging between her breasts.

The woman laughed. 'An old picture,' she said. She walked closer, moving with an efficient grace. 'Where did you get that?' she said. 'I haven't seen one of those for years.'

'Mrs Toth gave it to me.'

The woman smiled, and her teeth seemed to catch the Sun, so that her mouth, for a moment, appeared filled with light. 'Good old Mrs Toth,' she said. 'How is she?'

'Fine,' Julia said. 'I guess. She's got a computer.'

'Has she? Wonderful. Good for her.'

For a while they just stood there, the woman very still, Julia wishing she didn't sound so dumb. The gull who had led her to the building came and circled round her shoulders. 'Don't be afraid,' it told her in its loud gull voice.

Julia blushed. She said, 'I've got a message. From your husband.'

The woman shook her head. 'I've never married.'

'What? Oh. I mean, I'm sorry. I thought – '

'You haven't made a mistake.' A smile appeared, then vanished, as if she didn't want Julia to think this old lady was making fun of her.

'But he told me – a big man with red eyes? He said you were married, and he threw you out. And now he wants you back. I had to give you the message.'

The woman nodded. 'Thank you. You've done well. It's not your fault he told you something that wasn't true. I doubt that he himself knows the truth any more.'

'But the birds said – about the man and his wife – '

The woman laughed, the sound riding over the cries and whistles of the birds. She said, 'Just because they can fly doesn't mean they always get their stories right.'

Settling on the old woman's shoulder the gull said, 'We do our best.'

The woman stroked him. 'You do very well. All of you. I'm very proud of you all.'

Julia said, 'Then you never lived with him?'

'Oh, we lived together. He came to me – he looked so sweet then, so young and excited, so full of ideas and enthusiasm.' She sighed. 'And I guess I was curious. To see what he would do. That's always been my great fault, you know. Curiosity.'

'And he threw you out?'

The woman laughed again. 'Of course not. I left.'

'But why?'

'I just told you. Curiosity.' The light somehow shifted her face, so that Julia glimpsed a young woman, hard and bright. And then the old woman returned, patient, unmoving.

'He wants you back,' Julia said.

'No. He just wants to believe he controls everything. Me, the work, himself. There's really nothing I can do for him. I'm sorry.'

'Then what about us?' Julia said. 'Do you know what's happening?' She wasn't sure what she meant, only that a great anger had risen up in her. 'We need help. You and your damn birds –'

The woman held out her hands. 'Come here,' she said.

Julia backed away. 'What are you going to do?'

'Nothing that will hurt you.'

Julia didn't understand the panic that rose up in her. She couldn't breathe, it was like something was pounding on her heart. She looked at the triangles blocking the edge of the roof. She could climb over them, push aside the birds, get away – But what if she couldn't escape? What if something terrible waited for you after you died? She remembered the children in the photos, burned and broken. She walked up and put out her hands for the woman to take them.

At first nothing happened. Julia just stood there, feeling foolish as the fear subsided. And then she began to cry. She cried in a way she'd never known possible, huge whooping noises, her whole body a flood washing away pains she'd never known or else forgotten, pains she'd kept stored away all her life, like treasures hidden from the world. She looked down at the woman, expecting to see her crying as well. Instead, the ancient face looked up at her, impassive. The anger returned; Julia wanted to throw the arrogant old bitch to the ground. She tried to break loose, but the woman held on to her.

Julia didn't know if the pain was gone, but she discovered other treasures. Pleasure – rage – excitement – fear of excitement – thoughts of murder, of being murdered. And above all, desire. She wanted love. More than love itself, she wanted the power to make love happen or take it away, not just for herself, for everyone. It was the power that counted. She wanted to give life and destroy it. She wanted *her* words and *her* hands to make the grass grow, to give the birds their colours, to set the rhythms of the seas.

And then she looked at that face again, bland and empty. All of it – desire, anger, fear – dropped away in a last wrench of tears. When the crying stopped, Julia simply stood there, unmoving in the evening wind.

The old woman was still looking at her. Julia wondered if she should say something. 'Thank you', or 'I'm sorry'. Or maybe just laugh. Instead, she let go of the hands. The woman's arms dropped to her sides.

'It's getting dark,' she told Julia. 'Maybe you should be heading home.'

Julia looked around at the sky, a dark blue, almost purple. She noticed that the birds had left. Her crying must have covered the sound of the wings. She said, 'Did they go because of me?' Then she laughed, realizing how silly that sounded. She said, 'Can I come back and visit you again?'

'I won't be here long. They'll need to open the building soon.'

Julia nodded. She held out her hands once more and the old woman squeezed them briefly. At the door leading downstairs Julia turned around to see the old woman at the roof's edge, looking out past the triangles. In the evening light her hair had turned to silver and black.

When Julia pulled into her driveway the man in the pinstripe jacket was standing by the garage. 'Did you find her?' he said, even before Julia had got out of her car. 'Is she coming back?'

'I'm sorry,' Julia said. 'I did what I could.'

'What the hell am I supposed to do, come crawling on my knees? What the hell does she want from me?'

Julia took a step towards the house, then stopped. In one gesture, she took off Mrs Toth's medallion and slipped the chain over the man's head. Angrily he grabbed hold of it, as if to jerk it loose and throw it on the ground. Instead, he held it in his palm. Just before she went inside and closed the door, Julia saw the man with his hand up near his eyes. He was squinting at the disc. Moonlight made the silver sparkle in the night.

Rachel Pollack is a novelist and poet as well as a major authority on the symbolism of Tarot cards. Her recent novel *Unquenchable Fire* has been described as 'brilliant' and 'magical' for its vision of an America where myth and dream have broken through into the modern world. Her two-volume study of the Tarot, *78 Degrees of Wisdom*, is recognized in many countries as a standard text. Her other books on Tarot include the official text for *Salvador Dali's Tarot* and *The New Tarot*. She is also the author of the novels *Golden Vanity* and *Alqua Dreams*. Rachel Pollack's work has been translated into French, German, Danish, Dutch, Spanish, and Japanese. A former university lecturer, bar cleaner, IBM production planner, bottler of patchouli oil, and bookseller, she now writes full time. She has lived in Amsterdam in the Netherlands for the past fifteen years.